EMBERS

Books by Ronie Kendig

Dead Reckoning

Discarded Heroes Series
Nightshade
Digitalis
Wolfsbane
Firethorn

A Breed Apart Series
Trinity
Talon
Beowulf

Quiet Professionals Series
Raptor 6
Hawk
Falcon

Operation Zulu: Redemption

EMBERS

ABIASSA'S FIRE

BOOK ONE

RONIE KENDIG

ENCLAVE

PUBLISHING

Embers by Ronie Kendig
Published by Enclave Publishing
24 W. Cambelback Rd. A-635
Phoenix, AZ 85013
www.enclavepublishing.com

ISBN (paper): 978-1-62184-057-2

Embers
Copyright © 2015 by Veronica Kendig

Published in the United States by Enclave Publishing, an imprint of Third Day
Books, LLC, Phoenix, Arizona.

This is a work of fiction. Names, characters, places, and incidents are products of
the author's imagination or are used fictitiously. Any similarity to actual people,
organizations, and/or events is purely coincidental.

Cover illustration by Kirk DouPonce – DogEared Design

Printed in the United States of America

This book is dedicated to Steve Laube, a tireless reader, advocate, and champion of science fiction and fantasy.

You've helped a lot of authors' dreams come true—including mine! I think your cape is dipped in ultra-lightweight gold.

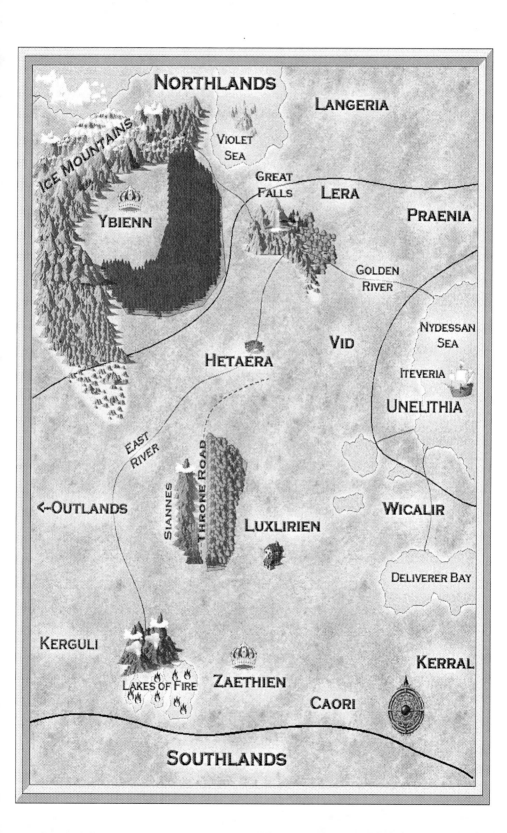

Once amid the fertile lands
Were proud and strong brigands.
Vain in their ways,
They numbered their days;
Then came the blight
With fire so bright.
It devoured hearts and pride.
In agony, their children cried
As roaring devoured every drop
Of life, livestock, and crop.
Red, orange, gold, and blue
Reshaped the lands—people, too.
Now they writhe amid the pyre
of Abiassa's Fire.

1

It was said the very soul of the land burned within her. The soul of the fire, of Abiassa. The thought drew Kaelyria Celahar's gaze to the Fiery Mount. She traced its spine in the distance. The charred slopes teemed with reddish-gold lava spilling down into the Lakes of Fire. So beautiful. Forbidding. Compelling.

"'Red, orange, gold, and blue; Reshaped the lands, people, too.'" Kaelyria's breath bloomed over the leaded glass as she recited the ancient rhyme. As the circle of fog shrank, she braced against the heaviness crowding her, sniffling out the joy she once felt at being the heir to the throne. The future ruler of a realm so powerful. "'Now to thrive on holy pyre, They unleash . . . Abiassa's Fire.'"

Blackened earth shifted, forced aside by the burning elements that glowed bright against the night-darkened land. Just as she would push aside the darkness pursuing her and her people. Gone were the laughter and merriment that thrived in the days of her childhood. At nineteen, she was an adult, no longer the child who once danced around the Great Pit singing the evensongs with her friends. With Haegan.

Things changed.

Kaelyria lowered her gaze. Hand on her stomach, she drew in a breath as synergy, hot and thrumming, surged against her palm. Answering. Churning. The very essence of who she'd been since Haegan's incident now infused her with the *abiatasso* that guided her, enabled her to someday rule. But more importantly it existed to protect the people of Zaethien.

Even the midnight sky seemed to shrink, yielding darkness to the territories beneath its heavy cloak. Or maybe they were shrinking because of her intended course—if her connection with the land was as whole as she'd been taught, could it feel her turmoil? The irrevocable path she'd chosen?

Grief anew threatened to strangle her. She closed her eyes. If she did not do this, the fires could go out. The land could die. But if she did, *she* could die.

"My lady-princess?"

The soft voice pulled Kaelyria from her somber thoughts. She straightened, smoothed a hand down her silk-embroidered gown as much to brush away the weighty thoughts as to compose herself, and turned from the window. Across the black lacquered floor, torchlight scampered up the gilded walls and tapestries, casting an odd glow against her handmaiden's young face.

Pulling the silk wrap tightly around her shoulders, Kaelyria lifted her chin. "Is he here?"

Kiesa gave a reluctant nod, no doubt held captive by the fear that shone in her eyes. This was the end, even her maiden knew. "My lady-grace, are you sure you—"

"Bring him." Kaelyria dared not trust herself to hear anyone's concerns or complaints, especially the one who knew her heart better than most. The one who attended her minute by minute. The one who dressed her, laughed with her, and shared confidences.

Kiesa tucked her head and stepped back. Once she'd cleared the threshold, she gave a quick bow and vanished.

One last chance to change your mind. Would Haegan ever forgive her for this? Would Father? And Graem . . . The thought cinched a tight cord around her stomach.

A large shape filled the doorway. Cilicien ka'Dur entered, followed by Kiesa. Hair smoothed back, facial hair trim and neat encircling his mouth, he brought with him a chill that defied the roaring fire in the hearth. Adorned in his Ignatieri overcloak and black breeches, he made an impressive figure as he bent before her. When he bowed, the firelight caught the gold threads and streamed down them, striking the rubies, orange sapphires, and—the most prized—citrines stitched into his mantle. Fiery prisms exploded from the gems and leapt around the room.

"Princess, it is an honor." His voice seemed oiled, slick. Though his gaze did not go to the fireworks cast by his bejeweled cloak, ka'Dur could not keep the pride from his eyes, from puffing his chest.

Kaelyria curled her hands into fists, her attention flicking to where Kiesa stood in the shadows, sensing the support of her handmaiden against this accelerant. His appearance had caught her off guard at their first meeting—he was not what she'd expected an accelerant to look like, especially not one of his caliber. Old, gnarled, she'd expected. This . . . Even as it pleased her eye, something about his beauty sparked unease in her heart.

With an amused look, ka'Dur strolled her private quarters, considering the paintings, the sofas, the gold tables, and brocade tapestries. "Quite a change from our last place of meeting."

Kaelyria ignored him, steeling herself. "Are you prepared to do this?"

"Are *you*, my lady-grace?"

Kaelyria walked quickly to the armoire and retrieved the pouch from the lead box. She rubbed her fingers over the velvet. Gems poked through the fabric and rolled against her palm. Half her inheritance, and the gems the least of the price she would pay.

Any price is worth protecting Abiassa's Fire.

And Haegan. He'd have a life of splendor and adventure, just as he'd always wanted. Deserved. Not a life of stone walls, drafty rooms, with a crippled body and a crotchety old guardian. For him, if not for the entire kingdom.

She spun around. Arm extended, she held out the pouch. "Your price, accelerant."

Eyebrow arched, he stalked toward her. Slow. Methodical. With a flourish, she released the bag.

Cilicien lunged and snatched the treasure from the air. Quick, for a man weighted by gems and pride. He could not be trusted beyond what they had agreed.

Watching her, Cilicien tugged the gold drawstring and dumped the blood price into his hand. He ran a finger along the jewels, their perfection capturing the torchlight and tossing colors along the papered walls. "You are sure, princess, that you want to do this? You've heard—"

"I am neither deaf nor stupid." Her voice trembled, but whether fear or conviction mastered her, she could not be sure. "I heard the conditions. Had I not agreed or understood, you would not be here. Time is short. Come." She pivoted on her slippered feet, her crimson gown fluttering as it stirred the air. In the hall, she hesitated at the portrait of two children, her eyes on the boy with wavy blond hair and a smile that rivaled the sun. Her heart ached. Was she doing the right thing?

"Your Highness?"

Kaelyria blinked. She continued down the passage and, lifting her skirts up, she mounted the stairs. At the top, she made her way to a small door. "Quickly. Let me do the talking." She speared Cilicien with a warning look, not moving until he acknowledged her command.

She allowed Cilicien and Kiesa to enter the musty, narrow stairwell huddled in the north corner of the castle. Behind them, she locked the door again, then slid past them both, meeting her servant's eyes. "Kiesa, remain here and watch the door."

Lifting her hem, she climbed the spiraling steps to the Upper Tower.

"You are aware, are you not, princess, that Poired Dyrth is advancing—"

Kaelyria spun and thrust a palm toward the man. Heat blossomed out like a blanket and pinned him to the wall. "Speak not that name again, accelerant, or it will be your last breath."

Cilicien smirked. With a flick of two fingers, he brushed aside her wielding, and Kaelyria flinched as the embers recoiled. "You would wield against the one who has agreed to help you in this scheme?"

Kaelyria swallowed, unprepared for the ease with which he countered her strength. Surprise tangled her mind, but she drew herself up.

"You would do well to remember whom you address, accelerant. That name offends House Celahar; it was the son of the Cold One who stole my brother's life."

"I meant no disrespect, princess. We are wasting time. The enemy sits on your doorstep."

Yes, she knew Dyrth was near. She could feel the icy tendrils of his wickedness blowing bitterly against the fires within her breast.

At last they rounded the final corner to Haegan's lonely chambers.

A venerable accelerant stood in the fore-chamber, flame-etched sword in hand. Scraggly beard and hair framed eyes that missed nothing. Though it would seem the brown robe hid a frail body, Kaelyria knew better. Once she had made the mistake of scoffing at the aged man. He'd flattened her and her pride in one fell swoop that left her trembling.

Kaelyria inclined her head, slipped a foot behind herself in a slight curtsey. "Sir Gwogh, forgive this intrusion."

He sheathed his weapon. His eyes brightened. "My lady-grace." Wariness crowded his welcoming expression as his gaze shifted behind her.

"Master," Gwogh said, bending curtly at the waist. "I was not aware House Celahar was given to entertaining someone of your . . . notoriety."

Smooth, sharp words. Kaelyria almost smiled at the thinly veiled accusation. Still, she did not need dissension, even between two masters of the Flames. "He is here at my behest, Sir Gwogh."

Confusion ruffled the elder's thick gray beard. He shifted his drab robe. "Forgive me, my lady-grace. I do not understand why you would come, and with . . . him. Not at an hour as late—" His bushy eyebrows sprang up. He gasped as understanding seemed to overtake him.

She should have known this could not be hidden, not from one so attuned. Kaelyria forged ahead.

"No, princess! Please do not do this." He rushed her, clutched her arm, propriety abandoned in his panic.

The thick door to Haegan's bedchamber stood ajar. Kaelyria's eyes traveled the twenty paces to her brother's bed. To the frail form cradled by moonlight. Though she visited him daily, the ache never lessened. "He is resting well tonight?" she asked softly.

"For once, yes, he sleeps in peace." Gwogh touched her again. "Please, princess. It was a story, an old legend. This should—*cannot*—be done."

Awareness of the finality of her actions flared through Kaelyria, pinning her, eyes locked onto her brother. "Legends are born of truth, did you not tell me that once?" Perhaps Haegan would take this gift and become a legend himself. He had it within. At least, he did once . . .

"When you were but five, my lady! Wh-when you were champing for adventure and excitement."

She remembered her days of innocence with a sad smile. "Now . . ." A light halo wreathed her brother's golden shoulder-length hair. She removed the old accelerant's hand from her arm. "Now, Haegan must have his own adventure."

"*No!*" Gwogh cried as she moved past him. "I beg you. Please—"

"Stop simpering, you old fool," Cilicien ka'Dur snapped. "Behave as befits your station."

Surprise darted through Kaelyria, and she saw it on Sir Gwogh's visage, but the reprimand almost seemed deserved. At least, that's what her guilt said.

"Cilicien!" Gwogh hissed. "I will not allow this. He is my charge, and I—"

Light and heat collided in a massive fireball between the two accelerants.

The aged flexed and rolled his fingers as he defended the door to Haegan's chamber. "You *know* the price!"

Drawing a hand back in a swift retreat, Cilicien drew in a deep breath, his nostrils flaring. He flicked his thumb then thrust his hand like a blade at the aged accelerant.

The blast of heat struck Gwogh's counter wield like a hammer, knocking him backward.

Kaelyria lifted her own hands, stunned. "What are you?"

But the slick accelerant slid his left palm toward her.

Stunned, bound by a band of Cilicien's power, Kaelyria felt a surge of anger. Righteous indignation and fear lent her strength, but not enough. She stood helpless.

Balance compromised by his attack on Kaelyria, Cilicien slid backward along the stone floor, his boots making a ragged scrape as they gave up traction. Closer to the stairs. Closer . . .

With a primal growl, he drew both palms back to himself in a momentary withdrawal of his wielding. Before Gwogh could fill the sudden vacuum, Cilicien shoved himself forward with a shout, ducking under Gwogh's line of attack and sending a blue-black wave of heat slamming into the older man.

Gwogh smacked against the wall. His head bounced off the stone. He collapsed in a heap of linen and robe.

The band encompassing Kaelyria vanished. She stumbled but caught herself, hand going to her mouth. "What have you done? How could you—"

"He would have stopped us." Cilicien smoothed back his hair and wiped the small trail of blood at his lip.

"I could have explained," she said, kneeling beside the man who'd tormented her brother with endless Histories and Legacies, who'd comforted him with faithful service for years. She brushed the white strands of hair from his face and fingered the singe mark on his temple.

"He'll live. But we will not if he regains consciousness before the transference is done."

Was she making a mistake? It might not be right in terms of legal wielding, but was she wrong to do this?

"Princess." Cilicien's tone was curt, dark. "Would you have Dyrth steal your gift?"

The words pulled her to her feet. She gazed at Gwogh once more, then eased into the room, crossing from wood floor to thick carpet that softened her steps as she reached Haegan's bed. She lifted her gown and hitched her leg, easing onto the edge of the thick feather mattress.

Haegan's dark blond hair lay against the pillow, silky and the color of autumn fields in the Northlands. Kept trim and neat by Sir Gwogh,

Haegan looked ready to attend court. A strong jaw mirrored their father's, but he also had a beauty that not many had the benefit of seeing, since he did not venture outside these walls. Maybe he would capture the heart of a lady, find love, once outside Seultrie. Once *free* of Seultrie.

Did he look paler than usual? She touched his cheek. All Celahar heirs held the fire within that burned hotter, even those, like Haegan, who did not wield the Flames. Were he ill, his flesh would cool. Not warm as most outside these fortified walls.

No, he was warm. Had he been allowed to grow into the man he should have been, Haegan would've ruled the kingdom with presence alone. Father had loved him so much. Doted on him. Afforded him every pleasure. Until that day Poired Dyrth's foul creatures poisoned Haegan and left him without the use of his limbs.

She drew a finger along his forehead, tucking aside a curl. Her brother, separated by a mere ten months. They'd nearly shared the same womb. Had shared the same toys. The same jokes, same every-thing. Until that day. She traced across his jaw again, so wishing he could run and laugh. And he would. Tonight. In a few months—before he reached the Falls—he would turn eighteen. He should be whole when he entered manhood.

The cost . . . *Oh the cost!*

"Do you know," he said softly, eyes still closed, "how rare it is to be touched?" Blue eyes opened and fastened on her. "I would know yours anywhere, sister."

Leaning over him, she smiled. "Silly fool. You would know not mine from any other lady's."

"Not true," he said, the words familiar, repeated at nearly every greeting. "Yours holds fire."

It was their joke. Because of the *abiatasso*, heat within her burned purer and more direct. And it often found escape in tiny aspects like her touch. Especially, for some reason, with Haegan. He *could* tell hers apart. Always had been able to discern. A lopsided grin worked its way across his face. Then he frowned as his gaze drifted past her.

To the skylight. Then back to her. "What . . . why are you here? It's past midnight."

The back of her throat grew raw. She drew up her courage and leaned closer. "I have a gift for you."

He chuckled. "Could it not wait till morning? I've been slaying dragons and saving beautiful damsels all day. I need my rest."

She smiled. "A thousand apologies, brother, but some gifts are impatient."

His gaze flicked to her right and hardened. "Who are you? Where is Gwogh?"

Kaelyria touched his lips. "Shh. This is a . . . friend. His name is Cilicien ka'Dur. I . . . I need him here."

Uncertainty twitched in Haegan's eyes. "Why? Why do we need another accelerant?" Clarity shone in those blue orbs so like their father's. "Kae, something is not right."

Smoothing the curls along his face, she spoke what she had practiced a hundred times in anticipation of his discernment. "You trust me, don't you, brother? Haven't I taken care of you all these years, visited you, loved you?"

"Of course." His gaze bounced again to the accelerant. "Where is Gwogh? Bring him." Such authority.

"Listen to me, Haegan." On his cheek, she felt the prick of stubble. A month shy of eighteen and already manhood crouched at his door. So strange to think of him as such. "Remember the Tale of Ruadh?"

"Our favorite."

Because I have longed for this day . . . "I have been doing research with Cilicien's help." Kaelyria considered the accelerant. Though her gifts warned her not to trust ka'Dur, he was the only member of the Ignatieri with the strength and abilities—and willingness—to help.

Right or wrong, it must be done.

"We can do it, Haegan."

"Do what?" Wariness clung to his words and his gaze.

"Change places." *You must sound more certain.* "Like Ruadh and his best friend."

"What . . . what do you mean?"

"We can trade places, of sorts—"

His eyes widened. "No!"

"—but only for a short while," she said, pressing against his shoulder. "Just like Ruadh."

"Kaelyria, this is madness. Stop this talk at once."

"No, it's not madness." She forced a laugh into her voice. "It's amazing—you'll be free, Haegan. Free!" She scooted closer, pulling both legs up onto the bed with him, feeding off the hesitation in his objections, off the longing in his eyes. And in her own heart. "We can do this, just like Ruadh and Manido."

Haegan half smiled at the mention of the great friends. But she saw the doubt: they were myths.

"You will recall that when Ruadh's wife was found murdered, her brother, Manido—though mortally wounded in the battle that had claimed his sister's life—transferred his gifts to Ruadh to rout the killer." They'd loved that tale, the sacrifice of friends for the love of one woman.

"I recall," he said with a snort, "the transference cost those friends their lives." His eyes closed. "I am too tired for tales of fancy. It's madness. Go to bed, Kaelyria. We'll talk in the morning."

"Haegan," she said, the merriment gone from her voice. "Sir Jedric has asked our father-king for my hand. In three months, I leave Fieri Keep."

He locked onto her once more and scowled. "You're betrothed?"

She struggled to smile. "Aye, but before I leave, I want to give you a gift. For one month, you will have all your strength, all your vigor."

"I care not about a gift. You can't leave. What of Graem?"

She shrugged, pretending she didn't know what he did not speak: *What of me?* "It is ordered that I marry. No use in arguing. So, please, let me bestow this upon you."

"How? How would you—?" Haegan shook his head. "No. No, we can't."

"I *am* doing this, Haegan. It is my gift to you. Do not refuse me, brother. I beg you."

He considered the accelerant for a long while in stony silence. And in that time, Kaelyria saw again what a strong king he would have made. A defender. Protector. "What will happen to you?"

Her heart thudded at the question, afraid she'd betray herself. "To me?" She scoffed, nearly choking on it. "Nothing. It transfers *gifts*. Not bodies." She laughed, but it sounded hollow even to her.

"There is a cost. There is *always* a cost." Haegan frowned. "It doesn't make sense. I have no gifts! Our father-king is on the fields, fighting for Seultrie. If you are without your gifts, Seultrie is undefended."

"Foolspeech, brother. Half the Jujak are quartered here in the keep."

"And as a capital city, there are accelerants within Seultrie's borders," Cilicien added.

"Look around you, sister" Haegan said. "I have a mind that works. That is all. You have that and much more, all of which are vital to the protection of Seultrie."

"No, I assure you—it does not eradicate my gift." She licked her lips, braced as she recited words she'd practiced over and over. "It is but a share of what I possess. And only for one month." *Remind him of his long-held dream—to walk!* "Go to the Falls, Haegan—the Great Falls. It's time for the Kindling. You remember the Kindling, yes?"

He hesitated, his eyes sparking with the realization of what she meant. "Once every hundred years . . ."

With a smile and nod, she grew impassioned. "Yes! And this is that year. Walk beneath the healing waters. Then, you will have your life back."

"Kaelyria, never did I imagine you'd be so short on intelligence. The Kindling is another flight of fancy." Haegan huffed, but she saw in his words and expression the faint hope to walk again. "Why must you persist? It's insanity!"

She lifted his limp hand and held it in hers, then crushed it against her lips. Tears burned. "Can you imagine? Being able to walk and feel again?"

He studied her. "No." His voice neared a growl. "It is not right."

"My prince, if I may speak?"

Fierce, discerning eyes sliced through the accelerant. Haegan had always been shrewd. "You may not. I do not trust you, accelerant. I would seek the advice of Sir Gwogh." He looked to the door. "Where is my guardian?"

"A bit tied up with duties, my lord-prince," Cilicien answered.

"I will wait then," Haegan said.

Kaelyria lifted both his hands, though she knew he could not feel or return the fervor of her grip. After pressing a kiss to them, she set her chin on their joined hands. "An adventure, Haegan. We've dreamed of this day for so long, and now that I have a way, you refuse me. You're breaking my heart."

His brows knitted. "You twist this on me."

"I only want to give you something you've long wanted, return what has been stolen from you before I am wrenched from our home and you." Tears blurred her eyes at the thought of being Jedric's bride. Heartless creature. "We've both talked of this so often. Please?"

"I want to know the side effects," he said.

"You may have a peculiar craving for lace and petticoats," Cilicien teased.

Haegan scowled.

Kaelyria could only laugh. "He jests!" It felt good to laugh amid this tension. "Do it for me, brother. Let my one gift to you be this before I am gone from my home."

"What would I do, Kae? I am nobody. To be sure, the kingdom has forgotten me. I have no life. No friends. Almost no visitors, besides you and Gwogh."

"Just . . . for me," Kaelyria pleaded again. "Let me have the pleasure of seeing you whole, at least for a short time, brother. Go to the Falls. What do you have to lose?"

He laughed. "It's not what *I* have to lose that concerns me."

Her heart caught. "Then you refuse me?" Would she have to force him? "But—"

"Be at peace." He closed his eyes and sighed. "You wear me down with your begging. In all our years, you've never persisted so earnestly."

Once more he glared at the accelerant before meeting her gaze. "I will do it. For you."

Tears sprang to her eyes. She might save the kingdom after all. "Thank you." With a nod, she looked at Cilicien. "Begin."

2

Zireli, ruler of the Nine, king of Zaethien, and Supreme High Lord of the Ignatieri, stood on the field with his eyes closed. He opened his awareness and tuned into the land spread before him. To the sweet smell of grass and the wildflowers dotting the plain. To the warbler joining the chorus of dawn, waking the slumbering valley, the melody a deceptive distraction from the danger lurking beneath the thin veil of mist. The dampness of the predawn hour soaked into his clothes, its temperature subtle yet significant. To some, unnoticeable, but to him—unmistakable.

He turned his senses across the hillock to the right. The coolness proved prevalent and welcoming. Zireli breathed softly, deeply, pushing from his mind weighty concerns: his wife, daughter, and son back at the keep; the fleeing refugees under his protection. And his fears—was his daughter enough to protect Seultrie and its inhabitants? Would she remain strong? She was the only hope, now that he had been forced into the field to war with the enemy.

He focused on the sweet grasses. The crisp, fresh field. Beyond the rising knoll on the other side, the temperature dipped as it spread over a small lake. Even farther north the lake-rich land of Caori taunted him with its faint but brisk scent.

Behind him, a throat cleared.

Ignoring his warriors, Zireli pushed deeper into his own senses, to what the air told him. His elite, the Jujak, were chosen for a reason, for their prowess, their ferocity. And even for their impatience to act.

But now, this morning, he must take time. Determine the enemy's location. If it took till the noon meal, so be it.

A soft *thwat* made him smile. No doubt General Grinda had used a glove to slap the warrior who had complained, silencing him.

Zireli craned his head to the left. Trees and utter calm. He brought his search back to the center of the northwestern quadrant of the plain, hidden behind a cluster of boulders. A balmy breeze drifted down across the grass, pushing his hair away from his face.

He lifted his head, inhaling deeply of the air that wafted from the cool center-north area. Then to the left again. Inhale. *Tepid.*

Pivoting, he opened his eyes. Stalked the half-dozen yards back to the contingent. He swung up onto his horse. "There, in the northwest."

Grim-faced Grinda glanced in that direction, using his looking glass. He lowered the brass piece and eyed him.

"You doubt me," Zireli said, his mount shifting beneath him.

"Nay," Grinda said. "But there's only one course of action around that area—burn the trees."

The trees flanked the enemy on two sides. He could burn the foliage, forcing the troops backward—out of Zaethien. It'd be easy. "Too easy," Zireli muttered, taking in the treetops. The rocks. "The woods are populated with pine."

"Easier to burn."

"Mm." Why could he not shake the ominous feeling? Pine was one of the easier woods to burn. Oak the harder.

"Perhaps Dyrth has become overconfident," Captain Mallius suggested, but his tone belied his words.

"He is always overconfident," Zireli said. "But not stupid." Would Zaethien bring about their own demise in this battle that felt more futile with each engagement?

"Whether a trap or not, we must drive them back." Grinda's gravelly voice grew dark. "If not here, then on the higher plains."

"Where we risk higher civilian casualties," Captain Mallius said.

Zireli pulled his attention from the valley beyond the boulders. Two villages and another that could be a city. Over a thousand people. What few farmers this region held had fled to Seultrie and even Caori.

Here on the plain fatalities would be limited to his men and the enemy's.

"Only my nine and you." Zireli jabbed his heels into his mount's sides.

"Valor Guard, forward! Captain," Grinda said, "hold here and make ready to return to camp."

"Aye, sir!"

Zireli was already in the open when he heard the thunder of hooves racing up. The nine Jujak chosen as his personal guards fell into formation with the ease of long practice. Within ten minutes, they were on the inner perimeter of the tree line. Zireli and the warriors dismounted and gingerly picked their way through the woods.

The hill spilled down toward a small pond not large enough to be marked on a map. Around the water, the Sirdarians sat talking, sharpening swords. Oiling leather and buffing shields. Skirmishes to the left exhibited the prowess of the enemy army. It was not so much skill but a penchant for brutality and cruelty that marked their kind.

Zireli gave a lone nod.

Without a word, Grinda sent the nine flaring out. They'd form the Fire Triangle—a triangle within a triangle three times over. The formation protected the wielder and yet still allowed the Guard to fight effectively.

On a knee, Zireli lowered his head. Closed his eyes again. Attuned his being to Abiassa, to her will and the blessed lands he was tasked with protecting. Fist on his chest, he bent his will to hers. "Guide me by the Flames. Protect me by the hand of thy Deliverers."

Zireli pulled himself to his full height. Opened his eyes, maintaining the calming. He planted his right foot back, crossing his wrists in front of him as he did.

"Eyes out," Grinda ordered the Valor Guard. He uttered an oath, grunting as he tried to shake off dried leaves sticking to the bottom of his boots.

Resin from the trees, no doubt.

Opening his fists to a palm strike, Zireli swept his hand along the forward-most line of trees. The branches. The leaves. He focused his attention as he turned his palm over and formed a cup, then drew his elbow back to his side, drawing the heat from the elements and into the trunks. Growing the heat.

Burning trees was a simple thing, conducted even by first-years. But isolating the burn, keeping it contained within the perimeter, to flush the Sirdarians out of the valley and back through the southern part of the Nine . . . that took focus.

Around him, the Jujak shifted, their boots crunching on forest litter. The dim glow of embers sparked.

He palmed the area, pushing and pulling, restricting the flames to the trees he'd ignited so the heat intensified. The fire more demanding. While navigating the burning trees with his left, Zireli lured a warm wind to blow against the flames, pushing the fire toward the Sirdarians—as well as the smoke.

"Sir!" a Jujak's shout sounded strained.

"What?" Grinda responded.

"Taps, sir!"

Fire could be so beautiful. So ethereal. It singed, burned, but it also cleansed.

"Taps in the trees!"

Zireli's gaze slid to the trunks near him. He saw no ta— Wait! There. Midway up the trunk. Hidden among leaves. Steel poked through, its shiny surface defiant against the dull wood.

He traced the trunk to its offshoots. The needles. Pine.

And it finally made sense. He skirted a look around them, around the base of the trees. The ground. Zireli's breath backed into his throat. "It's a trap!" He spun and used a gust of hot air to push the Jujak from his location. "Back! Get out!"

He followed swiftly, and they closed around him, running as a unit with him in the center. They reached the horses and swung into their saddles. Zireli's steed galloped hard, but he kept a watchful eye, trusting his horse to lead him from the woods. They were barreling through the wood sentries when the resin ignited.

Zireli shoved his hand out in a flash-strike, pushing back against the concussive boom of the explosion. His horse whinnied in panic as heat rushed over them. A blast of air wrenched him from the mount. Thrust him backward.

He hit hard, air punched from his lungs. Zireli slumped against a tree. Ash shook from the burning leaves and branches. He coughed but battled to keep the fire back. To restrict oxygen so the greedy tendril could not devour him or his men.

Hands grabbed him. Zireli let the men drag him backward as he wrestled the flames. Fought their advance. Sweat dripped into his eyes, the fire sizzling along his arms and trousers.

Struggling between wielding and the searing pain as the fire ate at his clothes, Zireli knew surrender for him meant death for his men. And Zaethien. That could not happen.

"Feet," he grunted, palming the fire that fought him more viciously than a sword-wielding Sirdarian.

His men righted him—Grinda patting down his pant leg to crush the flames—and Zireli once more planted his foot back and regained his central focus. He harnessed the oxygen in the air, though it was warmed and ready for ignition, and used it to fan back the fire. He pushed. His muscles aching from the exertion. Whether minute or hours, he knew not, but he held the ground he stood upon. And fought back the ambush fires of the Sirdarians.

At last, Grinda's voice broke through his focus. "We should go, sire."

Exhausted, clothing shredded, Zireli stared at the out-of-control fire consuming the once-quiet forest. Grinda pushed into his periphery, offering the reins to his horse. "Please, sire."

With a huff, Zireli took the leather straps, flung himself into the saddle, and gave one last look at the devastation. At his defeat.

• • •

Fire and torment held Haegan Celahar hostage. Everything hurt. Burned. Ached. Mind ablaze, he tried to claw free. A howl screeched through his mind. Creaking and popping. Echoing darkness. Had he been stretched on a rack and torn limb from limb, he would have felt blessed compared to this torture.

But then . . . like a warm bath, a red, fiery light blossomed across his field of vision. Bored through his being and swarmed his chest. His abdomen. Down to his toes. A thrumming resonated, vibrating against his ribs. Tingling through his fingers—

Fingers? *You can't feel your fingers, fool!*

"You should go. Now. Kiesa will take you."

"But—"

"If you are caught, they will kill you."

Who was Kaelyria talking to? The accelerant?

White-hot agony ripped through him like a spear piercing his heart. He screamed, felt himself fall as the heat exploded across his chest. His ears shrieked beneath the torment.

"Gwogh," he managed, reaching out, unable to see, searching for the guardian who'd been his right hand. Who had tutored him. Challenged him. Been his friend. Ally. Champion. He felt the man's presence and groped for him.

Wait. He *thought* he was reaching. Even in his dreams, he believed he could run, swim, ride. A fool's fancy. He couldn't feel anything. He'd been crippled a decade past.

Something caught his hand.

No. Can't be. I can't feel.

"You foolish girl!" Gwogh hissed. "What have you done?"

"It had to be done," came Kaelyria's unnaturally calm voice.

"No!" Gwogh growled. "No. Not like this. Blessed Abiassa, have mercy on him," came Gwogh's soft whisper against Haegan's ears. "The Fire King will singe you alive for this!"

Worse terrors plucked at Haegan's courage. "Why can't I see?" He struggled to control the panic. He'd gone years without the use of his body—now his eyes, too? "I've angered Her, Gwogh."

"Foolspeech, my prince. Just . . . be at peace. It'll come . . ."

"Are those tears I hear in your words, old friend?" Pushing aside his panic, he tried to calm himself. Then like a light, the aged guardian loomed over him. Sweet relief swept through him. "By the Flames!" He laughed. "I thought I was blind, too." An annoying sensation in his legs—how could that be?—drew his attention away from his gray-bearded guardian. He shifted. Felt a thump. Heard a crash.

A girl cried out.

Haegan looked down . . . his legs . . . Those weren't his legs. His were atrophied, grossly thin and pale. Embarrassing. Humiliating. These were strong, muscular legs.

The gray slate felt like ice beneath him. "The floor," he muttered and glanced around. "I'm on the floor. Why am I on the cold floor?"

Gwogh sucked in a breath. "You can feel it? The cold?"

Haegan stilled. Let his gaze drop back to the legs. To the slate. Saw a hand moving toward the strong limbs. *My hand!* A noise, strange and guttural, wormed through his chest. Laughter! "I can," he said with a laugh. "I can feel. And *move!*"

With gentleness that had defined his guardian, Gwogh slid away from Haegan, watching with a strange expression.

Every fiber of Haegan's being erupted. Tingling. Fire zipping from the top of his head to his toes. Feeling! It was *feeling*. Another bubble of laughter escaped as he again met his guardian's somber expression. "What ails you, Sir Gwogh? You look as if you've seen a ghoul."

"I fear I have."

Haegan drew his feet in, exhilarated when they responded. He reached for the windowsill—*how did I get off the bed?*—and drew himself up. Rising, he reeled as the world loomed into view. He drew in a steadying breath and let it out, a light fog clouding the leaded glass. He smiled that he could move—view the world at his leisure or pleasure. Disbelief spiraled through him. He shook his head. *Madness!*

I am whole. Tears stung his eyes. How many nights and days had he begged Abiassa to let him walk again? And now . . . it'd happened.

Haegan pulled his attention back to himself, to the limbs that had not worked, that could not even hold a goblet. Legs that certainly could not push him to his feet. Balling his fists, he felt the strength. Watched the tendons and muscles contract. Incredible!

Bouncing on his toes, he laughed. Glorious! "You spoke truth, sister. I am free!" A presence beside him made Haegan turn his head from admiring his hands.

Gwogh. Concern etched the gray eyes, as it had not done in a very long time. Since the day he fell to the poison. And in that second, Haegan had a wretched, awful feeling. *This is wrong.* Yet he could not let it go. Did not *want* to let it go.

It *was* wrong. This should *not* have happened. But all he could say was, "You're short."

"I'm afraid you've outgrown me, my lord prince."

Something in Haegan scrambled for reassurance, for Gwogh to say this *wasn't* wrong. That it was okay to be free. It was okay to walk and be normal. Strong. But his guardian merely stared. And for a second, that angered Haegan. Could the man not have one spark of joy for him?

The graybeard shook his head. "This should not have been done. Forgive me for saying so, my lord prince, but it should not." He turned and left the room, shoulders stooped. With more than age.

The urge to go after him pushed Haegan two steps forward. "Gwogh, wait!" He stopped, his mind whirling and unused to the movement. A gurgle of laughter trickled through him—*Walking! I'm walking!*

"It will take some time to get your land legs," Cilicien said with an amused laugh.

Haegan looked at the Ignatieri high marshal, then at his bed. Blanket and sheets clumped to the side—wait. No. Not sheets and blanket—a shape lay there.

Cilicien moved closer to Haegan.

Blocking my view.

"What will you do first, my lord prince?" The accelerant shifted again, pointed to the windows. "The lands of Zaethien and Luxlirien are plentiful with beautiful maidens, and since you have your youthful vigor back . . ."

Anger rose. Did he think Haegan so callow? So ignorant of his devices? Haegan swept aside the accelerant, dreading to know what the conniving marshal was hiding, and pushed forward. He stopped,

the world tilting at what he saw—Kaelyria. Laid out on the very bed
he had occupied for too many years. The bed that had held him,
cocooned him, imprisoned him, now did the same to his sister.

Breath would not fill his lungs. He stood, mute. *Fool!* "Kaelyria!"
Haegan lunged. "Kaelyria!"

She did not move, even as a tear traced her perfect face.

"What happened?" He spun toward the accelerant. "What did you
do to her?"

"Haegan." A whisper, faint and haunting, reached for him.
Clutched him by the throat. "Forgive me, my brother." More tears as
her delicate blond brows knitted. "It was the only way."

Revelation struck him as he stared at his sister. "You knew . . . you
knew this would happen." He groped for understanding that would
not come and dropped against the mattress. "Why? Why in blazes
would you do this?"

"It's the Year of the Feasts."

"Every hundredth year," he said. "But, Kae, the Kindling—'tis a
fancy, not reality."

Kae drew in a shuddering breath and a smile wavered across her
lips, her blue eyes locked on him. "No, 'tis real. True. I've read accounts
of those who've been healed there. A long time ago, I asked Father to
take you when the Kindling came . . ." She faltered, then went on,
"He, too, said it was fancy."

Her eyes sparkled. "But I'm convinced this is your chance to be
whole. This transference will last but one month, long enough for you
to reach the Falls." She blinked away tears that pooled in her eyes.
"You can walk beneath the waters and be healed."

"Then . . . then you'll be released?" He scanned her body, hoping
to see her leg move. Fingers lift.

"Yes," she breathed. "But if you don't get to the Falls, you will be
imprisoned again."

"This is madness! And supposition—there is no way to know if it
is true." Desperation strangled his words. He shook his head, fighting
tears he'd given up on long ago. "My stupid big sister," he said with
all the grief and love a brother could possess. He pressed his forehead

to hers. "Why . . .? This is—I don't want this. *You* have the *abiatasso*. Our people need *you*."

A rustle of fabric preceded Gwogh's return.

Kae's eyes flicked in his direction. "You must leave, Haegan. I think your guardian has realized that as well."

"I cannot leave you! Not like this." Haegan felt the tears. The strangle in his chest. Thrumming in his arms.

"If you stay, this is all for nothing." Kaelyria's eyes sought the guardian. "Get him to safety. When they learn what has happened, the Jujak will act swiftly. Hurry!"

"Come, my prince. She's right." Hands clapped onto his shoulders. "The queen and king will not be forgiving. They would see you thrown into the Lakes, for the truth of it."

"No. If I'm dead, she gets her legs back, right? This is my fault. I'll stay." He'd lived his life in this room, in this tower, watching the heavens. If he stayed, he'd die, true. But he would not abandon Kaelyria. She had not abandoned him when he'd lost his life to poisoning. "If they burn me—"

Shouts spiraled up from the courtyard outside. He could hear armor clanking. His heart skipped a beat. He'd not seen their father-king in years. A yearning burst within him to have his father laugh, clap him on the shoulder. Just once more. Treat him as the son he was born to be. But now . . . now that would never happen. Even if he weren't off campaigning, Father would see Kaelyria.

And kill me for what has happened here.

Fear crested his grief.

"You have one month. Only one," she said. "I watched you lie here for years. Think you I am not strong enough to take your yoke for one month? This was my choice, Haegan."

He wavered.

"If you go now, you can make it."

"No!" He could not let this happen.

"Do not waste this gift I have given you," Kaelyria ground out. "Go, brother!" Another tear escaped and slipped into the thick blond hair that formed a halo around her head. "Save Fieri Keep."

Before he could respond, a resounding thud echoed through his brain. His teeth clattered. His vision ghosted and went dark.

3

Darkness pervaded. Haegan blinked, digging himself out from the beneath the torment of pain and blindness. His mind scrambled for placement, clarity. For purchase against a torrent of dreams. Blazes! Not dreams—*Nightmares!* Only as the drums of a pounding headache assaulted him did he realize . . . *'Tis no nightmare.*

'Twas far worse: reality. "No," he croaked out.

As he tried to lift his cheek from the dirt he lay in, his head protested with a shrill ringing. He slumped back down. Someone must have clobbered him and removed him from the palace. With the darkness and the smells, he could not gain his bearings.

Shadows lightened as he blinked again. Just an inch from his nose, something moved. Startled him. Then he saw—fingers. *My fingers!* Scratching in the dirt, Haegan processed the fact that he had full control of his digits.

Grief wrapped its powerful talons around his heart and squeezed. Why would she do this? He could not wipe away the image of Kaelyria lying there, perfect. But perfectly crippled. "No!" He curled into himself, rage and grief warring.

He beat a fist against the dirt.

Shouts erupted.

Haegan lifted his head. Looked around. Darkness, shadows, stench, and dampness. *Where am I?*

Pounding footsteps jerked him up, and he winced at the pain. He scrabbled backward as several shapes burst from the shadows—straight toward him. His back thudded against something hard. His fingers traced the wooden barrier.

The first of the crowd bolted past, leaving a trail of stench.

Two more rushed onward. One wedged between the other and the wall. Too close! No gap—the one wearing a cap would trample him. Haegan drew in his legs, arms.

Thud!

They collided. The boy toppled over him. Feet. Legs. Screams. Confusion addled his mind as he fought to untangle himself. He struggled against the person, against the assault on his senses. Trapped. He felt trapped. And crowded. And weird—all these feelings rushing over him like a squall.

"Let go!" the kid shouted. Kicked. Slapped. Punched.

Knuckles collided with his eye.

"Augh!" Haegan struck out with his own punch, but stopped short, realizing the futility of the move. "I am not your enemy. Stop."

Hands pawed at them both as one of the others returned. Hot, rank breath skated along Haegan's cheek. "Up! C'mon, Thiel."

Darkness prevented Haegan from seeing straight. Tangles of arms and legs drew him up. Pushed him into the darkness of another tunnel.

"No, wait."

"Shut yer trap," the youth ordered, shoving him. "Want them to find us?"

Yes. Wait—*the guards.* No. He did not want to be found. Not till he could sort out what happened, how to fix this mess and restore Kaelyria.

They propelled him onward. Maybe it was just as well. He wasn't even sure where he was right now.

Light bloomed in the confined darkness, torches drawing closer.

"*Go!*"

Arrows thunked into the wood behind him. Haegan started. Jujak! His father's royal guards!

He flipped around and bolted, mind afire with the very thought that he *could* run. He hadn't done that since he was eight, chasing Kaelyria across the plains to the Lakes of Fire and down the forbidden passages. He'd chased her laughter more than her. And now . . . now she might never run again if he didn't escape and get to the Falls.

No! Don't think of her.

One month. That was all he had. There was no going back, so he just had to muster on. Get to the Falls, get healed, and return. This gift his sister had—*stupidly, foolishly*—given him would not be wasted. He would not dishonor her. He *would* fix this. She'd walk again. And rule Seultrie and Fieri Keep.

What if she didn't? What if he failed? The thought made him want to cry out again.

You're Prince of Zaethien, son of the Fire King. It mattered not that he'd never sit upon that gilded throne or harness the Flames. He had all the pride necessary to have been sired by the Fire King.

Running, he marveled at how long it took his legs to exhaust. It was as if those ten bedridden years had never been. Palming the slick, mossy stone wall for guidance, he hurried on through the blinding darkness, his mind on its own frantic rampage.

The wall curved out, away from Zaethien. Darkness lightened the tunnel fifty paces ahead. There the others vanished around another corner. His breath hitched. Having lived inside the walls, he did not know these routes. What if he got lost?

Haegan almost laughed. Lost would be the least of his problems if thrust before his father's Jujak. He'd gained his strength, use of his body, but he'd lose *everything* else.

"No! Don't slow," came a panting voice from behind. A slight figure brushed past him. "They won't."

He looked back. Torches bobbed and armor clanked as the guards ran. "Seal the gates," a guard shouted.

Haegan glanced at the boy. Grubby pants, a large tunic and vest marked the one who'd punched him, he was sure.

Stay and face the guards. Nobody would believe he was the prince. At least, not at first. But it wouldn't be long before the truth was discovered. His father would formally denounce him as he pitched him into the Lakes of Fire. They would not believe Kae had done this of her own will. What Seultrie lost . . .

Feet slapped the earth.

Haegan's head jerked up.

The boy had returned. Clutched Haegan's jerkin. Yanked. "Move!"

They broke into a run, the boy pulling him on when his feet tangled in unfamiliar motion. *Is this right?* If these street urchins were found with him and arrested, they would be killed, too. He could not be responsible for more lives. For more *loss*.

Though shorter than Haegan by a head, the kid was strong, tugging him onward. Toward the light. Toward freedom. "There!" He yanked again.

Haegan tripped. But kept going, his mind alive with conflicting messages. Warm stone. Fire in his shoulder. His gut—something felt strange there. After years of paralysis, now he struggled to orient his mind to what was happening in his body. He hit the boy. They slammed into a wall, Haegan tripping on top of him.

The boy rolled in his grasp. "Stupid!"

Haegan grabbed shoulders. Turned. Pushed him toward the opening not more than fifteen paces away. "Go," he said. Why wouldn't the boy go?

"You're hurt."

"I'm not. I'm fine." Haegan urged him toward the end of the tunnel.

The kid jerked back, but Haegan was already pushing, forcing him to keep moving. "Go!"

More arrows thwapped into the wood beams. Seared along his arm. Haegan howled against the pain that exploded in his shoulder. He jerked toward the guards, angry. Why would they hound youth in tunnels?

They're looking for me.

Why, Kaelyria? Why did you do this?

The boy's eyes were wide. He'd frozen.

"Go," Haegan growled at the boy.

"You're . . . you're . . . the arrow hit you."

As if he needed to be told. He felt the warmth sliding down his shoulder and arm. Felt the blazing pain. But that didn't help. "Go!" He shoved the boy. Jerked toward the guards. He didn't know what he'd do. How he would stop a half dozen of his father's elite. But he would. With lies. With tricks. Whatever it took. Then he'd have to explain to his father.

Right. When had he ever talked to his father in the last several years?

Rejected. Forgotten.

"Halt! By order of the Fire King!"

And now he was no less alone, abandoned even by Gwogh, unable to reach his sister. Why? Why couldn't Kae have left him to his books? Why couldn't the guards just let him go? He was no one. Had no friends. No power. Nothing.

Pain tugged at his shoulder.

Why must they all force him to do something he did not want to do? *Why?*

Anger pulsed through Haegan. Breathing . . . hard . . . Just once, for even a moment, he wanted control of his life. Of what happened to him. Something hot flared through him. As if fire ate at his chest. Or an arrow had pierced a lung.

How dare the Jujak try to kill me? Before I can reach the Falls, before I can return to save Kaelyria? Before my father could even be consulted?

But then . . . he would not put it past his father-king to condone their actions. Anger tumbled into rage. If he failed, if these guards stopped him—

Rage blew into fury. Kae would live his lot for the rest of her life. She didn't deserve that. Beauty, grace, purity . . .

The clatter of armor roiled toward him.

He raised his eyes toward the Jujak. Glared. *Why can't they just . . . leave . . . me . . . alone?* A growl rose in his chest. *"Why?"*

Light exploded.

4

Zireli stormed into his tent, his mind and the backs of his arms still scalded from the explosion. He yanked off his gloves and pitched them onto the table. Rage coiled around his heart and lungs, constricting. His fingers itched to throw the servant fussing over the platter of bread and cheeses. "Leave us."

The servant scurried from the tent without a word, leaving Zireli to his anger. Plucking free the buckles of his cloak, he wrestled his thoughts. "See to it Etru's family is compensated. Their mortgage paid."

Grinda nodded. "Aye, sir."

Yanking off the armor he'd worn, the simple plates that allowed him to wield but also protected him from arrow and sword, he chided himself. No, he *condemned* himself. Must. "I could smell it," he muttered as he set the armor on the stand. He gave a soft snort. "I could smell the resin, but gave no thought to it."

"No one could've seen that trap coming."

"Trap?" Zireli pivoted. "That was a blazing ambush! The amount of resin—the scent was too strong." He bent over the wood table, palms flat against the surface as he stared at the maps, the missives, the orders . . . "Yet, I allowed my arrogance and pride to block what was right beneath my nose."

"Sire, he took a risk—"

"He baited me." The maps he'd considered in the predawn lamplight revealed the trail Poired had left. The trail right to that valley. "He's playing with me."

"It makes no sense, this far north, to lay a trap like that. What did he hope to accomplish?"

"Why did I not notice the taps?" It was simple thing to note. To take into account. First-years were taught to search their surroundings and weigh the costs and effects of wielding in the area. "And because I didn't, I lost one of my guard."

The thought of Etru's body engulfed by fire pried at Zireli's conscience. Beat him. Tormented him. "Why . . .?" There were no villages, no main cities worth taking. "Why this far north . . .?" But he didn't need to ask that question.

Grinda shifted, but remained silent. A move that drew Zireli's attention to the man he'd called friend far longer than he'd called him general.

"Seultrie. He wanted me away from the keep." Zireli's mind flew to his queen and daughter, tucked safely within the walls of Fieri Keep. "She is not undefended."

"But she is not you, sire."

Zireli eyed the grim-faced man who stood across the table from him.

"Think you the princess's gift is strong enough to—"

"It must be," Zireli bit out, his chest tightening at the thought of Kaelyria facing down such a powerful adversary at her young age. Not even an adult, she was charged with the protection of Seultrie in his absence. "She's formidable in her own right. Even Gwogh said she had unusual wielding abilities. She's intelligent, as well." He'd left her there. Alone. He'd had every confidence in her. The threat against the Nine had come to a head, his presence on the battlefield demanded. "There is naught at the keep save my family."

"Aye, but if Dyrth takes the keep, he takes the heart of the Nine. It's symbolic—the loss would devastate the people."

"She'll hold."

"The princess is only nineteen, my—"

"She'll. Hold."

Grinda glanced at him, speculative grey eyes weighing. Assessing.

Thoughts twisted and churned through the man's granite-like visage. "She's your daughter—"

"And you send your son to battle as readily as I set Kaelyria to defend the keep." Zireli tried to breathe past the tinge of panic that erupted, thinking of his daughter protecting her mother and crippled brother.

"My son's a trained Jujak and has been through numerous battles. He's a leader among his peers. He—"

Shouts arose within the camp. Zireli strode to the opening and stepped out, eyeing a rider barreling up from the south end of the camp. The red sash across his chest marked him as a Seultrian guard.

"It's Captain Grinda, sire!" a guard shouted.

The general was there at his side instantly, his breath raspy. "This can't be good."

Ten seconds delivered the younger Grinda to the command tent. The young officer threw himself off his mount and dropped to a knee. "Your majesty, word from the keep."

Aware of the thickening crowd, Zireli turned back to his tent. "Inside, Captain." Back in the relative warmth of the tent, he stood at the table, his heart in his throat. Was it Adrroania? Kaelyria? Or had Haegan finally succumbed to the poison that had stolen his destiny?

"What's happened?" Grinda demanded of his son as the tent flap closed behind them.

The two were much alike in looks—both with the dark hair of their Zaethien forebears. The younger had not yet grown a beard, but the colorings and dark eyes were nevertheless piercing and intelligent. Breathless as his gaze met Zireli's, the captain gave a firm nod. His cheeks were flushed, his green tunic darkened to almost black by rings of perspiration. He'd ridden hard and fast.

Only bad news would come this way. Zireli straightened. "Go on."

"Your majesty," Captain Grinda choked out. "Information is short but I bring news of your son, Haegan."

Haegan? Zireli twitched, stopping himself from stepping forward. His mind raced to the tower that housed his son. *My son . . .* Had he died? Would Zireli's failure to protect Haegan from the enemy's poison haunt him forever?

"Speak!" Grinda growled at his son.

"The prince has fled the keep."

"Fled?" Zireli shook his head. "Forget you that my son is unable to walk, let alone flee?"

"He was . . . restored, my king. By some means. Nefarious, it is rumored." Posture tense, hands fisted at his sides, the young officer barreled on. "A banished accelerant was seen fleeing the keep through a servant's entrance." He swallowed, then a storm swept across his ruddy features. "The princess was found ill and bedridden. She's—she's paralyzed, sire. As if she traded places with the prince."

Zireli lurched. "Traded?" His mind twisted and churned through the words. The impossible words. Traded places? "Captain—are you on the drink?"

Dark eyes widened. "It's forbidden for a Jujak, sire. In earnest—your son, the prince, is gone and able to walk and your daughter now lies in a tower, bereft and paralyzed."

"Poired?" Grinda asked.

"No, sire," his son said. "It's worse."

"Worse?" Zireli couldn't laugh this time. His hands tingled with the urge to wield. To hurt someone. "Explain yourself."

"Facts are short and rumors long, sire." Graem's gaze darted to the ground, then to Zireli, but evaded capture once more. "It is said . . ." He huffed. "King Zireli, it was the prince. Haegan is responsible for what has befallen the princess."

Singed by the words, Zireli froze. "You realize the words you speak—you realize what they mean? What judgment would be against—"

"I do, sire. And I speak no falsehoods. I was sent here—"

"Why?" Zireli turned to the table again. Betrayed by his own son? No. No, he would not believe that of Haegan. The boy might have no use of his body, but he had a brilliant mind . . . and a good heart. "Why would he do this?" It made no sense. It was not in the boy's character.

I left him there . . . in that tower. Too ashamed of his own failings to give witness to what that had cost his son, the kingdom. Had
Haegan grown bitter after all those years alone?

"I know not, my king. But the princess . . . she sends for you."

"Sends for me?" He felt so witless. Dumbstruck.

"Yes, my king. Her gifts . . . they're gone, sire."

Numbness spread through him. Then panicked alarm. "The keep."
It sat undefended save the handful of Jujak left there. "Ready my horse
to ride!"

• • •

Thud . . . thud . . . thud.

Thud!

Haegan jolted upright. Bright light pierced his eyes, hurting all the
way to the back of his skull. He slammed shut his eyelids and dropped
back down. Pain bloomed against his head and shoulders. Groaning,
he wasn't sure what injury to nurse—his head, his shoulders, or his
heart. And beneath it all, a strange rocking motion that stirred nausea.

"You're awake."

Haegan tried to see in the blinding day. Shielding his eyes, he
peered to the side. Three others sat watching him, their backs against
a brace support in a wagon that carried them along a dirt road. A boy
with golden hair that framed his brow and face grinned at Haegan.
Two others sat beside the boy, one a dark-haired teen who looked about
eighteen. The other teen had brown skin and black hair. Kergulian,
Haegan guessed.

"Wh-who are you?" Why had they taken him, protected him,
helped him?

The golden-haired youth cracked a smile. "That's what we'd like
to know. Thiel there"—the boy bobbed his head to someone behind
Haegan—"says you're some pretender what stole into the castle and
tried to kill the princess so's you could nick the throne."

Something sailed past Haegan and thumped the boy in the head.
He held it up, triumphant. "It's so easy to get Thiel to give up food."
He chomped into the roll.

"Give it back."

The boy shrugged as he took another bite. "Your fault. Shouldn't 'ave thrown it." He bobbed his head toward Haegan. "Left you a roll and apple for when ya woke."

Haegan glanced down, saw the food, but what really snagged his attention was the fact that he no longer wore his jerkin. A grubby tunic draped his torso.

"Ah," the boy said, his cheek puffed with bread. "That's Thiel's doing, too. You was all bloody and stuff, but from what, we can't figure. What with the blinding light and all—anyways, you got no wound for all that blood, but what with that big red stain and all, we would've drawn the coppers, so Thiel changed you a'fore we got under way."

Haegan tried to peer at his rescuer but Thiel turned his back to him.

The golden-haired boy shrugged. "Anyway, Tokar here says since you was sleeping in the tunnels near the hidden gate that maybe you wanted to be an accelerant but didn't have the hang of the Fires."

"Flames," Haegan corrected.

"Wha'?" the boy asked.

"You wield Flames. The Fires refer to the Lakes," Haegan nodded, only to realize he wasn't sure which direction the Lakes of Fire were now.

"Wha'ever," the boy said. "Don' matter, do it, because you ain' got nee-ver." The boy wagged what was left of the roll. "But what with the gate being near Zaethien's Sanctuary, we all think you must be connected to that."

Three pairs of eyes waited, wanting him to prove he could control the Flames. Or had tried—as illegal outside the Sanctuary as being in the lower passages. Haegan would prove nothing. Would say nothing.

"Aw, blazes!" the boy muttered. "Look, you gotta talk cuz we already got someone what can't." He stuck a finger at the biggest of the four, the dark-skinned one. "They cut out his tongue when he stole and lied about it. That's what happens wif thieves."

Haegan straightened, his shoulder aching. "I'm no thief."

"Yes!" The boy thrust a fist in the air, his blond hair swinging across his face as he looked to the others in triumph. "That always works."

The dark-skinned fellow leaned forward and nudged the boy. "Don't listen to Laertes." For one who was purported to be mute, he spoke very clearly. "He's got more embers than brains. I'm Praegur." He stuck out his tongue. "Intact, as you can see."

Haegan gave a slight nod and worked to sit up. Plucking a dagger from his eye would've been less painful. Yet he relished the pain. Yesterday he could not feel *anything*. Not a touch. Not a pinch. But now, pain riddled him.

From what? The boy—Laertes—said he didn't have a wound. Haegan tested the spot he'd felt the arrow pierce but found nothing. So why was he hurting so much? He grimaced and grunted as he used the side of the wagon to haul himself into a sitting position. Heat rushed through him at the effort.

"What're you called?" Tokar asked.

"I'm—" Haegan's mind spasmed as it registered the terrain the rocking wagon lumbered over. A hill. Grass. *Green* grass. No fires? How long had he lain unconscious? A strange panic heated his chest. "Where are we?"

"Three days north of Fieri Keep." Laertes tugged the hat over his eyes.

"Three days!" So far from home? What would he do? He didn't know anyone. Had no means to provide for himself. No friends for help. No family or guardian to watch over him. How many miles . . .? He thought through his lessons with Gwogh—

Gwogh! What would his old guardian think? The old accelerant had tutored him in the sciences and maths. If they were three days north, then somewhere between fifty and sixty leagues stretched between him and all that he knew and loved. Were they in Caori, the kingdom that bordered Zaethien to the northeast? He struggled to breathe, to not be overtaken by fear and panic.

You are the Fire King's son!

Haegan practiced the calming Gwogh had taught him, but even that made him desperate for the old accelerant.

"You've been out cold since—"

Tokar elbowed him, and Praegur threw a terrible scowl at the young boy.

Their gazes bounced to Thiel but fell away just as fast. Sitting on the bench seat beside the wagon master, Thiel gave a sharp shake of his head. Laertes swallowed and swiped his tongue over his teeth, hunching his shoulders and burrowing into himself with a huff.

"Since what?"

Haegan might have been holed up in a tower for years, but he wasn't a simpleton.

Thiel shifted on the bench that hovered at Haegan's shoulder. Light streaked across his face, igniting brown eyes to a clear, wild gold. Suspicion rimmed his features. Grungy vest and tunic. This was the same one who'd tripped over Haegan, then punched him. The leader of these four, clearly. But Thiel seemed too young, too soft in the face. No whiskers yet. But there was much fire in the young leader.

In the tunnel, Thiel had yanked him onward when his courage flagged. He'd argued. Wrestled. Refused to budge when Haegan insisted they move. Shouted at him. Called him names. Haegan had to force Thiel out of the tunnels. Even to the point of pushing his chest . . . a chest that wasn't quite . . . flat.

Haegan hadn't thought twice of it then. Armor? Thiel wore only a simple tunic that hung loose. Haegan skated a gaze around the wagon. No hulky bundles that might be armor. So . . . if it wasn't armor . . .

Curves. His face heated as the realization sank in, the words on his tongue before he could stop them. "You're not a boy."

"And you're not an idiot," Thiel said. "Good to know."

The snickers of the others didn't faze him. "Why do you dress like that?"

Lips drew tight. She lifted her chin. "You've not given us your name. Who are you? What were you doing in the lower tunnels?" He—*she* leaned forward. "Are you a spy? An assassin?"

With a snort, Haegan shook his head. He'd spent a decade matching wits with one of the sharpest minds in Seultrie and all the Nine.

He would not be bested now by a girl dressed as a boy. "I could ask the same of you. It is forbidden to be wandering the tunnels."

Her eyes narrowed. "What are you hiding? One word from me and this driver will dump you."

Haegan knew better than to look at the man bent over his task of urging the beasts of burden onward. But he did. Because he couldn't look into her sun-lit eyes any longer.

"Why were you down there?" Thiel demanded. "I saw an accelerant dump you and lock the gate."

Haegan blinked. An accelerant dumped him? Who—Gwogh? His tutor wouldn't dare abandon him like a dog. But what other explanation could exist? He'd been standing there, refusing to leave Kaelyria, when—

Someone hit the back of my head. Knocked him unconscious.

"Answer, tunnel rat! Why were you down there?"

His heart sped at the demand. He'd never had anyone speak to him in such a disagreeable manner—well, except Kae, but that was her way. "A disagreement." It couldn't be Gwogh who dumped him—they had too much history. The bejeweled accelerant had fled. Then who . . .?

"What happened in the tunnel?"

Haegan's attention popped to Tokar. "I told you, a disagreement."

"No." Quiet confidence oozed out of the dark-haired teen's unusual gold eyes. "Not when the accelerant dumped you. After, when you were escaping"—he bobbed his head toward the lone girl of their company—"with Thiel."

Confused, Haegan looked at her again. "I . . . I don't understand." He frowned. "Are you talking about when I pushed you—"

"The light!" Her face reddened, whether under embarrassment or anger he wasn't sure. "The explosion."

"What explosion?" Haegan shook his head. "I have no idea. The guards must've thrown a cluster or something." His answer didn't satisfy them by the look in their eyes. "What?"

Tokar watched warily. "It's just that the light, it—"

"Leave off." Thiel slipped from the bench and sat between Tokar and the young boy. "We want your name, tunnel rat."

"And if I withhold it?" Something about her impudence steeled his resolve to conceal his identity and purpose. That and being pursued by the Jujak.

"We'll turn you over to the nearest accelerant once we reach Luxlirien."

Flames. Accelerants and Jujak were equally ominous. Whatever happened . . . whatever Kaelyria had done, he would be punished. "Rigar," he supplied the name unwillingly. But not in the manner they believed. Because he detested liars. There was an imperative nature to a false identity, so he felt justified. But still guilty.

Thiel gave a nod. "Rest then, Rigar. We'll camp soon. At this pace, we'll reach Luxlirien in a week."

His tutor had made frequent trips to the Light City, and he'd heard his father had as well. Staying there meant risking exposure. "I can't stay there. Not for long."

A smile tugged the left side of Thiel's lips up. "Neither can we, tunnel rat. We set for the Northlands during the full rise."

"Northlands?" Haegan cringed. "I need to get to Hetaera."

Confrontation crouched in her gaze. "Nobody wants to go there these days. The Ignatieri—" She broke off.

Thiel watched Haegan, he eyes narrowing. "The Great Falls." She smiled when he tensed. "You want the healing waters."

5

The embers of time spark and flash but they, like all else, smolder and extinguish.

Alas, it had happened far too quickly. Sir Gwogh held his robes as he descended the stone spiral staircase. His booted feet carried him quickly through the lower servant's passage to the kitchen, which was in an uproar over the events of the last days—including the Fire King's abrupt return to the keep. As Gwogh strode past the thick cook and his assistants tending the second meal preparations, Gwogh beseeched Abiassa to keep him from failing. Again.

He hurried through the kitchen door into a small courtyard and through the vegetable garden. His leather soles crunched over the dirt path as he made his way to the gate at the back of the bricked wall that traced a formidable line around Fieri Keep. With a grating sound, the key slid into the iron lock. Twisted. He tugged back the bolt.

A scrappy boy in rags straightened from beneath the tree across the worn path. Shifting from one foot to another, he traced the road then castle walls with his gaze.

Gwogh extended a silver dallion.

The boy stared at it. "*Flames,*" he whispered.

"The parchment," Gwogh prompted, stuffing kindness into his weathered features to lessen the severity.

The boy drew the paper from a half-torn pocket and handed it over, snatching the coin in quick exchange. Without a word, Gwogh turned, secured the gate, and entered the keep. Inside, he tucked himself into an alcove above the servant's quarters and pulled out the missive. Red wax stamped with a flame promised only two sets of eyes would see this message, his and the sender's. He broke the seal and read the single line: *The Spark takes the quickest route to ignition.*

Gwogh let out a breath he'd held for two days and leaned against the warm stone wall. Their proximity to the Lakes of Fire forbade the chill inherent in most stones. With his old bones and the evil he faced, he welcomed the warmth. He crumpled the parchment and looked down the passage, lit every twenty paces by torches fed off the natural gas pumped through slender troughs in the stone. Never consumed yet always consuming.

He lifted his hand, twisted his wrist and opened his palm. With a flash and puff, the parchment disintegrated. The uneducated might call his gift, his training, *majik.* It was not. The source was more pure, divine—when used and guided by Abiassa. There were, of course, those who had abandoned Abiassa and perverted her gift. Incipients. Their champion sought to overrun these very walls—Sirdar of Tharqnis and his puppet, Poired Dyrth.

Evidence incinerated, Gwogh headed toward the meeting hall. What happened to young Haegan should never have come to pass. He'd given every effort to make certain the boy was protected. Somehow he'd failed him. But it would not happen again.

As he rounded the corner and reached for the rail to ascend the last flight, he heard whispers. Hurried, frantic ones chasing each other down the dark passage. Gwogh paused, and cocked his head, listening. Sounded like . . . Adrroania.

The realization pulled him backward. He eased to the side, peering around the corner toward the royal residence. Queen Adrroania, resplendent in a buttery yellow gown, stood in the light of an intersecting passage. Hair rolled and tied up at the back, she wore the ceremonial crown fashioned with rubies and citrines that resembled dancing flames. The headpiece was worn only while holding court or attending the Fire King. Today was such a day. The two would meet with the Council to discuss the plight of their children, the heirs.

Adrroania glided past him without notice or comment. She sailed, it seemed, right over the black marble to the chambers where she and her husband would hold council. And she carried herself as if nothing were amiss.

All these years, all the service he'd surrendered in the hopes of guiding the Flames within this family—especially to guide Haegan after he was lost to his family, lost to the poison—had it all been for naught? The boy lived a pittance of an existence. Relegated to the towers with no visitors save his sister, his mother, and, on occasion, his father's top general, Kiliv Grinda. King Zireli had entered the passage once each year—on Haegan's birth morn. But only until the prince reached the age of acceptance, fourteen. Zireli had not darkened those halls again until his return yester eve with the Valor Guard.

Had Gwogh wasted a whole decade educating Haegan, teaching him? Even now he wondered if the plan he'd put into play was in vain.

Abiassa . . . dare I hope that there is *hope?* "I am old, Daughter of Flame," he whispered.

And it is your ageless wisdom from Me that is needed now more than ever before, old friend.

He'd had a feeling she would answer as such. With a sigh, he lumbered to his feet. Decided to take the servant's passage to the council hall, mayhap slip in unnoticed. Remain in the shadows and watch. Avoid conversation with the Brethren. They'd long ago closed their meetings and doors to him, when he was sent out to tend to a poisoned princeling.

When he gained the rear entrance, two servants waited in the butler's passage, heads down, staring at their trays. Prepared trays. Food going cold.

Incensed, Gwogh asked, "What—"

"Did you think I would not discover your betrayal?" a voice roared from the inner chamber.

Stilled, Gwogh hauled in a breath. He knew that voice. All within Seultrie knew that voice. Zireli! He rushed to the heavy wooden door that stood ajar and peeked through the sliver of an opening. The private antechamber, paneled in rich, dark searage—a fieri wood that had undergone a meticulous process of scorching till it blackened, then coated with a thick glaze—sat outside the council hall.

King Zireli, fierce and formidable in his red and black uniform of the Ignatieri, towered over a kneeling Adrroania. "How could you do this? To me? To Zaethien?"

Adrroania shook her head. "I did not."

The king glowered, his robes riffling the air as he spun away from her in a rage. "I have it here, the proof that you granted Cilicien audience with Kaelyria!"

"No, I—"

Face red, Zireli spun and thrust a hand at her.

Though he did not touch her, Adrroania cried out and threw her head back. The bejeweled crown tumbled off and clanked to the floor. Her chest heaved amid her sobs. "Please! My love!"

And Gwogh knew. Knew Zireli held his own wife in the halo, an invisible force of tingling fire that paralyzed its target. Could *crush* its captive, if wielded just so.

Grief tugged at Gwogh. The fragile tendrils of this family, of this line, this powerful race, teetered on the brink of collapse. And though Zireli blamed his queen, Gwogh knew the naïve but beautiful woman had not conspired against her own children. Not this time.

"Zireli, please," Adrroania gasped beneath the halo. "I love our children. I would *never* betray you or them. Kaelyria asked for training—"

He stepped sideways toward her, his face crimson. "*I* train her! *I* assign tutors. Not you. Not anyone else. Ever!" His shoulders rose and fell raggedly as he seemed to struggle against the torrent within himself. "I warned you—before they were even conceived. In doing this, you *have* betrayed me!" He slammed the heel of his hand toward her.

Adrroania flopped back a half-dozen feet. She slumped to the ground, groaning, her long, delicate fingers seeming to dig into the marble. But she was free. Free of the halo.

"Our daughter is a cripple, Adrroania—the *heir!*" Zireli's voice roared off the high dark rafters of their chamber. "The defender of Seultrie in my absence! The one who is to sit on the High Seat. The one to protect the Nine Kingdoms against Sirdar and his Fallen. *Augh!*" Veins bulging in his temples, Zireli spun, crossed his hands, and then flung them outward in a giant X formation.

Windows shattered. Silver toppled. Curtains ruffled. The concussion sent ripples of heat roiling over Gwogh. The door in front of him snapped back. Thumped him in the head. Pain exploded through his neck and temples.

Fool, he chided himself. *That's what comes of eavesdropping.* Touching the quickly forming knot on his forehead, he stepped into the private chamber.

"This, *this* is why I alone choose their tutors. This is why. How could you—?" Zireli flung himself around, rage mottling his face as his hands went out again.

With a yelp, Adrroania curled in on herself, prepared for her husband's fury.

"My king," Gwogh breathed, aware he'd breached protocol yet willing to brave the assault. After all, technically he was not their subject. The submission he gave was done out of respect for this royal family.

Zireli stumbled, the momentum of his anger tumbling over him. Another flashpoint bubbled up. He aimed his rage at Gwogh.

Who held out his palms, rotated his wrists and shielded himself as the blast barreled across the great hall. Flames licked the walls around Gwogh, but nothing more than a warm breeze wafted through his beard and gray hair.

Surprise trickled through the Fire King's expression, lessening the rage.

"Direct your anger, sire, at those responsible," Gwogh spoke softly.

Zireli's nostrils flared. "And who would that be?" He held out his hands again, and Gwogh could not help but flinch. "Show them to me, and I assure you, my anger *will* burn against them! Tell me who conspired with my son to steal his sister's gifts."

"My lord," Gwogh said. "Your son is a good man, and I can assure you on my life that he had no knowledge of what would happen in the tower."

"Were you not his protector? Why did you not protect, accelerant?"

"I was rendered unconscious to prevent my interfering."

Zireli's blond brows lifted. "You accuse Kaelyria." His anger simmering amid the words that held warning. He raised his chin, his breath slightly uneven.

"No." Gwogh dropped his gaze, offering humility and submission. "It is my belief even the princess did not fully understand what would happen in the transference."

"Transference." Zireli's hands went to his head as he turned, the hunger to believe his daughter's innocence plain in his torment. "You confuse me, Sir Gwogh. You suggest transference, yet all accelerants know it's forbidden. Yet you accuse my daughter of—"

"Whether it was the princess or not, transference was effected. The results are in that tower, King Zireli."

"You believe her . . . innocent, then?"

"Naïve, sire. Yes." Relief almost pushed a smile into Gwogh's face. "I also believe that many have been manipulated in the events that have taken place."

"Who?" Challenge roiled through the king's eyes. "Name the traitor."

Gwogh would not give more fuel to the embers of rage that burned in the Fire King. Not yet. Not until he knew beyond a shadow. "That is what we must find out, my lord." Though Gwogh had made no decision regarding the queen's guilt, he suspected she was more a pawn than a perpetrator. The man who used the gentle queen's grief over her crippled son against her was probably the same one who'd convinced the princess that transference was a gift. Not the curse it truly was.

Zireli stood still, eyes narrowing in understanding. When the king's hands lowered, Gwogh felt the squeeze in his chest lessen. Zireli had been the fiercest Ignatieri in centuries. The control he had over the Flames, the power he could exert, was unlike any other. Handsome, with his golden hair and blue eyes, he'd been a ready candidate for the throne and the hearts of the people across the Nine Kingdoms, not to mention the desire of women vying to be his queen. But with his power, with the intensity of his wielding, had also come a quick and fierce temper.

Zireli's lips quirked, making his strong jaw jut. "What do you know, my old friend?"

6

Four excruciating hours sitting on a stone bench did nothing for aged bones and weary minds. Especially Gwogh's. Because he had plans. Knew what must be done. The tedious dialogue among the elect, with which he no longer stood, gave him ample time to feed his plan, to weed out errors made in tactics, and water the hope that it might actually succeed.

Gwogh removed himself from the large hall as the council adjourned, sharing a meaningful look with King Zireli and Queen Adrroania as he did. Rarely had he seen Zireli use the gifts against his queen, but the tearing of the fabric of their kingdom had sheared the tightly woven cords of their family. In spite of it all, the weight on the monarchs was not evident in the meeting, except to Gwogh. They presented a forbidding front. Nothing decisive came from the hourslong meeting with the High Lord Marshal and his minions. Sitting there, aware that he had once numbered among the Ignatieri, Gwogh praised Abiassa he had fled their ranks before he could fall into the political machinations.

He climbed the stairs, grateful to be out from under the eyes of the accelerants. Up the spiral stairs into the lone tower chambers he went.

The princess's handmaiden sat with her feet drawn up as she stared out the same window he had while standing vigil over Haegan. And now, Kiesa would spend her days the same way, guarding her princess. The grief almost proved too much for Gwogh. Kiesa was young, of childbearing years. She should attend court with her lady. Find love. Maybe even a little adventure. Not sit, daydream, and wait as years ate the paralyzed body of the princess.

When Kiesa noticed him, she shoved to her feet. "Sir Gwogh." She gave a small smile and nodded to the bed. "She's resting . . . finally. For the first time since . . ."

"I'm sure it is a shock to be bedridden and immobilized."

"She says it's a thousand times worse than she imagined," Kiesa whispered, her chin tucked. Her eyes glossed. "It's awful, watching her cry so much."

Gwogh touched her shoulder. "It must be hard on you, too. You couldn't have known about her plan. Otherwise I know you'd have stopped her."

Her gaze shifted to the stones.

"Ah." Disappointment tugged at him, though her duplicity was no surprise. Kaelyria had always been a persuasive, strong-willed child. Gwogh sighed. "If you plan to escape the king's anger, you'll need to hide the truth better. Did I not know how convincing the princess could be, I would extend my own chastisement." He considered Kaelyria, sleeping like an angel. One of the most beautiful women in the kingdom, just like her mother. "Tell me what you know, Kiesa. How did this come to be?"

"I . . ." Her gaze darted to Kaelyria. "She forbids me to speak of it." Conflict pinched the girl's brow. "I can't betray her. Especially now. Please understand."

"But you know."

Kiesa ducked.

"Would that you—"

"Leave her," Kaelyria's soft, firm voice interrupted. "She will not speak of it, nor will I."

Resignation clung to the very tapestries in the room. "Princess," he said, unsure where to start. How to convince her. But then . . . he couldn't, could he? In her boiled the same fire that raged in her father. Perhaps not the anger, but the bullheadedness. "I want you to understand, child, what your actions have cost your family."

"You forget yourself, accelerant." She sniffed. "I know the price—can you not see where I lie?"

"Ah, only thinking of yourself again." Gwogh nodded. "Let me enlighten you. Your father very nearly seared your mother today in the private council chambers."

Kaelyria's eyes flicked to him.

"He learned that Queen Adrroania granted permission for Cilicien to tutor you."

"She did not grant anything—she . . . acquiesced." Sorrow laced her words as she licked her lips. "I would not stop hounding her." Kaelyria's gaze drifted to the leaded glass. "I saw a way and pursued it with all the fire gifted me by Abiassa."

"And then—you threw that gift away."

"I did not throw it away," she hissed, then closed her eyes for a moment. "I . . . lent it to Haegan."

"Lent it?"

"So he could be healed." She could not, would not hold his gaze.

"For all your breeding," Gwogh said, struggling to stem his anger, "you do not lie well, princess. I know why you did this—the *real* reason."

A hardness formed around her blue eyes. Resolve.

Gwogh traced the stone walls with a longsuffering sigh and shook his head. Had he not thought this through, determined his path already, he'd scald her ears with a chastisement the like of which she had probably never heard. "But for now, I will let you hold that secret."

Uncertainty flickered through her brows. "Why?"

"Because, child, unlike you, my priority is this kingdom. Your parents. All of Fieri Keep, Seultrie, and Zaethien. It cannot afford to fall. Too much will be lost." Too much.

"What . . . what of Haegan?"

"Ah," Gwogh said with a laugh and glanced down at her. "At last you think of the poor boy saddled with things he was not ready to face."

"We are nearly the same age—he has the same knowledge as I, if not more!"

"Haegan has been cooped up here with books and an old man!" Gwogh shook his head. "I fear the reality assaulting him as he makes his way through Zaethien. And I pray—you might join me, princess—that he does not encounter any incipients. Or that no one would recognize the son of King Zireli."

Her breathing grew quicker.

"I wonder what would be done to him if somehow Poired Dyrth learned Haegan was out there. All alone. Ignorant of what pursues him." Gwogh clucked his tongue. "Imagine, if they found him. What they'd do to that boy. His heart so gentle, so firm. But so very naïve." With a sardonic smile, he winked. "That won't last long, I assure you. I wonder, though, would Poired Dyrth kill him or torture him? Now that I think of it—no, Dyrth would have far too much fun slicing off pieces—"

"Stop it." Tears slid down princess Kaelyria's pale cheeks. "You are cruel."

"I believe, princess, the cruel hand was yours." Though he could not stand to see her pained, she needed to realize her error, the troubles she had forced upon her own brother.

"You know not of what you speak, old man!" Kaelyria sniffled as her handmaiden wiped her eyes and nose. Once more, fire laced her pale irises. "Go to him, Gwogh. You must. You must protect him!"

Make a mistake, send the old wise man. He never thought he'd live out clichéd legends of the wizened wizard—though he wasn't one—saving the realm.

He grunted. The irony. "I am but an old man, as you clearly reminded me, retired from the Ignatieri and in the service of our king." He smiled at her. "Your father-king, who is very angry this day, is unlikely to release me."

"You must help Haegan! Please."

"I beg your mercy, but I think this one is bigger than me."

"Please!"

Gwogh turned and left the weeping princess. He stood in the antechamber, staring at the steps that led into the belly of Fieri Keep. The same passage he'd fled down three nights past, when this nightmare unfolded.

"You know where he is." The calm, smooth voice of Queen Adrroania wrapped around his ears. Had she stood here all this time, listening to his conversation with Kaelyria?

Gwogh sighed without turning to her. "Those who spend time in the shadows are often consumed by them, my queen." He faced her now.

Tall and regal, she stood with her hands clasped before her. The gold circlet, returned to her brow once more, vied for dominance amid the thick brown hair she had passed to neither of her children. "I have made mistakes," she said as her chest and chin rose, "but not the ones you suggest. And I've been punished for both, real and imagined."

"You attempt to work my sympathies, my queen, but they are not available to you. Not at this hour." He supposed he did feel sorry for her. In fact, his heart could not withstand much more, watching this family and kingdom fall. "Yes," he managed. "What happens in the shadows is brought into the light." Oh, the weight of it all. Hands behind his back, he moved toward the stairs.

Adrroania was at his side, touching his arm. "Please, Gwogh. Go to him." Words earnest, fingernails digging into his withered flesh, she pleaded just as her daughter before her. "*Please*. Haegan needs you. He doesn't know what's out there. He's smart, so very smart"—her gaze grew wistful and burdened with memories—"but as you said, unschooled in the ways of this world."

He'd never seen anyone hungry for knowledge like Haegan Celahar. A mind keen and sharp. But if Poired Dyrth caught up with him . . . Yet, a graver risk existed. One that—

A delicate squeeze on his arm drew his gaze to the queen's. "I did *not* do this to my daughter."

He narrowed his eyes, feeling the old surge within himself. "But you *knew* Cilicien intended to convince your daughter-heir to change places."

Adrroania did not yield. "I had no idea Kaelyria would . . . that she . . . would be paralyzed in his place."

"But you *did* know what she intended. Her actions were not to heal Haegan, but to prevent Poired from stealing the gift." Gwogh pushed. He must. They were playing with a fire more dangerous than any had faced before. "You knew that."

Her hand fell away, and in her expression the realization of her guilt and the justice of her punishment came together. "Yes." Tears filled her eyes. "Hear me when I say, I did not think it would work. I thought it mere fancy, a generous gift she believed she could pass to her brother."

"I understand." And he did, so the gentleness he allowed into words was sincere. But so was his anger. "There is yet one thing I almost cannot forgive, my queen."

She stared down her perfectly straight nose at him. Daring him to defy her.

And defy her he would, and blame her. "You let it happen, knowing . . . *knowing* about Haegan. What would happen to him. What it would change."

Surprise sparked in her eyes. She took a step back, question—uncertainty—plain on her delicate features.

Why must I always be right?

Gwogh trained his gaze on the steps. On where they must lead him. On what he must do. "Pray, my lady queen, that I am not too late or too old to stop what has been set into motion."

Haunted by truth and pursued by the gravity of the situation, Gwogh made his way to his quarters, where he bundled up what little he owned, then hurried down to the stables. He lured a massive gray mount from the stall. Smoothed a hand over the horse's broad skull. "Tonight, we ride, my old friend."

The horse nickered and flicked his tail.

Gwogh tossed up his bag behind the saddle and tied it. He secured a food pouch and water skin to the other side along with blankets. Though he would seek shelter at an inn, he could not guarantee his journey would afford time for the luxury his aged bones demanded. He would ride, guided by Abiassa's Flame.

7

Drracien Khar'val tossed back another pint of fermented juice. Not quite as strong as ale. But then, the uppers couldn't accuse him of being drunk when he returned to Sanctuary. He wrapped his arm around the curvy wench perched on his right leg as she planted a kiss on his cheek.

"Are you really an incipient?" she asked.

Drracien tensed. Why must they use *that* word? Instead of unleashing his frustration, he sparked her. With a yelp, she leapt up, rubbing her backside. He laughed.

She grabbed his stein and tossed the remaining juice in his face.

Raucous laughter broke out across the small room, and Drracien chuckled. With a lunge, he grabbed her, stole a kiss, then used her apron to wipe his face. "Thank you, mi'lady."

She shoved him backward and spun around. But not before he saw her grin. He trudged out of the tavern and headed down the road toward the village, toward home. Fingering his hair into place, and testing his breath, he wondered after his mother's welfare. Well kept? Taking care of his siblings?

In a working village like theirs, his mother's sacrifice in surrendering him to the Ignatieri meant she lost a strong back and mind. Lost income and help. He worked hard to make sure her selfless act would not count against her. Or his siblings. They were forbidden by the Order from having contact, so he paid through the local moneylender, enough to keep his family clothed and fed.

The darkening sky cradled the moons, forcing him to hurry. He'd do well not to return to the Holy City late. Another hundred paces delivered him to the market. From there, he stalked to the collector.

Drracien stooped to enter through the low wooden door. Pushing in, he gave a double-rap. "Hello?"

"Who goes there at this hour?" a voice boomed.

Drracien moved into the lamplight. "Forgive me, Littien. I lost track of time." He lifted the pouch from beneath his cloak and grinned. "But I doubt it's too late for this."

Littien's face brightened. "Drracien! As regular as the tax collector."

"Ah, but I come not to collect, only to deliver." He dropped the pouch on the table beside a stack of long, thick ledgers. "You'll be sure to record it on her account. You'll see to it, yes?"

"Of course," Littien said as he eased into the creaking spindle-backed chair and raised his hands. "I do every month."

"I gave extra this time." Drracien leaned in. "Tell her last month was overpaid. Winter's coming. She'll need extra provisions and clothes for the young ones."

"Generous for an incipient."

Drracien clenched a fist. *"Accelerant."*

The man considered him. "Word is, you're not only practicing the arts, but teaching others as well."

Practicing the arts. As if he were a magician or conjurer. Drracien pushed aside the accusation in the man's comment and focused on his mission. He fingered the pouch.

"To think you were nothing but a beggar like the rest of us once."

She'd be proud of him, wouldn't she? For making something of himself. Building a life . . .

To do that, she'd have to know.

Something warm slithered across Drracien's shoulders. He recognized the heating. *Calm,* he reminded himself and mentally walked through the calming practice, so he would not be goaded. He'd risen above that. Learned to master himself. Master his temper. His desires.

Yes, she'd be proud. If she knew.

"You'll see to it?" Drracien winked. "I'll bring extra for you next time."

Littien roughed a dirty, ink-stained hand over his gnarled beard. "Of course, of course. I always do, don't I?"

Weight lifted from his mind, Drracien clamped a hand on the man's shoulder. "Thank you, friend."

"She asks." Littien's eyes met Drracien's. "Every time."

Hesitation held Drracien captive. "You haven't told her, have you? Tell me you haven't—"

"No." Littien swallowed hard, gaze bouncing to Drracien's hand. So the accountant was afraid of being sparked. "But I daresay she almost wouldn't take it last time."

"It's your job to make sure she does." Drracien squeezed the man's shoulder. "If it stops for her, the extra stops for you as well."

"No need to threaten me, boy. I said I'd do it." He waved blackened hands at him. "Now off with you. It's late. I wish to sup and sleep."

"Good eve." Drracien bowed and backed out of the small front room.

In the cool of the night, he made his way back to the Holy City. Back to a better life. For him, for her. For all of them. He knew not how the doors had opened for him, only that they had. That Aloing had sent for him. Ordered his training commence at once. Beyond that, how the High Marshal even knew a poor kid like him had the ignition necessary . . . It'd been too curious to fathom. There certainly was no affection between them. The High Marshal had been a hard taskmaster, always pushing Drracien. Compelling him to work harder, better, so much so that at times, Drracien hated the graying old man.

As he climbed the hill back to the city, he plucked an apple from a tree. Rather than immediately return to the accelerants, to the uniformity, the strict adherence to the guiding principles, Drracien allowed himself to linger just inside the walls. He sat on a boulder tucked into one of the crags. As he finished the fruit, he eyed the somber glow of lights across the walled city. It had been a good day. The indulgence of the juice. The stolen kiss. He chuckled. Girls had always given him more than one look.

You've the look of your father, the rogue. How many times had his mother swatted his backside as she sent him scuttling out of their thatched-roof shanty when he'd been rotten. Apparently, his father had been quite the looker, with black hair and blue eyes, both of which

Drracien inherited. He was also strong, of course. Drracien lifted his arm and flexed his bicep. *Naturally—strong.*

And yet . . . yet, Drracien was here. In the Holy City.

A rogue. In the Holy City.

Doing *well* in the Holy City.

Only because he'd set his mind to it. Determined to figure out what purpose the Fires had in drawing him out. His gaze rose to the blackened sky. As dark as searage. Twinkling with the fires of stars. *Even there . . . the universe echoes what exists within the Elect.*

Elect?

Maybe. He wasn't convinced it was a great thing to be an accelerant. But it provided for those he loved. Kept them fed. Clothed. Sheltered.

Unlike my rogue father . . .

Shouts rose and mingled with cries.

Drracien rose, eyeing the shadows, and searched for the source. He dusted off his pants as he moved in the direction of the noise. Sounded like an altercation. Shouts . . . laughter. Mocking laughter. He hustled through the inner arch just as the guards swung it closed for the night. Followed the noise to the right. Through a passage. Out into the market courtyard.

By the butcher's shop, a huddle. Laughter. Shouts. Cries.

And in the middle of it all—Tortook Puthago. *Should have known.* A heat halo warbled around the head and throat of a young boy pinned to the high wall at the back of the alley.

"It is said," Drracien spoke loud and clear as he closed the gap between himself and the taunters, "those who cannot earn respect prey on the weak."

Tortook's dark gaze flicked to him. "Come to join the fun, *Marshal Khar'val?*"

Drracien eyed the others. Some were initiates. The girl with pretty green eyes was not. She was pretty, though. Curvy, too.

No time . . . Both he and Puthago would both face needlings if they were late. Yet, if he pushed Tortook, perhaps his thirst for power would shift from the boy taking the punishment. "What? Could you not get Miss Green Eyes"—he pulled his gaze from her willing smile—"warmed with your charm, so you resorted to proving you had abilities?"

The girl's lips parted in surprise. She looked to Puthago, then stepped away.

"You're the one with a taste for ladies, Drracien. It's *your* weakness," he hissed.

Blazes. What would it take? "Novice Puthago, you know the Guidings of the Order. Release him or I will be forced—"

Tortook whipped around, his hands stirring the air as he did. "Forced to what?"

In a heartbeat, Drracien shoved out his palm. A bolt faster than the blink of an eye ignited. Shot through the air. Sparked past Puthago.

The heat bubble popped.

The boy dropped to his knees, whimpering.

"Who told you to interfere? I'm tired of your meddling!" Puthago took a step forward.

With a grin, Drracien flicked a spark at the novice. The brown-haired reprobate responded too slowly. The trail seared across his cheek. He cried out.

"Told you," a younger boy murmured. "Nobody can outmaneuver Drracien."

At one time, the words would have filled him with giddy excitement at being recognized. But now, it brought only awareness of his actions, of his temper. Guilt shrouded him as he felt the gazes of the others. He backed up. Even as the fear swarmed him, Drracien saw Puthago's smirk.

Straightening, the impudent novice stalked toward him. Bumped his shoulder as he walked past.

Who had been goaded this time?

8

Gravel crunched as he stepped from the clawing heat of the afternoon sun into the shade of a shop's bright yellow awning. Haegan glanced down at his boots, wondering not for the first time where he'd gotten them. Being laid up in a bed for years made shoes a nonissue, except on the rare occasions when Gwogh wheeled him into the private garden beneath the great kyssups, their massive trunks a stable base for the ever-reaching limbs that shielded much of the southern portion of the realm from sun. Much like most of his life—sheltered, hidden. But the last couple of weeks . . .

Standing in Luxlirien with the awning overhead and dirt beneath his feet nearly proved Haegan's undoing. To feel, to sense! He eased closer to the shop wall, taking a moment to gain his bearings. Stow the awe that unseated his ability to think. He had to stuff away the memories, the fact that he was removed from everything he'd known and loved.

Will I ever see home again?

What an ignorant question! Of course he would. Get to the Great Falls. Return home.

Thirty days.

No. Twenty. He'd lost ten getting to this point. He swiped a hand across his mouth, watching the bustle of people going from one place to the next. They had purpose. Had loved ones. Lives.

Who am I? What *am I?* Even if the Falls healed him, he could not return to Fieri Keep and present himself to his father. He'd been trained in no duties. Prepared for no role. To reign as the Fire King, he must possess knowledge, wisdom, leadership that—had he not been poisoned as a child—he would've had. In his stead, those instructions were given to Kaelyria.

Kae . . . *What have you done to me, sister?*

A woman with three children tugging at her skirts slipped into a bakery. A man escorted a woman in richly adorned brocade into a jeweler's shop. Pangs struck Haegan. He recalled Kaelyria's pleas about Jedric. Would father continue with the plans to marry the two? 'Twas a fool's errand, trying to bring peace to the realm through Vid and Jedric's family. True, they had wealth, but not a strong moral base. At least, not Jedric.

Two children erupted from an alley, shouting and laughing.

Haegan shifted to avoid a collision, and a rock popped beneath his boot. He glanced down. Lifted his foot. A benign thing, hearing a rock crunch against the dirt. But to him, it was the sound of a miracle.

"You step in something?"

Haegan flinched. Glanced to his right, where Thiel and Laertes stood. "What?" Stepped in something? "Oh. No, I thought so."

"Well, come on." Thiel took a few steps toward the town square. "We need to get supplies. You can get the dried meat from the butcher. How much money you got?"

Haegan blinked.

"Great fires!" Thiel gave him a soft shove and turned away. "Are you any good to us?"

He thudded against the wall. Embarrassment and anger burned his cheeks. Could he help it? This wasn't a *planned* trip. "Look," he said, pulling away from the slats.

But something tugged him backward—his tunic had snagged. *Rrrippp.* At the sound of coins spilling over the dirt, he jerked. When he glanced down, his breath caught as he took in the glitter of gold on the ground. Gold paladiums.

Eyes alive, Thiel stabbed her dagger at the money. "Explain that!"

"I . . ." He'd discovered the coins when he'd awoken in the wagon, but with his situaion and predicament, he had not given them a second thought. He'd had no money on his person in the tower. In truth, he'd only worn his cotton jerkin and bed pants. Like always. Occasionally socks in winter. Confined to a bedchamber, he'd had no need of coin. "I . . ."

There was a shout, and several children scrambled toward the spilled money.

Thiel and Laertes warned them off, deflecting the full effect of the girl's anger from Haegan. Where *had* those coins come from? Whoever put him outside the far gate in the tunnels must have tied the money to his belt. But why? And who? If they had rejected him . . .

"Hurry," Laertes said, his hair bobbing as he thrust the coins back in Haegan's hands. "If Jujak see this, they'll string us up for sure."

That snapped Haegan out of his stupor. "Why?" He knelt and retrieved a couple of paladiums that had rolled behind a barrel.

"Because we're poor beggars." Thiel punched to her feet. "And the only way beggars get money, let alone *gold* paladiums"—meaning and accusation laced that word—"is if we stole the lot." She shoved the coins toward Haegan. "Hide them."

"You think I stole them?" Stunned at her insinuation, he held up his hands. "It would be less noticeable, wouldn't you agree, if we all took a share?"

She stared, her hard gaze darting over his face. "Why would you do that? Do you *want* us to get arrested—that's it! A trap to get rid of us. You ungrateful swine."

He couldn't help the laugh. "No. Calm yourself, my lady."

This time Thiel barked a laugh as she held out her hands, motioning to the dusty breeches and smudged tunic. "As you can see, *my lord,* I am no lady."

Could he say nothing to her that would gain some measure of peace, or even civility? Haegan sighed and shook his head. "My point was only that if so many coins together might draw unwanted attention, wouldn't it be safer to split them up? Are you familiar with the proverb about putting all your flints in one tinderbox?" And he clearly wasn't perceptive enough to protect himself. "Prudence would have us split them up, use them wisely and carefully."

Thiel's eyebrow arched. "Prudence?"

"He has a point," Laertes said, snatching a paladium and pocketing it without a moment's hesitation.

"Just remember, young prince," Haegan said with a wink, "that doesn't belong to you."

Laertes frowned. "What doesn't?"

"The coin."

"What coin?"

"The—" Haegan caught on, but Laertes bolted off. "Hey!" He lunged after the boy.

Thiel caught his arm. "Chasing him will draw attention." She shrugged. "What do you expect? He's ten."

"He should be taught a lesson. One shouldn't steal."

"A lesson?" Thiel crossed her arms, the anger back.

Great. He couldn't manage to keep his mouth of fire shut. "He is young and should be raised in the codes, taught the morality of upright living. That's all I meant."

"The codes. Upright living." She snorted and started walking.

"What does that mean?" Haegan kept pace with her.

"What do you know of upright living, you who were in the forbidden tunnels and abandoned by an incipient?"

"Accelerant," he said. "There's a difference." Too many tried to imply that his family—in particular, his father—were incipients.

She frowned at him, gauging. "Not where I come from."

"And where is that?"

Thiel hadn't returned the paladiums, but she also hadn't secured them in the satchel strung across her torso. She hesitated, her face softening for just a second. Then, the rock-hard visage returned. "It's not your concern." Tucking three paladiums in a small pocket at her waist, she held his gaze. "I'll give one each to Praegur and Tokar. We talked it over last night. You can accompany us as far as Hetaera, but we'll need to secure supplies if we're to survive the trek. You keep the rest. We'll need them to get through the mountains alive. Buy dried meat and"—her gaze skipped over his attire—"better clothing."

Another insult? The girl was bold. "You are one to talk."

Her lips tightened. "Careful, tunnel rat. I'm dressed as one of my station should be. Now—the supplies."

"You trust me, then?"

"Call it buying your good graces."

"So," he said as he dropped the coins in his boots, "it's okay to keep my coins but not to tell me from where you hail?"

"It was your idea to split them up. Can I help it if you're not as smart as you look?"

Haegan almost grinned. "You think I look smart, then?"

She bristled. Sunlight streaked over her face as she stepped from beneath the awning, her eyes once more glinting gold. "Meet back at the wagon at dusk."

. . .

"He is only a captain."

"A captain with more experience than some of our current majors. A captain reared by one of the strongest and most savvy generals Zaethien has seen in a hundred years." A young man who was the contemporary of Zireli's son, whom his son might have sparred with, trained with, had Poired not wounded the Celahar by poisoning Haegan.

"You flatter only to silence me."

Zireli grinned at his friend. "Is it working?" He'd returned to camp that morning after his brief sojourn in Seultrie. He lifted a hand to quiet the objection and reply. "Flattery is the last thing on my mind." Finding Haegan, finding answers to what happened in the keep . . . that was his priority—along with saving the Nine. "It was your son who raced across Zaethien to warn me of what happened back at the keep. Graem's men respect him and will follow him." He lifted a cup of warmed cordi juice. "You yourself said he's had a natural ability since he was but a lad." Just as Haegan once had.

"Aye," Grinda groused. "But I am his father. I'm *supposed* to be unashamedly biased about my progeny."

Zireli took in the maps of the Nine and the placement of troops. "I need him to go, Kiliv. There are few who can track as well as Graem. You've raised him well. Now, leave him to his duties. "

After a longsuffering sigh, Kiliv lowered himself to a chair and rested an elbow on the arm, peering through his thick, bushy brow at Zireli. "Why are you hunting your own son?" Though Kiliv's question was not pointed, it still felt like a dagger. "You can't really believe he acted against you and the throne."

Did he believe his son had betrayed the Nine?

Zireli was no longer certain. In fact, the horrible truth lay in the reality that he did not know his son, save from the reports from Adrroania and Gwogh. All he knew now was that his son had, once more, been lost to him. He traced a finger over the northbound route from Seultrie up to the Great Falls. He'd go through Luxlirien and then on to Hetaera. That made the most sense. Afforded dense populations to hide among.

Explaining himself was not something he was accustomed to, but exploring the complicated waters of his relationship with Haegan . . . of their past . . . of this new injury inflicted by the son he'd already lost once . . .

Had I spent more time with him, would he have turned against me like this?

"The princess herself said it wasn't Haegan's doing," Kiliv continued.

"Kaelyria is protective of her brother. Always has been. She will say whatever necessary to stay my hand and anger against him." Since Haegan had first entered the world, a ruddy, screaming, strong baby boy, Kaelyria had wanted to be with him.

Kiliv arched a brow. "And why are you not as ardent in your protection and defense of your own blood?"

Anger churned through Zireli. "Careful, friend." Choking back the indignation, he sighed. "Haegan's actions have left Seultrie undefended."

"Not entirely," Grinda countered. "There is a contingent of your fiercest warriors within the walls. We reinforced defenses. The bulk of the Zaethien army is encamped between here and the keep. And Kerral has promised—"

"Kerralian troops will be too few too late. And now, for the first time in a thousand years, there is no accelerant guarding Seultrie. Haegan stole that—"

"You don't know—"

"What other explanation is there?" Zireli pounded his fist against the table. "He is out there, running free when his people, his *sister*, his own parents, are fighting for their lives." He shoved a hand through his hair and turned away, breathing hard. "He made the choice. If there is even a bone of truth to Kaelyria's story, Haegan made the choice to accept the transference. Now he's stolen the hope of Seultrie."

"I rarely disagree with you, Zireli, but in this, I cannot eat what you serve. Haegan may have been a cripple, but he is just as ardent in his pride as a Celahar and Seultrian. He would never set himself against you or the Nine." He lifted his hands as Zireli straightened and fixed narrowed eyes on him.

"How do you know my son so well?"

Grinda faltered for only a moment. Then he met Zireli's gaze. "I used to visit the boy on occasion. When I was in the keep."

Zireli felt as if he'd been caught in a halo. The air seemed to go out of the room.

Grinda's eyes softened. "I will say no more, but hear me in this: you are *wrong* to hunt your own son like a enemy."

The guilt stung like a branding iron, burning straight into his heart. Guilt that he'd failed Haegan. Guilt that he had not visited him more, guided his growing. Guilt that he had not protected his family.

"What if he was just as much a pawn in ka'Dur's scheme as Kaelyria?" Kiliv suggested. "How have you so easily clothed your own son in the cloak of evil? Haegan—"

"It's done!" Zireli shouted. "I will hear no more. He—"

A shadow broke the sunlight seeping through the tied-back opening.

Zireli seized the distraction. "Enter!"

Captain Graem Grinda ducked inside, acknowledged his father with a nod, then placed his fist over his heart and faced his king. "You summoned me, Your Majesty?"

"Aye." Zireli sighed and slid a glance to the young officer's father. "You've done well as a captain, Graem."

Brawny and focused, the young man shifted nervously before inclining his head. "Thank you, sire. It is my honor to serve you."

"Not me, Graem. You serve Abiassa and the Nine."

He thumped his fist over his heart again. "May they burn bright and long!"

"By the Flames," Zireli affirmed. "I'm sending you out. You'll take five Jujak and ride north."

Graem started. "Not return to the keep, sire? She'll be undefended."

"As your father has just pointed out, the keep is defended by additional Jujak and a battalion outside the wall. Fieri Keep and Seultrie will hold until my return. So, you'll go north."

"North, sire." Questions hung in his young face.

Zireli heaved a breath. "The prince has betrayed the Nine. I want Haegan found and returned to me."

"Dead or alive, sire?"

Zireli shot the captain a scowl. "We are not in the practice of execution without trial, Captain Grinda. Leave that to Sirdar's minions and bring my son back to answer for what he's done."

9

Thick, leaded glass did nothing to impede her vision or her desire as Thiel stood outside the mercantile. With her eyes, she traced each part of the dresses hanging on the wooden mannequins—the bustles, the puffed sleeves, the bejeweled necklines or waistlines. Ribbons, silk, brocade. Fur stoles and cloaks to fend off bitter winters. So familiar to her—both the winters and the fur stoles.

She lifted a hand to her jaw as she remembered the flutter of fur against her skin, even though it'd been years since she'd worn such luxury. The softer-than-new-fallen-snow feel of satin. Her favorite green dress.

But that was before. Before she made a decision no one else would make. A decision that cost every ounce of luxury and notoriety. A decision that hung loneliness and despair around her neck in place of her family's crest. An invisible hand from the past clutched her throat, strangling her happiness. Her dreams . . . relegated to a beggar's life.

Thiel lowered her gaze to her grungy tunic.

"What do you think?"

She flinched and whirled, coming face to chest with Praegur. "Think?" She blinked as she took a step back and looked up at her dark-skinned friend. "About what?"

"Our young ruffian." He nodded toward the blacksmith's shop, where Rigar stood at the smithy, apparently confused.

Thiel shook her head. "It confounds me how he still walks and breathes." And yet, something about him tugged at her curiosity. Her awareness.

"A little out of his realm, wouldn't you say?"

"A little?" Thiel held up the paladiums. "He told me to take these."

Praegur's gold eyes flashed. "*Take* them? What a fool!"

"No." Thiel felt the answer in her belly. The newcomer might be awkward, but he was no fool. Naïve, perhaps. But intelligence lurked behind those assessing eyes. There was no way to justify her gut instinct, what she suspected. The others would probably think *her* the fool if she mentioned it. "I think we're right to go with him to Hetaera."

Praegur scowled. "Nothing but trouble up that way."

"Mm, exactly. And how do you think our new friend will fare?"

Praegur grunted. "I see your point. But why are you so interested in this one?"

"Not interested," Thiel muttered. "Curious." When Praegur frowned at her, she shrugged. "Here. Take this. You can secure bread and pastries from Mistress An'sur, aye?"

Lifting the coin from her hand, he nodded. "Let's hope I can escape without a betrothal proposition this time."

"Surely her daughter isn't as unsightly as that."

"Mayhap . . . but the smell."

"I love the smell of bread."

"It ain't bread she stinks of—her father is the tanner." His lip curled as he turned and strode off the boardwalk.

Thiel smiled, but it fell away when shouts from the smithy brought her attention back round. Rigar stumbled out of the barn, offering an apology. A horseshoe hit him in the chest with a thud Thiel heard across the market square.

Something in her twisted into a knot, seeing his embarrassment. His shame as he tucked his chin and turned in her direction. She ducked into the mercantile. Hurrying behind a display of china, she watched through the pristine windows as Rigar rubbed his chest.

"Go on with the likes of you," someone growled from the back. "We don't need rabble in here causin' trouble!"

Heat flaring down her spine, Thiel glanced around, feigning ignorance. Then her gaze struck the shopkeeper. "Oh. Do you speak to me, good sir?"

"Aye, you know well I do! Go on"—he waved her toward the door—"out wit' ye."

Thiel slid the gold paladium between her fingers and held it up. "Is this not appropriate here?"

Surprised tugged back the man's scowl. Then it returned just as swiftly. "Where'd you get that? Stole it, I bet!"

"Sir, your words wound me. I came by it honestly, as any proper citizen would. Now, I have a few supplies to secure. Would you rather I went to Harket's?"

Muttering his disgust, he disappeared into the back of the shop, calling someone as he did. A minute later, the shopkeeper's wife came out and helped her gather the necessary supplies.

By the time Thiel had the dry goods and left the shop, dusk had settled. She stepped into the street. A girl's scream stopped her. Thiel shifted, holding the sack tight against her chest. Listening . . .

"Leave me!" a girl cried out.

The alley. Thiel ran toward it, suddenly bombarded by memories. Filcher's rancid breath. His meaty paws. She rounded the corner and saw him.

No. Thiel swallowed. Not Filcher. Some thug. Dragging a girl down the alley. In the middle of the day. "Hey!" Thiel threw herself forward, the supplies tossed aside. "Leave her!"

The man turned. Sneered. "Twofer, eh?" He grinned and reached for Thiel.

She shoved his arm, swinging him off balance. He stumbled forward with a curse. "Run," Thiel shouted to the girl, who stared in stunned silence. *"Run!"*

The girl finally found her wits and her feet.

A crunch warned Thiel of the thug. She crouched, feeling the whoosh of air over her head. She swung around. Clipped the back of his knee and shouldered into him. The man went down.

Thiel shot out of the alley, hauling up the dry goods without stopping.

She barreled into Rigar. "Move you oaf!"

"What happened?" He was looking back at the alley.

"Nothing." Because she'd stopped it. Wouldn't let some girl end up brutalized like she had been. "Did you get the supplies on your list?"

"Need to get—"

"Then do it!" Heart pounding, she raced for the wagon yard, feeling the after-battle tremor weakening her legs. *Just get to the wagon.* She'd be safe there. Outside town with families of refugees from the war, tinkers, gypsies, and even pirates. Yeah, safe.

Sack hoisted over her shoulder, Thiel rounded a corner. Saw portly Ah'maral, their wagon master, bending over a campfire. Relief speared her. She hurried across the road to him.

Thunder erupted from her left. A flurry of hooves and beasts. Thiel cringed and drew into herself. A throng of riders, dressed in black and bearing the mark—

"*No,*" she breathed, frozen at the sight. Then she rushed along the fringe of the gathering crowd, trying to glimpse the emblem on their long black cloaks that draped elegantly over the broad flanks of the massive horses.

Yes. There it was. The gold raqine.

Thiel stopped short, breath caught in her throat as she stared at the riders. And slowly, longing rose within her. Surged. The ache to belong drew her closer. Just a peek, she promised herself. *Just look at their faces.*

10

Villagers fled the road, some shouting at the riders for not being more careful, others screaming for children to get clear. As the wide path filled with horses and riders, both black and fierce as night, Haegan spotted Thiel rimming the crowd. Her face was pale. Strangely pale, especially for one with as much fire in her belly as Thiel.

The riders pulled up and dismounted beside the large fountain in front of the—*Sanctuary*!

The sight of the Ignatieri's insignia on the wooden structure sent Haegan backward. Spiked an icy chill down his spine. He would be easily discovered here. Haegan pivoted and scurried down an alley. He broke out onto the other side of the market and narrowly avoided a woman carrying an infant. To his left a cluster of children followed another woman, their grubby fists dug into her apron and skirts.

A man shouldered past him, a flank of meat tucked under his arm. A bit dirty, if you asked Haegan, but what did he know?

Across the narrow road, he spotted Praegur backing out of a shop, his arms loaded with a bag. He shook his head and kept walking backwards—right off the step. He fell hard against the dirt road but scrambled to his feet.

A woman and her daughter followed, laughing and smiling.

Praegur glanced around as if looking for something. His gaze hit Haegan's. His expression shifted from that of a cornered animal to that of—Haegan wasn't sure what. He said something to the ladies, who glanced in his direction, too.

Head tucked, Haegan angled away, not wanting anyone to take much notice of him.

A hand clapped on his shoulder. "You saved me," Praegur's deep voice boomed. "Start walking."

Haegan did, stealing a backward glance. "What was that about?"

"She's convinced I should marry her daughter."

"Why don't you?"

"Did you smell her?"

Haegan laughed. As they threaded through the crowds, his mirth faded. He felt as if something pressed against his chest, making it hard to breathe. "There are so many people."

From the side, a wail went up. A woman and her infant sat on a step, both crying.

"What's wrong with them?" He wanted to stop and hand off a paladium.

"Not enough to eat," Praegur said, urging him along. "Keep walking. If she's thought to be begging, they'll throw her in prison."

"They do that? But she's hungry!"

Praegur continued down the road, his hand never leaving Haegan's shoulder. "The greater crime is that there's not enough food. At least, that's what they say unless you can pay for it. Which we can, thanks to you."

"How can they do that—turn away the poor?" Haegan slowed when he thought he saw Thiel across the clogged street, but as he searched, he could find no trace of her.

Praegur shrugged. "Everyone's afraid of the refugees, afraid they'll bring disease and crime, or eat all the food."

"Do they?" Haegan suddenly questioned his education under Gwogh. "How can this be allowed? Why . . .?" *Why doesn't Father do something?*

"Because," a voice growled from the corner. A man in black—one of the riders—stood there, holding a cordi. "The farther into the Nine Dyrth invades and is allowed to lay siege to, the farther north and west the people flee."

"Oh, go on with you," a vendor said, waving off the rider. "We don't need your kind here. Bring the accelerants down on us, you will."

"Me?" The rider laughed. "I am here but to trade and be on my way."

"Then do it!"

The rider bit into the fruit with a decisive crunch and exchanged some coins with the fruit vendor, thanking him. Conducting his business politely, contrary to what the other vendor had said. But as he turned away, the rider slowed, his gaze narrowed on something.

Haegan followed it, but saw nothing.

"We should hurry." Praegur nodded. Then Haegan noticed Thiel lingering in the shadows of a tree that spread its branches over two small huts.

Without warning, the rider lurched forward.

Right toward Thiel.

"Thiel," Praegur muttered before breaking into a run.

Haegan rushed after him, his mind a tangle of questions again. Why would the rider care about Thiel? She'd hidden from them—was she afraid of being discovered? Had she stolen from them?

"What is this? Far from your lands, are you not, Asykthian raiders?" The voice from somewhere beyond the crowd hissed through the air, entwining Haegan's mind like a heavy mist.

Asykthian! The name pushed his gaze back to the rider. Why had he not recognized their crest from the tomes he'd pored over, studying the sigils for each realm and land? They were the Ice Dwellers, Northlanders. Why were they so far south, away from their ice palaces and frozen rivers? Assassins, betrayers, those who consorted with beasts. According to the Legends, which Haegan had read more fervently than the gilded pages of the Histories, the Northlands were home to not only the raqine, but the Unauri and Drigo, and their lesser kind, the Raeng—ruthless, lawless assassins. Much like incipients, only worse. All were extinct, relegated to ink and parchment rather than breath and body.

Save the Asykth, who were responsible for the murder of the Supreme King when they gained alliance with the Umelyrians. It was said Abiassa struck the Northlands barren and frozen for their part in the Rebellion. Legends held that the raqine and Drigo vanished in the fallout of that dreadful era, lost in the icy lands.

The rider who'd spoken to them in the market stopped. Uttered something Haegan could not hear.

"Blasphemy so close to the holy Sanctuary!" A sea of red, black, and gold streamed into the street, parting the crowd as if an invisible hand tossed them aside. There had to be a half dozen accelerants.

"Invading our lands is treason!"

"Since when is seeking food and provision—trading—a crime, Master Sentinel?"

Only then did Haegan see the pompous Sentinel, an accelerant who had achieved the rank of Electreri, which enabled him to rule a town. *"Beware those in power, Haegan. Power corrupts."* His old mentor's warning whistled through his mind. Yet drew him. Was this Sentinel corrupt? How could one tell?

"Since Dyrth and his minions swept over the southern plains. King Zireli ordered the borders closed."

"And how are we to know what is done in the south? We travel from the Northlands, in case you forgot where we are from."

"You are here as spies!"

"You know not of what you speak, *incipient!*"

A gasp trickled through the crowd—and through Haegan's own chest. Calling a duly appointed and honorably charged accelerant such an offensive term could bring more punishment. Even Haegan knew that, locked away most of his life.

The crowd quickly thinned as the rider's lip curled, disdain pulsing with each breath as the Sentinel assumed the first position. And that emptying of the street afforded the arrival of the other riders, who were now mounted once more. The leader swung effortlessly up onto his horse.

Heart thrumming, Haegan moved toward Thiel—or where he'd last seen her—but kept his eyes on the standoff. They needed to steer clear of this confrontation. Get to safety. Leave and get to Hetaera.

A plume of heat warbled in the afternoon light. "You will respect," the Sentinel said, his words again hissing as the embers of wielding bloomed around him, "the office which I hold while you are within our borders, Sir . . .?"

"Considering the force you stare down, *Sentinel*, I would consider your actions and words carefully." The man tossed back the long panels of his black jacket, exposing a scabbard and sword.

Haegan drew up short. A challenge? He had heard the Asykthians detested accelerants as much as his father detested their leader, Thurig the Formidable, but to give witness to such a challenge was more than he'd imagined of this chaotic city.

"I barter in these lands, but I do *not* owe fealty here. And there will be no respect where it has not been earned." The Asykthian's lips were so tightly drawn his nostrils flared.

"Easy," another rider muttered, nudging his horse around, then giving a low whistle.

A burning in Haegan's stomach tugged at his attention, but the almost tangible tension between these two refused to release him. He should leave. If the Sentinel spotted and recognized him, he'd be captured. Couldn't reach the Great Falls. Couldn't heal Kaelyria. *Go—run!*

"Let them make their purchases and pass," came a loud but disinterested voice. The sentinel swung around. A dozen yards behind him stood a high marshal. This one should be—Haegan strained to remember his lessons, remember who served over Luxlirien—Marshal Gelas.

"But sir—"

"Have you ill intent here, Master Asykth?"

"We have but one intent—to purchase supplies."

"Then do it and leave our lands. Your kind bring trouble and attention we do not need." Gelas looked around the crowded city. "As you can see, our stores are dwindling. Be quick and buy only as necessary." He started back to Sanctuary, his minions scurrying after him.

"Never thought I'd see that," Haegan muttered. "Asykthians are nearly as hated as Dyrth."

"That's the difference," Praegur said. "*Nearly.*"

But it annoyed Haegan that the lawless raiders his father had often railed about were allowed to roam so freely. What if they *were* spies? What if their intent went beyond mere supplies? Anger thrummed through his veins. Gelas should have had them questioned. Detained at the least!

Movement beyond the riders caught his attention. He strained to see and finally made out Thiel's form slinking along the edge of the trees. He wasn't sure why she wanted to hide, but if she came any closer, she'd be discovered.

The rider's massive horse swung around. Puffed air right at Haegan's face. Then shifted. Whinny-screeched.

As the horse reared, Haegan clenched his eyes shut, twisting away and using his arms to shield himself. He slammed into something hard.

"Rigar!"

The warbled call of his name sounded like a distant shout below water. Haegan shook his head. Shook off the hollowing of his hearing. Blinked. But there was no hearing. Or seeing.

11

Zireli stood at the window overlooking the Lakes of Fire. Lava and fire tumbled and churned, winding southward. Molten rock swirled, a hot spot flaring as a shelf broke away from Mount Fieri. It glided in a fiery dance along the river, its course altered by a massive, scorched boulder that neither yielded to nor overcame the fire surrounding it.

Just as Zireli would be in the assault by Sirdar. Span by span, his forces had given ground over the last week. Now what remained of his army huddled outside Seultrie's walls, waiting for Poired to execute his final push, to take the city, the keep—everything. Zireli had come to accept that there was little hope of overcoming Poired, but he would never stop fighting. No Celahar had backed down from a battle, from any challenge set forth. And that line would not be broken at his hand.

But days laden with dark foreboding and ominous reports tested the edges of his reason. Tempted him to doubt. Shame drew his gaze from the Lakes. He did not deserve the gift Abiassa had given him, his failings so complete.

"What else does your son say?" Zireli craned his neck to the right, to the overlook upon which Poired had mounted and sat in silent standoff against the keep. What he waited for, Zireli could not fathom.

Parchment crinkled as Grinda looked at the dispatch. "Haegan was seen just south of Hetaera."

"Isn't that the land of the Ematahri?" Adrroania's voice shook with the concern Zireli felt as well.

"It is, my queen," Grinda said.

"Let us hope Gwogh did a thorough job teaching him the lands and their threats—that Haegan will know better than to cross those savages." Zireli stroked his beard, thinking of his son against that fierce race. Neither ally nor enemy, they were best left alone.

"He has strength of mind," Grinda said, "but has he the heart and stamina of a fighter? Pitted against even one Ematahri, he—"

"We must trust," Zireli said, turning and cutting off his general, "that his way is guided by Abiassa and protected by Deliverers. And that Graem and his Jujak find him soon."

• • •

"Your mercy, mistress, but have you shelter and food?"

The woman paused as she pulled the teats of the cow. Face blanched, she slowly rose, hands wiping against the dingy apron encircling her waist. "I . . ." Her gaze started for the small cottage then dropped. "I have little, sir."

"I need little," Gwogh said as he glanced at her quaint home. The beams. The plaster protecting the south-facing wall against the heat. A fence, old but in perfect repair, created a pen that held two swine and wrapped around the small barn that abutted the cottage. She had little, yet her home sat in pristine order. He considered her. Aged, plump. Unlikely to be the sole tender of the property.

"Take his horse, Verusel," a voice spoke from the doorway, where shadows held its owner hostage.

In response, a young boy of no more than twelve jogged from the rear of the property and took Gwogh's horse. Looking strangely relieved, the woman strode toward the house.

Then the man's shape took form. He ducked beneath the doorpost, his dark hair long, shielding his face as he stepped into the late-afternoon sun. "You are welcome according to the laws of Alaemantu."

The local custom created by the Electreri demanded one night's hospitality to those who journeyed. "I thank—"

"One meal." The man's tone would brook no argument. "*One* night, Accelerant."

Gwogh suppressed his surprise at being recognized even dressed as no more than a traveler. He shot another look at the man's hidden face. "Abiassa favor you, kind sir."

Pale, pale eyes drilled him with silent warning.

A thought struck Gwogh like a sudden chill. In his days, there was only one manner of man who could recognize and be unafraid of an accelerant with such temerity. But they were gone—recalled to Abiassa like the Drigovudd.

Gwogh inclined his head. "I assure you, I seek only to eat, sleep, then be on my way before first light."

The man had neither moved nor shown any hint of approval. Jaw muscle bouncing, he held Gwogh's gaze. Tension roiled off him. Tall, though not as the giants of old, he seemed to contain a presence not his own. As if possessed by something.

Or Someone.

Gwogh felt a tremor of fear and awe trace his spine.

Finally, the man stepped aside with a slight bow, though his expression did not soften.

Gwogh advanced, every step a concerted effort, as if he climbed a steep mountain. And yet—a strange warmth saturated the air like a bidding. A yielding. Nervousness settled over him that he hadn't felt in a very long time. Had he chosen the wrong dwelling?

Where I lead, you follow.

Surrendering his jitters at the voice of the Lady, Gwogh entered. The main room spanned the entire length of the home, and a small passage led to at least two openings that he could see. All wood. Handmade. Simple but effective. A slight woman's touch with the curtains and skirt around the washbasin stand.

"I'll have the stew on shortly." The woman motioned to a basin. "Here, you may freshen after your journey."

With a quirk of his eyebrow, Gwogh washed his hands and dabbed his face, feeling refreshed. Drying off, he shifted.

The tapestry before him ruffled in the air. Beyond it sat a pristine pitcher and another basin in front of a round window no bigger than the metal plate on the table. Beneath the window lay an ornately threaded carpet. The wood floor did not shine, but no trace of dirt could be found.

All the elements for a ceremonial cleansing.

A round table tucked in the corner left the chamber feeling cramped rather than cozy. Or perhaps that was the overpowering presence of the man who had returned and now loomed behind Gwogh. The woman had vanished.

"A'tia will attend you when she returns," the man said, his voice low and deep. Retrieving a pipe from the mantel, the master settled into his rocking chair by the fire.

Gwogh lowered his gaze. *Had* he come to the wrong dwelling? His gaze struck the master again. No more than thirty-five, if that, though it seemed he wore experience and hardship heavier than his own age. Black hair—void of silver and gray. A sure sign.

But the pipe . . . and the woman. Abiassa's chosen never married, never smoked, and never indulged in any fleshly pleasure. And they were faceless in Her service. But as sure as he breathed air, Gwogh was convinced this man—

"Pardon the delay." A'tia returned with a pail of milk and retrieved the pitcher. "Rest and enjoy some warm milk." She went outside and returned a few quiet moments later to fill the large black cooking pot. She worked quietly, chopping carrots and a potato or two.

But Gwogh's gaze returned to the quiet man. "Are you long in this realm?"

Clank!

With a start at the loud noise, Gwogh looked to the woman, who was wrestling fur from a dead animal. Then back to the man. Indeed. Such a being, bound and producing heirs? "Your son is a fine lad—"

"Rabbit," the woman interjected. "He's good at hunting them."

"—master."

"Oh." Realizing he hadn't been speaking to her, A'tia jerked her gaze away, then stole a quick glimpse at the master. She wiped her hands and set before Gwogh a small bowl with bread and honey.

Interesting. Was the food distraction, something to stop him from talking or asking questions? "What word comes from the city?" Gwogh tore a chunk from the loaf and dipped it in sticky sweetness.

"We keep to our own," the master said. "Luxlirien and Hetaera are places of pagans and debauchery. We have no need of that here."

"Ignore Medr—"

"A'tia!"

Though not loud, the power in the master's voice seemed to echo in the small, heavily paneled home. Gwogh startled as if the man had shouted, and the effect was no less severe on A'tia, who dropped a bowl hard against the table.

Gwogh recovered slowly, his mind churning. Anonymity? Is that what the man sought? He cleared his throat. "I did not meant to encroach—"

"One meal. One night." The master returned to his chair. "We have little need of discussion here."

So they sat. In silence. After some time, the boy, Verusel, joined Gwogh at the table but kept his eyes down and made no response to Gwogh's gentle greeting. With each passing minute, Gwogh grew more convinced of whose presence he sat in. No, not whose. What's. It would explain so much—his unusually long hair, his dislike for conversation. The pipe he held but did not light. If this man were of Abiassa, well then he wouldn't be a man. He would care naught for pleasantries among strangers.

But neither did the man seem aware of Gwogh's quest. At least, he had not asked questions. Had not inquired of it, nor blessed it. He wasn't even sure they did that. After several moments, he roused himself to pose another testing query. "I wonder, do you have any ale?"

A'tia blanched. Cast a nervous glance toward the man. "Oh, he—we don't drink spirits. But I have more fresh milk." She delivered a bowl of hot stew to the table.

So he avoided fermented drinks. "Just as I thought—er, I mean, just as well," Gwogh said with a light laugh. "I need a clear mind when I set out." He glanced at the late-eve meal. "Ah, this looks as something Abiassa herself stewed, A'tia. Well done, mistress!"

The woman dipped her head with an obvious blush. "It's nothing."

"It's more than I've had in a day's ride, and it will provide the nourishment to continue my course. A feast could do no more."

As the sun settled into the cool embrace of night, she finished the washing up and begged leave to retire for the evening. The boy disappeared, and Gwogh was shown to a small room, no bigger than a closet, with a cot and wool blanket.

"It ain't much, but it's all we got." A'tia retrieved a few belongings from the corner.

"Is this your room?"

"No, Verusel stays here," she said.

"And would the master be upset with me for taking his son's bed?"

"Oh, he's not Verusel's father. He's watched over us the way a brother would—he don' much like us telling people, but he showed up when Ematahri raiders killed my husband and left me for dead. He's been here ever since. It ain't proper, I know, for a woman to be living with a man who ain't her husband, but there's naught but protection that goes on with M—him." She straightened, sniffing her mouth shut as she clasped her hands in front of her. "Will that be all, sir?"

"I'm well. Thank you." After she left, Gwogh set aside his pack then oriented himself in the room, deciphering which way the Citadel sat. Fingers splayed, he raised them out, warmed his inner being, then closed his eyes. And surrendered his mission, his life, his very breath to the cause of Abiassa.

Righted within, he sighed. Noticed the darkness in the room. His cleansing had taken longer this eve. But then, the things he had done, the thoughts he'd carried . . .

Something shifted in the shadows to his left.

Gwogh's heart shoved into his throat. He stumbled backward just as the form of the master filled his vision. He gave a shaky laugh, weakness trembling through his hands and knees. "Give care with the fright you throw upon this old man, master."

He stepped into the room. With the barest moonslight seeping through the curtain, the man's corded muscles tightened, pulling against his tunic. His hand was down and to the side in a way that bespoke a firm grip on a weapon. A sword.

Heat surged through Gwogh. *So, it is as I thought.*

"What is the purpose of your journey, Accelerant?" The question carried the authority only one type of man would dare wield against an accelerant of Gwogh's standing.

But would not one of his kind know the answer to that?

Hard eyes glinted—so pale. "I know only what She shares with me."

Startled, Gwogh inclined his head. "It is a sacred one, I assure you." No, that wouldn't be good enough. He must convince him. "I am sent by Abiassa to locate and protect one of her charges."

Jaw muscle popping, the man stood unmoving. Unanswering. *Judging.* Staring out the small sliver between the curtains to the night sky, the light stroking his strong face.

Gwogh swallowed. He'd been in many a frightening situation before, becalmed by Abiassa. But never before in *this* tricky position. A question burned through his chest and lungs. The thought terrifying. But he must extend the invitation. It was the way. It was expected. An accelerant who did not had something to hide. "Would you test me?"

The man lowered his head, his thick neck rotating as he slid his gaze back to Gwogh. "She would have you answer." In a blink, he placed his hand against Gwogh's chest.

Time and light vanished.

Gwogh struggled for balance as a searing, cleansing fire washed over him. He screamed at the pain of it, his arms thrown wide as he arched his back against the agony.

And as if someone had snapped a band, Gwogh stood in darkness. And yet . . . not darkness. For he could see plainly, though there was little to see. This was the Void, the space that bridged the gap between Primar and where Abiassa dwelt with the Creator.

In the yester of Nine and One, you set your hand against Me.

Before him laughed and darted a young boy, chasing his sister and tackling her, pinning her even amid her screams of protest. He yanked her hair as a brother would and took off running.

In a heartbeat, the boy lay stretched on a bed, surrounded by grieving parents and a confused sister.

Your oath was clear and well embraced, yet you stood defiant.

No, Gwogh replied. *I foresaw what would come.*

Say you now that you are like Me, that you have the ability to know the hearts and minds of My Children?

I beg Your mercy, My Lady, but I saw how fear would poison hearts. I saw what would come!

Say you now that you have more knowledge and wisdom than I, who have set this world in motion?

May and true—You set it in motion, but You also set upon men their own will. To act, to make their choosings. If I have exerted my best belief wrongly, then my life is Yours to take.

Fire crawled over his body, consuming, searing. Singeing. *I beg Your Mercy!* Gwogh cried out, feeling as if his flesh dripped from his body like water from an icicle. *I only sought to protect him.*

What you did was done in fear. You set your best belief against Me, against what I have ordained.

Not with intent, My Lady. I believed it best—I believed that was my purpose in life, why I was set on this path—to protect—

Think you that I need an aged accelerant to protect my chosen?

No, my Lady, he panted, his hair matting against his forehead and sweat slipping through his beard. *You have need of no one, but You choose all manner of people, no matter profession or age . . . or foolishness.*

Snap-clap!

Gwogh dropped to the hard floor, bumping against the cot. Sweat clung to him, chilling his flesh. And if he were not out of his mind—for there could be no certainty at this moment—he saw steam rising from his skin.

"Slumber well, Accelerant. Dawn comes early to a tired mind." Swift and silent, the man turned, and Gwogh drew in a sharp breath. No longer could the man's features be discerned, as if he had drawn a filmy veil over his face.

"W-who are you?"

"I am called Medric."

Wind swirled past Gwogh in Medric's wake, the pardon felt in more than the air. "I'm alive," he managed around a parched tongue as he climbed beneath the wool blanket to shake off the chill that seeped into his bones. Alive. With a shaky laugh, he closed his eyes, knowing Abiassa tested him even here. Pushed him to be excellent in Her service.

Now he stood on the cusp of a time in which brewed a heated battle that, were the sparks flickering within him right, could determine the course of the planet itself.

"Master Gwogh?" came A'tia's soft call. "Are you well, sir?"

He almost smiled as she peeked into the room, her face a curtain of concern. "Aye." He *was* well. And *alive*. That was the most important.

"Oh, thanks be to Abiassa!" She sagged, releasing a deep breath.

Gwogh clutched the rough wool blanket, his gaze on the ceiling. "He is a marked one." Thus, he believed, the reason for the man's long hair—to hide the mark of Abiassa on his neck and face. "A Deliverer."

"Aye."

"And I'm alive." He couldn't stop saying it. He'd encountered a Deliverer—the very hand of Abiassa, inordinately gifted, absolute in his reasoning, swift in delivering justice—and survived.

12

"I envy him the freedom he has now." Kaelyria could not keep the heaviness from her voice, though she knew this captivity was of her own making. A right decision, albeit a desperate one. Had there been any other way . . .

"I wonder, do you think he'll find a girl to love while he's gone?"

Kae almost smiled at that. It was strange to think of him out there, making his way to the Great Falls. "My brother will be so singularly focused and naïve, I'm not sure he would recognize love if it struck him over the head."

Kiesa laughed, her cheeks crimson.

"You still fancy him, then?"

"Oh, I—" Kiesa shook her head, the red rushing across her face and flaring across the tips of her ears. "I—" She looked past the beveled glass. "I know my place, my lady-grace. And I'm happy to serve you."

"Be at peace. I know your heart." As she had known her brother's. As she'd known he would surrender to her prodding. And prod she had.

Once more the green fields littered with tents and the embers of small fires lured her thoughts away from the room that had become her prison. He was out there. Dutifully making his way across the Nine . . .

A shadow shifted in the glass, drawing Kaelyria's attention. What had she seen? It moved again—and her breath backed into her throat. Cilicien? Her gaze darted to the left, to the shadows outside her chambers. Was he here? Father would kill him if he caught him in the keep again! But first she would give this daemon a piece of her mind for the half-truths he'd delivered.

"I . . ." She looked at her handmaiden. "Could you fetch me some warm cordi juice?" Kaelyria asked. That would only take a moment. "And some toast with jam?"

Kiesa stood and inclined her head. "Shall I remove you to the bed, my lady?"

The thought of being in bed with that accelerant in the room . . . "No. I thank you." Eyes to the window, she searched for the shadowy reflection again. "I prefer this view." Kae wet her lips as her handmaiden slipped out and vanished down the spiral steps.

Bedecked in a long black cloak that fastened at his waist and whose high collar poked into his jaw, Cilicien ka'Dur seemed to float into the room. "And how does my lady princess fare this eve?"

"Pleasantries do not become you, dark one."

His eyebrows rose toward his slicked-back hair, black as pitch. "Dark one, am I?" His cold, beady eyes slithered over her. "And how have I earned this title from one who not so long ago depended entirely upon my generosity and willingness?"

Oh, that she could wrap her hands around his throat! Or wield— she did not need hands to do that, but even that was lost to her now. "You were not forthcoming with me, not in the full."

"And how is it you believe this?"

"Consider my situation and be enlightened."

His mustached lip curled. "Forgive my boldness, Lady Princess, but you were convinced, were you not, that this should happen—*at any price.*"

"The transference—yes! But you did not tell me I would be paralyzed as my brother had been." She met his gaze evenly and there saw the glint of pleasure she'd anticipated. "You *knew* what would happen!"

"Nothing was written—"

"You *knew!*" The shout even startled her. "You knew yet you withheld the full truth of what would happen to me. Did nothing to prepare me for the cruelty of it." If she could feel her body, she would wager it trembled.

"Full truth." Cilicien repeated and drew near her feet, hands clasped as he stared out the window. "*Truth* convinced you, did it not, that the only course of action prudent to protecting your gift was transference."

"Truth?" Was it? She wasn't as confident any longer. "You call it truth, but I call it a shade of the truth you wanted me to see."

"One you were all too eager to capture."

Anger sparked through her at the veracity of words. She hated him almost as much as she hated herself for what she'd done. No more could she take his presence or what he represented. "What is your intention, Cilicien?"

"Intention?"

"Why are you here?" Her throat constricted, forcing her to swallow. It was the only indication that her heart pounded against her ribs. How strange not to feel it. "Why have you returned? Why are you not with your master?"

He frowned. "Which master is that?"

"Poired! Or Sirdar."

With a scoff, he shook his head. "There are more irons in this fire than Unelithien and the Nine."

"Then you did this—not for Poired?"

"Ah, my motives are my own. My intentions"—again, beady eyes roamed her—"are my own, dear princess."

"Surely you know my father-king has ordered your arrest."

A smirk slowly slid into olive complexion. "I have heard."

Maddening, petulant . . . "*Why* are you here? What do you seek?" Agitation and irritation coated her question, but she cared not.

"We had an agreement—"

"Which was fulfilled." Should she call for the guards?

He cocked his head, those eyes probing her. "To your satisfaction?"

She shifted her gaze to the windows once more, hating that *satisfaction* did not come close to what she felt. Yes, what she sought to accomplish had succeeded. But she had not fathomed the . . . rest. Haegan's wandering. Her paralysis. Her father's anger. Her mother's grief. The kingdom's despair.

Satisfaction mattered not. This was not Abiassa Day when children received gifts, debts were forgiven, and men chose wives. She had carried out what was necessary. No more. No less. "It is done. We have no further business. I would have you leave."

A half smile bared his teeth. "You think to dismiss me so easily?"

Kaelyria swallowed, unease coiling around her confidence and strangling it. "Yes."

"Forgive me, Lady-Princess, but I am not ready to leave." He bent closer, impressing upon her the awful truth of her situation—though she would have wielded against him at one time, now she could do nothing but watch him crowd her. He pushed his way onto the cushion beside her, making room where there was none.

Why had she not noticed before how his presence made her feel uneasy? "Get out."

He sneered this time. "You seem to forget yourself, princess. Or rather, forget that you are an invalid, weak in body." His eyebrow winged up again. "And abilities."

"One shout from me and the guards will be upon you," she hissed, her anger mounting. "They would drag you to the dungeons, where my father would sear that smirk off your face."

Chin tucked, he merely smiled, his eyes communicating his dominance and comfort therein.

She struggled to breathe. "Now. Leave me."

"I think not."

The air . . . so thick . . . "Wha—"

"Now . . . now you see who is in control."

"You serve Poired well." The air wouldn't move in her throat. Kaelyria felt the heady swell of panic in her breast.

Eyes dark and menacing, he curled his fingers into a fist . . . one . . . after . . . another. As if tightening them around her neck. "A little hard to breathe, princess?"

Her temples throbbed. Scream! She had to scream. But she couldn't. A hot tear slipped from her eye and slid over her cheek. Alone, with nobody to help, she would die here. With this putrid accelerant squeezing the life from her lungs.

"Perhaps a little fresh air . . ."

The edges of her vision ghosted as his other palm swam a circle over the pane. *Crack!* The tinkling of breaking glass grew faint in her ears.

Wind gusted across her cheeks. Where was it coming from? She couldn't see. Didn't care. *Air! I need air!*

Kaelyria felt herself sliding . . .

A scream warbled somewhere distant.

Pop!

The stranglehold broke! She gasped. Hauled in a greedy breath of air. Blinked away the grayness. All at once she saw and heard too many things. Green swam in her vision. Grass? How was she—

Kae screamed this time, realizing she hung out the window. "Help!" she shouted, long and primal. "Help me!"

A Jujak swung out from below a sheltered area near the main door. He looked around, then up . . .

Kaelyria's tears blurred her vision. Chilled winds smacked her face and yanked her hair from its knot. *Crack!* The window broke more. She shifted. Screamed again.

Hands gripped her shoulders. Pulled her up.

Kaelyria fought the wild panic as she was drawn back through the window, noting the blood smeared across the glass. The jagged glass.

"Easy, there. I've got you." Mother! Her mother had her. "Help me!"

Stronger hands caught Kaelyria's shoulders. Lifted her from the terrifying heights she'd hung from. Carried her from the cushioned seat.

Tears burned the backs of her eyes, but Kae refused to cry before this Jujak, this warrior.

"No, not there. It's too cold here now. To her chambers." Her mother swept ahead, motioning out of the tower. She stepped over something—no, not something. A body!

"Kiesa!"

"She's alive," her mother said without stopping.

A handful of Jujak clanked up the steps, slowing as they met on the stairwell.

"You," her mother said, pointing to two warriors. "Take my daughter's handmaid to the pharmakeia, then bring him here at once. His nurse can tend the girl, but the princess needs him immediately. The rest of you—Cilicien ka'Dur is in the keep. Find him and secure him until the king's return."

They hustled to fulfill her orders as the queen and the Jujak warrior continued down the stairs. It took several long minutes before they reached the royal residences and the Jujak plodded over the ornate rugs that lined the hall to her private chambers. Her mother's pale blue dress made her appear as a ghost, swimming in and out of rooms before finally throwing open the doors to Kae's room.

"The bed."

"Yes, my queen," the Jujak said, delivering Kae to the bed.

"Leave us. When her handmaid is recovered, send her here at once. And make sure the pharmakeia knows where to find us."

"Yes, my queen."

After a soft snick of the locks, her mother stood staring at the door.

Kaelyira could take it no longer. "Mother . . ."

Her mother swung around, and in a billowing cloud of satin and organza, rushed to the bed. Crawled up on the feathered mattress beside Kae and pulled her into her arms. "Oh, my darling girl!"

And the tears came. "I'm so sorry." Mentally, she clung to her mother. "I beg your mercy. I was a fool."

Hands cupped her head, her mother's heartbeat thumping against her ear. "Shh, shh."

"I had to do it. I had to. I could not let Poired deliver my gift to Sirdar. I could not. But I didn't know . . . I didn't know I'd feel so empty." The tears rushed down her face, cleansing Kaelyria of the terror she had invited into their family and realm. "I didn't know!"

13

I will have his head!

Zireli sprinted through the stone passages, the blood in his veins heated with the venom of hatred against the one who had brought about the sure destruction of his line and the realms. "Leave ka'Dur to me," he shouted over his shoulder as they rounded the last bend.

"He's not there," a voice called from behind.

Zireli slowed and glanced back. Kiesa stood, cheeks flushed and eyes rimmed in the red of tears. He started toward her. "What do you know?"

"He's fled, my king. Out the servant's passage," she said, bobbing her head toward the back of the keep.

"Go," he ordered six warriors. "Capture this miscreant and bring him to me." After sharing a glance with the remaining Jujak and flexing his hands as if stroking the embers of rage, he took a measured breath. Turned to the servant. "My daughter."

The girl curtseyed and tucked her chin. "In her chambers with the queen, sire."

He pivoted and headed back down the stairs to the residential wing. Though there appeared to be no imminent danger, his nerves itched to run. To fling himself down the passage. He quickened his steps.

Then slowed as sobs reached him through the thick doors of Kaelyria's chambers. Punched him in the chest.

Zireli stepped into the room, sunlight streaming in through an open window, dust particles dancing on a beam that touched his daughter's bed. What had possessed his wife to bring Kaelyria down here, where she could be seen in such a state by all? "Why have you brought her here?"

Adrroania stood. Stepped away from their daughter, her hands held out to the sides. She turned to him, haunted. Her face stricken white.

"What?" Zireli rushed toward the curtained bed.

"Nothing." It was Kaelyria's voice. But it also wasn't. He stared at her face, hearing the emptiness in the lone word she had spoken mirror the vacant expression she wore. Blue eyes still rimmed with red, she stared toward the window. "We should go to him."

A chill slithered down his spine.

"He would be our advocate. It is only right."

"How can you say that?" Adrroania gasped. "He is our sworn enemy, ravaging villages, murdering our people."

"It is necessary." Still focused on the window, Kaelyria hadn't blinked. A tear slipped down her cheek. She spoke as one without a will. One attached to the strings of—

"He's in her head!" In one fell swoop, Zireli swept aside his wife. Planted himself between his daughter and the beam of light. Palms splayed, he sliced an X in the air and stepped back, ready to spar. "Release her!"

A father's anger rose up within him. A righteous anger. Powerful and pure, unlike that of rage or arrogance. Zireli drew back his right hand and cupped the swell of heat he sensed there. A tendril, really. Nothing more. But powerfully focused, so much that it had at first escaped his notice. Curling his fingers around the thrumming force, he shoved it back. "She is *protected*! By her father, the king. By the Flames. By Abiassa!"

An angry roar spiraled up through the air and slammed into Zireli. The disembodied punch snapped his head back. Pain exploded between his eyes. His foot slipped. Warmth slid over his lip.

He recovered, gathering the heat and embers Abiassa granted. "Yield I will not," he yelled, his throat scraping raw with the effort. "You cannot have her!"

Shouldering into the battle unseen by the ungifted, Zireli honed all his righteous anger at the beam that had sneaked past his senses.

That had seized his daughter's mind and turned her own will against her. But he felt the resistance. Felt it pushing against him, as if a Jujak had his armor-plated shoulder against his own. With his left hand, bracing against the torrent, he drew on the heat. On the fire of Poired's anger . . . and sent the volley back to him with a swift flick.

The torrent snapped closed.

Yellow light blinked gray. A breeze rushed in through the window, tussling his hair. Behind him, he heard a choked cry. He spun back to his family, wiping the warm blood from his beard. "Adrroania, get the pharmakeia."

. . .

Kaelyria slumped. Breathing hard and vaguely aware as someone gathered her in his arms. Pain . . . fear . . . terror held her captive. Unable to think. She sobbed. Though she couldn't control her limbs, she imagined she trembled all the way to her toes. Hot tears streamed down her cheeks as strong, gentle hands clasped her shoulders. Righted her.

Surprise spiraled through her as she met her father's gold eyes. *"Gold amid the Flames . . ."* Accelerants' eyes turned gold while wielding, but the embers smothered and the natural color returned within minutes. But when? When had he wielded? She had no memory. Of anything since . . . "Fath—"

"Quiet," he said, tugging her back against his chest.

More tears fell, confusion rampant, but the relief of his presence thickened her throat. Then at once, it flooded back to her. "Poired." The tightening of her father's arms around her was a sweet comfort. "I . . . I let him in."

"It takes but a crack in the best accelerant's armor for the darkness to become a plague."

"I'm so sorry. About that. About trusting Cilicien. I've been a fool!" she muttered against the gold threaded jewels of his jerkin. Kaelyria wanted to clutch the fabric, clutch *him*. "I wanted to save—"

He eased her back against the mattress and shifted around in front of her; his skilled, strong hands tucked the blanket around her shoulders even as his gaze never left hers. Blue eyes so constant—like Haegan's. Blond hair lightly threaded with silver. Formidable and handsome. "You have done well, Kaelyria."

Tears stung her eyes again. "No!"

Again, he squeezed her arms. "He is strong. Practiced. Think you the incipient has had no training? He has had the best training at the Citadel, and when he was stripped, the most cunning master."

"Sirdar." Tears blurred her vision. "What have I done? I was desperate when I heard of him smothering accelerants' gifts and stealing others. I couldn't let it happen. I did the unthinkable . . . too late. I'm too late!"

Pensive, he looked out on their kingdom. Sat there for several long minutes. And even beneath his soft facial hair, his jaw muscle popped. Age had become an enemy to him in the last few years. "I never thought it would fall while I protected the Nine." He blinked and gave a quick, gentle smile as he cupped her head. "How do you feel?"

"Tired."

He nodded. "But your thoughts."

She blinked.

"Are they your own. Do you feel the traces of him? Do you taste ash in your mouth?"

"Ash." She frowned. "No. I sense nothing. And at first, I could remember nothing." The fiery shards of the moments before she found herself staring into her coverlets. "It was *terrifying*. Confusing. I could not breathe nor free myself. I heard him—in my head. Somehow my thoughts became . . . twisted. Tangled." She knit her brow, imploring him with sorrow. "How? *Is* that even possible? Am I losing my mind as well as my strength now?"

He sighed and looked over his shoulder. Only then did she notice her mother there.

"What . . . what is it?" Kaelyria felt her nerves fraying more. "What holds you prisoner in your thoughts as he held me in mine?"

King Zireli rose and walked toward his queen. Back to Kaelyria, he whispered something indiscernible, then started for the door.

"What?" Panic flushed her face. "Do not treat me as a child! Speak plainly, for we must find way out of the keep this very day—that is, if we are to evade what he said."

Her father pivoted. His face bright. Eyes challenging. "You heard him? His voice. Not just a touch on your mind, but he *spoke* to you?"

"Yes. No." She blinked again, struggling to breathe. "I don't know. I just—"

Her mother came and sat on the bed with her, smoothing Kaelyria's hair. "What did you hear, my sweet girl?"

Skirting a glance to her father, who stood as if ready for battle, Kaelyria inhaled. Again she smelled the carnage. Remembered the strewn bodies. "I saw . . . death. Destruction. And he said . . . he said I would yield."

"Don't you see, Adrroania!" Her father's voice reverberated across the stones. "It has begun—she has unleashed the demon from his boundaries!"

14

A shock of cold cracked his head.

Haegan jerked upward, water dripping from his face and tunic. Stunned, mind still clinging to the cobwebs of sleep, he grew aware of the crowd that stood around him, frowning down on him as he lay in the dirt—*water* and dirt. Praegur held a dripping bucket. Murmurs and concerned expressions mottled the crowd.

The attention stirred his pulse. He didn't want attention. No attention. Not when he was in the keep. Especially not now.

He struggled to his feet, wiping his now-muddied hands.

Praegur was there, his arm coming up under him for support. "Are you sure you—"

"Aye." He winced as scampering torchlight from a shop seared the backs of his eyes. "What happened?"

"Everything!" Laertes bounded ahead of them, spinning around to walk backward. "One second we was waiting for him what wields to blast the Asykthian to ashes, and the next you fall right down like what a sack of potatoes does."

Tokar fell into step, ever brooding and annoyed.

Thiel. Where was she?

"People was shouting," Laertes went on, animated. "The Ignatieri went branding hot and, next thing what we know—"

"Where's Thiel?"

"—Thiel's gone!"

Haegan stopped short. "What?"

"Keep walking," Tokar ordered, apparently having taken control of the group in Thiel's absence. Nobody had ever said the girl was in charge, but he dared one of them to challenge her to her face.

Tokar set a fast pace, his anger strong. "We've had enough attention for one day. Let's get to camp and figure things out."

"Figure what out?" Flames, the water must have shocked his brain, too. "Wait—what happened?"

"That's what I was trying to say," Laertes put in. "The accelerants were asking about us."

"No." Tokar trudged into the valley where more than a dozen wagons, including theirs, had encamped. "About him." He stabbed a length of stick at Haegan.

"Me?" Haegan's heart stuttered.

"You were fainting like a girl," Tokar said with a sneer. "They wanted to know about your parents."

"That's when I said you ain't got none."

"Don't have any," Haegan corrected Laertes without thinking.

The lad scowled. "It don't matter how I say it. Still means the same thing."

"Look, you're bringing a heap of trouble on us," Tokar said. "I'm thinking you should stay in camp while we look for Thiel."

"We must get Thiel back—the more eyes the better. When did you last see her?"

"When the big-mouth rider took her," Laertes said.

Haegan stilled, glancing to the others. "The riders took her?"

"She was lurking over by the trees," Praegur said. "Then the leader barreled past you and lifted her by the scruff of her neck like she wasn't anything."

"We must get her back." Haegan cringed as a pang stole through his side again. "Now."

"You're in no shape, and you are as awkward on your feet as you are in the way you act. If you go with us and the Asykthians hear us before we get Thiel out, we'll all be trussed before you can say 'raqine.'" Tokar held nothing back. Including his dislike for Haegan, which smarted more than Haegan would give voice to.

"Your feelings toward me should not engender ill will toward Thiel. If you know where they are, lead the way. Or would you like us to keep you informed as we search?"

Tokar stood straight, challenge glinting in his eyes.

"Very well. Let's go." Haegan waited.

Tokar spun, dropping quickly into a silent half-run toward the wooded area at the base of the northern cliffs. Leaves crackled beneath Haegan's feet as he jogged in a crouch. The taller, broader Praegur glanced over his shoulder. "Slower. Lighter."

Haegan tried—Flames knew he tried to be quiet. But adjusting to legs he could walk on, let alone sneak on . . . well, he hadn't perfected the technique of stalking just yet. Frustration wrapped around him as they closed in on the Asykthians' camp. A dozen paces from the riders' fire, they slowed. Beyond the reach of the firelight, shadows shifted and groaned like ghouls, spilling dread across Haegan's shoulders and down his spine.

Nearly laughing aloud, Haegan realized his folly. No ghosts in the night. Just those massive horses, tethered to a line. A branch snapped beneath his boot.

Tokar spun, whites of his eyes bulging. Lips screwed tight, he stabbed a finger to the ground. "Wait here."

What? "No! I might be new but I care just as much," Haegan argued in a whisper. "It is my—"

"What? Your right to mess it up?" Tokar interjected.

"Just . . . wait." Praegur knelt beside them. "Thiel is tough. If you can't keep quiet, you put her in danger. And I might not know you much, but I can figure out you wouldn't want her hurt. Right?"

Haegan had no reply.

"Besides," Laertes said from the side. "Isn't she one of them anyway?"

"Shut up." Tokar pivoted and started moving.

"One of whom?"

"Stay." Praegur gave him a look then followed the other teen.

I'm older and a prince. Yet among them I am nothing.

Of no use.

Much like at home.

Gritting his teeth, Haegan knelt in the forest litter as the others, even the much younger Laertes, sneaked toward the Asykthian camp.

Slumped against an aspen, he sighed. Wrestled with the truth of his existence. Despite having strength for the first time in more than a decade, he felt weaker than ever.

Haegan pushed off the tree and drifted away from the camp, deeper into the trees. He touched the bark. Bandra oak. He visually traced the tree to its canopy. Savored the rough feel beneath his hands. As he walked, he stared through the branches that had already begun to shed their leaves in anticipation of winter. He spotted a harkling, mostly found in northern lands and known for its vibrant colors. His wilds knowledge coming to life. What would Kaelyria think? That he should get his head out of the leaves and back onto more important matters.

His heart caught, remembering his sister—now afflicted with his condition. Paralyzed. Captive within limbs that refused cooperation.

He paused, hand on an aspen, mentally retracing his steps. Reminding himself he had a mission—get to the Falls. Stand beneath the healing waters and return to Seultrie to free Kae before it was too late. Before whatever Cilicien had done became permanent.

"No," Haegan ground out. He would not see his sister confined to a bed and wheeled chair for the rest of her given years. He would not see her relegated to the tower, her beauty and purity concealed within unfeeling stone.

Not like they did to me.

"It will not happen," he whispered his vow into the wind.

A voice answered.

Haegan flinched and looked around. Wait. Where was he? How far had he ventured? He hadn't been paying attention. Had he been followed?

Again the voice came. Haegan paused, head tilted as he homed in on the sound. Voices. More than one. He turned slightly, careful not to stir the floor litter or—as he had clumsily done before—snap a twig.

With each silent step, the voices grew louder.

Haegan willed himself to be stealthy. Patient but intent. Patient? How does one stay patient when a friend was in danger?

The voices sounded near now. He used trees as shields but knew with the white bark and his dark tunic, camouflage would be near impossible. Ahead, a fog-drenched clearing stretched a hundred paces across before colliding with the encircling trees. And there they stood, enveloped by encroaching darkness, their words swallowed by the mist. His boot hit a stump. Haegan caught and braced himself, eyes glued on the scene before him.

The Asykthian leader grabbed the arm of the other, who wrenched free. He knew that defiant posture. *Thiel!* His heart skipped a beat. Where were Praegur and Tokar?

The raider jerked her toward himself. Would the brigand try to violate her here, where he thought they were alone?

I will not let that happen!

Again, she ripped free of the man's grip.

Haegan breathed a little easier at Thiel's defiance of her captor, and yet he feared for her. Feared the retaliation the rider would exact against her. They were a violent sort, Asykthians, prone to use of their swords over words of peace. Preferred bloodshed to negotiations. In the Histories were many a telling of their bloodlust.

He should intervene now, before she was injured. Haegan shifted around the tree.

The raider held up his hands and took a step back, stilling Haegan. He tucked himself back behind the cover of the trunk. The raider stood a foot taller than Thiel, and his dark-brown hair seemed to melt into the shadows. He placed a hand on his scabbard.

Flames! Now would he run through an innocent girl?

Haegan gulped and took a step forward . . . yet nothing happened. Except discussion. Thiel spun toward the man, arms rising and falling. Angry? Yelling at him. What was this? She seemed to be talking to him as if she . . .

Haegan drew up short. *"Isn't she one of them anyway?"* Laertes's words invaded his mind. Haegan hauled in a breath. And drew back.

Snap.

He cringed.

A sudden wind swept over him as his gaze struck the two, who stood unmoving. Then something in the shadows drew his gaze. Movement—the shadows and darkness morphed into a hulking creature. Not the mighty horses the Asykthians rode. This was more agile. Lower to the ground—though not much. The beast swung around in a fluid motion, its ebony coat making it difficult to sort where it started and ended. But the horizontal spread of—

"Wings," Haegan gasped.

In terror, he watched as the beast crouched, dark eyes sparking, then lurched into the air.

Raqine! His heart seized. It could not be. He struggled to breathe.

Wits gathered with an effort, Haegan scrambled behind a tree, hugging the bark as he searched the sky for the creature. This can't be. This can't be. This can't be.

Though the raqine flew upward till it was naught but a speck, Haegan knew the second the beast locked onto him. A tingling zipped through his spine as the beast's black eyes stared into his soul. *Impossible!*

A roar like rushing wind filled his mind, deadening him to anything but the beast. *It's not real. They have passed beyond the Shadows. They're extinct!*

Yet he felt it crowding his mind. But . . . he could not . . . could not yield. Even as the raqine's gaze ensnared him, Haegan saw Thiel and the Asykthian turn in his direction.

Move, you idiot!

Holding his ears against the beast's roaring, Haegan slid into a crouch. No good. Still screeching. He turned and marked a crooked, stumbling course away from the raqine. Away from Thiel. What happened to his head? Why could he still hear the roaring?

Then as if someone had slammed a door shut, silence dropped. Haegan now only heard the thundering of his heart. The crunch of his boots over the leaves. Gasping hard, he worked to slow his breathing. To calm himself. He must to get back to camp. Tell the others.

No. They would not believe him. He would be made a fool. And Thiel . . . with the raiders. What did it mean? How could she even speak with those brigands?

"The Northern Riders are as violent as they are coldhearted," his father-king had said many times. Too many. The topic so distasteful his mother often fled the room. And Haegan's tutor had been similarly harsh regarding the Asykthian, especially regarding their king, Thurig.

Knowing the others would be merciless in their mockery, Haegan diverted from the path to camp and headed up a hill, desperate for solitude to sort all that had happened. Less than a half-month past he lay in a tower, all too comfortable in his paralyzed life. Now, he stood—*stood*—on this mount.

But he was alone. Perhaps more so now that he had not the comfort or love of his mentor.

Haegan trudged up the incline and broke into a clearing. No larger than a small dwelling, the area boasted a massive jutting of granite, one part broken off and smooth, like a giant—*throne*. He turned a slow circle, throwing off the weight of the last few hours and taking in the outcropping. Abiassa's Throne, the locals had named it. Something about the legendary seat of her wisdom and power drew him. Haegan hauled himself up and let the moment settle in his brain. His challenged, exhausted brain that refused to accept the beast.

It wasn't real. Couldn't be real. No way a raqine existed. Gwogh . . . Gwogh was smarter than anyone, and he said the beasts died with the Drigo and Unauri.

Can't be real. Impossible.

My mind is fractured.

In the far distance a glimmer of something pulled his attention. He could barely make out the delicate curve of a mountain against the ever-darkening sky. What could be there, sparkling as if stroked by starlight?

Haegan's breath caught in his throat. Could it be? He mentally referred to the maps Gwogh and he had scoured, the Histories. His gaze hit the faint lights of Hetaera, the glittering valley city, then slid up the base of the mountain, and once more he settled on the tree-darkened spine and the trail of silver.

"The Falls."

15

Sensing the hope and tug of freedom and healing—*restoration*—after seeing the Great Falls, Haegan jumped off the giant boulder, took one more look toward Hetaera. His gaze rose to the sky, to the Tri-tipped Flame, the place his people had long believed to be Abiassa's home before she came to Primar.

Help me, Abiassa. I'm alone. Verses said she was a friend to the lonely.

He wasn't even sure how to be a friend anymore. It'd been a decade since he had one, and even then he'd been a prince—a stranger, perhaps, to true friendship. Haegan turned as he slid his hands in his pockets. 'Twas a fool's errand to seek a friend in Abiassa when he had nothing to offer in return.

A shape shifted at the far edge of the overlook, shoving his stomach up into his throat. He froze as Thiel eased into the moonlight. His heart thumped hard. *Betrayer.*

And yet, this slight girl had been his only ally. One among their number who had given a measure of hope that he could make it to the Falls. Though she heaped condescension on him at every chance, he saw in her a friend. An intelligent one, who missed little. Endured much. For that reason alone, he held his tongue. What was he to say anyway? *I saw you with a raqine?* Cavorting with a coldhearted savage?

Yes, that would gain her trust and respect.

Her enduring silence pushed his gaze down. What would not sound as an accusation or insult? He should depart. Go in silence down the dark path that led to the camp, to some fledgling hope that he could reach the Falls and save his sister.

Haegan crossed the flattened overlook to the path that had led him down. He stepped around her, felt his sleeve brush hers. His boot hit a rock as he turned the first switchback.

"I know."

Stilled by her words, Haegan stared at the hard-packed earth, telling himself not to talk to her. That they stood on tenuous ground and should merely bide their time. Endure this journey without giving rise to the tide of anger. And yet, his strict upbringing, at first in the court of his father-king, and then under the gruff tutelage of Gwogh, would not allow him to walk away, delivering a slight.

How could she have knowledge of his secrets? He'd given no indication of his past or his birthright. He'd been careful and diligent. Haegan shifted in place. Looked to the side, then to her. "Know what?"

Hard light glinted off her cheeks as Thiel folded her arms over her bound chest. She tilted her head, the brown hair sticking out in angles around her face. "Did you do it?"

She would ask questions of him but not answer his? Haegan grew weary. "Do what?" A wind riffled the air, tossing leaves along the path he so desperately sought for escape. The more he talked to her, the more he'd soften. Because he'd never been one to hold grudges. Not even against his father. What rested in his chest was a raw ache grown in years of neglect and shame.

Thiel shot him an expression of frustration but then pointed to the boulder he'd just climbed off and went to it. "You saw me in the woods. If you have questions to ask of me, do it now." She made quick work of reaching the top, then crossed her ankles and sat down.

"Me? You are the one asking questions but not clarifying." *Just go back to camp.* But he was tired of being alone. Tired of not understanding things around him. Haegan trudged over to the rock. "I have no desire to pry answers from the unwilling."

She rolled her eyes. "Don't be so cross. Sit down. I'm not going to bite."

"No," he said as he hauled himself up next to her. "But that raqine bites."

Wide brown eyes met his. Moonlight caressed her pale face and shone against her skin. She recovered but not quickly enough. "You know they are things only of myth."

Haegan hated the way his stomach threatened each time she looked him in the eye. That was a reaction for a weakling. Not a prince. He pushed his attention out, toward Hetaera. "What do you want of me, Thiel?"

"Who says I want anything?"

He gauged her expression and saw the same hunger consuming him—one for friendship and belonging. "Your eyes."

Thiel flicked her gaze away. "Says the person who says he saw a raqine." When Haegan pushed to his feet, she caught his hand and pulled him back down. "I'm only teasing." Lingering light danced in her eyes, bouncing off flecks of gold. "You . . . you're"—she leaned in closer—"the prince."

Haegan drew back. How did she know that? In his panic that he might be revealed and captured, anger sparked in his chest. "I—No!"

"Don't deny it."

Challenged by her words, Haegan recalled the debates with Gwogh. The training. The tutelage to think and not necessarily speak. To weigh an adversary and rout weakness. "I could speak the same of you."

Her eyes widened, then narrowed. "The raqine? You jest!"

Haegan let his statement be his response. "Not just the raqine. The Asykthian raiders. You were with them."

"It's not what you think."

His cheek twitched but he steeled the smile.

"It's not." She glanced to the side, at the city of lights. Leaned in closer. Touched his arm.

No, not touched. *Gripped.* Held it tight.

"You must swear by the Flames—"

"That is a sacred oath." To take them lightly, to speak them casually, was forbidden. Especially for the royal line tasked with upholding them. Especially by him.

Victory danced in her eyes. "Do you count me as a friend?"

Did he? Associating with the Asykthians—the closest thing to an enemy of Zaethien without actually being an enemy. And she was connected to them? "We met but two weeks past. Is that what *you* would call me?"

Sultry and mischievous, she did this jig with her neck that threw her right eyebrow up. "I haven't driven my dagger between your ribs."

"And *that* is your measure of friendship?" Haegan chuckled. "No wonder you spend your days wandering the plains with rogues and thieves."

She looked away, pained somehow. "You know nothing of me. Of what I have been through and fought for." The searing reprimand stung the air between them. "Not every child of Abiassa can be raised in opulence with private tutors and servants placating your every need and whim. Some of us have had to fight to survive, deprived of warmth and safety." Thiel's brown eyes widened, as if surprised by the words that seemed to have fled a sacred vault in her heart.

Her words, the ferocity of them, and the now-present panic, tugged at his honor. Flooded him with guilt that choked his pithy reply. "I . . . I beg your mercy." He saw her then, not as the fighting girl hiding beneath the clothes of men, but the wounded young woman he would call friend. "My tutor . . . he said often that my tongue is quicker than my mind."

A faint smile tugged at her mouth. "I would think we were born beneath the same moon, then. I've been quick with many weapons and training, but none quicker than the retort." She drew in a measured breath and let it out. Thiel wet her lips, which now glistened under the tease of the moonlight. "I left my family when I was twelve. Of my own choosing. In fact, that is why I chopped off my hair and traded luxurious satins for rough wool. I did not want them to find me."

Haegan frowned. "Why?"

She tossed her chin at him. "You must answer first—did you do it?"

Should he play her game, would his secrets lay bare on the cool stone before the first rise of the sun? And yet, leaving her . . . "Do what, precisely?"

"Are you always so stiff?"

Haegan arched an eyebrow. "Stiff? I am confused—you ask an incomplete question, my lady."

She went serious, her dark eyes expressive and probing. "Did you betray your sister to take the crown?"

16

Haegan twitched. Angry at her question. Angry that she must ask to know the answer. That she believed him capable of such wickedness. He sighed, suddenly drowning in the volatile memories of that day. Of the moment that altered his life. Seeing Kaelyria lying there, weak and powerless as he had for far too long . . .

"No," he whispered, aching.

"Then you *are* him." Thiel hopped onto her knees, pressing intimately closer. Too close. Her face was vibrant. "You're Prince Haegan."

Jerking away did nothing but prove her right.

"But they said you were paralyzed!" She touched him, gripping his arm as she sat down once more. "Tell me what happened."

"You know too much already."

She laughed. "And I'm not leaving without more answers, prince."

"Don't." He glanced around, concerned. Hating the sneer that invariably came with the title.

"We're alone." She settled in, legs crisscrossed. "Now, tell me— what happened? How'd you end up in that tunnel?"

"I don't know."

"Oh, c'mon!"

"I don't—I woke up down there."

"Very well. But with the princess, what happened?"

"This is not some opera or jester's court," Haegan spat, pushing to his feet. He stood at the overhang, his heart beating out of his chest to escape the horrible truth. *Abiassa, what is this nightmare you have placed me in?*

A light touch on his sleeve startled him—that he felt it was one surprise. That it was Thiel's touch was another. "Now *I* beg your mercy, Prince Haegan. I meant no offense."

He studied her, curious at the formality in her language. Was she mocking him now? But the sincerity of her expression told him she was trying to reach him through the only world he'd known—court. "It's of no consequence." He felt foolish now, and tucked his head. "It was . . . a mistake." But if he spoke of it, if he explained what happened, would he betray Kaelyria? Which would ultimately be a betrayal of the crown itself.

"Whose mistake?"

Kaelyria's. No, he could not—*would* not blame her. "It matters not, Thiel. What matters is that my sister lies there, paralyzed, and I am here." Free. Whole. It hurt too much to admit, to recall. To speak out loud.

He wouldn't do this. He started for the path.

Thiel caught him. "Haegan."

It was strange, so incredibly strange, to hear her use his real name. It also pained him. No longer was he worthy of that name it or the attached title.

"Oh. Should I be calling you 'Your Highness' or something?" She looked around, and he was sure the question a jest until he saw her confusion.

He tugged his arm free. "*Rigar* must be my name. Jujak hunt me. Accelerants as well, if my father-king has done as I would expect."

"The king, your father, hunts you.?

"I believe he blames me. Believes me a traitor." He hunched his shoulders. Anything to get away from her and this conversation. "It's who I am now."

"Rigar, talk to me," she said. "You said it was a mistake—whose mistake?"

"An accelerant's." Yes, Cilicien ka'Dur would shoulder the blame for turning the ways of the Flames upside down. For using them for unintended purposes. In all the Parchments, use of the Flames as such demanded recompense. It was a wonder the Deliverers had not come for Cilicien. But they no longer existed. Having fled into exile, their kind had simply vanished after Zaelero II took the throne and established peace, returning the Nine to the ways of Abiassa.

Thiel angled to the side, trying to peer at his face. "You speak as if you hate accelerants."

Haegan remained unmoved, watching the twinkling lights and their varying colors. "It is hard to hate a line you are issued from, but I do protest the one who deceived my sister into relinquishing—"

Thiel touched his hand, the soft gesture pulling his gaze to hers.

He must change the direction of this discourse. "You were with the Asykthian in the woods."

She sighed. "As'Tili."

The name pulled him up. "A son of Thurig," Haegan muttered, his mind caught on the way she'd said the prince's name. With tenderness. Affection. "You have feelings for the king's son?"

Why did that anger him and stir up so many illogical feelings? He must protect her from the raider. Encourage her to be cautious. Clearly she did not understand the way of the Asykthians. "Waste not your breath or time on them, Thiel. The line of Thurig is filled with marauders, driven only by their thirst for power and—"

Scowling, Thiel popped his shoulder.

Haegan frowned. "I seek only to protect you. They are lawless—"

She punched his side.

Haegan doubled, groping for air. "Have you so firmly set your affections on him that you would injure a man you just called friend?"

"Man? *Hmph!*" But then she craned her neck toward him, her brows digging into that pert nose. "Wait—you're . . . you're *jealous?*"

"I assure you my intentions—"

"Now you have intentions toward me?"

Heat filled his face. "That is not at all what I meant. I only intend— *meant* to say that—"

"He's my brother, *Prince Haegan.*"

The way she spat his name warred with the words that hadn't quite caught up in his brain. Her brother? But that meant—

Sparks!

Haegan stepped back, realization flooding over him like the warmth of a new dawn. He remembered the Parchments, the lessons. He'd been forced to memorize every member of the Nine and the outlying provinces. Thurig's wife had given birth to four sons. And one daughter. "Kiethiel," he whispered.

She smirked. "Ironic, isn't it? Here we stand on Abiassa's Throne, two *friends,* heirs of two kingdoms who hate each other almost as much as they hate Poired Dyrth."

Haegan gave her a rueful look. "My father would have me singed for even sharing the same air with you."

She laughed. "Mine, too. And my brothers—well, after they beat me, you wouldn't want to see what they'd do to you." She rested her hands on the boulder and leaned back.

Haegan slumped against the rock beside her, his mind a boiling pot of confusion. Something niggled in the pit of his stomach. Something about the princess . . . "Why would you leave your family? Thurig is powerful and his land is fertile. One of the wealthiest of the Northlands."

"Wealth, indeed." Thiel toyed with the tassel of her tunic. "I left because at twelve, I was kidnapped. Held for ransom. What those men did to me as they waited for their blood money . . ."

Haegan stilled, his blood curdling in his veins. Anger roiled through him as he waited for Thiel to finish, not trusting himself to speak or move.

"When I returned to Ybienn, I pretended that the—" She swallowed. "That what they did to me had no effect. But I saw"—raw emotion choked her words —"*saw* what it did to my father. Heard the whispers of the villagers who felt if he could not keep his own daughter safe, how could he protect them?" Glossy eyes met his, her lips curled back in anger. "Just as the prophecy foretold." A tear broke free. "Shame followed me everywhere. Became my only friend. People knew and avoided me. As if I would dirty them."

"What prophecy?" Haegan chided himself—as if some prophecy mattered after her honor had been ripped from her.

"The Parchments were clear: *and the daughter birthed beneath the arch of the Tri-Tipped Flame will bring to those who love her pain, death, and shame.*"

"That could've been any daughter."

"Oh no," Thiel said with a hollow laugh. "No, only royal children are born beneath the arch of the Tri-Tipped Flame."

"The what?"

She looked at him, seemingly uncertain. "You jest?"

He shook his head.

"There is an arch that bears the image of that constellation. All royals are born there. It is said that Abiassa herself gave birth to her child there."

"Abiassa didn't have a child."

"She did," Thiel said with a growl.

Tender ground yet again. Haegan steered around it. "But still, another daughter—"

"No. There hasn't been a female born to an Asykthian king since"—she shrugged—"generations. Until me. What happened to me, my father's inability to prevent it, shamed him. Soiled his name. So I left. I left in the night, with naught but the clothes I'd snitched from a servant boy."

"Is that why you dress as a boy?"

"I ended up living with some forest people for a couple of years. Then I . . . joined up with Tokar and Praegur." She shrugged again, touching her hair. "It's worked for the last four years, hiding from my family. And men."

"Until tonight."

She nodded. "I did not realize how much I missed them, my brothers and parents. Tili said to come back, that our parents have never stopped trying to find me."

Haegan heard the hurt, the fear in her voice. But hope shifted away the distaste for Thurig and lodged itself in his heart. If a king could not find his own daughter in four years . . . If Thiel—*Kie*thiel had hidden from her parents that long, mayhap he could find refuge and evade his father's anger.

"Are you going back?"

She frowned. "Why would I? When I return, my shame returns with me." She drew in a breath and seemed intent on changing the conversation. "Would you go back?"

"I must. Kaelyria's life depends on it." His gaze fell on the glimmer of moonlight in the distance. "Kae told me to go the Falls. She said I would be permanently healed and then she would be restored."

"So once you take that swim, you're going back?"

Haegan nodded.

"Sparks," Thiel mumbled. Then she shifted and held up her palm.

"What?"

"Give me your hand, tunnel rat." She grabbed his hand as a warrior would grip another's, not as a girl might clasp the hand of a suitor. Not that he was a suitor . . . "A pact, Haegan, Prince of Zaethien and all the Nine. We will be each other's guardians and confidants, holding these secrets until our dying breaths."

Something in him warmed, ignited by how easily she conferred her trust upon him. "Agreed. Guardians and confidants. Protector."

"I think I have more training than you." Thiel smiled, and it seemed as if the stars themselves swam around her, for the angle of the mountain and the position in which he stood draped a dark blanket of lights around her. Her face glowed softly in the deepening night, and even with her short hair, the first hint of beauty shone in the girl borne of his father's enemy.

"Considering I've been a cripple for ten years . . ." He hated to admit it—men were supposed to be the champion for the fair maiden—but she was right. "However, by the Flames, I would prefer not to die at all on this journey."

17

Life could not get more insipid than when training twenty cold-palms. On the raised instruction platform, Drracien Khar'val crossed his arms over his black and white Marshal tunic, ignoring the way the stiff collar poked into the fleshy part of his chin. Eyes narrowed, jaw clamped, he watched the initiates gliding through their calming drills to the steady thump of a large drum in the far northern corner of the cobbled training yard.

He'd rather be down in the tavern. With a wench.

Or plucking out his fingernails.

A boy of eight stumbled.

"Markhul!" Drracien's voice carried like the crack of a whip as he pierced the young initiate with a glare. The drums stopped, drenching the yard in a painful silence. The others assumed their 'steady' pose, but tension radiated off their weary, sweating bodies.

Drracien didn't care. He'd gone through training, too. He'd seen the cost of carelessness. "You're clumsy, Marhkul," he said, with a growl. "Master your body before it masters you and someone pays the price." He motioned to the drummer. "Again. Everyone."

Though none dared utter a groan or complaint, several initiates shot the boy a glare. A promise of trouble afterward for extending calming.

"Begin!" Drracien hopped from the dais and walked the rows of inexperienced bodies. Those yearning for the power of the Flames. It was one thing to even be able to wield—only a select few could—but then to control that ability . . . He eyed their movement, their form that imitated the flow of the Flames. Elementary moves that would one day become more than just hand gliding and fist thrusting.

Markhul had promise. He did. But the boy was as clumsy as he was young. "Smooth, Markhul!" Drracien stood behind him, towering over the initiate. Tuning his heart to the drum, his eyes to the boy's forms, Drracien stepped into the calming with him. Guided the boy. "Easy," he said. "With care. Not jerking." Eyes closed, Drracien felt his own leveling. Then, like a warm current, he sensed Markhul's rhythms slow and fall into sync. Calm. Steadied. Controlled instead of controlling.

"Aye," Drracien whispered, nodding as the peace returned. Opened his eyes.

A flutter of material beneath one of the dozen arches lining the southern courtyard snagged his attention. The pale blue robe of the high marshal's personal attendant distracted him, but he said nothing. He kept his focus on the students.

"A snap, Dradith. Like so." Drracien fisted his hand and faced the closed palm toward himself. Then he stretched it out, snapping the wrist at the last second so his fist flashed a spark with the speed of lightning. One of the higher ranks among the initiates, Dradith held the most promise.

Drracien fully intended to recommend her for a black tunic. When she mimicked his instruction with perfection, he nodded. "Excellent." He removed himself from the line and signaled Korben to take over as he stalked toward the messenger.

"Marshal Khar'val," Galaun, the high marshal's personal attendant said, his chin and attitude raised. "You are summoned to His Lordship."

What did High Marshal Aloing want with him? He gave a curt nod. "I'll come immediately aft—"

"The high marshal, he said you are not to tarry." Galaun's pocked face remained impassive, but a flicker of arrogance delivered the pleasure he felt at ordering Drracien. "I am to bring you *immediately*."

Anger stabbed Drracien. The uppers were always pulling the leash around his neck tighter than the stupid collar of his tunic.

Why was he being summoned? Another indiscretion? No . . . he'd taken great care these last several months.

Jaw tight, Drracien met Galaun's annoyed gaze, then started for the archway. As he made the long hike up the stone stairs, past the Grand Hall, Drracien talked himself through calming. The tugs on his proverbial collar were annoying and plentiful. The accelerants of the Citadel found his quickly rising path suspect. Could he help it that his gift was natural? That he didn't need the hours upon hours of calming and instruction the way initiates like Markhul did? To him, wielding came as naturally as breathing. But he still had to attend lectures and meditation. Practice and teach. He was here for a purpose.

What in Abiassa's Fire that was, he didn't know.

He rounded the gilded halls to the high chambers . . . and slowed. Tortook Puthago.

Drracien chuckled. *Ah, burning flames.* It made sense now. He lifted his chin, threw off the heat kneading his shoulders and neck, and smirked at Tortook. The petulant novice didn't even acknowledge him. Arrogance.

Galaun stopped at the floor-to-ceiling doors carved heavily with ornate flames. He nodded to Drracien with a deferring incline of his head. *Wait.*

Of course.

Galaun knocked three times. After a pause, he entered and bowed. "My Lord High Marshal, Marshal Khar'val is here as requested."

Hands behind his back, Drracien almost laughed when he heard Aloing's loud sigh.

"See?" Tortook hissed as he passed Drracien and aimed for the spiral stairs. "Nobody wants to see you, not even your champion."

Drracien flicked his right hand, fingers splayed.

A spark struck Tortook between the shoulders. The man stumbled. Spun around with a growl.

"Drracien!" Aloing's voice reverberated through the marbled corridor, and Drracien knew he was safe from retaliation. Tortook had wanted Drracien's appointment as a marshal, but he'd never rise so high if Aloing saw him fighting in the hall before his chamber.

Straightening his shoulders, Drracien entered the long, narrow room that ended in a bank of windows. Sunlight glared through the thin panes and bounced off the highly polished black singewood and glass desk. Ornate carvings climbed its legs and surface, etching the sacred symbols and emblem of Abiassa's Fire.

In regal robes that made his shoulders pointed and his waist unnaturally thin, High Marshal Aloing sat in his high-backed chair. Glowering.

So, no commendations then . . .

Drracien went to a knee and tucked his head low, right hand extended and fingertips on the black marble, a sign of surrendering the Flames to his superior. "High Marshal Aloing, I present myself for approval."

Approval he had failed to gain no matter how desperately he'd tried. It was not his fault he'd been born to a wench who taught him many ways of ill-repute before he'd reach five. Before he'd been ripped from her bosom and thrust into the Heat.

A low, deep rumble sifted the chilled air for several long seconds. Behind Drracien the doors closed. "How long has it taken to beat you into submission, to teach you to bow when you enter?"

Nostrils flaring, Drracien focused on his right hand. On the ring of the Ignatieri.

An answer was expected. And no matter his distaste for certain elements, he would *never* disrespect the one who had championed him. "Twelve years."

"Truth," Aloing said with another chuckle. "Stand!"

Surprised at the terse command, Drracien straightened. Placed his hands behind his back, palms open, and spread his feet shoulder-width apart.

"You know, do you not, *Marshal* Khar'val that it is against the guiding principles of the Ignatieri to use your gift against a brother?"

"I do, my lord."

"And yet—and *yet!* Not a week passes without a report of you flinging sparks and bolts as if they were spittle!" Aloing's own words created a dribble as he came out of his chair. Rail thin, wrinkled with a lifetime of wielding, the high lord could flatten Drracien with a flick.

But the greater injury was the accusation, the chastisement by this accelerant who had taken an angry, passionate boy under his shield and trained him. Though Aloing was his champion, to say he was his friend would be a stretch. No, an outright lie.

Still, Drracien hated himself for failing his advocate again. But until the high marshal presented a direct charge, Drracien would not confess or defend himself.

"How do you explain your actions, Marshal?"

Freed to speak, Drracien expelled a frustrated breath. "You speak of Novice Puthago?"

Gray eyes burned with indignation. "You *know* of what I speak!"

Drracien tucked his chin. "Tortook had a first-year pinned and was bullying him. I told him to stop, but—"

"But what?" Aloing demanded. "He goaded you? Made you feel inferior? Reminded you of your past?"

"Yes." Drracien snapped a look to his champion. Where was this heated chastisement coming from? The high marshal had always been hard on him, but this . . . this felt different. Worse. "Tortook flaunts his placement over others, especially me."

"You find him out of order?"

Saying yes would bring Tortook up on charges. And doing that would only flay open Drracien's failings. His *many* failings. "I find him . . ."

"Abusive in his power?"

Same crime, different wording.

"Arrogant and—"

"Irritating," Drracien said between clenched teeth.

"And how did you find yourself tasked as protector and savior to the masses?"

The high marshal taunted him now. Drracien wouldn't be goaded. Sarcasm was *his* specialty. "I guess it's my birthright."

Slapping his hands on his desk, Aloing shouted, "Do you think I care that you made it to this rank in half the time as others?"

Vexation simmered. The source of high marshal's animosity evaded Drracien. He'd never been eviscerating. Not like this.

"Why Dromadric determined you would be granted fifth rating, I know not." The curl in the high lord's lip thickened in his words. "Think not for one minute that I believe you merited such a rank or position."

Defiance flashed through Drracien. "I worked twice as hard—"

In a heartbeat, an invisible fist lifted Drracien off the ground. Slammed him into the wall. His teeth rattled, the familiar scent of a singeing in the air. He landed on his backside with a thud. Fury ripped through him as Drracien flipped to his feet, ready for the fight.

No. Calm.

He resented the accusations. Struggled to understand. "My Lord, what have I—"

Another blast flipped him over, knocking him against the wall like pottery. He slid to the ground, groaning.

Singe him!

No. No, he would not be labeled an *incipient*.

"You are as unruly and foolish now as you were the day you arrived on the stoop!"

Anger welled, torrid and demanding a voice. Breathing through flared nostrils, Drracien dragged himself from the floor, resisting the urge to touch his head where he felt a trickle of wet warmth.

"You abuse your initiates—"

"*Not* true!" Drracien coiled his hands into his fists. *No, don't. Quell it! Calm. Calm.*

"That boy you sparked—Markhul. Just for stumbling?"

Flabbergasted, Drracien angled his neck forward. "He must learn—"

Wizened eyes blazed. "And so must you." Another wave of heat shoved him against the wall. Pinned him.

Caged. Alone. Wrongly accused.

Rivers of heat shot through his limbs, digging deeper and deeper into his bones. The riddling pain strangled his focus. His restraint.

He howled, a thousand searing knives peppering his flesh. His mind. His very blood.

Drracien pushed back with his own fire. But the effort was futile. He couldn't move. Could not strike back. *Release me!* This was unjust! He had not earned this punishment. The offenses were minor, at best.

Just like Madri. His own mother never understood his gift. He clenched his eyes and teeth against the memory, against the beatings. Against the taste of blood.

Anger rising. Power gliding.

Another howl.

Glass shattered.

The bubble that held him popped. He dropped to the floor, confused. The impact thudded up his legs, jarring him as slumped to his knees with another groan. A sudden chill swept around him, cocooning. Any morsel of penitence was gone. Submission vanished.

A great exhaustion coated his limbs. He braced himself against the cold floor, staring at his fingertips, haloed with a strange glow. Sweat slid down the black strands of hair that hung in his eyes and plopped onto the floor. "What?" he said with a sneer, breathing hard. "Growing tired, old man?"

No answer came, save the crunching of his own weight on the glass-littered floor as he shifted and came to his feet. Panting, he dragged his gaze off the shards, tracing the path to the—

Drracien froze. Sucked in a breath.

The high marshal lay on the floor. Unmoving. The only friend he'd had in this accursed place! Drracien threw himself forward with a strangled cry. "No!" He scrabbled to the frail form, glass digging into his knees and palms. "Sir!" Help. They needed— "Someone help!"

Dazed, confused gray eyes rolled to his. A crooked smile twitched the old man's mouth before vanishing amid a tremor. "M-mercy. I beg your m-mercy."

Drracien stilled, cradling the wispy-haired head in his lap. "What? No! I didn't . . . You—"

"F-for your . . . own . . . good."

"You're not thinking right. You must've hit your head when you fell." How *did* he fall? "Let me fetch the pharmakeia."

"*No*," the aged accelerant said forcefully. "Remember what I've taught you. Re—member. When . . . darkness calls . . . resist." Gnarled fingers gripped his robe. "*Resist!*"

Shouts came from the hall. Banging at the door. In that fiery second, Drracien saw the future. Saw what would happen if the aged and revered accelerant died. No! He could not die. This could not be.

Blame. He'd shoulder blame as he had all his life. He'd be—

"High Marshal, are you well?" came a stern voice from the foyer.

"Go," Aloing said, and his head lolled to the side.

"High Marshal, open!"

Heart racing, ears ringing, Drracien fought the urge to cry. To cry out. Heavy thudding at the door warned him they'd break through. Arrest him. He'd be sentenced to death by fire—the Lakes.

"High Marshal Aloing!" Dromadric's voice boomed. "Are you in there?" Voices. Questions. The worst: "Who's in there with him?"

"Drracien was," Galaun said.

Hands trembling, Drracien touched Aloing's throat. "Please." The only light in the whole of his miserable life lay in his hands. His own tear dropped onto the parchment-pale face—and sizzled. Only then did he notice the gray splotch on the side of the accelerant's temple.

Singed.

And not just a slight one, but a powerful one that . . . *I did this? But how?* "I beg your mercy. Whatever . . . whatever I did—truly, I beg your mercy." Tears blurred his vision. "Don't surrender your light, sir. Please. I need you." A sob beat against his chest, demanding freedom.

Eyes no longer saw. Flame no longer burned.

Crack!

The breaking door was the impetus to surrender his grief—for now. Gently but quickly, he laid Aloing on the cold floor. He stared at the old man. "Grant me mercy."

Drracien sprinted across the room to the high windows, empty of glass.

Crack! Groan!

They were through! He didn't stop to look. Didn't stop to give them a chance to kill him. With a leap, he hurtled into the open air.

"There—the window!"

"Drracien!"

He found purchase on the sloped tile roof. His right foot slid out and pitched him forward. He caught himself, listening to the chaos erupting behind him. He could not stop. They would assume the worst. Kill him on sight.

He darted over the rooftops. Jumped to a lower building, his body gliding on the unnaturally warm air. Feet hit, slipping then gaining traction. Without looking back, he sprinted as fast as his mind through this nightmare. What caused Aloing to turn against him?

"Drraaaacien!" Dromadric's shout boomed across the holy city.

Another jump tossed him onto the ledge of the dorms. One more building over and he'd be in the lower district. Even in the air, he plotted his disappearance. Planned how to vanish into the nothingness he'd been born from. Shed the Ignatieri coat. Meld into the teeming populace of paupers. He hauled himself onto the slate roof, flung out his arms to steady himself, then—

Crack! Tiles spat at him, others dribbling to the road below.

Someone sparked him! He jerked to a stop behind a chimney. Searched the high windows he'd escaped. The formidable shape of Grand Marshal Dromadric loomed like a warning beacon. Frozen by the sight of his order's supreme leader, paralyzed that the man he'd looked up to, the man he wanted to be like, now believed him guilty of murder, Drracien grasped for a tendril of sanity to understand what happened. Dromadric would try at all costs to kill him. Heart pounding a thousand times faster than the calming drums, Drracien huffed. Tried to swallow against a parched throat.

When the grand marshal's hands crossed, alarms blared through Drracien. Seconds. He had mere seconds—that was, if he could evade one of the most powerful accelerants on Primar. He launched across the roof. Angled sideways and slid down. Shoved his feet against a thatched roof. Tumbled forward. Used momentum to roll. Then pushed himself upright and ran.

A dead, blistering weight exploded between his shoulders.

Vaulted him forward.

Off the roof.

Darkness loomed.

And he was falling.

18

A friend. He had a friend in Thiel. For how many years had he longed for such a thing—beyond the gray-haired, short-fused accelerant who'd tutored him? Thiel stalked ahead through the unusual darkness under the thick growth of trees that bearded the mountain upon which they'd made their pact.

Shorter than him by a head at least, she had a slight frame. Narrow shoulders and thin arms that belied the strength he'd seen her exert. She may be little, but she was fast and quick-witted.

A good ally. Easily underestimated. Not easily outsmarted.

Thank Abiassa she was on his side.

"Stay close," she called over her shoulder.

About to retort, Haegan fell silent at the incredible number of campfires dotting the plain. There must be a hundred! "Where'd they come from?"

"Village east of Luxlirien was razed by the Sirdarians. The survivors fled. They were setting up camp when I set out to find you."

"Find me? I was looking for you!" Haegan hustled closer, navigating around a cluster of tents that hadn't been there before he climbed the hill.

"Yeah, well, the others and I met in the woods." Thiel nodded to an older woman tending a pot while her husband pounded tent stakes into the ground. "You weren't around, so I volunteered to find you."

"Alone? They let you go alone?"

"I'm a girl, not a weakling, tunnel-rat."

A sobbing woman caught Haegan's attention, killing any desire to talk. He could feel the density of the population wrapping cold fingers around his throat. Too many people. Entirely too many. Never thought he'd feel that way before now.

"Sparks, you're back!" Laertes said when they arrived, pushing from a stump he'd been sitting on. "Knew what with her skills, she'd find you. We got trouble, Thiel."

Thiel scowled. "What kind of trouble?"

Praegur took a step forward, unfolding his arms. "You're well then?"

"Who cares?" Tokar muttered, not moving from his sleep sack, where he lay with eyes closed and an arm draped over his face.

Thiel kicked his feet. He shot up like a snapping bowstring, glaring at her and stabbing a finger at Haegan. "Don't kick me. Thanks to your new sweetheart, we're back to being dirt poor. And you know what that means."

"What do you mean?" Thiel said, her words suddenly sharp.

"I mean we've been robbed. All because dung-for-brains over there doesn't have the sense of a halfwit calf."

Haegan blinked. "I don't understand . . ."

Tokar pinned him with a glance. "Where are your coins?"

Filled with a sick feeling, Haegan looked to his pack. Once he'd secured it at a shop, he'd transferred the remaining paladiums from his boots to a small inner pocket of the sack. Then he'd neatly stowed his supplies from the day's purchases on top. Now the sack lay open and lumpy. Unkempt.

Haegan snatched up the burlap and rifled through the contents. Dread choked him.

"You left them in your pack?" All trace of the warmth had fled Thiel's voice. Her eyes accused him with an intensity that left him baffled. Yes, he'd lost the coins, but they still had their supplies. They could still make it to Hetaera. Why this sudden fury?

"Bed down." Thiel stomped to a pallet laid out by the fire. "We need every strong body we can get to earn back what was lost tonight."

Light danced over Tokar as he lay down again, angrily kicking his blankets into order. "We have to find work tomorrow."

"Work? Why?"

Laertes sat cross-legged on his sack now, looking up at Haegan from beneath a wheat-colored fringe of hair. "No coins is a big problem if we wanna get to Hetaera."

"Why?" Haegan asked. "We have supplies—"

"Emata—"

"Shut up and go to sleep," Tokar growled at the boy.

Irritation clawed up Haegan's spine, digging its fiery talons into his heart and pride. He swallowed, his gaze sliding over to Thiel, who lay still and quiet, as if she already slumbered. Would she not speak up? Tell them . . .

No. No, she couldn't, now could she? Break her silence. Bare her secrets. And nor could he. But still—they were friends.

At least, they were on the mountain. Their camaraderie had vanished with the coins. But why did she not defend him? Speak for him when his absence had been in pursuit of her?

But still she lay silent.

A fool he'd been for thinking of her as friend.

You are alone. As it had been since he'd sipped that tart ale at his own Awakening ceremony. Since he'd been ushered into the round, isolated tower of loneliness, thanks to that poisoned cup.

"Bed down," Tokar muttered. "We start early."

"Shouldn't someone keep watch?" Thiel asked.

Praegur stood. "I'll take first watch."

Haegan stretched out on his back, staring up at the blanket of stars. They all seemed to agree that they now had to work for more coins. But work meant delay. Longer to reach the Falls.

Where was the purpose in it all? *A spark does not ignite without a purpose.* How many times had Sir Gwogh's gravelly voice raked over those words? And yet—here Haegan lay beneath a black night with no purpose and no friends.

Anger spiraled through his chest, unsettling his breathing. Burning his eyes. *I just want to matter. To someone. Anyone. For once—just once.* He wanted to be of use. Not a blister someone gets after journeying a long while.

Abiassa . . . He searched the sky. Searched the stars. Searched the emptiness of the world around him.

What would Kaelyria say?

"Burn the whine, you singeling."

Haegan gave a quiet snort, a smile stealing into his face at the memory of his sister. Strong. Confident. She had not tolerated his moodiness then. And he was sure, in light of the reversal of their situations, that she would tolerate none from him now.

There. There is your answer.

Only then did he feel the tingling heat in his body. A strange warming that started at his core and spread through his chest. Like the moment one sips cool water from a chalice and feels it spill through his body. He lifted his head from the cool earth and glanced at his stomach, half expecting to see something glowing there. Instead, he found only the dancing shadows of the dying campfire.

Mystifying.

He lay back and closed his eyes, mentally tracing the warmth as it slid away, leaving an uncomfortable chill. Again the anger surged. Alone. Cold. No possible way to get to the Falls.

I'm holding them prisoner.

Without him, they'd be free to follow their own course, no worse off than when he met them.

Go.

The word burned. Pushed him upright. His heart thudded. Should he? Just leave and head to the Falls? On his own, he would not burden the others.

Yes, he should go.

Haegan leaned forward.

"You're smarter than that," came a soft mumble from behind.

Haegan glanced over his shoulder to Praegur and found the gold eyes staring back.

"It's safer in numbers."

Haegan slumped. "I . . . I can't stay here and work. I have—" He severed the words. Stopped himself from giving away the truth.

"Time is never our friend," Praegur said. "But neither is foolishness."

"But working to regain all the paladiums "—Haegan shook his head—"I don't have that much time."

"Not all the paladiums," Praegur said. "Just enough to get us to Hetaera. A couple nights working in a tavern, and combined, we'll have enough." He lifted his chin toward Haegan's sleep sack. "Sleep. Even if you ignore my sage wisdom—"

Haegan couldn't help but smile at the sarcasm.

"—you don't want to wander the darkness with the beasts."

19

"Wake, you fool!"

The hushed, urgent voice drenched the thick sleep blanketing Haegan's mind. He lurched up, awareness and heat flooding him. "Wha—"

"Quiet," Tokar hissed.

Haegan swallowed hard, his nerves thrumming.

"We need to leave." Tokar's gray eyes blazed with meaning and warning. "Now."

"Why?"

"Jujak."

That small word severed any objection or complaint that lingered on Haegan's tongue. Instantly, his mind cleared and he saw the others working to gather their belongings. Morning had not yet fully crested, bathing the camps in a wash of blues and oranges. Thiel knelt, rolling her blanket and pallet. Beside her, Laertes shrugged into his pack.

With quick work, Haegan secured his bundle and slung it over his shoulder. Pushing up and pivoting, he barely saw the shadows of the others skittering into the tree line. A glance around told him most in the other camps had not yet awoken. Two or three women stood over steaming pots, but only the dogs and firelights stirred. He rushed into the trees, giving care to ensure his steps were light and fast.

He listened ahead, uncertain of which direction the others had fled. It would make sense to head north. Toward the Falls. With or without money, he had to get to there. But with each step he took, courage leaked from him like an old water skin. If he had a plentiful store, Haegan would not surrender to the fear that dogged his steps. But it weakened him. Frightened him. Angered him.

A thorny bramble caught his pant leg and clenched, its viney fingers tripping him. The razor-sharp talon sliced his leg. Haegan bit through the sting and yanked hard to free his leg. Defiant, the thorn only seemed to dig in harder.

Haegan picked himself up.

"Down," Thiel hissed, her hand on his head as she pressed him to the ground.

Chastised like a child, Haegan gritted his teeth. Fought the humiliation and gave no heed to the warm trickle sliding down his ankle. Something in him latched onto the smell in the air. The tingling, prickling sensation rippling across his shoulders and the back of his neck. Through the spindly legs of towering trees and beyond the fluttering leaves, he spied the green and gold uniforms of the Jujak.

An officer shifted into view, motioning and calling out. The knots on his shoulders indicated a captain. Why send a high ranking officer after Haegan, rogue son?

The truth hit him with a painful blow. When it came to Kaelyria and her gift, his father would do everything in his power to track down anyone who hurt her. The lethal precision, the speed with which this Jujak had determined Haegan's location—it was clear he was one of Zireli's best.

"Move," Thiel whispered as she spun away. Half bent, she ran through the trees as elegantly as a deer would navigate the forest, the others easily matching her quick pace. Her brown cloak riffled on the wind with no more sound than a leaf makes.

Deeper into the woods and farther from the Jujak they fled. His heart and mind raced between the thick bark, around the massive trunks that were more like the gnarled fingers of a Drigovudd digging into the ground.

Splash. Squish.

Haegan slowed, glancing down.

"A marsh. Don't stop." Evidence of Thiel's own displeasure at the swampy water could be found on her curled lips and repeated grunts.

They trudged onward. And onward. Haegan's lungs squeezed in objection to the rigorous path, but he would make no complaint.

With earnestness, he longed to tell her he was not up to the journey. But the argument fell mute before it reached his tongue—would he not have to journey to the Falls? A far more dangerous and arduous path lay before him. He would save his complaints. And his breath.

Heart pounding, he kept pace. Refused to lose her. To be found wanting in endurance. In determination. But his head—it pounded each time his boots suctioned against the muck. His thighs burned with the exertion of prying his boots up with each step. Then came a jarring step. One that made him slip. But then there was stability.

O blessed Fire! He whispered his thanks as they hit the rock path again. Somehow, stepping out of the muck and plodding along the uneven path, the way seemed easier. Quicker. No longer fighting to plant one foot in front of another, they were moving faster. Then Thiel and the others started running. Haegan bit back his frustration. He was slowing down. Growing more tired.

Haegan tripped.

"Just a little farther," Thiel mumbled. "There's a cave."

A child. She thinks me a child. "I'm . . . good." He hadn't meant the words to be so labored, so burdened with the exhaustion tearing at his limbs, but it was a futile effort to appear unaffected. "Where are we going?" Haegan lumbered over a fallen oak.

"Hetaera."

He stopped, causing Tokar to crash into him with a curse.

With a look over her shoulder, Thiel sighed. "What?"

"But we've no coin. Tokar said—"

"Would you rather beg off the Jujak?"

He blinked. "Nay, nor would I have us walk till our legs fell off, but you seem bent enough on that."

Thiel whirled, her face alive and pink. "Ematahri." Her lips flattened. "That name mean anything to you?"

Startled, he shook his head and a shrugged. "Gypsies." What else could it mean?

Tokar snorted. "*Lawless* gypsies. Some of the meanest you'll ever meet."

By the Flames—the boy was stoked with more embers than any Haegan had met. His anger roiled off him like a heat wake. But was his attitude any worse than the one soiling Haegan's heart even now? The one that wanted him to take Tokar to task for speaking so poorly to and of him? "By definition, aren't all gypsies lawless?"

Thiel cocked her head in a half-shake as she ruffled Laertes's hair and moved on down the path. "I've met gypsies who are better and more law-abiding than royals."

Haegan's heart thumped. The words were a dig at him. He was convinced. However, her words were true.

"But the Ematahri—they take pride in *protecting* the Way of the Throne," Tokar said, referring to the main road between Abiassa's stone seat and Hetaera. "And by protecting, we mean raping, murdering, plundering . . . whatever they want."

"That's not entirely true, but the danger is real enough," Thiel said. "We are on the edges of their territory. They are ruthless with invaders—and anyone not of them is against them."

Tokar sidled up alongside Haegan. "Ematahri earn rank according to the number of those they capture or kill."

Haegan shook his head. "Then why are we heading that way?"

"Yeah, see?" Tokar spun so that he walked backward, pointing at Haegan. "That's where you messed us up. We had planned to use the Cloud Road."

"The what?"

"Cloud—" Tokar popped the heel of his hand against his temple. "Singewood. That's what you are, Rigar." He tapped Haegan's head. "Do you even have a brain in there?"

Praegur pushed Tokar along and took up pace with Haegan. "The Cloud Road is the name for the hidden routes in the mountains, among the clouds. Only they're not hidden. Not anymore."

"They was once," Laertes said. "That's how me mum got us down to Seultrie before she went and died."

"People avoid the Way of the Throne now," Tokar explained, "especially since Zireli called all the regular soldiers down to fight Sirdar.

But it's the main road between Hetaera and most of the southern kingdom, so they found passage through the mountains. But the Ematahri, they figured out something was going on. They followed people into the hills, tracked them through the mountains. Now, they have spies up there who demand payment for letting them live."

"We have to pay to live?"

Praegur shrugged. "The Siannes and East River are on the other side—the waters are too treacherous, feeding off the waterfalls, so boats can't make it. Deadly waters, deadly roads, or deadly mountains. At least in the mountains you can pay your way out."

Haegan said, "So, if we can't pay—"

"Which we can't," Tokar growled.

"Then we . . .?"

Praegur lifted a shoulder. "Hide."

"And if we can't hide?"

"We fight."

20

It is of great irony that the mighty bow before the ignoble. That the powerful seek the counsel of the powerless. That darkness should shroud itself within the pretense of great light. Of honor. That Poired Dyrth, once a lowly prince to a crumbling kingdom, should rise on the tide of Nydessan waters to become the most feared creature crawling Primar.

He stands now before a man clothed humbly in brown, the shade of slaves that Poired once wore. But in his regalia, silver and black to symbolize the power he possesses both day and night, he strikes a terrible pose. His face marred with the blood of victories. His jaw set with the legacy of war.

"Tell me, Auspex," Poired Dyrth demands, "what you see. Is it time?"

Tongue tethered to the will of Sirdar of Tharqnis, the Auspex must speak what is seen or the fire he drank so many years ago will consume him. He has no will. "It is written," the hollow voice rings, echoing the haunting one who seeps through his thoughts, "that Poired shall mount once more upon his black steed and wait in the shadows of the fortress."

The wood table shatters beneath Poired's fists as his temper again outweighs control. He utters a curse and jerks away. "How long must I play this game? Sit there and stare?" He swings toward the Auspex, fury in his icy irises. "She is in my head! I sense her. I can smell her. *Taste* her breath in my mouth." Suffering the consequences of touching thoughts of one She possesses, he spits to the side and growls, slamming his armor-protected fist against a large outer tent post. The heavy draping fabric ripples beneath the exertion of his anger. Soon the table, incense wisping into the air, topples and yields to the greater power.

Brawny General Onerid remains steadfast immediately before the tent opening, a hand on the hilt of his Caorian blade, hewn from the fiery chasms of his homeland. With his jaw bearded and eyes a stony hazel, he reflects none of the rage his master exhibits. Beside the general, the younger, weaker Jedric shifts uneasily, affected by the surge of anger. An anger he knows has fueled fury against friend and foe alike. None are protected from Poired's temper and his fierce decisiveness as he pursues victory against the Flames and all the gifted.

But the will of Sirdar is unaltered. Spiraling through the Auspex, the waft of strong odor vanishes on a hot wind. Drained, the Foreteller sags from the abandonment. Eyes now hooded and body hunched, he stumbles to the side, out of view and reach of the High Lord Commander.

Recognizing he is now alone with his generals, Poired growls. "How long must I *sit*?" he shouts. "How long must I suffer inactivity against the Celahars?" A silver platter whips through the air and into a post that shudders in response. "They gloat in their towers, exalted above me when I could demolish that high seat with a tenth of the army!"

"The army?" Onerid flashes a lazy grin. "You would only need the Maereni."

Poired stuffs a hand through his hair, tugging at the leather thong that secures it. "Would that I could send them. Then"—his eyes flash with meaning—"*then* they would see weakness! But not in me. In Zireli! He must be brought down."

"Agreed," Onerid says. "And it will happen. On my oath!"

Sneering, Poired is unappeased. "Your words are filled with promise, with things not yet come. Things no man or beast can guarantee. A blade *guarantees*. Bloodshed *guarantees*." He drags a leathered hand across his mouth and heaves a futile sigh. "If only he would release me. But he plays this game—"

"Sir, with caution," Onerid says quietly, his gaze bouncing to the Auspex.

"He is nothing but a bag of bones without Sirdar." His lip curls. "Anyone can see he is now empty." He whips around, searching for a target. A pathetic Jedric stumbles back as the High Lord Commander rages toward him. "Blazes! If he would have me speak let me speak. Have me act if I am to act! But to sit—"

Fierce heat blasts from the Auspex's mouth, unexpected. Unwanted. The distinct stench of burnt spices stings the nostrils of Onerid and Jedric as an amber haze fills the tent. A scent so searing and acidic, drawn by anger and bloodlust, consuming the host. Those assembled remain still and wary, watching the bony, pale face.

"High Lord Commander," the Auspex speaks, a trail of amber spiraling out at the mighty general, along with a hefty dose of sarcasm.

Poired stands frozen, his muscles stiffened by the will of Sirdar.

"*You* chose this path. *You* said you would do what was necessary to overthrow Zaethien and her allies. To take Primar back. To return the Demas heir to the throne." Bathed in austerity and conviction of his vassal-state, the Auspex stares with ambivalence through vacant eyes at the warrior. "Answer now forever and hold your peace, Fallen One. Are you the champion of Unelithien?"

It is not a simple question, the one posed by Sirdar from his High Seat. The question holds promise. Promise of bounty should he yield. Yet another promise lingers therein—one of death should he deny the oath he swore a decade hence.

Hand fisted, Poired extends it, then snaps it back against his chest as a Maereni warrior salutes. "I am her champion."

"The days are numbered before the Fierian will rise and quench the Flames. You will face the Fires of Demas yourself if the Fierian succeeds."

• • •

"This wasn't supposed to happen."

From the valley floor, as they skirted the Throne Road, the Siannes range appeared monstrous and forbidding. White blankets of snow draped its spine, allowing for an occasional intrusion of spruce and pine against the pristine backdrop. Haegan stared up at the peaks, glittering in the sun that cast shadows on him and the others, deeply embedded in the trees. There on the mountain, they'd have found safe passage.

"You're right," Tokar said, challenge etched in his words. "If I remember, you lost our coin."

"If *I* remember," Haegan countered, "those coins were mine. In truth, you neither lost nor gained anything."

"I've lost time and precious advantage being stuck with you." Tokar turned toward Haegan, his shoulders squaring.

"I set forth no petition for your company nor protection." Haegan wanted to take back the words as soon as their bitter taste hit his tongue.

Tokar's eyebrows winged up. He took a step back. Gave a nod. "Good, Stiff. You're on your own, then. You're cursed anyway."

"No." Thiel stomped forward, her brown hair dusting her amber eyes. "We stay together. Now more than ever." She pointed to the road. "The Way of the Throne is no place for ego or temper. We will need every blade and every strong back—"

"Then he's disqualified already. He has neither." Tokar smiled down at Thiel, his gray eyes sparking with laughter at his own joke and with his obvious attraction to her. "Until now, he had one thing going for him—the paladiums. Now they're gone, as he should be."

Guilt and embarrassment pressed against Haegan. "It's true. I have little training, and I am not strong as"—he dare not mention the boy and worsen the damage—"one trained in warfare." He noted Laertes heading toward the trees. "But I will not back down. I do not abandon my friends. I *will* see this through."

"Friends?"

"*Yield*," Thiel snapped to Tokar, then glanced between him and Haegan. "Once we are safely in Hetaera, decisions about who stays and leaves can be made. Until then, anyone who abandons this road has no character or honor."

"Don't do that, Thiel," Tokar said, his voice soft but filled with warning.

"Then—"

"No, it was a different situation. No comparison." What looked to be grief roiled through Tokar's expression. "No call to assume I—"

"That was not my intent, Tokar." Her expression softened with a fair amount of compassion.

Clearly, a story lay behind that conversation. One they were unwilling to divulge. Somehow it reminded Haegan that Tokar was more than someone with a chip on his shoulder. He had a past. As did Haegan. And neither of them knew the other's story.

They were close to the road and, by logical extension, closer to danger. Haegan eyed a small, dilapidated structure less than a league ahead as the two conversed quietly. Wooden boards leaned to the side, some propped on top of others. Holes gaped like missing teeth.

And yet—no weeds had sprung up around it. The path to the door was worn. Heavily. Unease slithered through Haegan as he noticed narrow ruts around the perimeter. What were those for?

"Where's Laertes?"

Haegan glanced back. "He's—" But only a copse filled the spot he'd pointed to. "He was right . . ." The words died on his lips when he saw the boy's blanket at the base of a mauri. Alarms blared in his head. He sprinted toward the trees. "Laertes!" He threw himself into the forest, ears ringing with panic. "Laertes, where are you?"

A scream rent the quiet day.

"This way!" Thiel launched between the thin trunks. "I see him!"

Haegan, though not as nimble, gained on her. He would not let the lad be hurt. Not if he could help it. He darted around trees. Jumped over shrubs and fallen logs, and ran, using the bark to propel himself faster.

Ahead, a large man—a large *naked* man?—had an arm hooked around Laertes's neck, carrying him off the ground as he thudded through the woods.

"Laertes!" Thiel shouted. "Stop! Release the boy."

Haegan eyed the path the naked man ran along. Thought back . . . it seemed to—

He banked hard left. Pushed himself faster. His legs burned. Lungs squeezed. No matter. They must save Laertes.

"Haegan! Wrong way."

He might not have fighting skills, or weapons skills, but he had brain skills. At least, he hoped so.

"Haegan!" Thiel's voice grew dimmer with each second as he covered the distance.

A second later, he burst from the trees and flung himself forward. Like a big cat, he lowered his head, hoping for greater speed. Though he kept a straight course, he bounced his gaze between what lay ahead and the naked man carrying off Laertes.

Shouts tangled air as he ran, the wind blotting out clarity. Had he been wrong in his calculations? Hesitation slowed him.

But then he saw them. The naked man barreling ahead.

Not close enough.

Now!

The man broke into the open with a shout, no doubt calling for help.

Haegan lunged, landing a foot on the trunk of a tree, and then arched his back, throwing himself directly into what was—or would be—the path of the naked man. In three . . . two . . .

Oof!

Nailing the man in the side felt like dropping from a hundred meters onto a flat rock. Something cracked. A howl rent the air.

They were on the ground. Haegan rolled and felt pain spike through his arm. He paid no heed, jumping around, aware of the danger the man posed. He turned just in time to avoid a thick, meaty fist slamming into his face.

Haegan leaned away from the punch, seeing Laertes scrambling for safety.

Praegur and Thiel erupted from the woods at the same time. The naked man—who wasn't naked but wore a leather skirt-like contraption around his hips, growled. More leather straps around his thick arms seemed to exist for the sole purpose of emphasizing his muscles.

"Fool," the man snarled down at Haegan. Seemingly from thin air he produced a scimitar.

"Get Laertes to safety," Tokar shouted, bringing his long blade to bear.

Haegan resented the order to leave the fight.

"Go!" Thiel shouted. "Help him—he's hurt!"

He was? Haegan glanced at Laertes, who lay coiled on his side, limp. Haegan scooped him up and backed away from the fight. The one chance he had . . . nobody said anything. Admitted he wasn't as useless as they believed. Now, Thiel and Tokar stalked the Ematahri warrior. Thiel was more fierce than he'd ever seen her, with a dagger in hand. Where had she gotten that?

"Come," Praegur mumbled, head low and eyes on the fight. "Hurry."

Haegan nodded, and together they made their way back into the safety of the woods with an unconscious Laertes. The boy had a gash on his forehead and his arm hung at an unnatural angle. Guilt pursued Haegan. Had his attack on the warrior injured the boy? They hustled deeper into the woods, but not so far that they couldn't see the others. From the place he'd identified as a type of guard hut, a half-dozen warriors flooded out.

"No!" Haegan tripped, his concern over Thiel and Tokar tangling his feet and mind. But he righted himself and started toward them. Forward into the fray. Back into the thick trees.

"We must hurry. Let me take him," Praegur said.

"I'm good." Haegan readjusted the boy in his arms, grateful Laertes wasn't conscious to experience the jostling and humiliation. No doubt the boy would object to being carried. "We have to go back. The others are in trouble."

"No, we head out. Toward Hetaera." Praegur's dark face was etched with a fierce determination Haegan had not noticed before. "They'll catch up."

"What if they're hurt?"

At this, Praegur hesitated, too. "That's normally not an issue, but with those bloodthirsty gypsies . . ." He patted Haegan's shoulder and nudged him onward, suddenly decisive. "Come. We should hurry. Laertes is pale and needs a pharmakeia."

Looking back often, Haegan moved deeper into the woods, his mind lingering on Thiel in the thick of battle. Blazes! Was he a coward that he would yield and allow a girl to battle fierce warriors?

She said to go.

And you went because weakness fills the marrow of your bones!

A high-pitched scream riddled the air, smacking into Haegan like a vat of icy water. He froze and glanced back.

"No, keep—"

Something howled on the wind, severing words and thought alike. Haegan pushed his panicked gaze to Praegur, but the taller youth was staring back, the whites of his eyes bulging. His mouth fell open.

Heat washed over the back of Haegan's shoulders, drenching him with terror.

"Give him," Praegur barked as he grabbed the boy from him.

"But—"

"Now!"

What had he seen? Haegan glanced over his shoulder and hauled in a thick, heavy breath. The forest, once laden with trees, now had been overrun by a flood. Not of water. But of moving, writhing Ematahri warriors.

21

"Run!"

Something in Haegan twisted and clenched at the sight of Thiel sprinting toward him. The warrior-girl, who was never frazzled, now looked terrified, her face flushed and bloodied from the fight she'd already put up. Behind her, Tokar scrambled, fleeing a sword-wielding Ematahri.

"Go, idiot!" he shouted.

Haegan started running, realizing Praegur had left him. Apparently the only one with a brain. He scrambled for purchase on the slippery moss of a rocky outcropping, then pushed forward. He beat a hard path over the incline. He slipped and hopped down the other side, all the while feeling the danger like an icy bucket of water down his spine.

"Faster. Go! Now!"

I'm going! I'm going! Haegan worked to keep his feet moving and his body upright. The terrain fought him, slick from an earlier rain. Feet thudded against the ground, which shook under the onslaught.

Splash—behind.

Snap—to his left.

Warriors everywhere! Surrounded.

Panic tore at him, but he resisted the urge to look back.

"Keep going!" Thiel's voice echoed as she burst from the trees into a wide valley that opened up and spread before him. "Don't stop. No matter what."

Of course he wouldn't stop. Not with twenty Ematahri hunting him. Tokar tore past, sprinting as if he'd just started running. Agility and athleticism were his strong suits. Strength a bedmate. Envy spurted through Haegan, feeling the pains of the exertion. But he couldn't stop. Wouldn't. If he did, he'd die.

Something snagged his arm. He wrenched free.

"Haegan."

He kept moving. But his brain caught up with her voice. The use of his birth name. He glanced to the side. Thiel ran alongside, her eyes on his with an expression that seemed to berate him. Then it hit him—*I am slow.* She was having to slow down to protect him, wasn't she? "Leave me. Go. I'll be okay."

"You can stop this, stop them."

He laughed as he scrabbled over a boulder. "Were that true—"

"It is! The light."

Throwing a scowl at her, he dared not slow down further. "You mock me." He focused on the trees on the other side. Searched for a way to hide. He couldn't run any faster. Neither would he stop.

Something whooshed past him. The singe of the air startled him as he watched a wide scimitar plunk heavily into the dirt, cutting deep, sinking nearly to its hilt. He sucked in a hard breath, stunned. Had that hit him or Thiel—

Dead. They'd be dead.

"Stop them, Haegan!"

"I . . . can't!" Pushing the words out proved great effort, his lungs squeezing hard with each breath.

"You can—must!"

"What . . .?" He looked to her.

Something sailed into the air. Hit her. She snapped out of view behind him. Haegan glanced back. A warrior had tackled her. Meaty grunts sounded as they thrashed on the grass. Rolled.

Haegan skidded, searching for help. Assessing the rest of the warriors. A half-dozen yards back and closing fast.

"The light," Thiel shouted, fighting the Ematahri atop her.

Haegan threw himself at the warrior, knocking him backward. Somehow, the rogue flipped him, landing on top, straddling him.

Grinning, his bared bloody teeth as leathered hands beat at Haegan's face.

He shielded himself, wrestling to be free. In vain. All in vain.

Screams came from Thiel.

Haegan tried to look at her, but there were a half-dozen warriors pouncing on her. She screamed again.

A heat in him roared to the surface. Shrieked.

Surrounding him, the warriors crowded in, beating him. Punching. Kicking. Cursing. Spitting. One drew a dagger and thrust it at Haegan. He deflected with an arm. The blade sliced his flesh with a fiery eruption of pain. Haegan howled. He arched his back, the move giving him a glimpse of his friend.

The Ematahri stretched Thiel out, one at each arm and leg. Another kicked her in the side. She yelped, then whimpered.

Anger exploded through him.

Something swung at his head, rolling him onto his belly. The impact seemed as if he'd flown at a brick wall. His teeth rattled. Pain knifed down his head and neck.

He'd die. He'd die here. So would Thiel.

And he'd be to blame.

Kaelyria.

O Abiassa, send your Fires!

On all fours, Haegan shook his head. Felt the kick to his side. Grunted. Spit up blood. Coughed up more. Another blow to his back and he slumped to the ground. His fingers dug into the damp earth. Come all this way to die. To let Kaelyria die. And Thiel.

No.

"*Ïmnæh wæithe he-ahwl abiałassø et fhuriætyr.*" He knew not where the words came from but they resonated in his mind. Roiled across his chest. Expanded in his lungs. Beat against his heart. "*Ïmnæh wæithe he-ahwl abiałassø et fhuriætyr.*" Warmth spread through his body. Muscles found strength. Wounds healing. Thoughts life. "*Ïmnæh wæithe he-ahwl abiałassø et fhuriætyr. Ïmnæh wæithe he-ahwl abiałassø et fhuriætyr.*"

A blow to his head nearly dropped him into a chasm of darkness. But he refused to embrace defeat. "*Ïmnæh wæïthe*"—punch to his gut, he clenched his eyes and gritted his teeth—"*he-ahwl abiałassø*"—searing pain dug through his shoulder blades—"*et fhu*"—a warrior jerked him upright, eyes glowing yellow with hatred—"*rïætyr.*"

Howling rode the wind as Haegan dropped into the endless abyss of nothingness.

22

Haegan jolted upright, expecting danger. Expecting the Ematahri to finish what they'd started. Instead, he found darkness. A stone ceiling and walls. He was in a cave. And free of pain. Where was the headache? The fire of knife wounds? He felt nothing of the agony that should be riddling his body. He scanned his limbs, bewildered.

"It ain't right, I tell ya," came Laertes's strong objection. "Him what keeps fainting in the worst parts and missing the best parts."

"Him that brings trouble on us, is more like it," Tokar muttered, glancing at Haegan.

Haegan met his gaze. And where he expected hatred, he saw . . . What was that? Unease? Wariness? And what about— "Where is Thiel?"

"On watch," Praegur said, easing into view, a small fire crackling and spitting shadows over his face. "How are you?"

"How is he? He isn't wounded!" Tokar snapped. "I want to know how that's possible." He stood with his arms folded.

"What do you mean I'm not wounded?" Haegan's hand went to where the dagger sliced through his arm. Though there was a clean cut in his sleeve, there was no scab, stitches, or even a scrape against his flesh. What? How?

He stretched his spine, testing and expecting shards of pain to pierce him. But again—nothing. "I . . . I don't understand." His gaze rose to the others, feeling their unease as his own now. "How is this possible? I was—"

"That's what we'd like to know. How is it you keep causing this trouble, yet emerge without a single mark?"

"Foolspeech!" Haegan spat. "'Tis not possible." He only realized he'd come to his feet when Tokar took a step away and drew his arms back, as if ready for a fight.

No, not a fight. To defend himself.

"Just . . . keep clear," Tokar said, an edge sharper than any before in his voice. "And once we get to Hetaera—it's close enough to the Falls. Go your own way. Leave us. "

Fear spirited through Haegan. If they left him, he'd be alone. As much as he didn't want to admit it, he needed them. Needed their help. "I don't know my way."

"North," Tokar said, his eyes dark. "Head north, then, when you hit the river, follow it upstream."

"In earnest? You will abandon me?"

"I want to live!" Tokar snapped. "And I won't let you hurt them."

Haegan jerked at the accusation. "Explain yourself—how have I injured anyone?" His mind leapt to Laertes, who had been unconscious and his arm most likely broken the last time he'd seen him. Now, the boy sat ambivalent and in peace. The arm supporting him, unbroken. How was that possible?

Perhaps I simply over-read the situation.

"You just do. Every town, every people we meet, someone ends up hurt because of you."

"Now, that ain't true," Laertes said. "Not wholly."

"It's true enough to be justified," Tokar argued. "Besides, we've had nothing but trouble since we got stuck with him in Zaethien."

Laertes nodded, tugging a strip of jerky from his pack. "Now 'at's true." He chomped into it, giving Haegan a speculative look. "But Tok, I gotta say, he don't exactly look for the trouble."

"Yeah, but it finds him all the same." He waved a dismissive hand at Haegan. "Once we reach Hetaera, it's time to split up."

"I plead with you—I am alone." Did he truly sound so pathetic? "I need your help, and Thiel promised to see me to the Falls."

Tokar edged closer. "Listen, you care about her. I see it in your eyes. In the way you talk to her."

Heat climbed Heagan's face but he ignored it, swallowing against the truth of the words. "My pleas are not about her, but her promise."

"Do you want her to get hurt?"

The memory of her battered at the hands of the Ematahri hit him. Hurt him. He remembered thinking she'd die. "No," he said quietly.

Victory danced in Tokar's eyes. "Then do what's best. Protect her in the only way you know how."

Leave. Leave her and look back no more.

"You know who she is, right?"

Haegan looked away. The daughter of his father's near-enemy.

"And you know what her father and brothers would do to you if she were killed because of your unique ability to find trouble."

Danger whispered through the cave, bringing back that night on Abiassa's Throne when he'd seen shadows become impossible things. Things his mind had clearly conjured. Things that could not exist. Even that did not lessen the threat of her ice-hearted brothers.

"I'm telling you this for your own good." Was Tokar now gloating? "I know it'd upset her, but she would be powerless against an order from Thurig the Formidable."

But I have neither the means nor the knowledge to reach the Great Falls. Without her help, he would not touch those blessed waters.

Yet what was his life if it cost others theirs?

Kaelyria. "My sister . . ." Haegan chomped down on the words, reminding himself they did not know his true identity. To them he was Rigar, a bumbling, wandering idiot. "I must make it to the Falls, or my sister will die." It was vague enough not to injure his secret. But threat enough, perhaps, to persuade.

Tokar angled in, his left cheek twitching as he stared him down. Beneath the fire and animosity lurked a steel forged in the fires of the hard life of a roamer. In five years, Tokar would be a man who could put a petulant equal in line with a stony look or stare down the fiercest of enemies. "And if we help you, we all die."

Was it true, that if he stayed, their deaths would be on his conscience? Would the others see it that way, too? Haegan glanced to

Praegur, who looked away. Blond-haired Laertes, normally quick-witted and the first to tell it straight, slumped against the stone wall, chewing jerky, and shrugged.

Those he had thought to call friends apparently were not. And yet, he a man of honor and integrity, would not will danger or the threat thereof on any he might call friend. It seemed there was but one recourse at this dark hour.

"You are right. I should leave." Everything in him railed at the thought. But he would spend the rest of his life knowing he caused their deaths.

Then a different thought poked his conscience—what had happened back there that Tokar would be so ready to pitch Haegan from this circle? "Back in the clearing . . . I can scarce recall what happened." Yet it pulled at him. Told him it was important.

"Look," Tokar said, handing him his sack. "I don't know what happened—"

"That's right!" came Thiel's sharp, decisive intrusion. "You don't!"

They all turned to the entrance where she stood. Haegan drew in a breath, awe spreading through him. Her brown hair lay askew, most likely from the probing fingers of the wind. But beyond that, she appeared uninjured, unbruised . . . unaffected by the battle that should have claimed her life.

But that warrior—nearly twice her size—the other half-dozen beating her . . . And yet not a mark on her. How was that possible?

What *had* happened out there? The question injected fear into his veins.

"You'd do well, Tokar, to stop fearmongering." She entered, snatched up a water skin, glared at Praegur. "You should have stopped him, instead of conceding."

The biggest of them all, Praegur suddenly seemed to shrink beneath her admonishment.

She turned those amber eyes on Haegan. Plucked his sack from his hands and tossed it aside. "I would talk with you." And she walked out.

Haegan started after her.

"Wha'?" Laertes said around a piece of jerky. "You know som'thin what we can't know?"

Hesitation held Haegan at the lip of the cave where darkness crouched, and he looked at the boy, then to Thiel, but she hadn't stopped. Uncertainty chased him into the chilly night air.

Where had she gone? The only path lay before him because the other was too treacherous. He glanced around, scant moonlight casting strange shadows along the rocks as he followed a narrow trail coiling around the hillside. Though he moved forward, he wasn't sure he wanted to have the conversation that was coming. One that would bring questions. Questions he couldn't answer.

"You frighten me."

The words stopped Haegan. He, too, was frightened. But also because the one person he didn't want to scare off, his only semblance of a friend, spoke them. At the base of the winding path, Haegan turned to the right, where Thiel waited with her arms folded, leaning against a tree.

She pushed off and ran a hand through her short brown hair, then wrapped herself in a solitary hug. Shoulders hunched, she paced. "How did you do it?"

Though he still didn't want to admit what he'd done—was it truly *his* doing?—Haegan merely shook his head. "I wish I knew."

"Do you even know *what* you did?" She started forward.

Haegan held her gaze, gauging what was the right answer because he had the strongest inclination that providing the wrong one would tear the fragile threads of their friendship. "I didn't—"

"Those words!" Her brow knotted with heated emotion. "What were those words? Are you an incipient, Haegan?"

He started. A rush of anger shoved through his body. "No!" The repulsive nature of those creatures made her words bitter and cruel. "How could you suggest such an abomination?"

"Because you *healed* me! Healed yourself—with strange words in some language. What did you say? What did it mean?"

Stunned, he scanned her body, disbelieving. Thought of his own vanished wounds. And Laertes's. "I have no idea."

"You said them—how can you *not* know what you said?" She raised her hands in frustration.

"Answers evade me." Now he sounded stupid.

"You're not making sense, prince!"

"Well I know that none of this makes sense!" He spun away, caught in some wicked scheme that had brought ruination upon him and any future he might have had a few months ago. "Nothing has made sense since leaving my chambers that horrible night."

"So, what? Now you're the victim?"

Haegan glared at her. "I see no victim, nor do I perform as one."

"So, you're performing in another manner?"

"You twist my words."

"They're easy to twist when you're hiding—"

"I hide nothing." He sighed and let his shoulders sag. "Not even my own ignorance, though it shape me into a imbecile worthy of ridicule."

"You hide everything! Haegan, Prince of Zaethien. Brother to the heir apparent, brother who can walk when Princess Kaelyria is now bedridden. The kingdom is falling and you are running."

Her words ruptured the thin hold he had on his anger. "How dare you turn this on me. Would that I still lay in that musty tower cell, rotting and bored out of my mind with a seventy-year-old tutor who felt the Histories were a better subject than real life!" The edges of his vision blurred white. "Would that I could track down the accelerant who betrayed Kaelyria's naïve trust. That I could undo what has been done. That I could—"

"Haegan." Her voice was breathless as she swooped forward, capturing his hand. Her touch silenced him as she held him hostage in a gaze so deep and true he could not breathe.

Something broke in him, riveted him to her. He heard in his head, her thoughts, her voice, her tears. Haegan stepped back, but she did not release him. Instead, she lifted his hand between them, cupped between her delicate fingers. A strange glow cast upward, illuminating and yet shadowing her eyes.

Slowly, Thiel peeled her fingers away as one would an onion—and the glow brightened, emanating from her palms.

Haegan sucked in a breath, staring at the strange light. "What is it?"

Thiel looked from the glow to his face, hers awash with amazement and the pale gold halo surrounding his hands. "Your anger." She sighed. "I wondered if anger was the trigger."

Haegan jerked free. Took a step back, shoving his hands into his pockets. "Of what do you speak? What trigger?"

"Three times I've seen the same light—"

A thundering roar filled the night, devouring her words. The ground shook beneath them, and Haegan wondered if he was to blame for this, too. Noises cracked and popped, pushing past the roar. Haegan looked around, wondering . . . Guilt tugged him.

No, that was Thiel.

He turned and saw her mouthing something. No, *shouting*. At him!

"Go!" She grabbed his tunic. Pushed him. Desperation dripped from her face as she shoved him harder. "Hurry, before—"

A massive horse shot from between two trees and skidded to a halt. It reared, hooves raking at the air as if fighting a mighty enemy. Mounted bareback, the Ematahri warrior lifted a hand and made a horrible, wobbling noise.

Haegan tripped, his mind and body tangling in panic as Thiel again shoved him.

But somehow, warriors were there, too.

Haegan whipped back and collided with Thiel. Her momentum toppled them. She scrambled up, moving like lightning, yanking at him.

Why would the Ematahri not leave them alone? Haegan turned to the first warrior and stopped. Long black hair, half secured away from his face, draped his broad, bare shoulders. Orange paint streaked his torso, three bands circling his right arm. Poking up over his right shoulder, a massive blade seemed more an extension of the warrior than a weapon. Daggers and blades lay strapped over his leather trousers. He was every bit as terrible as the night terror stories Haegan had been told as a child.

Head high, the warrior once more yelled to the dozen ravagers. Whether orders or some war cry, Haegan could not decipher. However, the chill running down his spine grew unmistakable.

No more! They would not have a chance to finish off Thiel. No more would he tolerate brigands who upended his plans to reach the Falls. Who threatened his very existence and that of his friends. Haegan inched forward. Angry.

"No!" Thiel yelled at him, once more grabbing his hands—his glowing hands—in hers. "Don't." Her eyes were bright with alarm and foreboding as she tightened her grip over his. "The archon—he'll kill you! They—"

A metallic taste filled his mouth as a sensation ripped through Haegan, drowning her words. He felt the fierce black eyes lock onto him as tangibly and sharply as if an arrow had struck him. Haegan shifted his attention and found the dark irises his mind conjured boring through him, virulent.

With a whip of the Ematahri's hand, something sailed through the air. Cracked against Haegan's skull. He pitched forward. Went to a knee. His vision blurred, but he refused to succumb. Refused to surrender his acuity again.

Hand against the cool, damp grass as he steadied himself, Haegan struggled to shake off the ache worming through his neck and shoulders. The same one that fought for control of his eyesight. The unmistakable vibrancy emanating from his hand. With a growl, he pushed upward in a world still smeared gray and black.

A shout went up.

"No," Thiel ordered in a loud voice. She spoke with authority, which confounded Haegan as he dragged himself to his feet and cleared his mind. Firmly, she stepped in front of him and held her fisted hands to the side, legs shoulder-width apart. "I claim Kedardokith!"

Like a whirl of black smoke on a strong wind, the warrior alighted, his ebony cloak swirling around him. The beast of a man stood at least a head taller than Haegan. He stormed forward, the rest of his men gathering on their horses. He sneered, not at Thiel, but at Haegan. "Who are you, worm, that this woman defends you? Where is your honor?"

Shame silenced Haegan. That and confusion—what was Thiel doing?

Although the Ematahri warrior glared, the muscled mountain did not cross the invisible line Thiel had drawn, when he could have easily sent her sprawling with a swift backhand. Instead, he stood before her, their boots touching. Finally, he turned his foul gaze down. To Thiel, who stood resolute in her defense.

Haegan took a step forward.

The *tsing* of drawn swords sang across the darkening hillside. Each of the ravagers sat tensed, eyes on him. As his gaze returned to Thiel and the Ematahri warrior, he twitched. The two stared down as equals.

There could be no sense made of it. The ravagers *ravaged*. Why wasn't he attacking her? Killing her?

"I seek an audience with Seveired," Thiel demanded. She seemed to grow several inches as she faced the leader. "This man is under my protection by the laws of Kedardokith."

Keda—what? Haegan scowled at Thiel, confused.

"Seveired is gone," the warrior growled. "You will counsel with the new archon." He spun, the effect no less dramatic at close range. The cloak even stirred the air, puffing Haegan's curls from his damp forehead. Mounted once more, the warrior glowered at Thiel. Then yanked his reins and vanished into the woods.

The others followed, leaving them alone.

Thiel pivoted and shouted up the small knoll for the others to come and bring their packs.

"We're—we're leaving?" Haegan glanced over his shoulder, a prick of giddy but wary release bubbling within him. "We can go then?"

Thiel scalded him with a look. "Only if you want your flesh boiled off in a vat of oil."

Was she serious? His answer came in the form of brutes on massive gray horses. The two warriors were twins in both their dress—gray-

and-white streaked hair—and their impassive mirrored expressions. From their high seats, they stared down at the group in silent contempt.

"Should've just given him to them." Having emerged from the cave with the others, Tokar shouldered his way into his pack, eyes on the waiting ravagers. "He's solid enough they would've accepted."

Thiel's dark, angry eyes speared Tokar. "Before the new archon," she said, "nothing we have is a high enough price." She gave Laertes and Praegur a nod.

As if her nod had been meant for them, the twins shifted their horses apart, effectively creating a passage between them. What was going on? The question about leaving once again formed on his tongue, but he forbade it voice. But were they leaving?

"Again, you bring trouble," Tokar grumbled as he trudged past Haegan, soundly thumping shoulders with him.

Haegan could do naught but stare as Praegur ushered Laertes through the beastly "gates" before them. Fantastical visions of the two warriors swinging fiery blades and severing heads from torsos paraded through his mind. With that gruesome image, Haegan inched on, the muscles in his neck tightening when he neared the massive horses. As he passed between them, their long, broad skulls lowered as if telling him to keep moving. The beasts were so large even *they* looked down on him.

Brown marble-like eyes locked onto him. Dark shadows above the large orbs moved like eyebrows. Speculative. How it was possible for a horse to seem to possess the same hatred and cruelty as their masters, Haegan knew not. Tangled and black, the forelock draped over one eye, reminding Haegan of the Ematahri leader.

A twig snapped beneath his boot, sounding as loud as a club cracking against stone. Heart thundering, Haegan flinched. His leg lifted and swung to the left, away from the beast. Though in opposite directions, he was quite sure his heart and lungs ran. Something he wanted to do, but fear held him captive.

The horse swung his head with a nicker.

Haegan veered to avoid the enormous nostrils puffing steamy clouds in the cool morning air. A snort and whinny blasted against his ear. With a yelp, he resisted the urge to leap right. Instead, he threw himself forward as a shudder raked down his spine.

Taunting laughter followed him, as did the heavy clops. Only as the hooves continued and warm, wet breath brushed his nape did Haegan realize these warriors were here to *escort* them, not watch them leave.

Clip-clop. Clip-clunk. Clip-clop. Clip-clunk.

A cadence. Marching him. To what? His death? Something inside stirred him to fight back. But what could he, a longtime cripple, now healed—temporarily—but untrained, do against the battle-hardened Ematahri?

The image of his hands leapt into his thoughts. Of them glowing. Thiel holding them. Tight. *"No!"* she had warned him. But how had she known what would happen when he didn't? Walking through the trees behind the others, he rotated his wrists and stared at his palms. What . . . what was it? Why had they glowed?

It made no sense. He had no gift, and that would have been his first assumption—somehow he had a gift that manifested itself. But Abiassa had not chosen him to wield the Flames. She'd bestowed that honor on Kaelyria. A fate his father-king celebrated after Haegan fell into the cruel sleep and woke a cripple. So what was it? How had Thiel known? Not only known, but *anticipated* and prevented what he had not realized existed?

He rubbed his thumb against his forefinger, trying to remember what he felt when the glow happened. Nothing. No different from any other day he'd felt angry—there was heat. The kind that spilled across his shoulders and down his back. As well as the answering coolness that swirled in the pit of his stomach. No strange affliction. No unusual side effect.

But her touch—

A solid jolt against his back sent Haegan sprawling face-first to the ground with a mucky *splitch*. Lifting his hands, he heard the slurping of his fingers, suctioning free. Amid the laughter and the humiliation, stench stung his nostrils. An odor so foul it coated his tongue.

Guffaws snapped through the woods, the ravagers enjoying his situation far too much.

"Kedardokith protects this man from any harm," Thiel shouted angrily.

"We didn't touch him," one of their escorts stated. "I believe your Kedardokith is . . . intact."

"Though he smells like the pig wallow," the other added.

Slick and sickening, the mud clung to him. So did the odor. He wasn't sure there was a remedy to the stench that reeked of the humiliation he'd felt most of his life.

Abiassa, I would have preferred you left me a cripple to die in that lonely tower than endure this.

A strong grip cuffed his arm. Hauled him to his feet. Haegan stumbled and found himself staring not into eyes, but into the leather vest of the Ematahri leader. *Dwarf. I am but a dwarf to him.* And were the venomous gaze latched onto Haegan, he might be a *dead* dwarf. But it was locked on the escorts. The leader shouted something in their foreign tongue, then shoved Haegan to the side.

Hands plied at him, pulling him through a thick throng of villagers, seeping from the woods like ants from a disturbed hill. Two women, their grips like iron, dragged him backward. Away from the others.

Haegan searched for Thiel. For his friends. But he saw none of them.

The women hauled him through their camp, a chaotic assembly of tarps and poles, fires, and what looked like stone wells. Children darted from one shadowed place to another. Gathering his wits, he weighed his options and tried to regain his feet as they wrenched him around and towed him onward. He needed to break free and run.

As if his thoughts had been spoken aloud, two warriors emerged from the tent that lay in his path.

Stomach tight, Haegan tensed as the women led him into the tent, past the warriors. Immersed in darkness, Haegan's vision slowly adjusted. A lone glow emanated from the center of the tent. The light came from a fire with an enormous black pot over it. Steam rose from a liquid that gurgled and roiled under control of the flames.

Oil.

23

"No!" Haegan writhed to free himself of the matrons' iron grips, but they dug their nails into the soft flesh beneath his arms and yanked him toward the boiling vat. They shouted at him, and he shouted back, digging his heels in.

But together, they gave a shove that pitched him forward, and he tumbled into the terrible pot. His mind blanked and a shriek rent the air. Immersed, he felt the sizzling of his flesh. Ached with the burning of his muscles. He held his breath and scrambled up for air. He broke the surface and gave a shout.

The women laughed, pointing at him.

Murderous, foul wenches! When he was in such . . . a . . . Haegan glanced down, half expecting to see his own fat bubbling to the surface. Instead, the only thing floating there were clumps of muck. He lifted his arm, surprised to find not welts and burns but a slick material coating his skin. Strangest of all—it ate clean through the clothing he wore but didn't touch his flesh. "What . . .?"

"Medicinal."

He lifted his head, surprised to find a warrior there. "I . . . I don't understand."

Left bicep corded with a black and red braid, the warrior stood fast. A jagged scar traced an ugly line from his mouth to above his ear, where a brown braid ran along his head and down into the rest of his hair, secured in a leather strap. Only when the warrior searched for more drink did Haegan noticed the other braid had been dyed red. "You cannot go before the archon reeking of muarshtait."

"Right." Haegan lowered his arm hesitantly into the—whatever it was. No one had been allowed into his father's court without proper attire, so why would it be any different here?

Perhaps because they were ravagers.

The two women came at him with buckets and Haegan shrank, aware of his nakedness.

"Boy, they're healers," the warrior growled. "They've seen more than you have and wish you had." The warrior laughed as he stalked over to a bowl of fruit and a pitcher.

"They may have, but I have not."

The warrior sipped from a wooden cup, then grinned. "Shy? Never been with a woman?"

Haegan ignored the comment, shaking his head at the two matrons. "I'll clean myself."

"No." The heftier of the two leaned toward him with a bristled paddle that he supposed was their version of a brush or comb.

He reached for it. "Thank you."

She smacked his hand.

Haegan yanked back. "Now see here!"

The woman ranted, her arms moving as fast as her mouth set into a dark-red face. Though he might not know her words, he did not need language to know he'd angered her. But anger or not, he would not let a woman scrub his nakedness.

The warrior laughed then set aside his cup. "*Umwæithietïel.*"

The women started. Glared at the warrior, then slapped the bristled paddled into the water—splashing the concoction into Haegan's face—and huffed off.

Those words . . . they sounded familiar. Like a faint echo of something he'd heard. But his attention fastened on the way the women heeded the warrior's barked command. They left, and Haegan waited for the warrior to follow suit.

"Your tantrums will not work with me, boy. Clean yourself and get dressed."

Haegan scowled. "And how am I to dress when this"—he waved his hands over the bubbling vat—"evaporated my clothing?"

The warrior filled the cup with more amber liquid and pointed toward something behind Haegan. "There." He tossed back the contents, swallowed, grimaced, then set the cup aside again. "And you'd do well to hurry or you'll stand before him in all your glory."

So . . . naked. Haegan scrubbed himself down, surprised at the way whatever this was managed to clean him and leave him smelling woodsy but bathed. A noise outside drew the warrior's attention, and Haegan seized the moment to lunge up and hurry behind the dressing screen where he found classic Ematahri attire. Pants. *Just* pants. "Right." Hearing voices on the other side, he quickly shoved his legs into the rough material, then gave one more desperate search for a shirt. Feeling a draft across his chest, he stepped out, rubbing his arm.

The warrior's eyebrow arched with a smirk. "You haven't seen much daylight."

Haegan resisted the urge to glance down at his pale, *un*muscled chest and arms. "I was . . . raised indoors." The warrior's assessing gaze raked over Haegan, making him feel more naked than he had with the matrons. He shifted uneasily on his bare feet. "Is there something wrong?"

The warrior stalked closer, every move rippling with power and threat. He tucked his chin, staring hard. "Who are you, boy?"

Why did he care who Haegan was? Had he somehow discovered Haegan's identity? "I . . ." He swallowed hard, afraid that if this warrior knew his father was the Fire King, Haegan would either be held for ransom or killed for sport. "I'm nobody."

In the space of a blink, Haegan registered two things: the fist and the ground. He flew back, the breath violently knocked from his lungs, and his throat squeezed tight beneath the powerful hold of the warrior, who had effortlessly pinned him. Rocks bit into his shoulder blades. Gasping, Haegan tasted the bitter metallic taste of blood. Felt warmth sliding across his upper lip and down his cheek, right into his ear. Hands wrapped around the man's thick, hairy arm to stop him from choking him, Haegan shook his head, unable to breathe.

On a knee, the warrior dragged his hateful glare from the dirt to Haegan. "Etelide wagers her life for *nobody*?"

Can't breathe!

The tent flap fluttered, light broke in, then a shadow. "Zoijan."

The warrior didn't move.

The newcomer said something in their tongue.

Zoijan growled something over his shoulder in Ematahrian, then swung his gaze back to Haegan. "You better be worth her life, or I'll take yours." After yet another disapproving glare, he stomped to his feet.

Haegan hauled in greedy gulps of air, turning on his side and coughing.

"Let's go."

Clawing his way to his feet, Haegan shook his head and felt an acute awareness that disobedience would cost him more than a choking. He trailed the warrior, feeling like a child behind this man. The ridges and scars across his spine back proved he'd fought—and probably killed—many. Was he one of the border marauders? The lawless ravagers.

Head pounding, Haegan realized as he cringed at rocks and forest debris poking into the bottoms of his feet, that his nose was bleeding.

Trickles of laughter poked out from various places. He'd never had to concern himself with his appearance, and living without the use of one's limbs made it impossible to have the brawn these men wore as easily as clothing.

Zoijan stalked a corral and gave a nod to two armed men. He shifted Haegan toward it. "In."

The gate swung open. Haegan frowned and look into the partially covered area strewn with hay. Sitting against a far slat wall, Praegur, Tokar, and Laertes stared back. Rubbing the back of his neck where a new ache had begun, Haegan entered, anxious to be rid of Zoijan.

Hatred poured from Tokar, who turned away with folded arms. It was here more than anywhere else that the youth seemed at home, with brutes like Zoijan.

"What'd ya do," Laertes asked, grinning. "Sass the big one?"

Haegan shook his head.

"He doesn't have the embers to talk back," Tokar muttered.

Hanging his head only made the throb worsen. Haegan slid down against the wall. It was hopeless. Ever since Luxlirien, they couldn't seem to go more than a day without encountering trouble. He'd never make it to the Great Falls. Kaelyria would be permanently paralyzed. And he . . . he would live out his humiliation. Where, he didn't know. Maybe he should just die.

"Did you see Thiel?" Laertes squatted with his spine against the slat wall. "We ain't seen her since they drugged her off—"

"Dragged."

"—and threw us in here where they keep them muars." He glanced at Haegan. "How's come you got their clothes on?"

"They boiled mine off me."

Tokar snorted. "Are we supposed to believe that, you stupid muar?"

Haegan jerked his head up—and immediately regretted it. "It's true."

"Then why aren't you hurt, if they boiled clothes off you?"

"Because—"

"Hey," Praegur said, tapping Haegan's leg and nodding toward the gate.

The meaty Zoijan stood close to an Ematahri woman and touched her shoulder. With a nod, she smiled at him.

"What's Thiel doing with the likes of him?" Laertes asked.

Haegan froze as the realization washed over him that the woman in leathers, the woman he'd thought an Ematahri, who behaved with affection toward this ravager was indeed Thiel. With another nod to the barbarian, she turned into the corral.

On his feet, Haegan searched for some sign of coercion. Of being forced . . . but she wasn't forced. She hadn't been escorted to the corral, had she? In fact, she seemed to move about freely.

"What's going on, T?" Tokar asked, his voice coated with suspicion and wariness.

Haegan glanced to Zoijan and found the warrior glowering once more.

"Listen."

"We're all ears," Tokar bit out.

For once, Haegan was with the turbulent boy. He closed up their circle around Thiel, intentionally not turning his back on the fierce warrior.

"We will go before the archon," Thiel said. "You must all remain silent. I will answer and speak to him. I alone."

"I'm not understanding things," Tokar said. "Like how you know so much about these people. And how they know you."

"It's more than that." Haegan quickly connected the facts. "They respect you. You're"—what was that Zoijan had said—"etta . . ."

"*Etelide*," she said softly. "It's my Ematahri name. They know"—she nodded to Zoijan—"and respect me because I lived with this clan."

"You what?" Tokar growled. "And you didn't tell us? We attacked them!"

She held up a hand.

"Etelide," a deep rumbling voice spoke from behind. Zoijan. "It's time."

Irritation and what seemed like some level of panic churned through her features. "There is more, but once we enter the Inner Chamber, do not speak." She met each of their gazes. "That is my task. And mine alone."

"Why?" Haegan asked. "Because of this kedar-thing?"

She gave a slow nod.

"Zoijan said you wagered your life." *For me.*

She stepped closer, then hesitated. Looked to the others. "I want to speak to him, please. Go on. We'll follow."

Scowls and surprised expressions raked Haegan as the others started for the gate.

Thiel inched even closer and touched his hand. "Promise me, Haegan, that you will control your anger."

As they stood toe to toe, Haegan noticed the light sprinkling of freckles across her nose and the gold flecks in her brown eyes. Noticed the golden hue to her complexion, so obviously a Northlander, with that dark brown hair.

"Haegan."

"I pro—wait." He frowned. "Why are you—"

"It's imperative. Will you trust me?"

"Thiel, this makes no sense."

"Trust, Haegan. It's about trust. Will you trust me?"

"Yes, but how? What are you talking about?"

She squeezed his hand. No, she was squeezing something into his hand. Haegan scowled, but she smiled. "If you feel your anger rising during the—once we go in there, swallow this."

"What is it?"

"Just promise you'll swallow it. I'll need your help, but not your anger." She leaned in, her expression softening. "Will you promise to swallow it? I have to trust you with this, Haegan."

"What is it? How will it help you?" He tried to look down, but she held his hand between hers. Whatever it was, it felt large. And hard to swallow. Like the pit of a peach or cordi fruit.

"You said you'd help me and trust me. Did you lie?"

"No!"

"Then you'll swallow it."

Something about her expression tugged at him, as if a tether had been tied between them. "Yes."

Relief washed over, parting her lips as she took a breath. "Good." Her eyes seemed to gloss. "Thank you." Her chin started dimpling. As if she was about to cry. She clenched his hand. "Thank you."

With that, she turned and left him. Left the corral.

Zoijan waited there, his countenance more fierce than ever before. "Move, boy!"

24

Haegan was led to the front of a large Ematahri gathering before an enormous shelter. Too large to be a tent, it was more of a pavilion. As he inched closer, nudged by the all-too-tight grip of Zoijan, Haegan slid the large pill into his pocket. At least, he hoped it was a pill. She hadn't called it that, but what else would she want him to swallow?

"Say nothing and do nothing," Thiel whispered to Tokar and Praegur, who towered over her, agitated and alert. A glimmer of challenge glinted in Tokar's eyes, and Thiel must've seen it too. She arched a warning eyebrow at him. "No matter what is said or happens—"

A shout rang out, and the thick crowd of warriors surrounding them snapped to attention, facing the pavilion entrance.

"Do nothing." When neither of her friends acquiesced, Thiel threw another glare at them. "Do you understand me? Do no—"

"Do not ask me to stand by if they attack you," Tokar snapped.

"I asked nothing. I *commanded* you!"

Tokar's face darkened. Haegan might have found it amusing had the situation and Thiel's measures to assure their compliance not yanked at his inner alarms.

"What good will it do if you are killed?" Tokar asked.

"And what good is it if we are *all* killed? Then what of Hae—Rigar?"

"Rigar?" Tokar scoffed, then lifted his chin and set his focus on the structure. "I care not. He's naught but trouble. If it weren't for him, we'd be in Hetaera by now, enjoying hot ale and a warm fire."

"Swear it, Tokar," Thiel demanded with a ferocity that made Haegan blink. "Swear you will do nothing."

From within the great pavilion came the sound of drums, drawing Haegan's attention from his friends and toward the flaps adorned with gilt vines and green jewels in a pattern of the Ematahri crest—wings encompassing a fist clenching a sword.

"Abandon sword and strife. Enter the sanctum of the Archon!"

Thiel hauled in a breath and slowly let it out between her lips as the flaps snapped back. Her reaction concerned Haegan. How long had she lived among this clan to be so intimate with their customs and even their language? It must've been years.

The large pit at the center of the tent crackled and hissed, its welcome also a warning. Thiel seemed to cringe and swallow hard as the press of the warriors forced them forward. The twin warriors appeared at her side, severing her from Haegan and the others. The stream and Zoijan guided the boys to a boxed-off area, but Haegan never removed his gaze from Thiel, who was escorted to stand at the edge of a large hole in the ground.

"What's that smell?"

"Wild boarbeasts. That's their cave below," Zoijan explained.

Haegan jolted. "Boarbeasts!" Though he could not see the monsters, he heard their snorts and smelled the foul odor rising from the pit. They lusted for blood, and with their razor-sharp tusks, they killed any quarry they stalked. Much like the Ematahri.

Thiel stood unyielding, her gaze on the tri-level wooden dais directly in front of her. The first platform spanned ten hands and sat empty, unlike the second with its matching levers on each side. And the highest boasted a seat of power with an intricate design.

"Braided wood and steel—the symbol of Ematahri power," Zoijan said, "The wood for our lands. The steel for our hearts."

"That explains a lot," Praegur mumbled.

Jaw set tight, Thiel gazed straight ahead. But then she shifted, angling her head slightly to the right. Her lips moved, but the distance and din of the crowd made it impossible to hear what she'd said to the warrior.

The man seemed to snarl his reply, the curl of his lip proof of his attitude. Haegan wanted to punch him. The rhythm of the drums produced a writhing dance that seemed to make the pavilion pulsate with energy. Shouts. Drums. Thumping. Haegan's head pounded.

On the other side of the great gathering, the crowd parted and a lithe woman emerged. Draped in a pale green dress with a shimmering overlay, she paused and stared apathetically at Thiel. Black-as-night hair hung in flower-adorned ripples, woven in a thick braid over her bare shoulder.

Haegan looked to Thiel, surprised to see recognition flicker through her eyes.

"Verilla." Zoijan's voice rumbled in Haegan's ear. "My sister and consort of the archon. She was once as a sister to Etelide."

Then an ally, perhaps?

When the woman's green gaze slid over Thiel like an icy bath, Haegan knew there would be no ally. Not in that woman at least. Verilla lifted the pale sheath overlay of her dress, climbed to the top of the dais, and stood beside the seat of power, placing long, elegant fingers on the finial.

A horn blast silenced the thrumming chatter of the pavilion.

Haegan jerked at the noise.

"Grow a spine, boy."

• • •

The sudden intrusion of the horn signaling the archon's entrance squeezed Thiel's confidence as the curtain behind the dais parted and a stream of warriors—the archon's blood-brothers, his fiercest fighters—stalked up a flight of invisible steps at the rear. They flooded out around the seat of power, forming two perfect arcs sweeping from the braided throne to the edge of the upper tier.

Gripping the waist-high iron cage that held her, she stole a glance at Zoijan. The warrior was Cadeif's best friend. So where was Cadeif? Why had he not shown himself since she'd confronted him in the woods?

A creaking noise seemed to move the ground beneath her feet.

She shifted, but with a loud crack, a cage of mahrki—a hollow, steel-like reed—snapped around her. The dirt beneath her feet seeped through slats of wood. Wild panic punched the breath from her lungs as she grabbed the waist-high barrier.

Snarls and grunts reached up from the darkness, making her squirm.

The twins, Raleng and Ruldan, marched forward and stepped onto the second level of the dais, each taking position beside a lever. They bowed to each other, then pivoted and faced the crowd. With a stomp, each moved a hand to his heart and the other to a lever. "He fights on wings. He wields the sword. He has been chosen. Yield now to him!"

A resonating shout thudded through the room, then the warriors chanted, "He has been chosen! To him swords we yield!"

A flurry of movement to the side drew her attention. Laertes writhed against a warrior, his face crimson, his legs blurring as he kicked. Thiel moved to the side, trying to capture the lad's attention, to beg him to keep still. The warriors would not hesitate to kill him if he broke free. Her finger curled around the bars encasing her. She pushed her unwilling gaze to Haegan, who stirred. She silently willed him to calm down. It would be disastrous if he didn't. The pill. *Please remember the pill.*

She motioned to Praegur to silence the boy, but the large, well-muscled teen angled his neck, and she saw then the blade resting there.

Tokar . . . He stood stiff, his back arched. A warrior held him at dagger-point, too.

Anger soared through Thiel. She jerked to the front, ready to demand they release her friends. Instead dark brown eyes that had once probed her soul stopped her short. "Cadeif," she breathed, her anger washing away in the shock.

Wreathed in a tangle of black coils, his face seemed at first soft. Until she recognized the intimidating cloak and the bindings criss-crossing his chest, dark red—literally dyed in the blood of his enemies.

Cadeif. Cadeif was the archon? Her heart beat harder.

And he stood now to hear her claim. Her promise of protection over a man.

O Beneficent One . . . have mercy on me! If she had hoped for an ally among the Ematahri, she had been foolishly naïve. Seveered was dead. Cadeif—he was dead to her as well.

He whirled around, deliberately flipping the long tail of the cloak in her direction. It snapped the air. He strode up the dais and took his place on the seat of power, cutting an imposing figure. Always had. But especially now that he led not just his clan, but the entire Ematahri nation.

A lot had happened since she left nearly two years ago.

He leaned to the right, elbow propped on the armrest. Intense disapproval radiated off him as he stared her down. "Etelide, you claimed Kedardokith," he said decisively, his voice booming in the now-silent space.

"I have," Thiel replied, feeling small. Vulnerable. As she had four years past when she stumbled into the Ematahri camp, starving and terrified.

"And you recall the rites involved in this sacred oath you've claimed?" He eased forward, his eyes narrowing. "Is it not wrong for a woman to claim two warriors to her bed?"

Thiel started. Two warriors? To her bed? The accusation hung putrid before her nostrils. Set aside the fact Haegan was far from a warrior . . . she'd had *no* warrior to her bed. She'd been too young. They had been forbidden.

Worse, Cadeif had just stained her honor before the clan. "I have made no claim or move of such a nature."

"But you have," he barked, slapping the armrest and pushing to his feet. "Kedardokith is a lifeoath."

"Y-yes, I—"

"And this twig of a boy . . ." His thick muscles rippled as he motioned to Haegan. "You would bind yourself to him?"

"No, I—"

Cadeif stepped forward, his left foot now on the lowest tier, flanked by the twins. "Then you deny him before your brethren?" In his eyes she saw a spark of hope, one mirrored by the slight lift of his chin.

He *wanted* her to deny Haegan.

Her every step in the woods had been carefully placed so she would not cross paths with this clan of the Ematahri. To avoid the warrior she now stood before. "I would speak, Archon," she said, lowering her gaze . . . to the bars of the boarbeast den.

"Speak."

Thiel slowly raised her head, her gaze still down. "When I arrived here four years past, a brave warrior prevented his brothers from raping and murdering a pitiful girl with no home and no hope." Slowly, deliberately, she met Cadeif's eyes, remembering that day. Remembering the way he'd saved her. "By claiming Kedardokith, he saved my life. But I was an outsider to whom the rules did not necessarily apply, so Seveired gave me a choice—remain with the brothers, or be delivered to a village."

"And if I recall," his deep voice rumbled as he stalked down the dais to the ground, "you chose to stay."

He'd always been able to make her heart race. And looking into his eyes would work against her as it always had. She inclined her head. "I chose to stay." *He* had been the reason she made that choice. His kindness, his laughter, and in the end, his attraction—and hers.

"And you were accepted." Another step closer.

"I was." She held her shaking hands tightly before her so he wouldn't see.

"And you grew and fought. Became one of our own." As he circled the den, his voice grew firmer, until he stood within reach of her. No longer could she see the bars of the den. Instead only the cords binding his chest and upper arms. The ones that marked him as the archon. The mightiest, fiercest of the Ematahri.

"I grew." So had her feelings for him. "And I became one . . ."

"Do you find us repugnant now?"

"No!"

"And yet you withhold your eyes from your archon." His words were quiet and soft, mostly likely not heard by those at the farthest reaches of the Great Hall.

Her gaze traveled up his broad chest, past his thick neck, straight up to the dark-as-night eyes that had cocooned her heart and mind every time she looked into them. "I meant no insult, only deference and respect, Archon Cadeif."

Cadeif inched forward. She twitched, swallowing hard against his nearness. He lifted a hand slowly, each inch stalling her next heartbeat. His large, calloused fingers traced the side of her cheek. She drew in a breath, surprised that what she had left, what she remembered, still existed. He still cared. She had not expected him to understand. And she'd broken a half-dozen Ematahri customs returning. Could she truly be welcome back? Would he—

"And yet!" The storm raged once more, his breath hot and angry against her cheek. He nudged her back then pivoted and stomped back to the dais as he said, "You left your brothers. Without a word or explanation. You broke faith with our people. With me." He glared from his throne. "You were forbidden from our borders and yet you return with these"—his lip curled and disdain dripped from them—"these twigs who could barely heft a sword let alone wield one."

"I did not mean to cross the border. We were . . ." It did not matter. She must seek mercy for her friends. Her life was in Cadeif's hands. "They are my friends. We were trying to make our way north—"

"Yes, make your way through Ematahri Nation. Through our lands! Lands we are right to defend. And what does your pale friend here do but slaughter twenty of our brothers."

Thiel pulled in a hard breath. *Twenty?*

"What?" He cocked his head with a smirk. "Did you think I did not know? That I could not taste the spilled blood of my own brothers? That we could not smell the terror burning the air?" His arms drew back, his chest heaving. "And you would have me give his life to you? A life that is our right to wipe from Primar in penance for twenty Ematahri lives?"

"Cadeif, please—"

"Know your place!" he shouted, his visage marked with fury.

Thiel pulled in on herself, realizing her mistake too late. "Have mercy, Archon." Trembling, she noticed a soft glow to her right.

Haegan! She snapped her gaze there. His brow was knit tight. His lips taut. His hands . . .

No, please. Haegan, take the pill. Please take the pill. This . . . this could not happen. She could not let Haegan kill Cadeif and her friends here, even if they'd forced her to leave.

"You fled the safety of our warriors and now return for what? To bring us all down?"

"No," she cried. "I did not want to leave. You know better than anyone, Archon, that it was not of my choosing."

"It was mine," came a firm but quiet voice that shook not with anger but old age. A wobbly woman hobbled forward with her walking staff.

Thiel cupped her hand. "Cranna." She shook her head, overwhelmed by the memories. The heartache.

"I warned you not to return," Cranna said

Thiel fought the tears. "I didn't mean to. We . . ."

The glow brightened.

"He *must* be destroyed," Cranna said, pointing a gnarled finger. "Or he will destroy us all."

Through her tears, she looked at Haegan and finally found his eyes on hers. She touched two fingers to her lips, reminding him of the pill. *Take it*, she mouthed.

"She does not take this seriously," someone grumbled. "Even now she prefers the twig over her archon."

"Please," Thiel said, dragging her gaze back to Cadeif, who stood conferring with Cranna and—*O Abiassa, no*—Fut, the one warrior who'd hated her from the start because Cadeif had claimed her beneath the banner of Kedardokith.

"She should be hanged as we should have done when she stole into our camp years ago," Fut growled.

"That is neither here nor there," Cranna countered. "She is Etelide and an Ematahri by lifeoath with Cadeif. She must face the punishment for abandoning him and her people. For bringing this abomination before us."

"Truth," Fut said in his gravelly voice. "What purpose is there but to kill us all with this twig?"

Thiel turned her attention to Haegan again. Pleaded with her eyes for him to take the pill. But he shook his head, the glow and his anger brightening. If he did not—he may very well kill everyone.

What terrified her most is that he had no idea what was happening. Or how to stop it. In truth, neither did she, other than what had happened under his wrath previously. She would lose everyone here all over again. This time it would be permanent. He had to take the pill. She tilted her head, pleading through her tears.

"Bring her!" Cadeif shouted. "Remove the twig."

"No!" Haegan stepped forward.

Thiel's panic peaked. "Rigar, please!" She knew his heart. Knew the only way to end this. "Help me. Take it."

Grief-stricken, he hesitated. Stared at her. Then finally broke. His shoulders sagged. He lifted the pill to his mouth, and she nodded encouragement. He took it.

She closed her eyes in relief. At least she had prevented that much.

"Secure the twig!"

"No!" Hot tears coursed down her cheeks as the warriors closed in on Haegan. "Please! I beg your mercy, for myself and for my friends."

"*No!*" the answer boomed, deafening its own silent wake. "No, I will not give you his life! His life is mine to claim for my brothers he killed."

25

Waves of dizziness crashed over Haegan as two Ematahri warriors cuffed Thiel and trailed their leader to the back of the great pavilion. Haegan wrestled against Zoijan, whose powerful hands crushed his resistance with ease. Spots whirled in his vision and his hearing hollowed.

"No!" Even his own words sounded as if he'd been pushed under water. His limbs were leaden, heavy and cumbersome.

Darkness swallowed him, but his mind still fought. He could not see or hear, but he could feel. The thuds against his body. The punches he landed . . . or did he? In the thickness of his mind it grew impossible to discern.

His eyelids felt glued shut. He tried to open them, but his eyes rolled. He saw beams. Or were they bars?

Boarbeast den!

• • •

"Leave us," Cadeif said, flinging the archon cloak at Raleng, who caught it, shot Thiel a strong warning look but left without a word. Cadeif stripped off the cords of the archon. Coiled them up and tossed them to the side as he faced them. "Fut."

The tall warrior gave a stiff bow of his head then backed out. The flap dropped shut, a quiet snap, but it felt like a hammer's blow against her conscience. They had never been alone, even when she lived here. Cranna had forbidden it. Among other things.

"I have no power to protect your twig," Cadeif said, pacing before a small fire. "I cannot give you his life. Unless you can deny he killed Cerar's clan."

She couldn't. She'd been there, seen it with her own eyes. Except she hadn't realized so many had died in order for her and Haegan to escape.

"Do you understand the position you have put me in?"

Thiel didn't know what to say, how to act. When she'd been here last, he was her friend. He'd taught her to hunt. Taught her to track. To fight. To blend in.

Now, he was her archon. And not, all at once.

Fists at his side, he stared at her. "Do. You. Understand?"

Confusion riffled through her like the wind tugged at the tent. "I . . ."

"You claimed Kedardokith." Now he looked tormented. "In doing so, you have made his victories yours. His training yours. You are responsible for him."

"But you refused to release him to—"

"Because you are *mine*!" he roared, the veins in his temples bulging. "Mine!" He beat a fist against his chest. "Mine to teach, mine to train, mine to victor with, mine to l—" He pivoted away. His broad back heaved with ragged breaths. His shoulders sagged. "Mine to share failings."

Failings?

"My failings? But I made them. I—"

"We are one!" He slammed his fist against the table that sat to the side with maps and a wooden pitcher and cup. "Lifeoath!"

"Then . . . when I left . . ."

Palms on the table, emphasizing his large arms and shoulders, he closed his eyes and hung his head. "Seveired was forced to try me."

A wash of cold rushed through Thiel. "Try . . ." *Try to kill him.* "He's . . ." Seveired died forcing Cadeif to defend his honor.

"He lost." Cadeif straightened.

"He was like a father to you!" Pained for the price he'd paid because of her choice—one that had been forced, but still hers—she started forward.

"The choice was *mine*. Just as it was yours to walk out of the woods and leave me."

"That is not fair."

"No, it wasn't." His meaning, twisting her own words back on her, hung clear and sharp between them. "You left me to answer to the Ematahri. You left me shamed and dishonored among my brothers." His words morphed into a growl, his lip curling. "You were mine to defend, mine to lead—and you left!"

"Cadeif—"

He held up a hand. "It is not for us to argue the past." After a sidelong glance, he walked around the table so that its slats stretched between them. "What is for us to argue is your fate."

"My fate."

"You claimed Kedardokith with a second male. It's forbidden."

"I—how is it forbidden? I hadn't claimed it before. You claimed it."

He banged the table with his fist. "You are mine!" Again, he stood tall, daring her to challenge him.

And only this time did she understand. "I thought the lifeoath was protection."

"It is a bond between brothers—between men. But between a man and a woman . . ." He swallowed and looked away.

Heat spiraled through her as the realization finally washed through her. A realization that had not come in her two years spent here among the warriors. Not only had Cadeif claimed her as his protégé, but as much more. "But they forbade us!" Her mind tangled. Back then, she had wanted his love. Ached for it. "You sought permission as any warrior would do. Cranna and Severied refused."

This time, he sighed. "I cared not what they said, Etelide." His words were tender. Soft. "You were *mine*." This time, his fist rested over his heart.

"You would have defied the Counsel?"

He smirked. "I am Ematahri."

Grief crushed the breath from her lungs. "But they told me it was impossible, that I would bring destruction upon the nation." Her chest ached with the pain of that night, walking away, believing she'd never see him again. "I left to protect you. To free you—" A cry choked her words.

Cadeif rushed at her. Pulled her close. Cupped her face. "If you had not left, this night would not have come to be."

She collapsed, surrendering the tears she'd fought for so long. The ache for his laughter and for what the Counsel had forbidden. She clung to him, siphoning strength she no longer had. "I did not want to leave you. They told me . . . They said I should leave. Fut said you'd be released from the lifeoath. That it'd be as if you had never claimed me." She dug her fingers into her grip on him.

He arched back, his chest pushing her head up so that he could look at her. "He said this?"

She gave a nod.

Cadeif shook his head, but slowly the consternation gave way to something . . . more. Thiel's stomach knotted, remembering that look. She hesitated, thinking to resist him.

But his mouth was on hers. The years, the heartaches, the trials of the last month vanished beneath his warmth. He pulled her against his chest, deepening the kiss.

But reason, the purpose behind their moments alone, rushed back at her. She pulled away, pressing her forehead against his well-muscled chest.

He held her tight. Kissed the top of her head. "Your claim on my heart will never die. And I will deal with Fut for his lies. But Etelide—" He again held her face. "Look at me and tell me your twig did not do this—that he's not responsible for Cerar's people."

Thiel held his gaze, willing at this moment to do anything for Cadeif, as she had been when she lived among his people. Wanting, too, to save Haegan. But lying to Cadeif . . . would mean he would speak untruth, however innocently. And if discovered in that untruth, he would be condemned. Removed from his position as archon. Forcibly.

"If you do not, I must condemn him."

Thiel's resolution held fast.

"Do you understand what your silence means?"

She would not answer. Would not place that burden of guilt on Haegan. He hadn't meant to kill anyone. She had prodded him. Encouraged him to use the light. Or whatever it was.

"Because you declared to the nation that you are his protection, I must also condemn you." Cadeif's arm slid around her waist and tugged her tighter. "Do not make me do this, Etelide. You are my life."

Snugged against him, she rested her cheek against his chest. Listened to his heartbeat as she had done for so many moons. It was safe here, peaceful in a strange way. Wonderful in so many others. He had claimed her. Trained her. Loved her.

"Is it him, then?" His hand cradled the back of her head. "Is he the one Cranna foretold?"

At this, she found her voice but not her courage. "I . . . I fear he is, yes."

Cadeif released her and moved to the chair, his elbows on his knees as he bent forward, rubbing his scarred knuckles. "Then the Ematahri are at an end."

"Do not speak it!" She knelt before him, holding his hands. "You know these things are not clear. A future that has not come cannot be known."

"It is the present then, and we know futures *can* be known. Cranna said you would bring him here. That is why she and Seveired forbade our intimacy."

"What she saw could have different meanings." To believe she had brought destruction upon the people she'd grown to love shattered something deep inside Thiel.

Cadeif's fingers traced her jaw and lips. "Death has but one meaning, Etelide."

"Cranna never said *death*—she said 'an end.'"

"As always, you seek happy solutions where there are none."

"I seek peace."

He smiled softly on her. "You are an Ematahri by lifeoath. Peace will never be yours."

Thiel closed her eyes, feeling another rift opening in her heart. On the one side, Haegan, faith, and duty. And on the other, what might have been. "Perhaps you are right—I will never be at peace."

Cadeif leaned forward and kissed her again.

"Archon!" The slap of tent flaps severed the quiet moment. Raleng plowed in, his assessing eyes watching as Thiel stumbled off to the side.

Cadeif straightened, head high and his bearing authoritative.

"Something's wrong with the twig. He's not breathing."

26

"No!" Thiel darted forward, only to realize she did not know where Cadeif's men had taken Haegan. "He cannot die, Cadeif."

"His death releases us from—"

"You cannot let him die!"

A dark shadow passed over his handsome features. "You care so much for the twig?"

"He is . . . his father is very powerful. If something were to happen to him here, among the Ematahri, the consequences could be unfathomable."

Cadeif lifted his proud head. "The Ematahri—"

"Would not stand a chance against his father's armies."

Confusion knotted his expression. "*Armies?* More than one?" He frowned. "Who is the twig?"

"He has forbidden me from speaking it." But perhaps she should, to spare the people she once thrived among.

"There is only one king in the Nine with more than one army," Raleng said.

"Indeed," Cadeif muttered, once more studying her. His suspicions were growing. No doubt thinking unimaginable things of her.

"I did not say his father was a king," Thiel countered.

"Only a king commands armies." His words edged toward anger. "You trifle with words when the lives of my people are in your hands!"

A great shout went up from outside.

Cadeif rushed out, and Thiel followed, her heart thrumming. Torchlight littered the night and brightened the camp—but the congestion of bodies made it impossible to make their way through.

What was happening? Had Haegan died? Had he—

Oh no! What if he'd wiped out more people? What if his power or whatever it was, decimated these people, those she'd once called family? The thought shoved her ahead. She wove through the bodies. "Move!" She pushed harder, wishing Cadeif had taken the lead. Where had he gone? She glanced around and slowed . . .

Searched the faces. None were looking at her, but she saw the fear all the same. Fear? Since when? Ematahri were notorious for their boldness and unrelenting nature. Their reputation as ravagers had been well earned. But this crowd had all focused on something.

No, *someone.* Cadeif stood with the Raleng, Ruldan and Zoijan. The four were talking with another warrior, who motioned frantically behind him. There, coming up the main road of the encampment was a silver-cloaked man, a gleaming sword strapped to his back. He walked straight through the warriors, determined. Focused. He stopped before Cadeif.

Words drifted back to her through the crowd, like a teasing wind. Words like *deliverer, rider, lucent.*

Her mind turned the words over as she watched the fierce warriors, their faces etched in fear. Their fear and words coalesced into a terrible name: Lucent Rider. The Ematahri had dozens of stories about the faceless riders who delivered judgment on behalf of Abiassa. It did not matter if you believed in the Beneficent One. She sent her Deliverers regardless of faith or conviction.

A chill rippled through her. Why would a rider come? She had to get to him. Thiel grabbed the nearest warrior. "The boy, the one Cadeif calls Twig—where is he?"

The warrior scowled and wrested his arm free, taking steps closer to his archon and clearly putting his back to her.

If the Deliverer had come for Haegan, to stop his terrible power . . . She cornered a younger warrior. "If you want your people to live," she said, fierce in her pose and words, "tell me where to find the one they call Twig."

When his eyebrows started to come together and his lips tightened, she shoved her forearm into his throat and pinned him to a tent support.

"Now! Tell me now!"

Eyes wide, he froze. Pointed to the left. "S-stables."

Thiel sprinted through the settlement toward the stables. She had to get Haegan out of here. Must get the others to help. What if only Haegan were there? What if he were guarded?

Worries she would take care of later.

She lunged around the corner, aiming toward the structure of wood and branches that served as the horse shelter. As she raced up the foot path, she slowed at the sight that met her. A guard lay prostrate across the threshold. The gate hung crookedly from its hinges. Across the yard, she saw no more disarray. Haegan. He'd already attacked the guards?

No! She threw herself across the stable yard. Using his power would no doubt draw the Deliverer. He could harm no more warriors. She must get Haegan out before Cadeif could bring the Deliverer back here—which he would do, since the Lucent Riders had complete autonomy. No man or beast dared oppose one.

But as she drew closer, she spied more bodies on the ground. Dead? Quickly, she assessed them, but saw no wounds. Stealthily, she knelt beside one warrior and felt his neck. A pulse thumped steadily. Strange. Quietly, she relieved him of his weapon. If someone had done this, she might need to defend herself. And ferreting Haegan out of the camp would require one.

At the gate to the stables, she hesitated. It was quiet. Way too quiet. No nickering. Bleating. Nothing. Had the livestock and horses been freed?

She firmed her grip on the hilt and inched forward, nudging the gate inward. Great warmth swelled over her, stopping her. Forcing Thiel to swallow her fear and surprise as marble-like eyes of a horse gazed quietly back at her. Didn't blink. Head didn't swivel. She moved to another stall. Another set of brown eyes. What . . .?

The horses . . . they were there. In every stall. But they weren't moving. Impossible. The beasts were as restless as the warriors who rode them.

An eerie feeling traced her spine. She shivered involuntarily as she crept toward the open corral, where they would most likely keep

Haegan tied up. Where she'd last seen him. She inched forward, praying nothing crunched or gave her away. As she rounded the interior corner, she stopped. Sniffed a quick breath.

Praegur and Tokar lay to one side, unconscious. Yet again, no wounds.

Standing in the middle of the corral, Laertes stared at the door—at her.

She hurried forward, opening her mouth to call his name when she saw the massive dark form bending over something in a corner. Bending over Haegan!

Lucent Rider! Two—there must be two here. How else could she explain his sudden appearance and the bodies strewn like hay across the yard?

Frantically, she waved Laertes to her. He neither acknowledged her nor moved—only stared. Eyes wide. Frozen.

He would spoil her attack against the intruder. Again, she repeated her gesture. But the boy did not move. Thiel shifted forward, deliberately placing her foot so as not to make a sound as she reached for the ten-year-old. Her finger scraped against the rough fabric of his tunic, but a thrill of cold shot through her.

"He cannot hear you."

The deep, resonating voice vibrated through her chest and head like a resounding gong. Thiel jerked. The large form faced her. Draped head to toe in black, features shielded but by what she knew not for there was no fabric over his face, the Deliverer straightened to his full height. He seemed to grow and grow until she thought he'd knock against the beams.

Thiel took a step back.

"You gave him the pill."

She hauled in a breath. *How could he know that?* Fear tugged at her, willing her to move away.

"Nothing is hidden from Her."

He reads my thoughts!

"You are chosen as his protector." The Deliverer shifted aside, drawing away his cloak and revealing a sleeping Haegan. He seemed so peaceful. So handsome. So unaware. "Leave not his side until the time is fulfilled. Give him no potion." The Deliverer inclined his head. "Am I understood?"

Dragging her mind from the fog of his power and the incredible events, Thiel nodded.

"You sought to subdue what Abiassa has placed in him—"

"To protect him!"

He shifted and in that second, he seemed ready to attack. His right arm swung to the side, hand on a hilt she hadn't noticed before. He stared at her, and suddenly his eyes were there. So white and pale it seemed they had no irises. Power and intensity illuminated them, the glow so bright it reminded her of a smithy's kiln. "The potion *killed* him."

Killed? A gargled cry shot from her throat as Thiel's gaze darted to Haegan.

"He is restored. You must remove him from here."

"But the warriors. He's . . ." Surely he knew the men in this clan wanted Haegan dead. "They will kill me if I try to leave with him."

Once more his eyes receded into the black veil of nothingness. Though the black shadows hid him and she could not see his face, somehow she knew he smiled. Felt his amusement at her words. "He has them distracted. Go at once."

Her mind wrestled free of the fog. What? What was he smiling at?

That's when she realized there was no sound. Not only here in the stable, but . . . everywhere. Keeping her eyes on the Deliverer, she turned her head, listening. She glanced at Laertes, who remained frozen. She hesitantly moved to the archway that opened in the rear yard and revealed the camp. No movement. No chatter, shouts, laughter. Thiel dragged herself back to the Lucent Rider.

"Wake your friends. Take Haegan to the Falls. What happens there must happen. Remain at his side, steadfast warrior. He will need your sword and your counsel." The Deliverer turned away, and as he did, he vanished in a blur with the word, "Go!"

"But we're being hunted!" Instantly, in her mind's eye, a route through the forest streaked out, glowing as it progressed. Was it his way of saying that was the safest way?

At her feet came rustling. Praegur and Tokar pushed upright, confusion clouding their faces as they looked up and found her there.

"Wha—" Tokar jumped to his feet. He scowled at her. "Where did you come from? How did I get on the floor?"

"Ah!" Laertes shouted, stumbling forward. He stopped, as if he'd been cut short when the Deliverer had frozen him. He whirled in a circle, frantic. "Where . . .? I saw him! He—" He spun toward them, his chest bouncing up and down with excitement. "Did you see him?"

Praegur rustled his hair. "Easy."

Haegan groaned, a hand going to his head as he peeled himself from the stack of hay. Suddenly, he straightened. Glanced around, searching the room. Then his gaze darted to the ground, the stalls, and each of them. "What was in that pill? I feel like I died."

Ignoring the question and the guilt that came with it, Thiel knelt in front of him, her thoughts overwhelmed in a tangle of disbelief, worry, and astonishment. "We need to leave." She touched his leg, surprised at the thrumming warmth that poured off him. "Are you well enough?"

His gaze hit hers. "I feel"—he shook his head, disbelief in his blue eyes—"stronger than ever." Then he frowned. "A second ago, everything ached. What was in that pill you told me to take?"

"Later," she muttered. He lived. Explanations could wait. She hooked a hand beneath his arm. "We need to leave. Now."

"But we don't have any supplies," Praegur said.

"And I doubt those warriors are going to let you go anywhere with him," Tokar said. "They want him strung up and dangling from a tree."

Thiel pushed them toward the gate and opened it. "We have our lives. That's all we need right now."

"But—"

She spun. "If you do not move, we will not have that!"

"Ain't nobody gonna answer my question?" Laertes demanded, wagging his hands. "Did anybody else see what I sawed?"

Thiel gave him a gentle push into the woods, remaining at Haegan's side.

"There you go again," Tokar said. "Making up wild tales to cover your nightmares."

"I know what I sawed."

"*Saw.*"

· · ·

Captive. Behind bars the Auspex sits caged in corporeal form to the unbending general, and in mind and spirit to the will of Sirdar. Never his own, he watches. Understands. Within the person who existed before being tethered to darkness. Though a glimmer of his old self exists within the frail frame, he can no more bring about his own designs than he can speak his own thoughts.

Even now, he sits, watching.

In walks Onerid, adorned in battle dress. The high, thick collar molded from the hide of a boarbeast protects his neck from a death blow. His long red coat that marks him as the right hand of the High Lord Commander covers much of the black and silver breastplate that bears the image of Sirdar with daggers of fire shooting out like a thick, flowing mane. He cuts an impressive, forbidding figure.

Tossing down a pen, Poired slumps against his richly carved chair, the blood-red velvet fabric silhouetting his broad shoulders. "Time already?"

Onerid nods in deference to his commander. "Think of it as a break from the tedium."

"From one tedium to another." Swiping a hand over his bearded face does nothing to wipe away the frustration. "What is the point?"

"It's a psychological battle." Onerid swings the silvery helmet to the right and tucks it beneath his other arm.

"Against whom? Me?" Poired pushes up from his chair and heaves a sigh. He detests the ritualistic standoff.

The great one struggles to restrain himself. His restlessness has become apparent to all who have given witness to his comings and goings. Though he does not sit in a steel cage as the Auspex does, Poired is caged nonetheless. His movements are caged. His thoughts caged within a fortress of hatred and a thirst for Celahar blood. A thirst fueled by Sirdar's venom coursing through his veins. The curse of his power lay in the little-known truth that he could not stray from Sirdar's Eye or Voice. He was as dependent on his host as a person is on the organ thumping in his chest.

"The battle *is* psychological—against me. They sit up there in their high places and mock me," he growls loudly. "The battle would be won if he would release me!" Poired snatches his greaves from his servant. He sits, his strong frame defiant of the years he abused it.

"My lord commander." A private guard enters and goes to a knee, knowing not to speak until granted permission, lest he end up staining the ground with his blood. "A messenger from Hetaera."

Poired glares at the intrusion, then waves off the servant, no doubt glad for the delay in sitting on his mount for the next three hours. He moves to his desk and drops onto the cushioned seat. "Bring the messenger."

The sentry steps out, never showing his back to his commander, then reaches to the side. He hauls in a boy garbed in all black. Eyes wide, face pale, the newcomer is as terrified of the commander as anyone with common sense would be.

"Speak," Poired growls.

The sentry nudges the boy, who stumbles forward. "Your Grace—"

"I am no king, boy." Agitation and meanness are the hallmark of the great military leader. "No need for titles since you are not owed to me. Get on with your news."

"Y-yes, High Lord Commander. Word comes from my master. He says the people continue as normal, confident the fires of Zaethien will burn, and the"—his gaze travels the tent, replete with armor and weapons—"Tharqnis armies will remain south."

"As planned," Onerid says with a satisfied smirk.

"They are but a bunch of fattened cows, comfortable in their lives." Poired snorts and flings a paper to the side of his desk. "It amazes me how blind and complacent people are until you step on their necks."

"Apathy and selfishness give us more room than fear."

"Weak, putrid . . ." Poired flicks a finger at the sentry. "You're still in my tent, boy."

With a half-bow, the boy wrings his hands. "S-sorry, sir. I just . . . I get scared when I see uniforms." He dusts brown hair from his eyes. "I mean, not scared the way I was when I had to get past the Jujak, but here—all these warriors. I could wet myself!"

Poired stands, seeing in the boy something he has not seen in many. Bravery. He lifts an apple from the sideboard and hefts it in his hand. "You saw Jujak?" His mood is less cordial now. "In Hetaera."

"Oh, no. They wasn't in the city." The boy has locked onto the fruit, hunger numbing his brain. "Were it not for the fires, I would've run straight through their camp with them sitting there in their fancy uniforms and all. But it's a good thing I'm watchful. My master tells me I'm quick and quiet, which is why he sends me here."

"Where, boy?" With a gentle move, he places the apple in the boy's palm.

Wide-eyed wonder glosses the boy's eyes at the treat he now holds. But confusion knots the boy's gaze. "Where? Here, sir. To you."

"No," Poired says, squeezing the boy's hands in his own. "Where were the royal guard, the Jujak?"

"In the hills. Outside the city." He whimpers, pain crushing his small fingers. "Please, High Lord Commander—my hands."

With a thrust that sends the boy spiraling backward out of the tent, Poired frowns. He ambles back to his seat, fingers tracing the desk, and then looks to Onerid. "*What* are Zireli's lackeys doing in Hetaera?"

"Feckless cowards—probably fled the city when we first razed the outer villages. They are good, but they're not the Maereni." Onerid lowers himself to the other chair by the fire pit.

With a slow nod, Poired considers his general's suggestion. Then his face clears and hardens. "No," he says slowly with narrowed eyes. "The boy said they were in uniform. If they were hiding, they would've shed those cloaks before leaving Seultrie." His expression once again clouds.

Onerid leans forward, oozing intensity. "Think you Zireli has fled the capital?"

"No," Poired mutters, leaning back in his chair, his gaze lost in thought. "I saw him watching from the balcony of his chambers." He snorts. "Thinking to defy me."

"Then the queen or princess?"

"Adrroania would never leave Zireli—or her daughter. Zireli is foolish enough to believe himself untouchable in that fire-walled fortress."

"Who then? The prince?"

"The cripple?" With a barked laugh, the high lord commander dismisses the idea. "I've seen the light in the high tower. Still relegated to isolation and a dull existence with an addled accelerant. I think not."

"Then . . . why send the Jujak to Hetaera? Could he have learned of our plans?"

Poired sits still and silent for several long minutes. "Bring the Iteverians."

Onerid hesitates for only a second before leaving Poired with his tumbling thoughts. The worry hangs off him like an ill-fitted tunic. He remains motionless until his general returns. "Trale and Astadia Kath, sir."

Behind him stand a plain young man and woman. Wearing belted green tunics that drape to their shins, they go to a knee as one and incline their auburn heads, long hair twisted and secured down their spines.

"You summoned us," the young man says as they rise effortlessly to their feet.

"How do you like it here, Trale?"

The young man seems to glare, but that would be foolish. "You'll forgive us, sir, but we find it too hot and arid." His green eyes go to the woman. "We would wish for a greener climate."

"Good. Perfect." Poired stood. "Go to Hetaera."

"Hetaera." Agitation coats the way Trale speaks the name of the great city.

"Zireli's Jujak are there. Find out why and return."

Trale does not move or comply. It is obvious to all who know them that the two long for their home, Iteveria, and the lush woods and cliffs overlooking the Nydessan Sea. To be sent farther inland, toward the Sanctuary . . . it is an affront to all they hold dear. "Sir, you promised—"

The young woman stiffens suddenly, gasping for air. She clutches at her throat as if that can release the fiery hold on her. Distress lines her delicate, elegant features.

Fury ruptures the quiet veil over Trale. He lunges for Poired, but the woman's hand stills him, her other scratching at her neck as she pleads with glassy eyes for Trale not to confront Poired. She gasps, her face reddening.

Though power roils through him and skill unmatched in the realms rests with his touch, Trale stops short. Draws up his shoulders, his green eyes, and snaps a modicum of acquiescence to the high lord commander. "Because you command us."

27

The dream wouldn't leave him. In the days following their escape from the Ematahri camp—surprisingly uncontested—the words consumed his thoughts. Unfathomable words, saturating his mind as he trod over rocky knolls and up steep inclines. Those words and the pill. He'd felt himself falling into a bottomless pit after swallowing it. Had Thiel tried to kill him? Could he trust her after that? He didn't want to, but she seemed to know what she was doing. And staying with the Ematahri would not be good for his health. That much he knew. So, for now, he'd hike, camp, and keep watch. He'd follow her direction.

They trekked single file to hide their numbers and because the path often made it impossible to pass in pairs. Thiel set a relentless clip, stopping for only a few hours each night, leaving no time or energy for conversation. Even when darkness hung like a thick blanket, she moved on for hours as if she had a torch. Which she didn't. In the days since leaving the Ematahri camp, she had spoken little except to give orders and tell them to hurry.

As darkness settled at the end of the eighth day, tempers ran short.

"It's night," Laertes whined. "We ought ta be sleepin'. Like what normal people do."

"It's late," Tokar said. "He's right that we should rest."

"No." Unrelenting, she maintained her pace. "We have to get to the Great Falls."

Tokar huffed. "It's been days since we left the Ematahri. No one's following. We need a break."

"We must get to Hetaera."

Laertes tripped. Pitched forward. Haegan shifted to avoid stumbling on top of him. The ten-year-old grumbled but picked himself back up.

"Rest would do us well, Thiel." Haegan felt bad for countering her, but they all needed to recover. "One decent night's sleep."

With a huff, she glanced up the hill, as if she could see. Which she couldn't because the trees blocked the moonslight and nightfall blanketed the rocky path. "Fine. There's a cave ahead. We'll rest for a while inside."

"And how do you know that?" Tokar asked. "And why do you listen to Twig but not us?"

"Just move." Up around another turn, then a dozen paces farther and she turned off the beaten path. Soft, plush grass, slick from the damp air, softened their steps as Thiel hiked to a small clearing. "Here," she said, squatting beside what looked to be an ordinary boulder. "In."

On all fours, Laertes peered not around the boulder, but under it. A second later, his shadowed form disappeared beneath the earth. "Whoa!" he called, his voice echoing. "Watch yerself."

"You slide down," Thiel explained. "Then it widens." She met Haegan's gaze. "You next."

He tucked himself into the thin sliver of space and felt gravity pull him. He slid and his feet thudded against a rock. He blinked but saw nothing. The *scrriiitch* and thud of others descending pushed him backward, but he was afraid to move much more, concerned there might be another drop-off.

A spark hissed as a flame flared to life and chased darkness from the cave. Tokar waved the torch around, squinting past its brightness to their surroundings.

"Where'd you get that?" Laertes asked.

"In the corner." Tokar motioned toward a small pile of torches. "Now, bed down."

"Where's Thiel?" Haegan peered up at the pale light at the opening of the cave.

"At the entrance." Praegur nodded to the top even as he lowered himself against a wall.

A second later, Thiel whooshed down, maneuvering as if she'd been here before. As if she knew this cave. "Dawn comes early, so sleep." She knelt in a corner and reached beneath a stone ledge. She tugged out a pack and grinned.

"You've been here before." It seemed dumb to state the obvious, but Haegan couldn't not mention it.

"The first time I left the Ematahri, I camped here for a few days."

"And met me." Tokar grinned. "The cave is on the path from Hetaera. If you know where it is . . ."

"Then are we at risk of being discovered?"

Thiel tugged the pack of supplies to the side. "Not at this hour. Those who would seek shelter would've done so hours ago." After unfolding a twine-wrapped package, she handed out jerky.

"Why'd you leave this?" Haegan accepted the food.

"I didn't. Well, not this exactly. It's a custom to leave provisions, a welcome gift for those hard on their luck."

"But if we take it . . ."

She shrugged. "We leave some. It's a tradition."

"Some say if you don't," Tokar said, "the mountain won't let you pass."

"Deliverer!" Laertes's voice filled with awe. "What if he's tracking us?"

"Oh, leave off!" Tokar gave him a playful shove. "You and your creatures and stalkers. I thought you'd dropped it."

"I saw him!"

"Enough. Rest. We leave whether you have slept or not," Thiel said.

It was enough motivation for Haegan to curl onto his side, facing the stone wall. After too many years spent in a tower aching to be free, he suddenly yearned for that solitude. *Needed* it. There were too many faces and voices in the Ematahri camp. Too many voices taunting him in his dreams. A forbidding shadow filled his mind. Though the shadowy form was pitch black, Haegan remembered the hand that had reached from the ebony void and touched him.

A slight breeze stirred near his legs. He peered down the length of his body. Thiel had positioned herself against the wall by his boots.

She was looking down, then at him as she extended her hand. "You didn't eat."

As if he'd trust her to feed him anything ever again. "Not hungry."

"I beg your mercy," she whispered, lowering her head again.

"Why'd you give me the pill? Were you trying to poison me?"

"No!" She sighed, then shifted, moving around him so that she sat by his head. "Haegan, you have a gift that—"

"I have *no* gift!" He sat up, irritated. "Kaelyria has the gift." He adjusted, looking away from her. Away from the truth of his existence. "I am cursed. Have been since someone poisoned me as a boy." His upbringing and training forbade him from speaking his full mind. It would be rude. "Why did you give me the pill?"

"I know Cadeif and his people. Their laws. I knew if they believed you killed one of their clan, the only price they would accept was a blood price."

"*My* blood."

She nodded. "And mine, since I claimed Kedardokith. And they are . . . I see them as my people as much as I do my own birth family." With a sigh, she folded her arms. "The Ematahri are . . . Most people do not understand their ways. I knew things would grow . . . tense." Rolling her neck toward him, she once again met his gaze. "And your anger arouses whatever is in you, the light. And people die. I could not let that happen. Not to Cadeif or the others."

It ate at him that she had a fondness for this leader of the ravagers who apparently had quite a few laws that he'd broken. "You believe I killed the warriors."

Sadness clung to her brown eyes. "I *watched* you kill them, Haegan. With . . . words." She shook her head. "I cannot explain it, but you did."

Guilt snapped his head down. "No." He ground his teeth. "You are wrong. It . . . I couldn't." He shook his head. "If you believe I did this, and if you truly see the Ematahri as your own people, then it makes sense that you tried to kill me." It was hard to accept. Bitterly hard. And it crushed him that she wanted him dead.

"I've never sought your life," Thiel said, her words hard. "I don't know if the pill reacted with something in you, or if the healer intentionally created a deadly concoction, but I would never try to kill you. I asked her for something to make you sleep. That's all."

"Why?" He turned to her. "Why not kill me? You clearly have a past with the archon. He said you were his, so why would you not want to kill me?" He shoved a hand through his hair. "I would!"

She touched his arm. "Shh, the others."

Haegan tamped down his frustration and confusion. "I don't know what's happening to me. I just want to go lie in that stupid bed in the tower and listen to the droning of an old accelerant." With a snort, he drew his legs up. "Every night, I wished to be free of that tower and Gwogh's endless lectures. Now, I'd give my life to be back there. To have things as they were."

"Would you?" Her soft question pulled at him. "There are times I wish I was with my family, if I am truthful." She leaned her head back against the stone. "I wish I . . ."

Haegan watched her, waiting for Thiel to finish. Studying the lines of her face, the soft caress of the torchlight making her skin appear like honey. Beneath the stroke of the flame, her brown eyes were once more amber. Even with her impish haircut, Kiethiel was beautiful. "You wish what?" He wanted to hear her longings. Her desires.

She flinched and straightened, sighing. "Nothing." She adjusted again. "You should rest."

Haegan thought of his dreams, of the dark form . . . touching him . . . the howling of some great wind or beast. *What is happening to me?* He looked at his hands, turning them over. Thiel had said they glowed. His palms looked normal. Lines etched into the soft flesh like anyone else's.

Anger. She'd seen it when he'd been angry.

And when he felt those he cared about were in danger.

I have killed.

He coiled his hands into fists and swallowed hard. What *was* happening to him? Why had Abiassa allowed this? He just wanted to go home. To Kaelyria. His only friend these last ten years. But if he didn't get to the waterfalls . . .

A light touch rested on his hands. Haegan blinked and found Thiel's delicate fingers on his. "We'll figure it out." Amber eyes came to his. "Together."

A dribbling noise followed by a *tink-tink-tink* seemed to scream through the cave.

"Oh, are we going to talk about the obvious?" Tokar asked. "How he—"

"Shh!" Thiel hopped to her feet. "Someone's outside. "Douse the torch."

"Why—"

"Do it!" She moved toward the incline that had swept them into the cave.

A dull light broke through.

A man tumbled down the ramp, arms and legs akimbo. *"Augh!"* He flopped at Thiel's feet like a fish out of water. She dropped on him without hesitation. To Haegan's surprise, the torchlight flared against the blade of a dagger Thiel held to the intruder's throat. Her knee pressed to his chest.

Tokar came forward with sword and torch.

"Wait wait wait!" Messy black hair draped over the man's face as he held up his hands. "I mean no harm to any of you."

"What are you doing here?" Thiel demanded.

"I . . ." Hesitation grasped at the air as the man took in the group. "I came to warn you."

Jaw jutted, Thiel leaned down, applying pressure to blade. "How did you know we were here?"

"Warn us about what?" Tokar asked.

The man froze, his chin tilted up and away from her dagger. "Jujak." He gave a breathy laugh. "Easier to talk without fearing I'll slit my own throat."

Thiel glared and lifted the blade—only a fraction. "How did you know we were here?"

"I saw you on the path, watched you hide here."

"Nobody saw us," Thiel growled.

"Right," the man said. "I just randomly figured out five people were hiding in a cave that I didn't know existed nearly a league outside Hetaera proper."

"Let him up." Haegan stood over the man, taking in the stringy black hair, the clothes that didn't fit. He'd tumbled into the cave . . .

"An' what—let him rip our hearts out?" Laertes asked.

Haegan extended a hand and helped the man to his feet. Watched as he brushed himself off. "You made a lot of noise out there." Too much noise for someone slinking around. He'd tried to warn them of his approach.

Wary brown eyes came to his. Then flicked away.

"Amazing fall through a hole without getting injured."

The man sighed, accepting defeat. "I didn't want to advertise your location but also didn't want to get killed."

Haegan nodded. "You have a name?"

"Do you?"

Arm extended, Haegan offered his hand. "Rigar."

Clapping his forearm, the man gave a firm shake. "Drracien."

"Where are you from, Drracien?"

"Hold up—this ain't no meet and greetin'. He's trouble right there. Look at his boots!" Laertes stabbed a finger at the man's leather footwear. "Them right there are expensive. If he ain't stole 'em, then I say he's working with the Jujak, not warning us against them."

"Laertes is right," Tokar said. "You're not adding up."

Drracien held up his hands. "Fair enough. I'm running from something, just like you." He shrugged. "But I am no danger. And yes—there is a unit of Jujak within a half league of this cave."

"Are you wanted by the law?" Haegan asked.

Drracien met his gaze. Breathed. "No."

But he was wanted by someone else?

"I only seek shelter," Drracien said as his gaze lingered on Thiel—too long for Haegan's comfort. "And some company. That's all."

Something sparked in her eyes. "Sorry, not interested. Back out the hole you go," she snapped, pointing to the incline.

"I can help you."

Arms folded, Thiel flared her nostrils. "No."

Haegan asked, "How?"

Drracien held her gaze again—far too long and too hood-eyed. Haegan shifted and cleared his throat as he broke the newcomer's line of sight.

The man smirked. Swept a hand toward Tokar. The torch flickered then extinguished.

"Hey!" Tokar complained.

Soft and dull, a flame grew . . . directly in front of Thiel, the effect bathing her cheeks in a warm hue. So beautiful. But where was the flame coming from?

She gasped and stepped back. But thumped into Drracien, who had somehow moved behind her, his arm extended around her. The glow emanated from him!

"Incipient!" Tokar growled.

Something in Drracien's expression darkened. He held out his right hand toward Tokar, who jumped and rubbed his backside. "I am no incipient."

Haegan's thoughts pulsed with the excitement of what had happened. "But you can wield the Flames."

"As you see." Drracien moved away from Thiel. "And I'd say your group could use some protection."

"Flames are designed not for thuggery, but for the Pro—"

"—tection of Abiassa's children and the dissemination of Her will." Waving a hand, Drracien sighed heavily. "Would you have me recite the First Year's Tenets, the Guidings of Wielding, or the Creed of Hetaera the First, who outlawed use of the Flames by anyone other than an officially trained accelerant?" His dark brows wagged beneath a thick mop of hair. He turned a circle and held out his hands. "Or would you challenge me?"

"Enough!" Thiel stomped forward, her shoulders squared and the dagger still in hand. "You pushed your way into our shelter. It is not your place to mock us or make demands."

Though he looked and behaved older, as Drracien smiled at Thiel, it became clear that he was barely a man. No more than twenty or so cycles. And smart enough to recognize when he was not the one in control. Drracien inclined his head toward Thiel. "Right you are, mi'lady." He held out his hands again.

Haegan stepped away.

Drracien snorted. "How many times must I say I mean you no harm?"

"Many more times, accelerant." Thiel's eyes flared with anger. "Until we are satisfied."

He smiled. Broadly. "Then I am to stay. How can I satisfy you if I must leave?"

Would she allow him to remain with them? And for how long? Something in Haegan knotted at the thought of this accelerant moving in. He was too much like his father—handsome, smooth-spoken, powerful. Besides, his ability to wield could expose them.

Yet, when Thiel glided toward Haegan, holding his gaze, he felt sweet relief. And maybe a little smug satisfaction that she placed herself with him and not the newcomer. "On a condition."

"Name it."

"Supplies." Thiel folded her arms. "We ran out of most everything two days ago."

Laughing, Drracien sat against the incline and held his arms out. "As you see, I am empty handed, so I fail you already, mi'lady."

"*Get* supplies for us."

His eyebrows winged up beneath the fringe of dark hair. "And what makes you think I can get supplies for you?"

"The very boots that betrayed you. They are worn, but not from an arduous journey across the territories." Thiel glanced at Haegan. "The boots are from a cobbler in Hetaera. I recognized the mark on your sole when you fell. Your clothes are not your own—the pants too short. The shirt too tight. I'd suggest you've only recently found yourself in this situation and those clothes."

He pushed to his feet. "Perhaps my muscles are simply too large for the tunic."

"Your ego too large for it, more like," Tokar muttered.

"Supplies." Her insistence flared as she stood with her back to Haegan and arms crossed. "Find us enough supplies to make it to the Great Falls and you can remain."

"Falls!" Drracien coughed. "You jest. The routes are littered with disease-riddled believers, refugees, but more importantly—Jujak!"

Haegan shot a nervous look at the others but said nothing, unwilling to give away his secret.

"Remember, Drracien," Thiel said. "You wanted to be with us. Not the other way around. We don't need you."

"Apparently you do," he countered. When she opened her mouth, he held up a hand. "I'll go. But I want him"—he stabbed a finger toward Haegan—"to come with me."

"No," Haegan said.

"Why would you want him?" Tokar asked. "He's—"

"Because mi'lady looks to him when she speaks, and that speaks of his importance. I want reassurance that when I return you'll be here." He grinned. "I'd wager she won't leave without him."

"Why do you want to be with us? What's in it for you?" Praegur asked.

"Let's just say one man is missed in a crowd."

"So, you *are* hiding," Haegan said.

Dark eyes probed him. "Aren't we all?"

"Rigar's not going with you," Thiel said with finality.

"Him, or no supplies." Drracien crossed his arms over his chest. "I can get the supplies and be back in an hour, but I can't carry them on my own. And I want him."

"No."

"I'll go."

Thiel tucked her chin, heaving a frustrated sigh. "I would talk to you." She arched an eyebrow at him, motioning him toward the back of the cave. Back to the others, she lowered her head as Haegan inched between her and the cave wall. "We don't know him."

"No," Haegan said, eyeing the newcomer. "But he's skilled."

"*Too* skilled. I find it highly suspect that he singled you out. What if he's working with the Jujak? What if they hired him to lure you into the open? He's an *accelerant*, just like your father."

Haegan snapped his gaze back to her. "Yes, exactly. If his goal was to deliver me to the Jujak, he could spark me and knock me out. Knock us all out." With a shake of his head, he watched the man, who stared back unabashedly. "I don't know his game, but it's not about any of us."

"You can't know that."

"Mayhap, but neither can we know he has ill intent." Haegan smiled. "Be at peace, Thiel. We'll be in and out."

"What if someone recognizes you in the city?"

At that he snorted a laugh. "The crippled son of the Fire King?" he whispered. "Nobody even knows what I look like. I was put in the tower and forgotten." Though he patted her shoulder, Haegan found little comfort in his own words. And he didn't like her scowl. Because Thiel had a great mind for strategy and predicting trouble. "What's wrong?"

She shifted on her feet. "I'm not supposed to leave you."

He blinked. "Why? Who says you can't?"

She touched her forehead. "That's not—I meant—it's dangerous!"

"Hey, lovebirds."

Haegan angled back toward the others, feeling the heat of embarrassment rising up his neck.

"Daylight's coming and with it, plenty of elite fighters."

Thiel widened her eyes as if to say, "See?"

"Rest easy, Thiel. It's the only way to get what we need. All will be well," Haegan said to her, then started forward. "Let's hurry."

28

Making his way through the city felt a lot like drowning in a sea of people. A life of hiding from the citizenry and now an existence spent on a fuse, hunters breathing down his neck, left Haegan with little hope of surviving the day and crowds, let alone making it to the Great Falls. But he moved as casually as he could muster in the wake of the all-too-at-ease Drracien. In the four hours since entering the city, the accelerant had procured blankets, food items, and had a hint on the loan of horses—if they could find a certain gambler with a debt.

"You know the city and her people well," Haegan muttered as they pressed through a passel of people in a narrow alley.

Drracien smiled and patted someone on the shoulder but did not respond to Haegan's comment. They banked right, and a stench that reminded Haegan of the boarbeast muarshtait coiled around his nose. A few more steps, and he spotted a small pen of pigs snorting and squealing as their owner bargained with a man in a white apron who stood in front of a shop window boasting hams, sausages, even a side of beef. Drracien edged over to the shop and raised a hand. The burly butcher acknowledged him, and the accelerant lifted a bundle of jerky hanging on a pole. Without a word, he nodded and kept moving.

Stupefied, Haegan glanced back to the butcher, who had returned to his haggling. When he turned again, Haegan found himself alone.

A cold feeling washed over him as he searched the crowded market for the accelerant. He checked the cobbled road to the other shops. Dozens of citizens, but no black-headed, scraggly accelerant-in-hiding.

With a rush like ice water flooding his veins, Haegan pushed through the Hetaerans, glancing at faces as if rifling through a box of clothes. But as he slogged through the crowds, he grew disoriented, unable to see the sun for the buildings that huddled against his efforts. He stopped and once more searched for Drracien.

A woman bumped into his back. "Watch where you're going, love," she muttered as she came around, adjusting the large sack of produce to the other hip.

"I beg your mercy." He took a step back. There came a sharp thud between his shoulder blades.

"Oy! Beg off!" The gruff tone matched the foul breath of a burly man with a length of wood over his shoulder—the very length that had no doubt rammed into Haegan's spine.

"Mercy." Haegan shifted to the side.

A small girl shrieked as if he'd run her through. "Owww!"

"Mercy," he said touching her shoulder to reassure her.

"Get your hands off my child!" A portly woman swung a lumpy sack of something at Haegan. It thudded against his arm.

"Mercy. I meant no harm." Frustration coiled around him, with a heaping dose of suffocation. Too many people. Too many buildings. "The gate," he breathed, warning himself to calm and find an exit to remove himself immediately. This absurd plan to follow the accelerant into the city had been an elaborate ruse. He'd been duped. Lured. Abandoned again.

He whirled and searched the faces for some compassion—or at the least, wariness. He spied a young girl who blushed when he smiled at her. "I beg your pardon. The gate—which way to the gate?"

The older woman whose child he'd nearly toppled, stepped in between them. Sprigs of gray hair stuck out of a loose bun atop her head. She laughed. "Which one?"

More than one gate? "Uh . . . the closest one."

Skeptical eyes assessed him. "That'd be the Sheep Gate, straight that way. But you don't want to go there, love, unless you plan to graze on rocky pastures." Her words elicited a trickle of laughter from the crowd.

Blazes. He was drawing the very attention he wanted to avoid. "Thank you," he mumbled and started left.

"No, love," she said. "Go on the other way. You'll 'ave better luck there."

Haegan ignored her, spotting an opening in the sea of bodies and aiming for it.

"Fine, but don't go asking for help if you ain't gonna take it," her words chased him.

The clamor, the voices, the breathing, the smells closed in on him, tightening around his chest and constricting with every step. He needed air, needed to breathe. He'd do anything now for that lonely tower with its dampness warded off by the distinct scent of searage in the fireplace, and the isolation. Blessed isolation!

And Gwogh.

He almost laughed at the thought of his aged tutor. What would he think of Haegan wandering the largest city in the Nine? What would he say of the encounter with the Ematahri? Oh, the anger of the accelerant. He'd be outraged at the treatment Haegan had received.

Or perhaps he'd say Haegan deserved it for caving to Kaelyria's begging. For not being strong and following his convictions. It had been wrong. He'd known that. But her pleading had undone him.

Kaelyria. Heaviness tugged at him. What was she doing now?

A question without thought. She was prisoner in a bed, that's what she was doing. And he was wasting his time here. Gathering supplies.

He should just head out. Return to the cave.

So . . . the Sheep Gate.

Halfway down the street and slightly to the right, he saw shaggy black hair. Drracien? In order to see better, Haegan had to shift. But that hair—it was no doubt the accelerant. He was there talking to someone. Not just talking. *Laughing.* Then like a shot, the accelerant's expression changed, he slapped the man on the shoulder, and turned to his left, weaving away through a small family group.

Haegan started in that direction to catch up with the rogue. But where had he gone now? What had sent him scurrying?

Red smeared into the drab market. A pair of sentinels, the official police of the Sanctuary, strolled past, talking to each other. Were they the reason Drracien fled? Why was an accelerant fleeing his own Brethren?

Hurrying didn't provide an answer or a better view. Instead, it only served to move Haegan farther from his point of escape.

But . . . Drracien! Agitation tugged at Haegan. Why had he agreed to come, trusted the rogue? The sentinels were closer. He had no doubt his father-king would have every accelerant looking for him, including these two, though they may not know who he was or why the king wanted him.

Haegan slid out of view of the sentinels, filled with sudden paranoia. He knew they didn't have powers other than the gift to wield the Flames, but how many times had he wondered if Gwogh could read minds for the way he reprimanded unspoken thoughts and chided Haegan's willful reluctance?

Nudging along a small child who seemed to take a fascination with him, Haegan searched the family group. The others. Drracien in a blink had managed again to vanish.

How does he do that?

Forget the impudent man. Haegan had to get out of here. Already he'd drawn dubious attention to himself, and now sentinels were nearby. The old woman said the gate was straight ahead. Determination pushed him in that direction, his focus solely on—

A green-clad figure stepped into his path.

Haegan drew up short. Jujak!

A captain stood tall and forbidding, staring around the crowd, two officers at his side.

Heart in his throat, Haegan diverted to a side alley. He rushed through the anemic space, walls nearly touching his shoulders.

"Stop!"

The command propelled him faster, his ears tuned to the commotion that erupted behind him in shouts and screams. Running as fast as his legs would carry him, Haegan spotted an obstacle ahead. He jumped over it and crashed into the wall. A blaze of heat scored his elbow, but he pushed on.

Behind him a familiar whoosh and hiss warned him that the sentinels may be helping the Jujak. A woman stepped out of a small doorway. Right into Haegan's path.

He whipped around her, mumbling apologies when she lurched with a yelp. He rounded another corner and shot up the wider road, grateful for a little more room to breathe and a lot more distance between himself and the Jujak.

Getting lost in a crowd had never been so hard. It seemed as if his presence repelled the clusters of people. Each time he moved toward one, they broke up. He went to the right, where a man in a dark cloak stood talking with a handful of others. Businessmen. When he stepped closer, the man glowered and turned away.

In a corner, people his age huddled, talking quietly. After a glance back and seeing neither red cloaks nor green uniforms, he melted into the group. A girl spoke of the tedious hours spent at the tavern serving men with large bellies and appetites—and not just for food. The thought turned Haegan's stomach.

"I don't think you should stay here," a soft whisper came at his ear.

Haegan met a pair of murky brown eyes.

The girl shifted her gaze to something behind him. "They're after you, aye?"

Though he said nothing, Haegan knew she understood his dilemma.

"Go on in through the door," she muttered, nodding to her left. "Up the stairs. There's a window you can climb through at the back. But don't be botherin' no one, or I'll send them up after you myself."

"Thank you," Haegan breathed as he tucked his head and stepped back. He leaned into the door and slipped into darkness. He hesitated for a second, focusing on a long bright spot up and to his right. The window waited atop two flights of steps. He scurried up the first, letting the rail guide him.

A door opened straight ahead. A robed woman emerged, clinging to the arm of a man. Haegan's mind awakened to just exactly where he'd taken refuge—a brothel. Sparks! He ducked and hurried up the next flight, feeling humiliation where there was none. Perhaps for the girl. She didn't look any older than Kaelyria.

At the window, he knelt and eased it up. An iron landing welcomed him into the midafternoon sun. He hustled down the stairs, then hopped from the four-foot dead space. Scurrying through the back alleys and wandering for what felt like hours, he headed away from the main market, deeper into residences.

Quiet draped the dwellings in relative peace, the chaos of the market a distant thrum. Haegan folded himself into the shadow of a crooked tree behind a half-dozen one-story dwellings with a communal yard. He pulled his knees to his chest and wrapped his arms around them. Mouth pressed to his arm, he sat, willing the Jujak back into the hills. Away from the city. Away from him. *Return to Zaethien.*

Rest. He just wanted to rest.

He sniffed at the thought. The last four years, he'd wailed about how he wanted adventure, to be out of the tower, to walk with other Seultrians. To see cities and meet the violent Ematahri. Run missions with the Raeng.

He'd been naïve and foolish.

Mayhap he was even now, believing that sitting beneath a mauri tree would save him. But still, he could neither gather the courage to move nor the fear to flee. So he sat. And thought. Of Kaelyria. His parents. Gwogh.

Thiel.

Was she worried about him? Or mayhap she'd given up on him, thinking he was captured. It had been hours, after all, since he'd let Drracien lure him into the city. Had Tokar convinced her to leave without him? He'd made no bones about abandoning him if Haegan brought more trouble on their group.

He sat thinking through the route that delivered him to this residential park. And worked his way backward . . . back to the Sheep Gate.

Lights flickered to life in the homes, alerting Haegan to the fact that he'd let his mind wander much longer than he should have. Picking himself up, he plotted his course out of the city. Which was guaranteed to fail because he did not know where he was. If he could make it back to the pig pen, he was sure to find his way out of the city. But therein lay the challenge—finding the pigs.

Dusting off his pants, he made his way out of the small neighborhood. But not before he glanced back and surveyed the place of solace. He liked it here. This suited him. Cozy and warm, friendly.

A rustle in the shadows stabbed him with fear. Was someone there? He let his gaze probe the darkness, but he saw nothing. *Go on. Get moving.* It would follow, would it not, that the poor section of town would have the taverns and—he shuddered, remembering the half-robed woman—brothels. When the sun went down, the lesser morals of low cities came to life, wasn't it said?

So he traveled in the direction of the dim glow of city life. As he trailed down one street after another, it grew brighter, as if drawing him onward. A crunch behind him sent a trill of fear up his neck, raising his hackles. Haegan looked to the side but kept moving. If someone was following him, he didn't want to betray that he knew.

Couldn't be Jujak. They would seize the opportunity and attack. So who would track him? He couldn't see for the darkness.

Scritch.

Resistance crumbled. Haegan hurriedly glanced back but saw only shadows and walls. A couple stumbled from a tavern with their arms wound impossibly around each other. He jerked forward, looking up again to the halo of light rimming the city, growing brighter still. At least he was on the right pa—

A ripple of green.

Haegan stopped. Jerked against a building, watching the shadows. Staring hard into the darkness ahead, he took a few more tentative steps.

A glint. Light on . . . a shiny surface. Not a sword. Armor!

Jujak!

A lone figure strode across the road where Haegan had seen the glint, then vanished into the darkness. The same captain. He stepped back into view, the place the others waited obviously not deep enough to conceal him. Or perhaps, the young officer was overly confident in his belief that they could ambush Haegan.

A door in front of Haegan swung open. Light spilled onto the street, along with a cloud of smoke from the tavern

Haegan whirled around, spotted an alcove and whipped into it. Palm against the wood, he peered around the corner.

The captain and at least three other Jujak moved toward the tavern.

Haegan jerked back. And found himself not staring at wood slats, but eyes. A woman's eyes!

A yelp catapulted up his throat.

"*Shh!*" A hand clamped onto his mouth. Another caught his tunic and yanked him forward, right against her as they hid in the alcove.

Awareness of their bodies pressed together flared through Haegan. Propriety demanded he remove himself. But living demanded he not move. Writhing internally, he closed his mind to her curves. The floral scent of her hair.

Boots thudded closer.

Haegan held his breath, focused on the Jujak.

The thuds slowed, hesitated.

Palms still on the door, he pushed his head against the wood, his nose pressed into her hair. She stiffened, and he squeezed his eyes tighter.

Rocks crunched beneath boots. Then the steps fell away.

Haegan relaxed and stepped back. "I beg—"

"No!" She again pushed her hand against his mouth. "They will find me," she whispered and peeked out, then slipped beneath his arm. "Hurry. This way." Her small hands dug into his tunic and pulled.

Haegan followed but argued with himself each step of the way. Until she led him into an inn. Her warm hand slid down his arm and her fingers threaded through his as she drew him to a table at the back. "Sit," she hissed.

With a frown, he shook his head. "I beg your mercy, I—"

"Sit or you will betray us." Her features softened from panic to pleading. "They will arrest me." She lifted a roll from beneath the table, one she'd apparently stolen. "We were hungry."

"Look." He eased onto the edge of the chair across from her. "I am sorry for your troubles and situation, but it is impossible for me to remain with you."

"They will not think to look at a woman and her husband."

Haegan felt his eyes widen, stunned at her suggestion. "Mercy, but I—"

"Oh, I do not expect *that* of you. I just need to buy some time."

"And buy some food, if you plan to take up that table," came a gravelly voice.

"Sorry, si—" Haegan met the steely eyes of a very thick woman with a hard expression that could rival the young captain's. "Ma'am. We—"

"Stew and grog, please." The mystery woman produced two pitz coins and handed them to the tavern lady.

She had coins but stole a bun? Haegan wrestled with the thoughts as the innkeeper tucked the pitz into her apron and disappeared, mumbling about a girl thinking she's prettier than everyone else and lording it over them.

Haegan leaned closer. "I thought you were poor. Why steal when you could have easily purchased it?"

She gave him a shy smile, her face framed by long reddish-brown hair, and bit into the roll. "You're a gallant type. I saw you were in trouble, what with those Jujak stalking the streets and you ducking out of sight when you saw them." She lifted a thin shoulder. "Knew you wouldn't take a girl's help unless you thought she was in trouble."

Disbelief wound through him. "You—what?" He shook his head. "How did—"

"Sitting under the tree, you wasn't doing nothin'. Then slinking through them shadows till you set eyes on the soldiers." When she shrugged again, her hair rippled like fire beneath the wall-mounted torches. "Not hard to figure out."

And to think, he never saw her. But he'd heard her, hadn't he? The scritch. Then finding himself pressed against her. "I beg your mercy for—in the alley—" Heat flared across his cheeks.

She smiled. "I've been pinned by worse."

Surprised at her casual disregard of a substantial offense, he considered her. "For that, I am truly sorry. No lady should be in such a situation."

The innkeeper returned and dropped two tin plates on the table, along with two mugs. "Eat up and clear out. I've no patience for loiterers." And with that, she was gone.

The girl giggled. "It's a wonder she has any customers." Her accent had faded. She seemed to have noticed too, but quickly lifted the spoon and ate.

"Might I have the name of my rescuer?" Haegan asked.

She hesitated, then raised her spoon again. "You'll eat, then be off like the witch said."

A few things struck him then—her authoritative tone, though the way she led him into this tavern indicated she was used to being in control; her wavering accent, as if she wasn't good at it; and the way she called the woman a witch. That implied either she was very familiar with the innkeeper's disposition and had granted her the epithet, or she didn't know her at all and relegated her to a disposition rather than a name.

"Excuse me," she said, pushing up from her chair. "I need more grog."

Haegan's mind spun. He didn't know whether or not to trust her. That called into question the stew, of which he'd eaten but a few bites—and hadn't felt an overwhelming urge to cut out his own stomach yet. So if she wasn't trying to kill him, why would she help him?

A hand grabbed his tunic and yanked him upward. "Sparks! Are you a fool or what?"

Black hair. Light blue eyes slowly took focus. Drracien. Indignation surged through Haegan. He pushed the accelerant back. "You left me!"

"Yeah? Well, now we need to get out of here. Get back to the cave before that pretty friend of yours decides to have my head cut off." He glanced at the plates. "Who were you eating with?"

"I . . ." Haegan looked over his shoulder to the bar that was empty save for two potbellied men and the innkeeper. He spun around, searching for the girl. "She—"

"Oh, blazes, you are a fool." Drracien slapped his shoulder. "Good thing you were already poor, or she'd have made you that way."

"You know her?"

"No, I don't know a prostitute—unlike you." Drracien dumped the leftover stew into his mouth and wiped his face. "C'mon. We have to get out of here." He was moving before Haegan's brain caught up.

"No, she wasn't—"

"Quiet," Drracien hissed as he stepped into the night. "Police and sentinels love this district after dark. We don't need to end up in the stocks."

"Don't leave me this time."

"I didn't leave you." Drracien looked down the street. "You didn't follow."

Haegan snapped up his head. "I—" A blur of green and gold silenced him.

Drracien darted beneath iron stairs. Though Haegan followed, he gave the space a hard search to be sure he hadn't yet again pinned someone. Satisfied they were alone, he leaned himself against the wall.

Drracien glanced at him. His left cheek twitched as he studied him. "You know them?"

Know the Jujak? If he meant personally, no. Most of his father-king's elite warriors had never seen or met him. But yes, he knew they were Jujak. Knew they were hunting him. "How could I?"

"You're cowering."

Haegan felt the night darken at the accusation. "And what are *you* doing?"

Drracien grinned. "Breathing air not infected with the stench of a thousand poor city dwellers." His probing gaze came back to Haegan. "And apparently, protecting you."

Haegan pried himself off the wall, digging into the dregs of his courage. "No need to protect me. I can do that myself."

A rumble of laughter. "As you did with the prostitute?"

"She *wasn't* a prostitute."

Drracien gave him a look. "And you know this how? Have you that much experience with *experienced* women?"

Balling his fists, Haegan bit back the searing words begging for freedom. "That—"

A stream of Jujak emerged from a building.

"Back," Drracien hissed, planting a hand on Haegan and nudging him farther into the darkness. Only then did Haegan realize the building was the same one he'd escaped through—the brothel. Had someone seen him? Betrayed him? Or . . . had he brought trouble upon those . . . women?

"Why are they looking for you?" Drracien whispered.

Afraid he'd betray himself and the truth, Haegan moved to the other side and feigned heavy interest in the Jujak's direction.

"You deflect poorly, *Rigar.*"

"They're not. I—"

He slammed a crumpled paper against Haegan's chest. "Lie to me another day, *prince.*"

29

It felt as if the hard-packed ground had grown roots around his feet and legs. Haegan stood, unable to move, unable to believe the dark lines etched into the paper and illuminated beneath the moons' revealing light. An image of him, perfect in likeness. And beneath his image, a searing phrase in bold lettering: WANTED FOR HIGH TREASON. Below it read: *Known to associate with incipients. Capture alive at all costs. Large reward for his expedient return to King Zireli.*

Incipients? How could his father think this of him? The Jujak were one thing, but how could his own father turn an entire realm against his son? Believe that his flesh and blood would commit such a heinous act? Believe that he'd try to take the life of his beloved sister? *I love her!*

The poster mentioned nothing of his title "Prince." At least that much he could deflect for now. He tried to laugh, but seeing the proof that his father had put out a warrant for his arrest nauseated him.

"You may not have been in the public eye, but with that hair and those eyes, there is no doubt whose blood runs in your veins."

"So a person with blond hair and blue eyes *must* be the offspring of the Fire King?" Haegan glanced at the paper once more and squeezed his hand into a fist, the poster crumpling noisily. When he looked up, only the cobbled street and alleys running up to one stoop or building after another lay before him. Drracien had vanished. Again. Irritation clawed at Haegan.

"You trying to draw them to us?" Drracien growled.

Haegan spun to find the accelerant standing at the end of the alley, backlit by a torch. "Where did you go?" he demanded as he stormed toward him.

Hands out, Drracien shrugged. "Right here, princeling."

"*Don't.*" The words ground between Haegan's teeth. "It is imperative that you take this situation seriously. For once! What of the supplies? I've—"

Glowering, Drracien turned.

"I'm talking—"

"Yelling, actually." Drracien bent, hooked something, then pivoted.

A weight barreled into Haegan, thumping against his chest. He scrambled to catch the hefty, knobby sack. "What—?"

"The supplies you were whining about." Drracien slung another burlap bag over his shoulder. "Now shut up and get moving." Weaving through the alleys seemed as effortlessly familiar to the accelerant as lectures had been to Gwogh.

Questions piled up in Haegan's mind. Only the sound of their boots on the cobblestones met his ears as they slunk through the shadows of the city. When they passed not one but two gates, Haegan grew concerned. They were headed close to the alabaster walls of the Citadel Sanctuary. Unease increased. The accelerant never slowed or wavered.

And then a third gate.

Haegan slowed. Glanced at the thick wood barrier and the half-dozen guards. "Shouldn't—"

"No."

"But—"

"Quiet," Drracien threw over his shoulder.

Insult added to indignation. Haegan quickened his pace to catch up, give the rogue a piece of his mind.

Drracien stopped.

Haegan stumbled into him. A strong pressure and warmth kneaded into his chest where Drracien restrained him. "Let—"

"Shh!" Drracien's hot reprimand dashed along his cheek. "Sentinels," he breathed.

Haegan froze and spotted the red cloaks patrolling in their official overcloaks and helmets. Not just one pair. Several. Two leading up an endless flight of stairs. Two in between a pair of pillars, barely discernible from the darkness and shadows. And another set in the courtyard below, patrolling.

Haegan gave a curt nod so Drracien would release him. They both knelt at the corner of a retaining wall, eyeing the imposing setting. He had sketches of the Citadel at Sanctuary, but actually seeing the Spire of Zaelero, his ancestor who fought the Mad Queen's consort and ripped back the realm from his greed, stunned him into silence.

Two-storied buildings surrounded the courtyard on three sides. The fourth held an imposing structure that rose four or five levels—nearly as tall as Fieri Keep. But this building had innumerable columns at each level and atop it a dome adorned with a spire that glowed oddly bright beneath the moons.

How were they supposed to get out?

There was no way out. No gate. No alleys. Enclosed.

This had to be a mistake. Had Drracien grown confused with the darkness? He'd deftly managed to break away from Haegan many times, losing him altogether for a few hours. What had he done in that time? Contact accelerants? The Jujak?

Was Haegan, even now, cowering on the doorstep of an ambush? Had Thiel been right?

"Wait here," Drracien said as he pushed up and darted past Haegan.

"What?" Haegan's pulse vaulted over his panic. "No!"

But the accelerant was nothing but shadows and ebony against a blanket of blues, grays, and black. And heading—until Haegan lost sight of him—straight into the heart of the great Citadel.

Haegan dropped back against the wall and banged his head on it. Again. And again. What a fool to have trusted that rogue! To have placed his life in his hands. Swiping a hand over his face, he harnessed his frustration. What should he do? Wait here?

Right. *Make yourself a fool and just wait for the sentinels to invite you into a cell.*

So. He'd leave.

And go where?

The last gate. Could he remember how to get there from his position? He glanced in the direction from which they'd come and mentally back-traced his steps. Right to the last gate he'd seen. Yes, he could find his way.

Confident, Haegan hoisted the sack of goods in a firm grip and pushed to his feet, bent. Was he making the right move? What if Drracien returned?

Yes, the rogue would return—with the sentinels. Who would give up the reward on Haegan's life? With that much money anyone would be set for life. A king's ransom.

And a king's fury—for Haegan. He'd known his father's anger. He wouldn't be on the receiving end of that again if the power rested in his hands to prevent it. Scurrying through the night and alleys, he kept his head low and his hope lower. He knew not why Abiassa had set her hand against him, but he would not give her more reason to continue her aggression. He would get back to Thiel and the others and set out for the Falls as quickly as possible.

A thought stopped him cold. They had been gone all day. What if Thiel and the others were gone? What if they'd fled? It would make sense—the city crawling with sentinels and the hills with Jujak.

Fear pushed him back. He hesitated, crouching at a half wall. He felt the cool stone through his tunic as he leaned his shoulder against it. What if he was wrong? He did not know this city, and getting caught . . .

A swirl of emotions—fear, grief, anxiety—tore at his courage and determination, leaving him in thin rags of weakness. He thumped a fist against the wall. Life and its riddles had seemed so simple lying in a bed with a tutor and fire for company. But one mistake out here could make the difference between freedom and lifetime captivity, if not death.

And for now, he was a captive to indecision.

The only thing he knew for sure: He was tired of being weak. It had been Haegan's lot his entire life, first with paralysis and now with a lack of experience and knowledge. Enough. Gwogh had always said he had a bright mind, so he'd use it.

He hurried along the half wall and banked right. Yes, this was right. He remembered the cobbler's shop on the corner. Hefting the bag over his shoulder, he kept to the shadows. Down past the bakery. Yes, yes. This was the route they had traversed. Next should be the confectioner . . .

He scanned windows and signs searching for the one with the mound of chocolate squares. But . . . Haegan glanced back up the street he'd just come down. Then to what lay ahead. Wait. No, this wasn't right. He back-stepped, hand tracing the bricks, trying to remember. Sense the right direction.

But suddenly, nothing seemed familiar.

Panic stabbed his gut. He switched the weight of the bag to his other shoulder. Hurried back to what he'd last recognized. The bakery. He found the bowed window with the eyelet curtain across the top. Hand on the glass, he scoured the rest of the street. Then trod to the nearest intersection. Peered up and down the darkened streets. A curse hung on the tip of his tongue. None of it looked familiar. Why didn't it look familiar?

His gaze swung back to the curtain.

There hadn't been a curtain on the bakery window when he and Drracien had come. Wrong bakery. Blazes!

A clatter sounded in the darkness.

"Stop there!"

Haegan jerked toward the shout. A shadow flickered here. And there. But nothing moved at him. All the same, enough time had been wasted. He raced up the street and found a juncture he hadn't noticed. One that was a crossroads, an intersection that wasn't a hard turn, but a gentle blending of two streets. That would explain why he didn't remember turning. He hurried on the new branch and found the bakery. Confirmed it was the right bakery. Continuing, he easily found the confectioner. And then ahead should be—

Thwump.

Oof.

Hiss.

Haegan spun, listening past the thundering of his heart as he probed the veil of night. The rubbish bin. An empty slatted chair. Flowers riffling in the gentle breeze. Unable to discern a threat, though he felt one keenly, he pursued his escape.

Ahead, the gate. Exultation surged through his veins, but he restrained it lest he betray himself at the last minute. He shimmied up to a corner and peered at the larger gate and its smaller footgate. The wagon gate barred entrance for the night.

Four guards maintained watch over the footgate.

Why hadn't he thought of them? How was he supposed—

A shout went up somewhere to the right. Haegan ducked, afraid the guards might see him now. With extreme care, he eased his head around the corner. Spied two guards darting through a narrow passage, shouting for someone to stop.

The gate. Haegan traced it. The hut beside it. Two guards remained, distracted, watching their comrades disappear down the side street.

Now or never.

He threw himself out of the alley before he could change his mind. Over the powerful thump of his heartbeat, he could hear little other than the two muttering. He scooped up a rock as he ran and shoved himself into the relative safety of the darkened alcove.

Breathing came only with great effort, his fear of being discovered smothering him. Back plastered against the cold stone that formed the gate wall, Haegan stole a glance at the guards. They stood at an angle to him, their light chatter reassuring him that he had not inadvertently betrayed himself. Convinced of their obliviousness to his presence, he stuck his head out and peered at the gate. A heavy beam secured the smaller door.

A shout from one of the guards spiked his pulse.

Haegan sucked in a hard breath and jerked back, smacking his head against the stone. Biting back an oath, he flattened himself and slid a sidelong gaze toward the gate.

They were calling to someone else. Then laughed.

Hefting the rock, Haegan plotted his course. Executing the plan would take more courage than he possessed. But it had to be done or he'd be stranded or captured here in Hetaera.

With a quick flick of his wrist, he pitched the rock into the street. It clattered across the footpath and into the road.

The guards stilled. Glanced in that direction. But didn't leave their post.

Blazes. What would it take?

Only then did Haegan note a wooden platform hoisted and secured, towering over the two guards. The wagon gate, it seemed, had a counter-measure—a drawbridge. When the gate was open during the day, the bridge was lowered, affording passage into the city. When the gate closed at night, it lifted the drawbridge in an added measure of security so that only the East River, which traced Hetaera's southern boundary, moved in the night.

So. Brute force. If he could—

Enough thinking. Haegan examined the moonlight area, then launched himself at the guards. He cuffed one on the back of the head, pitching the guard forward. He bent over the small, waist-high fence but caught himself.

Haegan plowed into the second guard and shoved hard. The armored guard flipped over the barrier.

The first guard swung at Haegan with a shout. Clipped his cheek. Pain scored his face. He shouldered into the guard, lifting him off his feet and thrusting. The guard grabbed at Haegan, catching a fist hold of his tunic. The stiff fabric pulled against his lower back . . . his middle . . . his shoulders.

Haegan's heels lifted. If he didn't push now, they'd both end up in the narrow river. Fear and anger collided. He punched the guard in the side.

With a howl, the guard tipped backward.

Free! Heagan was free. He darted for the foot gate

He eased up to the heavy bar over the foot gate and squeezed through. He ran into the trees, praying with what was left of him that he wouldn't be seen. The slope grew steeper and his breathing more labored. Haegan slowed out of necessity, unable to breathe and half afraid he'd end up lost. Again.

"You stupid fool!"

Haegan spun.

Trudging toward him, Drracien seemed no more out of sorts than a man taking a quiet stroll in the woods. "I told you to *stay!*"

"I am not a dog that I take commands."

"No, but you are an ignorant, impudent prince who thinks he can do whatever he likes without considering the risk to others!"

"Says the accelerant who abandoned the person he was supposed to help get in and out of the city with supplies."

Having caught up, Drracien thumped the bag of stores. "Supplies." He popped Haegan on the head. "The person I was supposed to get out."

"You left me. Again!"

"With instructions to wait!" He was hiking up the hill. "But no, you had to dart off at the first chance."

"I had no way of knowing if you'd set me up. What were you doing anyway?"

With a barked laugh, Drracien kept moving. "You are not worth so much, prince, that I would expend my own life. I only had to follow the trail of bodies you left to find you." He patted Haegan's face, condescendingly. "Be more tidy next time."

Haegan slapped the hand away. "I do not need instructions from you."

"You need instructions from someone! I found four bodies—three sentinels and a gate guard. I would have caught up with you, but I had to conceal them so we weren't discovered. You have a lot to learn, princeling."

"This is madness. I killed no one!"

"I followed those bodies to the Purple Gate—which was unguarded, thanks to you."

"It wasn't me! I killed no one, you stupid, arrogant—"

Drracien stopped, his brow knotting. "I warned you once about lying to me, princeling."

Hands fisted, Haegan tossed aside the supplies. "And I warned you about—"

"Whoa-whoa-whoa! Stop!" Eyes wide, Drracien dropped his sack. He slid his hands in a swooping arc, crossing them over each other, then drawing the right over the left and pulling it back to his side while thrusting the left at Haegan. A glow warbled around his hand.

Haegan froze, recognizing the heat signature of an acceleration. "You'd wield against me?" The shock was surreal. No matter how hard he tried and no matter what he did, it seemed the world pitted itself against him.

"Only to stop you."

"Stop me?" Haegan held out his arm. "From what? You—"

"Stop, please!"

Right. Look away and the rogue would wield. "No more games. You weary me!"

"Please. *Stop.*" Drracien's expression changed as did his tone. And his posture. He wasn't just wielding. This was . . . advanced wielding.

Confusion and curiosity collided in Haegan. His anger abated somewhat. Who or what was Drracien? "You hid from the sentinels. Why?"

Drracien frowned. He straightened, his hands falling to his sides. "I know who you are."

"You're an accelerant. Of course you know who I am—the crippled prince whose father your order answers to." He shoved a hand through his hair, defeat clinging to him like the dampness cloaking the mountain.

A small sound disturbed the silence down the hill from them. Drracien immediately turned toward it, his eyes narrowed. "Debate later. Right now we have a bigger problem."

"What?"

"You're being tracked."

30

Torchlight skittered into one shadow after another as Gwogh followed the bent servant into the foyer of the great hall of Hetaera's Sanctuary. Above them, colorful glass windows slept, waiting for the morning light to spread their glory. Stone arches swung upward . . . all the way to the mural bathed in the somber glow of torches. The ever-lit depiction of Zaelero's mighty battle served as both a reminder and a charge to the Ignatieri to maintain the Flames and instruct future generations.

Gwogh shivered in the chill. It was cold here. Where it should not be.

"This way, Sir Gwogh." The servant shuffled onward, away from the private residences of the marshals, and toward the offices, training cellars, and courtyards. The farther they went, the more the chill pervaded Gwogh's bones. This wasn't right. Something was wrong here. Very wrong.

The silence. The darkness. It wasn't just the shadows of night. Gwogh flexed his hands, ready for whatever purpose this servant, whom he had once called friend, had in dragging him to the school. When they rounded the corner to the reception hall, Gwogh broke his silence. "There must be some mistake. I requested an audience with High Marshal Aloing."

"Yes." Eliatzer continued onward. "You asked me to take you to him." He unlocked a heavy steel door.

"Yes, but his residence is on the ninth floor." The physical representation of the Nine Kingdoms the Ignatieri were charged with defending.

"Indeed." Eliatzer did not slow as he shuffled, undeterred by the questions, across the open auditorium. Hauntingly empty, the gilded bannisters and seats seemed to mock Gwogh's subservient stature in the last decade, since he was sent out of Sanctuary to Fieri Keep to watch over the crippled prince.

"I fear I do not understand—"

"None of us lessers do," Eliatzer mumbled as his sandaled feet scraped against the passage that curved down . . . down . . .

"I beg your mercy, old friend, but what—"

"Here we are," Eliatzer declared. He placed two hands on an enormous door, his whole body shuddering as he pushed with great effort.

It wasn't until the barrier angled inward and light caught the ornate carvings that Gwogh's lunch squirmed in his stomach. "The morgue."

He entered the open room with one stone slab after another jutting from a center cavern that dripped frigid water. Cold enough to hold a body until burial. Cold enough to make Gwogh feel as if spikes had been shoved through his limbs.

"Why are we here?" But even as he asked, he saw the body, carefully laid out. Garbed in the ceremonial high fashion. Black and red intertwined among the rubies stitched into the thigh-length cloak. A massive citrine joined the collar, and tipped up the chin of the high lord, whose white-gray hair had been neatly combed back. The thick tapestry of his office draped elegantly over his waist and down the sides of the stone edifice. The red sash of his office.

Gwogh's eyes slid closed, his mind refusing to take in the truth: Aloing was dead.

He moved closer, but kept his hands to his sides, though they itched to touch the high marshal. His mentor. Friend. Unrivaled, Aloing had trained Zireli, raised him when his gifts were made known at a very young age. One of the grandest and gentlest accelerants Gwogh had ever known and trained with. And the fiercest when angered. When the Flames were violated. When the Codes rejected. His gifts bordered on Deliverer strength. Not even Dromadric could touch the level of his wielding, though it had been close. Something he had frequently taunted his oldest friend about. "What happened?"

"Now, that'd depend on who you asked."

A spark crackled through Gwogh. He flashed a glare at the servant. "Explain yourself."

He cocked his head to the side and shrugged. "It would be my advice, Sir Gwogh, that you speak with the high marshals and the grand marshal."

"Why will you not speak truth and release me from this anger?"

Eliatzer's eyes widened in understanding, his gaze flicking to Gwogh's hands.

"You've been around novices and conductors too long if you seek to gauge the depth of my anger through the embers." Gwogh held up his hands. "What do my embers tell you?"

Uncertainty shook the man's head, but the eyes told much more—that he felt the circle of heat around his throat and mind, though he saw no indication of Gwogh's wielding. That Gwogh's gifts were far more advanced than the young patrons and sparkers who practiced in the training yard. That he'd underestimated the wrong person.

"I would have the truth," Gwogh said.

Gasping, the man rubbed his throat and temple, scowling. "That's what I been trying to say—there are several truths floating around. I heard them." He swiped a hand at the air. "There is no call to hurt a poor man."

Unaffected by the false humility, Gwogh maintained his ground. "You led me to this morgue to shock me."

"I led you here to show you the truth." Eliatzer shuffled toward the high marshal's body. Bending, the aged man unfastened Aloing's collar.

"What are you doing? Unhand him!" Without thought, Gwogh sent a focused spark at the man's right shoulder.

Eliatzer swung back, gripping the spot that sizzled with spirals of smoke. "Look! Look at his throat." Tears streaked the man's face. "I meant no disrespect."

Gwogh reluctantly dragged himself to the high marshal's frozen form, such an unnatural state. Eyes still on the servant, he sent him a searing glare.

"Look," Eliatzer pleaded.

Finally, Gwogh turned his gaze downward. First to the face nearly as gray as the neatly combed hair. The pale lips. And finally, the throat. Thin black lines snaked up and around his neck. Dozens of them. "Scoriae."

"See?" Eliatzer surged forward, victory in his wrinkled, hooded eyes.

"This makes no sense." His mind tripped over the implications. The ramifications. His gaze flicked to the old man. "You've had your fun. I've played your games. Now, you will tell me what happened." When the man opened his mouth, his expression clearly set to challenge, Gwogh pressed on. "All versions."

Eliatzer sagged, lowered his head, and nodded. "Let's leave this cold place. We'll go to my room and talk there."

"No." Gwogh sensed an urgency to gather truths and leave the Sanctuary. "I will have the truth—truths—here. Now."

"But it's so cold."

"The truth usually is." Gwogh nodded. "Please. Begin."

"First, I should say I wasn't witness to none of these stories. I just hear them, that's all." Eliatzer rubbed his neck. "First truth going around is that the high marshal's protégé killed him during an argument. Then the young accelerant jumped out a window and escaped over the rooftops of the Citadel."

"What level was his protégé now?"

"Just tested and passed for marshal."

So quickly? "You're so certain. How is it that you know so clearly the rank of a student?"

"Everyone knows Drracien. Powerful, that boy. I heard some liken him to Zireli. A prodigy, they called him." He shrugged. "But he was wild. Powerful and wild."

"Indeed." Gwogh remembered Aloing's words about the wild boy of the lessers. He also remembered the destiny Aloing believed the boy born to.

"And what with the way young Drracien Khar'val vanished, it would seem that was the right truth."

"Except for the scoriae."

Eliatzer's cheek twitched with a smile. "Except for that."

Gwogh scowled. "I will take my leave of you now."

The man's eyes nearly fell out of their sockets. "Oh, no, sir. I—" He gaped. "Don't you want to know the other truths?"

No, he had heard more than enough. Gwogh inclined his head. "I thank you for your time and consideration. You have been truly helpful." He ducked and stepped into the night, moving at a pace that would tell others not to interfere. And a pace that put great distance between himself and Eliatzer, who was scrambling to perform his duty of seeing him out.

Back in the rotunda, he hurried as quickly as his seventy-two-year-old legs would carry him and turned left toward a small alcove. He palmed the wall and a panel slid back. As soon as he entered, the door closed.

Even after all these years away, he remembered. To the right, he found the rope. Pulled down. Then worked it hand over hand.

His mind rang with the singularity of the events that had taken place in the last weeks. Losing Haegan. Kaelyria bedridden. All those years he'd been convinced the Fierian was at least another generation away. That he would die in peace, that the worst time of Primar's history would not open up before his eyes.

But had he been convinced? Or had he convinced himself, desperate not to be a part of that bloody prophecy? He pinned himself in the corner of the lift, gripping the half wall with both hands. He closed his eyes. *Please let it not be in my time.*

But only an old blind fool would believe it was not. As only a blind fool would believe Abiassa's timing could be influenced by a mere mortal. His gaze rose to the darkness, where the shaft ended. The chill had already invaded Sanctuary. And he wasn't referring to the winter chill. But the chasing away of Abiassa's Fire.

31

"Tracked?" Huffing as he struggled to keep up with the agile accelerant, Haegan stumbled. "Wait." Cursed weak legs. They might look like warrior's legs, but they were clearly not. Or maybe he just hadn't perfected the art of using them. "What"—he gulped air—"makes you think"—huff—"I'm being tracked?"

"The bodies."

"But how do you know that's connected to me?"

"Because they were in your wake. Same path you took." Drracien stopped, one foot on a boulder, and glanced at Haegan. "Did you not hear anything behind you?"

"I heard plenty." Sweat dripped off the fringes of his hair plastered to his forehead. "Grunts and crunches mostly."

Drracien did a double-take. Turned away, his hand going to his mouth, then swung back. Held out his arms. "What did you expect? A formal announcement by herald?"

Haegan's face flushed, making him suddenly grateful for the darkness. "It was a city! How was I supposed to know—"

"You're a wanted fugitive. You should be hearing trouble in every creak and pop. When you have Ignatieri watching for you, Jujak hunting you, and Deliverers—"

Haegan hauled in a breath. "Deliverers?" His panic screamed, squeezing tight against his ribs. "They're disbanded. When my grandfather—"

Brows knotted, Drracien angled toward him. "Deliverers are never disbanded." He sliced a decisive hand through the air. "They live in peace and anonymity until Abiassa calls them to judge."

"Judge?" He hated the way his voice squeaked. "What—why?" His head hurt trying to make sense of things. He just wanted to get to the Falls, to just . . . survive.

"What did you do, prince?"

"I told you not to call me that!"

"Hey." The firm fierce voice of Thiel cut through their tension as she slipped into the open, moonslight softening her olive complexion. "You might as well light a fire and summon the Jujak." Her scathing expression scraped over Haegan, then Drracien, upon whom she turned her full attention.

Good. Mayhap she would carve that smug expression off his face.

"What happened?"

"The prince here got lost."

"Lost? You abandoned me! I turned my head and you were gone!"

"Quiet." Thiel touched his hand, her gaze still on the accelerant. "I trusted you to protect him—"

"I don't need his protection!"

"No, you need a babysitter!" Drracien's hair dipped into his eyes. He shoved it back. "I had things to take care of that I could not do with him latched to my side."

"Like what?" Thiel folded her arms.

He huffed. Looked away.

"Let's go." Thiel was looking at Haegan, anger blazing through her amber eyes.

"Wait." Drracien caught her arm and moved in close. If the proximity was not enough to set a new anger ablaze in Haegan, the way Drracien peered down at Thiel was. Haegan drew straighter, positioning himself alongside the two. "Release her."

After skating a sidelong glance to Haegan, Drracien focused on the winsome beauty between them. "We all have our secrets. Mine are . . . dangerous."

Why didn't Thiel push him back, the way she had with Haegan? "Most are, or they wouldn't be secrets."

"If I were caught in the city—"

"Sanctuary," Haegan corrected. "He snuck into the Citadel of the Ignatieri."

Eyes wide, Thiel did step back then. "Why?"

"I'm an accelerant," Drracien said in a condescending tone as he slid a hateful glare at Haegan.

Shaking her head, Thiel said, "No, why sneak? You belong there. Why not just walk in?"

There was a long pause as Drracien's gaze shifted to one then the other. For the first time, Haegan noticed weariness behind the arrogance in those eyes.

As if realizing his slip, Drracien sneered. "As I said, I'm an accelerant. A sought-after one." He smirked. "*Highly* sought after. As in dead."

"A good reason, then, to *avoid* them, not seek them out."

"Who wants you dead?" Haegan asked.

"Every accelerant in there. But mostly Grand Marshal Dromadric."

"Of what do they accuse you?"

Drracien stretched his jaw. "Murder." His dark eyes met theirs. "Of which I am *not* guilty."

Thiel stumbled out of his grip. "You bring death to us, Drracien."

"What of him?" He swung a finger toward Haegan. "Prince Haegan, son of King Zireli, wanted for high treason by his own father, who sent Jujak after him! Tell me, which do you fear more?"

Thiel let out a frustrated breath. "Both." She pressed her fingers to her temple. Then turned back to Drracien. "You specifically singled out Haegan to accompany you. Why would you do that, then leave him? Were you trying to get him caught?"

Drracien snorted.

"Explain yourself. How you justify abandoning him, then returning to me as if with a clear conscience." She was fiery when angry. And that had been a lot lately. "Were you hoping he'd be caught?" She whisked away from him, holding her head. "Why I trusted you, I don't—"

"I wanted him with me because I knew you had feelings for him."

Thiel's mouth hung open.

So did Haegan's.

"You know not of which you speak," Thiel hissed. "He is under my charge. I have feelings for all of them—Praegur, Tokar—"

"Then you knew."

She eyed him warily.

"You knew he was the prince."

Thiel looked down.

"And you let him go with me. Into the city. Knowing it could be an ambush."

"Do not turn this back on me, you—"

"I said I would go. It wasn't for her to say yes or no, as if I were a child." Haegan stepped closer. "But if you knew I was the prince—"

Drracien curled his lip. "I did not know. Not until I was in the market. A friend slipped me the paper—the wanted poster. I knew then that if I stayed with you, we'd both get caught. I knew if I broke away from you, you'd hide."

"That doesn't make sense, to intentionally leave him in a crowded city where he's clearly wanted."

"Look." Drracien brushed his dark hair off his forehead again. "The truth—I overestimated him. He looked strong. But once we were in the Citadel, I saw he was slow and that he didn't belong in the city. The crowds affected him. Shut him down."

Haegan flared his nostrils. "I am not used to crowds."

"I know the passages of the Citadel—better than most." His lips compressed, a truth—or lie?—hidden behind them. "I was confident I could escape or fight my way out. I knew he could not."

"All the more reason for you to remain at his side!"

Humiliation coiled around Haegan, pushing his head down.

"It is not meant as a slight, Prince, but a truth." Drracien faced him now. "I know not how you have come to be here, but I have doubts. Questions."

"Pray, speak your mind." Haegan balled his fists.

"You were known as the crippled prince. Was it true?"

"Was what true?"

"Were you crippled?"

"I . . . I was poisoned as a boy. I've spent the last ten years in a tower with an aging accelerant as my only friend and tutor."

"What happened to your sister, Princess Kaelyria? Rumor holds she's been injured."

"Please," Thiel said. "Can we speak of this in the cave?"

"No." Drracien squared his shoulders, though he did not have anger about him. "I would have the truth now before I set my course. If he hurt a member of the very family my order is charged with protecting, then I will turn him in myself."

"And risk your own capture?"

"Securing him would bring me pardon."

"Truly, you are not naïve enough to believe that." Haegan stared at him

"Perhaps not naïve," Thiel murmured. "Desperate."

Something sparked in Drracien's eyes.

"And you want a pardon so terribly, do you?" Haegan felt a strange surge through his chest, as if he could sense what this man felt.

"Yes!" Drracien's shout held a distinct scent to it.

Haegan stepped back, images of his father's anger curling before him in a wisp of smoke.

Thiel grabbed the sack of supplies from Drracien's grip. "I think you should leave. But I'll take these, since you have broken our agreement and endangered one of our own—because that's what it was, right, Drracien? As soon as you found out who Haegan was, you wanted to use him to buy your pardon."

"Would you not do the same to regain what you have fought so hard for and lost, through no will of your own?" His chest practically pressed into her chin, forcing her to look at him and him alone.

Haegan wanted to punch him.

"Then why did you stop? Why aren't we overrun by sentinels this very moment?"

Deflating, Drracien turned away. "I don't know."

No one spoke for a moment. Then Thiel touched the accelerant's arm. "What do they hold over you?" she asked softly. "Why are you running?"

He turned a bitter gaze on her. "Why are *you*? Where is your family, fair one?"

Thiel moved away.

Drracien stepped into her path again. "I meant no harm, my lady—"

"No harm?" Haegan growled. "You wanted me captured! You challenge a woman—"

"You're here, aren't you? And is there a reason you will not answer my question, prince? Did you bring harm to your sister?"

"Why would I harm the only person who saved me from the endless prattling of an aged accelerant who taught me nothing but useless information and skills?"

"You find education so lowly?"

"Only when it comes from Gwogh, who seemed to not only know but have lived through every battle and conflict in the Nine since Zaelero himself." He laughed but his agitation had not lessened.

Drracien's expression flashed. "Gwogh." His face hardened as he advanced toward Haegan. "He was your tutor? Gwogh?"

Uncertainly rippled through Haegan, and he eased away from the intensity roiling off the accelerant. "Yes. Why?"

"The why does not matter," Thiel said, her brown hair riffling in the pre-dawn wind. "We have the supplies. Now leave."

"I would go with you." Drracien retrieved the sack and slung it over his shoulder.

Thiel froze. Straightened. Lifted her chin. "Why would we allow you to remain when you have inflicted so much damage and tried to sell out Haegan? When you have already proven that we cannot trust you, that you would abandon us as quickly as it is to your benefit?"

"Neither will happen again. I swear it by the Flames." Ferocity akin to what had been seen in the Fire King emanated from Drracien. "I am at your service, my lady."

Shock held fast to Haegan. That was the equivalent of a lifeoath. "You realize the words you speak are binding at the highest level. No court, king, or ruler, will release you from that oath."

"Nor would I ask it."

"Why?" Haegan shifted uneasily. "Why would you do this? How can you change from a rogue to a hero in a blink?"

Drracien clapped him on the back. "Relax, prince. It's not your worry. I did this for her." He wagged his dark eyebrows at Thiel. "Someone has to protect her from you."

"Protect me? You have done more damage in this clearing than he could do in a lifetime."

"How do you—?"

Just then Tokar burst out of a copse of trees. "*Run!*" He was half-way across the clearing when he announced, "Jujak!"

32

"Go!" Drracien dropped the sack. "North, into the woods. Cross the river, and I'll follow." He bent and dug through the contents. "I'll hold them off."

"No." At the thunder of hooves, Thiel glanced back. "There's a dozen of them, if not more."

"Go!" Drracien shifted on his haunches to Haegan. "I'll meet you by the river. Get her out of here!"

Surprised the accelerant charged him with the task, he jolted. "I should help you."

Drracien thrust a hand at him. A puff of hot air bounced off the ground and blasted at Haegan. He stumbled back, realizing he was out of his depth. Again.

"I see the prince!"

The words sent Haegan spiraling. He sprinted toward Thiel, shoving her around. Together, they launched toward the woods. As he sped between two mauri trees, he glanced back. And stopped cold.

Drracien stood in the center of the clearing, now adorned in a red and black Ignatieri cloak. The red and black intertwined flames crawled up over his shoulders and down his arms, ending in an exploding fire burst of gold threads.

Haegan froze. Not gold threads. *Gems!* Those were gems encircling the cuffs of Drracien's cloak. And not just any gems, but the imperial topaz. Which meant Drracien was a marshal, a mere two steps below Grand Marshal Dromadric, who technically equaled the Fire King. But why was he wearing the cloak? He would reveal himself!

Drracien moved his hands in elegant patterns, swirling in a circle, hands and one leg extended. The elements responded to his dance. A thin circlet of golden light spread out like a halo across the clearing. Leaves overhead rustled as a wave of heat whooshed through them, brushing the hair from Haegan's forehead and shoulders. An explosion of light shattered the darkness.

Jujak barreled into the clearing.

"Drracien," Haegan whispered, lurching forward.

"No!" Thiel caught his shoulders, having apparently been as spellbound watching the accelerant as Haegan had been. "He can handle this. We should go."

"Right." But he could not move.

The horses, large and powerful, pranced around Drracien.

"Surrender the Flames!"

The captain with gray eyes challenged Drracien, his presence so intimidating that it nearly squeezed the breath from Haegan's lungs. This would end very badly.

A crackling in the air pulled Haegan's gaze toward the halo around Drracien and the clearing. More shouts from the Jujak, the elite guard circling the lone accelerant, who had yet to pay any attention to the orders shouted at him.

"When they wield," Thiel whispered over his shoulder, "it is rumored they are not even mentally in our world, but with Abiassa. Standing before her in the Void. Ignatieri believe they are protecting her or her children when they wield. The gems are said to harness the Flames, focus them."

Of course, Haegan knew this—under Gwogh's instruction, he had gained a basic understanding of what was believed to happen in wielding and with other forces, like Sirdar's Auspex, though Gwogh had said the latter was darkness—mahjik—not gifting. Haegan's father was once a high marshal, but he'd never seen his father conjure something like this.

"Take him!" Raising his sword, the young captain appeared almost heavenly in the power of the ethereal light.

With a wide arc, Drracien drew his leg straight under him and stood, bringing his right arm behind him then up and over his head until he clapped his palms together with a loud *pop*.

The air wavered, warbling like a dying bird, one that seemed to be flying directly at Haegan. His ears popped, spearing him with fiery shards. He cried out, covering his ears and bending in half. Mind addled with pain, he leaned against the tree, bark digging into his shoulder. He felt a weight drop against him but couldn't draw himself out of the agony to sort out what happened.

Shouts and cries of similar agony rippled through the royal guards. That's when Haegan realized he'd closed his eyes. He opened them, surprised to find Thiel curled against him, her head on his chest, her face pressed against his abdomen. Across the way, Jujak writhed on the ground. The others struggled between holding their horses in check and covering their ears.

Light drenched the clearing. Crackling and popping resonated through the atmosphere like thunder and rain, but heat and fire. Dark became light. Chill vanished. Dew hissed in response to Drracien's wielding as he brought both hands over his head again. Then pushed down and out.

The halo! The halo Drracien created finally surrendered and snapped blankets of fire straight down, sealing off the Jujak.

"He'll be captured." Tokar was at their side.

"No." Cringing, Thiel wiped blood from her ears. "He won't. Drracien knows what he's doing. Move so that his efforts are not in vain."

They hoofed, once more, through the woods to where a rope bridge spanned the narrowest part of the river. Like the little warrior he was, Laertes scampered across like a mouse, agile and quick. He stood on the other side, cheering Haegan. Though it sounded more like taunting. Haegan tucked aside his fear of falling and traversed the makeshift bridge with slick hands. He'd never been so glad to face a steep, rocky mountain. The trek proved arduous, but there was no time for complaint, even with burst eardrums causing imbalance and difficulty. They pressed on. They had to.

Haegan's mind was alive with the images of Drracien . . . the man's skills. His power. And that invariably brought him back to his sister. She had the gift. She'd been learning wielding. Not that he'd seen her, but she'd shared some of her experiences. The way their father yelled at her for not focusing her mind or her wielding. How, as much as she knew it was her right and a gift, she hated it. How she tired of the studying and practicing.

"Our father bores me with his lectures on proper handling of the Flames, correct techniques. 'No, Kaelyria, with the heart. Not the gut.' Ugh!" She dropped against his bed, her head on his pillow, their shoulders overlapping. "You must save me, Haegan."

"Of course," he said, staring up at the map of the realms Gwogh had commissioned to have painted on the ceiling. "I'll jump right out of this bed and march down to our father and demand he leave you alone."

She laughed, curling closer and hugging him. "You are the hero as always, Haegan."

Her laughter had bled into his heart, done wonders for his boredom that, at times, hovered on insanity. She'd hidden from further lessons that day—and many others—by reading to him from the Parchments. She preferred the decidedly dark ones, believing them to be more folklore and symbolic tales of higher truths than actual history.

He lay in that bed the whole time, listening to her, encouraging her to stay the course, be strong. Trust their father. Learn and be the best Fire Queen she could be. But he'd ached. *Ached* to be in her place. To have purpose. To belong.

Hero. She'd called him that all the time, but he was not a hero. Not the crippled prince. Not even now, the able-bodied prince.

"I wouldn'a let him leave you in that dirty city, Rigar." Laertes trudged alongside him, a long stick in his hand as he walked down the slope. "We're brothers, us four, and we don' leave no one behind."

Haegan almost managed a smile—until a thought struck him. In order for Laertes to know about Drracien leaving him in Hetaera, he had to have heard the entire conversation. Including the part about Haegan's identity. Somehow, he liked that the boy had heard, that he knew and didn't care. But the others? Did they know? He peered ahead to where Tokar and Praegur walked a few paces in front of Thiel.

Praegur held up a fist.

Immediately Tokar and the others stopped. Haegan followed suit, glancing around as his heart skipped a beat, then another, remembering the Ematahri. The Jujak. Ignatieri. Feeling small and insignificant in a world of fighters and warriors, Haegan detected a tingling against his skin. Like tiny sparks. He glanced at his arms. His flesh stood on end, hairs standing out. What was going on?

"Do you hear that?" Praegur's brown eyes slid around to them, alive with . . . what?

"I hear water, like—"

"The river!" Laertes shouted and spun to Haegan and Thiel. "That means—"

An exultant cheer went up, but Haegan stood mute. The river. He couldn't breathe. The Falls.

• • •

Cold and damp, the passage offered no forgiveness or comfort for invading its darkness. But Gwogh pushed on, scaling the long widow's walk that stretched across several buildings, right into what appeared to be no more than a shuttered window. Tucking himself through the small opening tightened muscles he'd long forgotten about. Inside, relative warmth offered no more comfort than the previous passage.

Gwogh eased himself out of the fold, sensing an ache and twitch here and there that slowed him. He glanced around the room, taking in the long table with ten chairs. The small couch and books lining the east and west walls. A desk below the slanted ceiling windows. Beds built into bunks along the remaining wall. All prepared. All as it should be.

"Best start a fire and brew some tea," he muttered. In the small pantry, he went to work digging out supplies. When he had laid them out on the table, he knelt and tugged chopped wood from a small alcove next to the bricked fireplace.

Carefully setting the wood in the small stove, he soon had a fire crackling beneath two kettles of water. He was about to turn aside when a movement jerked him around. His gaze flung to the corner, where the Deliverer stood, a long, thin sword in hand.

"You have summoned the Nine."

The daunting voice buzzed in Gwogh's head as he swallowed. With a slight bow, he searched his heart to make sure he had not erred, that he was not performing this act to please anyone but Abiassa. But even as he weighed his motives, a sound came through the walls. Already, the Council were coming through the hidden passages of the city. Each would take a different route as a precaution. A protection.

Aware he had not yet answered, he said, "I have."

The man-yet-not-man seemed to melt into the shadows even as he said, "I will remain."

His heart stuttered. "I beg your mercy, sir, but the Nine will be reluctant to converse openly in your presence." As if their words and intentions could be hidden from Abiassa.

"They will be unaware." His voice had come from everywhere, yet nowhere. How . . . how did they do that?

A few moments later, the first council member slipped through the secret door. "So it was you, Gwogh," came a nasally voice, nonplussed.

Refusing to be irritated by the man's rudeness, Gwogh gestured to the table. "Welcome, Aoald."

The Caorian representative grumbled and took his seat at the table, hands folded, round face pinched beneath a scowl. "Saw Griese and Voath in the city. They'll be along soon."

Witnessed entering the city. That might be a problem.

"Seems . . . stuffy in here. As if the room is already crowded," Aoald said, sniffing.

Gwogh refused to let his gaze drift to where the Deliverer stood, instead busying himself with preparing the tea.

Over the next ten minutes, the council room indeed became crowded. First to arrive were the pair Aoald predicted. Right behind them, even before the door could close, came Adek, a burly accelerant and one of their youngest, and his mentor, Bæde. Traytith and Kedulcya slunk in almost unnoticed from the southern panel. Kelviel was the last to join them.

"This is most unusual," Kedulcya said, her Kerralian accent thickening her words. "Two meetings within a cycle. We risk exposure."

"I'm afraid it was imperative."

Voath threw back the cup of tea. "Strange goings on are plaguing the realm. Word came from an Ematahri clan just inside the border that dozens of its warriors were wiped out in an explosion."

"What's unusual about that?" Adek asked, his arms muscular and his beard long. "There are explosions all the time—miners, people trying to make a new way over the mountain without paying a tax or being enslaved."

"Why have we not remedied that yet?" Kedulcya asked. "The Ematahri gain in power and usurp the rule of Zireli."

"Explosion—with no explosives. A bright light," Voath explained.

"Traytith overheard whisperings of a Deliverer walking the woods around the Way of the Throne."

"Deliverer," Aoald muttered as he shook his head. "They've been gone since Zaelero the Great made peace and unified the Nine."

"Kelviel," Gwogh spoke up. "You've been quiet."

Lifting one shoulder in a shrug, Kelviel pursed his lips. But even as the others went on, mentioning everything from raqine to Drigovudd, Gwogh watched as the Hetaeran representative maintained his silence . . . his gaze continuously drifting to a particular corner.

"So," Bæde said pounding a fist on the table. "Enough prattle. Why are we convened?"

Gwogh rose to his feet. "My brethren and sister"—he nodded to Kedulcya—"I've called you together because . . ." Would they think him a fool? Again? "I think you should be aware of events I have witnessed firsthand, and ones I believe will be forthcoming."

Adek barked a laugh. "What? Will you tell us the Fierian is coming?"

Piercing the man with a glare provided little satisfaction. "Yes."

Silence gaped.

Then just as swift, laughter mocked. Adek laughed again, this time bellowing. Bæde joined him. Though Griese gave a laugh, he shifted, uncomfortable. Traytith and Voath remained unmoved—as did Aoald.

"By the Flames, Gwogh, have you lost your mind?" Aoald shook his head, his thoughts revealed. "The Fierian is more myth than truth."

"The day we believe what Sirdar speaks is the day we are useless as a council." Gwogh's anger crested. "That day—*this* day, if you are earnest in your mockery of Abiassa's Parchments—we are nothing more than over-gifted accelerants, who should be singed by the very breath of Abiassa!"

Kelviel watched Gwogh, a storm in his gray eyes.

"What proof have you?" Bæde demanded, his balding crown catching the light of the candles and wall torches.

"Much." So Gwogh shared the truth of what happened in Fieri Keep. Of Haegan's temporary healing. The princess's paralysis and apparent loss of her gifts.

"You were sent there in shame to babysit a crippled prince, and you could not even do that," Bæde said. "Why should I listen to your rantings, old man?"

Stunned at the disrespect, Gwogh stared at the accelerant.

"Ask him what he was paid by Sirdar to betray those who sit at this table." The voice came from behind—and yet in front. The Deliverer.

Gwogh pivoted and looked to the dark corner, yet still saw nothing but wood slats and a grimy window. He turned back, and found the others watching, their expressions wary. Had they not heard the Deliverer?

"Something wrong?" Kedulcya asked, touching the back of her neck, as if she could feel the presence of Abiassa's judge.

"No." Gwogh cleared his throat.

"Ask him!"

The vehemence sent a rush of heat over Gwogh's shoulders. He swallowed hard. "Tell me, Bæde, what price Sirdar paid you to betray this council."

The man paled. Shifted his wide girth on the hard chair. "What are you talking about, you old fool?"

"Speak truth!" The voice boomed from the corner.

Chairs squawked as the others shoved them back and pushed to their feet. Bæde didn't move, his expression like stone. Defiant. Angry.

"The judges return to the land," Kedulcya whispered.

"I am Medric," the Deliverer said, his voice echoing and yet calm, "sent by the will of Abiassa." He glided across the room, the others flocking to opposite corners, stricken.

Adek took a step, no doubt thinking it his place to defend his mentor. "What right—"

Medric did not blink or detour from his path. Yet Adek collapsed in a heap. At his side, Kedulcya glanced down but then away. Like the others, she did not want to appear to side with those who had set themselves against Abiassa.

Bæde slowly came to his feet.

Medric tucked his chin.

Bæde went back down hard, as if pushed into his chair by an invisible hand.

"Bæde of Dradith, you have stained this council with the blood of innocents, the coin of Dyrth, and the scourge of Sirdar." Silver glinted in the torchlight.

His sword. Gwogh drew in a breath, unable to move, remembering how, in A'tia's home, his hand had seemed to hold the blade that was not visible.

"Do you seek the mercy of Abiassa?"

Skin mottled, Bæde stared unabashed at the judge advancing on him. The whites of his eyes revealed his rage. "I have no need of Her mercy!"

"Your heart is revealed for all to see. Your guilt is decided." Medric knelt, bowed his head. "Judgment delivered."

Unbelievably, Bæde lunged.

And Medric was on his feet somehow. Towering—head and shoulders over the forty-something accelerant. The hideous beauty of his movement, of his supernaturally fast movement, roared through Gwogh's mind. Like lightning, Medric's blade flashed.

Tsing!

The sound hit his ears late, the strike happening in the space of a single heartbeat. Strangest of all—there was no blood. No body. Bæde simply ceased to exist.

Medric turned, faced the council, his blade again unseen. His purpose apparently concluded. "There is no shame in doubt," he spoke, his gaze on Kelviel. "What you do with doubt decides your judgment. But make no mistake—it is *your* choice." His fiery gaze swung to Gwogh. "Upon your shoulders rests the burden of his protection. He is in the forest near the Great Falls facing four enemies. Save him."

3 3

Raging and tumultuous, the river rushed past Haegan. They'd hiked through the night to put distance between them and the Jujak. Thiel had pushed them mercilessly, only allowing a short break in the hopes Drracien would catch up. His continued absence haunted them the farther they went. Now as dawn once more climbed from its slumber and tore back the veil of night, they trudged onward.

They traced the path of the tumbling waters up to the Great Falls for another half day. Exhaustion weighted his limbs already, the trek arduous and long—a day spent at a breakneck pace. With his gaze, he followed the river's path. It barreled past them, running south and straight off a cliff, where it dove down and crashed into enormous boulders, which split the water into two heads. From his spot at the head of these Falls, the lesser sibling of the colossal waterfall to the north, Haegan stared out over the wooded mountain range and eyed the two sparkling lines that broke from this mighty river. The larger of the two rushed out toward the east, dumping into the Twin Cities and the Nydessan Sea. The other, the branch they had crossed, swung outward, its girth slimming once it left Hetaera and arced into Kerguli territory where the badlands blew its hot breath against the waters, thinning the river until it vanished altogether among the mountains—the Shields, the range that twisted around Seultrie and ended in the Lakes of Fire.

"Oy, if I fell into that, it would make mincemeat pie of me," Laertes mumbled.

"More like soup." Tokar ruffled his hair again.

"Get off me," Laertes said, shoving Tokar's hand away. "I might be only ten, but I'm not a kid."

"We should keep moving," Praegur said, but his gaze never left the waters. Wonder becalmed him.

"Have you not seen waters like this?" Haegan said.

"It is much smaller in Kerguli—passable, unlike here."

"Does your family live near the East River?" Haegan asked. "Will you go back to them?"

"My parents were taken by the Ematahri. My sister was slaughtered. I have no reason to return."

"Mercy," Haegan mumbled. "I . . . I had no idea. You said nothing when we were held by them."

"It was a different clan. And you were not with us long enough. Let's move." Praegur stalked ahead.

"Shouldn't we wait for Drracien?" Thiel hiked the sack of supplies over her shoulder. "He shouldn't be too far behind us."

"He told us to meet him by the river." Haegan eyed the rapids once more, hating the trickle of jealousy at her concern for the accelerant.

"But it spans leagues!" Thiel swiped at a fly. "How are we to know where?"

"He said he'd meet us, so if he keeps moving along the path of the river, he'll find us."

"If we wait, he'll find us. If we keep moving—"

"If we wait, he won't be the only one to find us," Haegan said.

Her amber eyes found his. Though her expression told him she wanted to argue, Thiel nodded. "You're right. I just . . ."

His gut twisted. "You're worried about him." Had she ever worried about Haegan? When he and Drracien had been late returning—did she wonder if he survived? "It's natural," he forced himself to say. "But as you saw, he's quite capable of taking care of himself."

Sticking to the path of the river challenged the group. Moss-covered boulders hugging the trail made the path treacherous. Laertes scampered up the long incline like a monkey, but with the supplies, Haegan and Thiel took their time of the journey. Hours bled into evening.

"Were you close?" she asked, hopping from one rock to another.

"To what?"

She gave a small smile and jumped to another spot. "Your sister."

"Oh. Yes—quite." Haegan cringed every time she made a leap, his steps more deliberate, careful. "You should watch yourself. The rocks are slick."

She jutted her jaw, defiant. "I've covered worse territory than this, tunnel rat."

"So we're back to condescension and names, are we?"

"Did we move past it?" An eyebrow winged over her amber eyes. And had he not known better, he would've thought she was flirting. But what would a woman like Thiel want with a weakling like him? Wasn't she more suited for the dapper Drracien?

"After four weeks, I would hope so."

"Only four? I've held grudges for years."

"Then I am truly sorry for you," he said, reaching for a high rock and pulling up onto it with a grunt, "for nothing rots a soul faster than bitterness."

She glanced down, her brown hair dripping into her face, the boyish cut now shaggy but not quite enough to be pretty. Perhaps cute, in an *"I'd rather trousers and horses to silks and ribbons."* way. She had that manner about her. With another rueful look at him, Thiel again hopped.

"I wish you wouldn't—"

"Relax, tunnel rat." She grinned and flung herself to a rock.

One that was too far away.

"No!" Haegan sucked in a hard breath as she hit hard with a meaty *oof*, that no doubt knocked the air from her lungs. "Thiel!"

She bounced off the ledge. And slid. Down . . . "Augh!"

He lunged to the right, groping for her hand. Her fingers grazed his. And slid right through. "Thiel! No!"

Her scream faded with her.

Haegan eyed the incline.

"What happened?" Tokar shouted.

"She fell." Haegan dangled his leg over the edge, determined to slide after her.

"Rigar, don't! It's too dangerous," Tokar called, his movements thumping overhead.

But Haegan was already sliding. The rock warmed the seat of his pants as he skidded with his feet, trying to slow his descent. He kept his gaze below, looking for her. "Thiel!" A rock flung him off the sheer edifice. He went airborne, his hands sweating out his terror.

Boulders raced up at him. Clipped his arm. Flipped him, the rocks slick and the raging river icy.

Thud!

Pain jarred through his back and neck as he hit, then continued down.

There! He saw her. Bent. Still. "Thiel!"

She moved. Pushed upward and glanced up at him. Her eyes went wide. "Haegan!"

Then he saw why she panicked. A large rock jumped into his path. He rammed into it, his shoulder hitting first. Pain spiked through his back. His head thumped off the rock as he flipped, water rushing down on either side of the rock. Joints and head screaming, he blinked. His vision slowly focused as spots faded. He groaned. Though the landing had been awful, he didn't feel anything horrible—until he heard Thiel's crying. Then he felt pain similar to the night Kaelyria carried out the transference. He rolled onto his side and found himself facing Thiel.

And beneath them, mere inches away, the soaring emptiness of a thirty-foot drop. He felt his stomach plummet with the depths. Shifted backward. Focused on Thiel. Her face was screwed tight in pain, a sheen covering her.

"What's wrong?"

She grimaced, pushing back, breathing hard. "My ankle—it's trapped."

Careful not to pitch himself off the ledge, Haegan glanced at her leg. Caught in a crevice. He didn't see blood, but she'd surely broken it with the way it had wedged into the tiny space. And there was no way down from the ledge. They were stuck. And she was injured.

Blazes! What would they do?

"Hey, you two okay?"

Peering up the incline, Haegan stilled at the length they'd fallen. Had to be twenty yards or more. "Her leg is trapped. We have no way of getting down."

A whistle shrieked behind him. Haegan glanced toward the base. What was that noise? He searched, then saw movement. Drracien waved his arms.

Haegan turned away, annoyed. This wasn't a time for fun. They needed help.

"What is it?" Thiel asked, her face pale and sweaty.

"Drracien. Waving at us."

Another shrill whistle.

Haegan turned, glared.

This time, Drracien motioned both hands to the left. "Move away. I can wield—"

Thiel gasped, her knuckles white as she gripped Haegan's shirt. "No! Don't let him. The ledge will give way."

When Haegan looked back to Drracien, he had scaled half the distance that separated them. "Protect her!"

"No," Haegan shouted, but the accelerant's arms were arcing and swooping. He threw himself around, pinning Thiel between himself and the rock.

Her fingers dug into his shirt, her body trembling. "He's going to kill us," she whimpered.

The rock rumbled. "No, he won't." He better not. Or Haegan would kill him.

Thiel's arms snaked around his waist, holding tight.

"I've got y—"

Crack!

Ground beneath them tilted. Thiel's scream pierced his aching ear, but it went deeper. Through his brain. Down his heart. Into his soul. When he felt invisible hands pulling him back, toward the drop-off, Haegan crushed her against himself. They fell away from the rock.

Air tore at his tunic and hair.

Thiel clung to him, her body rigid with terror that matched his own. They were going to die. He would die, not make it to the Falls and Kaelyria would never walk away. Falling . . . falling . . .

Abiaaaaassssssa!

A weight slammed into his back.

Oof!

They flipped midair,. Once more, Haegan tensed, sensing the ground rushing up at them.

Splash! Thud!

• • •

"Rigar! Rigar, wake up!"

Pain riddled every move. Haegan swam through the thick sludge of unconsciousness, aiming for the voice. The urgent, panicked voice of Thiel.

"Rigar, please. Wake up. They're coming. They're right there."

Alarms blared through his mind. He jerked upward.

Shrieking pain stabbed his head and back. He arched his spine and threw himself backward. "Augh!"

"Careful, careful!" Thiel hovered over him, her hair mottled with green moss and mud. "You . . . you hit hard."

His head swam, the memory of that impact thudding over and over in his brain. Eyes closed, he tested his hands. Feeling there. Feet. He hissed, sensing a fracture or sprain. But his back . . . *Blazes, it hurts!*

"Get him up. Someone's coming. We have to hide."

That snapped open his eyes. Thiel lifted his right arm, Praegur his left.

"Move," Tokar said, nudging Thiel aside. "He doesn't need his arm around you, and you need support yourself with that broken ankle."

Jealousy—at least they had that much in common, vying for Thiel's affections—tore at Haegan, but he focused on getting up. But then it struck him. Praegur, Laertes, and Tokar had made it back down the rugged path. "How long was I out?"

"Just get up!" Tokar bit out as he and Praegur hauled him off the ground. Haegan's knees buckled. Pain punched him. Was the transference lost? Was he crippled again?

"Stand, you weakling!" Tokar growled. "I'll leave you before I carry you."

Mind shaken alert, Haegan jerked forward. Told his feet to get under him.

"Go go go!" Laertes said.

They half-dragged him to the thicket and dove for cover just seconds before a wagon lumbered over the knoll, then rolled quickly down into the small valley. Packed into the cart like cows in a pen, the people stared out with vacant eyes. Arms and legs dangled over the sides and through slats, the same slats stragglers clung to on the outside. The cart labored up the next hill, and the oxen struggled, hooves failing to find purchase. Their muscles strained. The wagon creaked. Groaned. And started rolling backward.

With a shout, those clinging to the outer slats hopped off and pushed. Stopped the defeat and succeeded in helping the beasts heave over the incline.

Grunting with a twinge of sharp pain, Haegan watched. "What's over that hill?"

"More of the same," Drracien said. "It's this way all the way up this mountain to the Falls. Like someone wanted to make the journey as difficult as possible."

"Abiassa's good at that." Tokar huffed.

"Tests our character, our mettle," Haegan agreed through gritted teeth.

"Got to have that to be tested," Drracien muttered. "We should get moving."

Haegan bit back his frustration. "Scouts." He adjusted, cowering beneath a wad of pain. "We should send scouts. Find a good place to camp."

"Agreed," Thiel said. "Laertes, you're the best at that. You up to it?"

"Sure I am." And he was off like lightning.

"I'll go with him." Praegur jogged behind Laertes through the thick shrubs and broad-leafed fronds dotting the riverside.

Quiet draped over the small group as they waited in the brush for the recon reports. Haegan seized the chance to rest his aching back, pressing his spine flat against the earth. What had he hit? A pike? It felt like it. Where had he landed? He didn't know. He remembered falling. That had been a terrifying feeling, knowing he had Thiel tight in his arms as they plummeted, that he must protect her.

"You saved me," she said softly, easing down beside him.

He would never, as long as he lived, forget that fall. Or holding her. Smelling her hair—which carried the unique scents of the forest. And though she had concealed herself for the first few weeks, Thiel's curves were no longer hidden.

He should be ashamed of himself. But there was not enough in him to feel that way. She was amazing. Brave. Courageous. Beautiful.

"Can I ask a question?"

Haegan turned his head toward her, tensing at the pinch of pain.

"When we were falling, something . . ." She wet her lips. Looked away. Then smiled. "Do not think that I banged my head too hard—but did something hit us?"

Haegan frowned. "I beg your mercy?"

"We were knocked sideways. Quite noticeably."

We were? Haegan thought . . . fought to recall . . . The pain. Between his shoulders. The distinct shift in their descent. Yes. She was right. "I think so." He shook his head. "I'm not sure what hit us. But I think that's why I'm in so much pain."

"Well, I thought that might have been my fault." She blushed. So pretty. "I landed on top of you . . . and well, you bounced."

"Ah." He wanted to laugh, but he had no memory of landing. Or bouncing. "Did you get hurt? From the fall, I mean?"

"No," she said, her voice soft. "Thanks to you."

"Hey, lovebirds!" Drracien hissed at them. "They're back."

Thiel spun around, yelping as she twisted her leg.

Haegan sat up, grinding his teeth. Whatever it was had nailed him squarely in the back, possibly saving their lives.

"You won't believe it," Laertes said, his brown eyes wide with excitement. "There are hundreds—"

"Possibly a thousand," Praegur said.

"—encamped all up the side of the mountain." Laertes knelt in front of Thiel. "It's a small city up in here what we can get lost."

"How are we supposed to get to the Falls?" Tokar growled. "All those people—"

"Make the perfect cover, like the boy said," Drracien replied.

Haegan turned to Laertes. "Did you see Jujak?"

Laertes frowned. "I just saw them people."

"*Those* people," Haegan corrected, his mind on the crowds. On the ability to hide in a sea of bodies.

"You think it's safe?" Thiel asked him.

"What are you asking him for?"

"Because he has a good mind. He thinks things through." Thiel held her leg as she guided it around Drracien and Tokar. "Unlike some of you."

"Right. Jumping off the side of the mountain after you is really thinking things through." Tokar shook his head. "I don't know—"

"If he hadn't come after me, I'd be dead."

Silence hung like a black void between them.

"I heard 'em talking about soldiers, I did, when I was walking through the crowds. They was all in a bother." Laertes shook his head. "But what made them say that, I can't tell. I didn't see no soldiers."

Haegan nodded. "If we can hide, so can the Jujak."

"Word has probably already spread about my confrontation with them," Drracien said.

"This is a string of right bad luck," Laertes said mournfully. "This journey is cursed."

"No, *Rigar* is cursed. He's the bad luck," Tokar said.

"Easy." Thiel glanced again to Haegan, then Tokar and Drracien. "I think we should try the crowds. See if we can blend in. If we sense things are off, we can slip out.

"At least they aren't Dyrth's Maereni or the Raeng." One were part of Poired's army, the other a band of assassins. Both merciless fighters.

"Thankfully, neither venture this far west," Thiel said. "Let's get going. I want to make camp before dark."

• • •

"There they are."

Trale Kath eased behind the trunk of a tree, chomping into a ripe cordi fruit as he monitored the group of six. They were a little younger than Astadia, the white-skinned teens closer to eighteen than her twenty years. But they were all more innocent. Less corrupted.

The six had broken up before entering the camp, most likely to avoid drawing attention. But Trale had no trouble identifying them. It almost disappointed him how easily he and Astadia had followed them after leaving the city.

First to enter the encampment of hopefuls were the Kerguli and the young boy, not more than ten cycles but as alert as they came. He wore his blond hair longer than Northlanders, but normal for Iteverians. Perhaps that was what made Trale admire the boy. Even now, his brown eyes came to Trale and lingered. He scowled, then looked away, muttering something to the Kergulian, whose gaze swung around the crowd but never rested on Trale for longer than the barest of seconds. More practiced at avoiding detection than most, Trale guessed. Good for him.

It didn't work, of course. Trale had no equal. No Iteverian on the plains of the Embers did. One only had to look around this encampment of hopefuls, crowding the forest for a chance at a fantasy—a chance for a miracle.

Fools. Blinded by their selfishness. Nothing was ever enough, though they had more than he had, including their freedom. And gullible fools at that. Believing the lies of accelerants and politicians. Ruled by the vicious Fire King.

The Kergulian kept walking, talking, and feigning casualness. But to trackers, to those who preyed on others, their nervousness was as obnoxious as if they had painted themselves red.

Ah. Here. The girl who played boy with her chopped brown hair, trousers, and tunics. Despicable. And she limped—could she not handle herself in the wild? Then she should return to the halls of her people and continue their legacy with children. Aiding her was the one he did not like. Black hair shorn to his skull, tall and impetuous. He hooked an arm around the impish girl as she hobbled to a tree stump.

"That's him," Astadia spoke from the shadows behind him. "With the accelerant."

Trale smiled at her prowess. She could smell an accelerant leagues away. Probably because she so desperately despised their master, Dyrth.

But she wasn't speaking about the accelerant. Trailing everyone by a dozen paces or more walked a moderately built man. Well, not quite a man. Not a boy either. Someday, he might be formidable. But for now he was a shaggy boy working too hard to blend in with the others flocking to this wetland. Long gold hair, nose in the air—nobility. Fool. He should know to crop that hair or those around him would guess his identity.

But was he the reason the Jujak had scoured Hetaera and come so far north? "You're sure?" Nobody in his party had paid the boy particular attention. In fact, the shorn-head blaggard seemed to hate him.

Astadia crossed her arms. "He's the prince."

Trale took another bite of the cordi, surreptitiously monitoring the Seultrian heir. "This should be enough to remove our shackles." He could not think what Dyrth would do to this boy if he captured him. But that was not Trale's concern. Freeing his sister was.

At his side, Astadia touched his shoulder, her green eyes reflecting the desperate hope he sought but knew was out of reach. At least for him. He warred on. Tracked on. In the hope that some day, she could be free.

After pitching the cordi core into the brush, he turned back into the camp. Swiped a hand over his mouth as he knelt and drew out a dagger. Holding it tightly, he returned to her. "You know what to do."

34

Thiel's scream raked through the din of the camp. Her hand crushed Haegan's as he knelt at her side, his stomach roiling at the thought of the excruciating pain she experienced as the healer set her broken ankle. Trembling, she slumped against the cot and closed her eyes. The sight of her in such agony tore at him. He wanted to hold her. Reassure her.

"There now," the healer said. "That's the worst of it. I'll have it bound in no time."

Thiel's head lolled to the side, and her amber eyes, still hooded in pain, brightened as she looked at him. A half smile worked its way into her lips. "You look worse than me."

"Have you seen yourself?"

Releasing the knot she'd formed in the blanket, she weakly smacked his bicep.

"It was poor of me," he said with a laugh, "to make light of your discomfort."

"Discomfort?" Her eyes hinted at mirth, though she sounded indignant. Yet the pale sheen clung to her like an early morning mist. "Let me give you some discomfort, tunnel rat."

"There you go. Keep it elevated," the healer said to Thiel, who brushed the sweat-soaked hair from her face. "I've bound it, but you'll need to stay off the leg so it can heal."

Thiel rolled her eyes.

The healer huffed, shaking her head that sported multiple braided buns sticking out all over the place, like knots on a tree. "Don't you come complaining to me if you break it again or worse. I told you what you need to do. It's up to you." The healer turned to Haegan. "Keep her off that foot, even if she don't want to listen to you."

"Yes, ma'am," he said as Praegur passed her a pouch.

Money? Or was he divesting for her payment what little supplies they'd secured before leaving Luxlirien?

"What about 'im?" Laertes thumbed to Haegan. "He got hurt, too."

"Oh?" A healer lives for the hurting, and this one seemed especially glad for the work.

Haegan raised a hand. "Mercy. I'm fine." When he bent to acknowledge and thank her, he jerked, pain catching his spine.

"Your back, is it?"

With a shake of his head, Haegan came to his feet. "It is of no bother. Truly."

She twirled her finger in the air. "Around, you. Let me have a look."

Spearing Laertes with a glare, Haegan tugged his tunic off as he turned.

"O beneficent, merciful One!"

Haegan frowned and glanced over his shoulder. "Is there concern?" The lad's eyes were bugged, and the healer stood shaking her head, pale. "What?"

"You're—the whole of your back is covered in a monstrous bruise of some sort."

Haegan scowled. Jerked around, cringing and arching away in a vain attempt to see the mark. "No surprise," he grunted out. "It hurts as if someone used me to beat out their clothes."

"Let me make sure nothing's broken." The healer's firm hands moved over his spine, nearly buckling Haegan's knees. "Mercy," she whispered. "I think everything is where it's supposed to be, but how you got such a wicked mark . . . I think"—she rifled through her bag—"ah, here. A salve. Apply it twice a day. It'll help the ache and swelling."

Haegan took the small container. "Thanks."

The healer headed for the tent opening. "Find me if you need more help."

"I hope that won't be necessary." Haegan lifted his tunic and turned it around, straightening it to put it on.

Tokar slipped beneath the tent flap as the older woman left. He hesitated, staring at Haegan, then Thiel. "What? A bare-chest contest?" He whipped off his tunic. "I have you beat, Twig." He flexed his muscles. Real muscles. Not the muscles Haegan had, which were twice what he'd had as an invalid. But Tokar's were toned and spoke of his strength and agility.

Haegan's gaze flicked to Thiel, who snickered. Humiliated, he stabbed his arms through the sleeves. Would he ever measure up? To anyone's standards? "I beg your mercy." He moved toward the tent opening.

"Rigar," Praegur called. "We must talk."

Hand on the tent flap, Haegan hesitated and slowly glanced at the foursome. "Of what?"

"Do you know the ritual for entering the Falls?"

A frown gave his answer.

"It's . . . it's costly." Praegur's dark features were carved with concern. "I think we should just move on."

"How can you say that?" Haegan stalked into the middle of the tent. "I've worked for weeks to get here. I *must* enter the waterfall."

"Why?" Tokar joined the dispute, almost anxious to have an argument with Haegan. "Why must you do this? You seem healthy enough. It's cost us everything. Thiel broke her ankle—"

"And I risked my life to save her," Haegan snapped. "Where were you?"

Tokar lunged.

"No!" Thiel shouted.

But Tokar's punch landed true and hard on Haegan's jaw. Pain exploded through his face and neck as he fell backward. A fresh wave of pain—from his back this time—clawed his body. Blinking, he expected additional blows. When they did not come, he braved a glance at Tokar.

Two arms hooked him from behind and held him—Drracien.

Gritting his teeth, Haegan pulled himself off the ground. His lip was swelling, and a metallic taste glanced across his tongue. He spat blood.

Thiel hobbled toward them, her injured leg held at an awkward angle. "What is wrong with you?" she demanded of Tokar, pushing him backward. "You know he does this for his sister. He has spoken of her since we first encountered him. We are here, and there is no reason to leave when he's so close." Then to Haegan. "Badly done, Rigar. That was uncalled for."

Chastised, he knew she was right but could not bring himself to speak or tear his gaze from Tokar.

"Let go of me," Tokar hissed at Drracien and wrenched free. He shrugged, straightening his tunic.

Hauling himself out of his anger and frustration, Haegan forced his mind to Thiel. "The healer's orders were explicit—you are to rest. Stay off your leg."

"And I would if you two would stop acting like children who need a mother!" She threw herself back on the cot, wincing as she lifted her leg back onto it.

"I shall remove myself, so I am no longer a burden to you." With a slight bow, he left the tent. Shaking his head, he reprimanded himself for lowering himself to the level of Tokar and taking the bait. For lashing out. He was not himself. Had not been for the last four weeks or so.

"Might I show you something?"

Haegan glanced back and found Drracien hiking up the hill after him. "I am in no mood for another remonstration. I am duly chided."

"Indeed." Determination marked the man's brow. "But no chiding or lecture." He swept past without much of an effort. "I believe you will want to see this, prince."

Haegan stopped, irritated that the accelerant continued referring to him as such in public. With a sigh, Haegan followed him up the hillside, around a path that twisted and switchbacked until Haegan was certain they were lost. He searched for a marker to gain his bearings, but nothing was familiar. Even the trees were foreign. Why was he even trusting the accelerant?

A niggling at the back of his mind wormed deeper and deeper into his brain. Drracien knew Haegan's real identity. He'd already once

admitted he'd tried to turn Haegan in to regain his position. What if
this was another attempt to do that? Separating him from the others.

"You tired?" Drracien pulled himself up onto a rock and through
two narrowly set trees.

"Mercy?"

He slanted a glance back. "You're slowing."

Am I?

"Just a little farther."

"What are we—"

"Shh." Drracien dragged himself up on a large boulder and squatted behind a copse of trees with a bluish trunks. He motioned Haegan
down into the same position.

Heart thumping from the exertion and the anticipation of trouble,
Haegan hunched into the small space, surprised to find a cleft jutting
out before them, just beyond the reach of the tree limbs. A rush of
cold swept over him at the thirty-foot drop. He'd already had a fall
and would rather not repeat the unfortunate incident. It went straight
down, right to a clearing just east of the Great Falls.

But not just a clearing. A clearing that played host to—"Ignatieri."
Richly adorned, two rows of tents arced away from where the waterfall
crashed into a large pool that fed the river. The far lip spilled the icy
water down into the head river. A dozen accelerants lingered around
a campfire. Another ten or so were off to the side setting up more
shelter. With their red and black uniforms, they were a fierce sight.

And yet—they somehow paled to the smaller, simpler tents going
up along one flank. "Jujak." The royal guard were still settling in, their
movements precise and sharp. Haegan had longed to be among their
ranks as a boy, and he could not deny the admiration still lingered.
"There must be . . ." His heart crashed as violently against his ribs as
the waterfall did against the pool. "Twenty. Maybe a few less."

So many? At a time like this? Why? These couldn't be the Jujak
that had dogged their steps since Luxlirien. Though they had clearly
arrived just that day, they had already accomplished hours' worth of
work—on this rough terrain, even with horses, the group chasing
Haegan never could have gotten so far ahead of them.

Drracien studied him. "Why are they after you?"

They blocked the route to the Great Falls. To reach the blessed waters, he'd have to get past both Jujak and Ignatieri. How? Going around would take too long, since the river above was thick and impassible with its violent rapids.

"On second thought," Drracien said, "*why?* Why are you doing this? Why the Kindling?" He squinted. "You have your health."

"But she does not." Haegan spoke quietly, Kaelyria's sweet, beautiful face taunting him yet again.

"Your sister."

"If I do not enter the waters, she will forever be captive by the ailments that once bound me."

Dark brows drew tight. Seconds of silence grew into minutes. "I do not understand. You stole your sister's health?"

Haegan sniffed. "I would not even begin to know how to steal it." The memory still proved painful. "She had an accelerant assist her in the scheme."

"Impossible. If what are you saying is true, then they performed a transference. Those are forbidden!" Drracien's hair hung over eyes aflame with indignation. "No accelerant worth his wielding would be caught performing such an act."

"Then maybe that's the problem. Maybe he hasn't been caught."

"Aye, I heard rumblings in the camp earlier that they're still looking for the prince and the accomplice. Yet you claim innocence."

"Because it is truth!"

Drracien expelled a frustrated breath. His gaze went back to the clearing. "Who was it?" Another shake of his head. "No, do not tell me. There is nothing I could do."

"I should not have relented when she pleaded with me. I only did it because she was so eager to change what I had accepted long ago— that the bed would be my existence until I died. She kept mentioning Ruadh and Manido . . ."

"You and the princess were close?"

An almost imperceptible nod acknowledged the truth and Haegan's grief. "I would have given her the world had I but the tools. She is good and pure, not at all spoiled as most would expect." He slumped against the tree. Leaves rustled and rattled.

Hand up, Drracien snapped his gaze below, his eyes wide with alarm that they might be noticed. A few seconds went by. He leaned to one side, watching a detachment of Jujak, who trotted quickly out of view. But they returned almost as quick. "Drills." Drracien eased onto the ground and drew a knee to his chest. "If you loved your sister so wholly, why did you allow this?"

"Do not think me so poor of character. She withheld from me the full of what would happen. And though I cannot make sense of her motives or her effort, my sister is strong and her character infallible. Young she may be, but Kaelyria's purpose and very breath are for the Nine."

"What happened—tell me of the transference." When Haegan hesitated, Drracien shifted. "I'm an accelerant. I'm curious . . ."

"I am not sure how much I recall. Cilicien—"

"*ka'Dur?*"

Haegan paused. "I am not certain. It was not until I spoke his name that I even recalled it."

With a scowl, Drracien bobbed his head. "Go on."

"He said some words, did some dance—"

"Form."

"What?"

"It's not a dance," Drracien said. "It's a form."

"Of course. He danced *the form*." He could not help but annoy the man. "Next thing I knew, I felt like my very body was on fire. It was incredible to feel again after so many years. I was ecstatic. I had not realized how much I wanted to be whole again." He sighed, suddenly remembering the tears sliding down her cheek. "But when I turned, she"—burning started at the back of his throat and eyes—"was crippled."

Drracien tilted his head, frowning. "So she then had your paralyzed body and you were whole?"

"It was wrong. So very wrong." Haegan knew it in the deepest part of him. When the accelerant seemed to weigh the answer, his eyes darting back and forth to nothing in particular, Haegan grew alarmed. "What?"

He shook his head, then gave a small smile. "She gave you an opportunity."

"Perhaps. But to what end?" Haegan's gaze rose to the waters tumbling from a great height not visible to him at this vantage. "I'm not even sure the Kindling will heal me." It seemed surreal and peaceful, the foam, the churning wake, the mist rising off the falling waters.

Hesitation seemed to hold the accelerant in a firm grip. Then he finally spoke. "Have no fear—they *will* heal you."

"How can you believe so wholly?"

"I'm an accelerant. If I didn't believe, I couldn't wield." Drracien hopped onto his feet, but remained in a crouch as he looked down at the clearing again. "Our challenge is figuring out how to get you to the pool without being captured or killed."

35

"Wait." Haegan caught Drracien's tunic. "Tell me."

"I don't know how we're going to get you through. That's what I just said."

"No, tell me what concern lay in your hesitation." He would not go darkly into another trap. This time, he would go with his eyes open. No more falsehoods or hidden truths. "The look on your face is the same one my sister bore when she gave only partial truths. What lies behind yours?"

Drracien stilled. Looked down. Then something rippled through his face. "We should go."

"No." Haegan moved in front of him. "I would have answers, truth."

"Only Abiassa can provide what you seek, Pr—" He bit off the end of his word, his gaze again flicking to the side. Something changed in his posture. He'd tensed.

Haegan's pulse sped up, noting Drracien was not paying attention to him but to something in the brush around them.

"Come." Drracien hopped off the very rock Haegan felt would protect them. Uncertainty followed him down the trodden path. Had the accelerant deftly avoided his question? Or was there a danger Haegan had not noticed? Tension knotted the muscles between his aching shoulders.

After a few minutes of confusing trails, his patience thinned. "What—?"

Drracien threw himself to the right, hands moving in quick circles.

A cry went out—a woman's.

The accelerant rushed into the brush with Haegan on his heels. Tucked into a thicket lay a young woman, holding her shoulder.

No. Not just a woman. "This is the woman who helped me avoid the Jujak in Hetaera."

"The prostitute?"

"I'm not—"

"She's not—" Haegan stopped when they spoke simultaneously.

"Why are you following us?" Drracien aimed his palms at her.

She held up her hands. "I am no threat, Master Accelerant."

"I am no master," Drracien said. "On your feet."

Haegan felt the compulsion to help her. She flashed him a small smile and set her fingers against his. He tugged her up and waited to ascertain if she was injured.

"Why are you following us?" Drracien repeated.

"I saw him"—her brown eyes came to Haegan—"and . . ." Her cheeks pinked, even in the dim light of the forest. She chewed her lower lip and refused to meet his gaze again.

"Well?" Drracien demanded.

"So I's got a soft spot for him." She slapped her hands against her skirt with a huff. "I wanted to talk with him."

"Alone? To what end—to damage his name or to entrap him in a marriage bond?"

Haegan could not help but take a step back. Did girls really do that?

"What?" Her wide green eyes snapped up, her mouth agape. "No! I wouldn't ever do that to a man that I be likin'." Again, her eyes widened then flicked away.

The air warbled, and the girl leaned back, whimpering. Haegan could barely detect the heat plume around her torso. He frowned at Drracien, whose expression had grown fierce. "What are you—"

"Who are you?" Drracien growled.

"Just a girl—"

Drracien's fingers widened as he pushed his hands toward her. "The truth!"

She cried out. Sweat trickled from her temples and slid down her face. And yet, she didn't defend herself.

With a drawn-in breath, Drracien stepped back with his right foot, pointed his thumb and drew his hand back along the length of his arm.

The girl wilted for a second, and Haegan's sympathies were touched. This should stop. It wasn't right to wield against the innocent. And such a pretty girl. Had she truly sought him out because of romantic interest? To force him into a relationship? The thought made his head spin. His fingers twitched toward Drracien.

She stiffened, sweat beading on her lips that grew tight. Her nostrils flared.

That wasn't agony or pain. That was anger. Why was she angry?

"Who are you? *Name!*" Drracien, hair dangling in his eyes again, dragged his right hand in an arc until it swung up and over his head, then rested at eye level in front of his face. "Or I will singe the hairs off your body."

Alarmed, Haegan darted a look to his friend, then back to the girl.

She curled her lip at him. What . . . what was that?

"C'mon, she's just—"

"*Name!*"

She trembled, fighting the pain.

Drracien flicked his middle finger.

That simple move seemed to crackle the air. The girl cried out, her head tossed back. Tears streaked down her face. "Astadia," she cried out.

Drracien froze. He shot Haegan a look. "Get back to the tent."

"But—"

"*Now!*"

Haegan stumbled backward, but then looked at the girl again. Her face had reddened and her muscles convulsed uncontrollably. Even her neck and arms were turning red.

Burning.

"Stop." Haegan reached to the accelerant.

"She's not an innocent woman."

"I don't care. You're hurting her."

"If you knew what she's done and who she works for, you would order me to kill her."

Stunned, Haegan again looked to the girl. Her green eyes held a spark of red in them, turning a dull, flat color into a rich, deep one. And they resonated with her pain. Her . . . regret.

She slumped, tears streaming down her face.

"Enough. She's surrendered."

"Until I release her. Then she'll attack."

Haegan went to her. Knelt, staying clear of Drracien's wielding. "I must have your word that you will not attempt to harm us—"

"Or any in our company," Drracien added.

Haegan nodded. "Or any in our company," he repeated to be sure the terms of her surrender were clear. Though he ached for the pain in her eyes, he was not foolish enough to think she wouldn't lash out.

"Her word means nothing. She is—"

"Where are you from?" Haegan switched tactics.

"Iteveria," she whispered, a trail of blood escaping her nose and racing down her jaw.

His lengthy years enduring Gwogh's lessons were coming in useful after all. He remembered the Twin Cities, Iteveria and Tharqnis. The birthplaces of Poired Dyrth and Sirdar. The latter had abandoned the tenets of the Iteverian faith. The former had not. "Family above friendship," he began, watching her. Hoping she understood what he was doing. "Duty above family . . ."

Lips, now cracked and parched beneath the heat drawing the moisture from her muscles and skin, parted and tremored. Her words were almost inaudible over the hum of the wielding. "Honor above all else."

"Yes." Haegan nodded at her. "Give me your word, and I will believe and hold you to it."

Unbending, she did not yield, though she locked onto Haegan visually.

"Your word," Haegan insisted. "Or I can make no promise of what my friend may do."

Drracien, who stood behind him wielding, must have increased the intensity, because she yelped again.

"Yes," she cried. "You have it. I will not bring harm to you or this murderous accelerant."

"Or our company."

"I know not of your company." The field must've dropped or lessened because she dragged herself a few inches to a tree and pushed up against it. Panic gripped her, eyes wide. She held a hand to Drracien, who must've threatened more wielding, because she quickly added, "But I will do them no harm."

Haegan eased back to the accelerant, who seemed especially disturbed and agitated at relenting. "How did you know?"

"I just knew." Drracien watched her warily. "You cannot trust her."

"She gave her word."

"It does not mean anything." He nodded at her. "Not to trained assassins."

"Assassins?" He stared at the accelerant. "What—?"

"My brother will kill you, accelerant." She dragged a shaking hand across her face, wiping the blood from her nose.

"I would like to see him try," Drracien said.

She sneered. "You will not *see* anything when he comes for you."

Haegan touched her shoulder. "Friend, you gave your word not to harm us."

"It is not me who will do the harming," she growled.

"Then you have no honor?"

She lifted her chin. "I do what I am commanded."

"And who commands you?"

Lips tight, she turned away.

"Let me end her," Drracien said. "Her refusal to answer tells me who holds her leash—Poired Dyrth."

Shock washed through Haegan like a cold, biting wind. He looked at the girl. She'd been so nice. So friendly, though she couldn't fake her accent well enough. He'd liked her. Trusted her and been alone with her. There were many opportunities for her to have killed him. And she hadn't.

She hung her head, burrowing into her shoulders. As if cowering from his gaze. Shame? But her defiance still sparked through those eyes.

"Why?" Haegan heard himself ask. "Why would you choose to serve him? How can you not see what he's doing?"

Her green eyes rammed into him. "With the Cold One, there is no choice."

"The tenets of Iteveria demand honor above all else," Haegan said. "Being commanded does not excuse your actions, Astadia. Duty is overruled by honor, and that is guided by the edicts of Abiassa."

"That is easily spoken when you are not under threats—"

"Silence, Astadia!"

Haegan spun, but was stunned to find Drracien had already turned and aimed his wielding at the intruder. The brother, he guessed by the look of the man, with his matching brown hair and green eyes. But also well-muscled and hardened.

"Release her to me," he said.

"She threatened us." Drracien was ready. For a fight. For blood.

The man said nothing. Just stood there, a bow and arrow clutched in his left hand.

"She gave her word," Haegan said, moving forward to end the stalemate. "Not to harm us or our company."

The planes of his face were like stone. Hard, chiseled. "But I'm sure she made no such assurances about what I would do."

Haegan gritted his teeth.

"No." Drracien crossed in front of Haegan, his hands stirring the warmth in the air. "But over that rise are twenty Jujak and ten times that number of Ignatieri. Now, unless you are willing to take us all on . . ."

"You are alienated from your Brethren, are you not, accelerant?" the man said. "And what fear should I have of the king's royal guard—"

"Every fear," Haegan said. "We know you do the work of Sirdar of Tharqnis. Think you not the Jujak would take your very presence seriously, even as a threat, since the Unelithiens are ensconced about Fieri Keep even as we speak?"

The man said nothing, but his upper arm muscle flexed. "Release her to me."

"We have no obligation—"

Haegan touched Drracien's shoulder. "We will release her. Unlike the two of you, we have no ill intent."

"Don't you?" the man sneered. "A fugitive prince and master accelerant together and so close to justice? I think those over that rise would welcome news of your whereabouts."

Drracien stopped.

A stalemate again.

"We are Iteverians. If we say we will leave—"

"Your ethnicity only means you are seasoned at deception, as we have learned from your sister." Haegan didn't know what to do, but the thought of being discovered by the Jujak proved terrifying. Especially when tomorrow he could walk beneath the waterfall and everything would return to normal.

"What price would you pay, prince, to have knowledge of what hit you in the river?" The man seemed to have all the cards. "Would you want to know why you have that mark on your back?"

Haegan flinched. "How—?"

"Healers talk. You should be more careful with strangers. And—it's no bruise." He motioned to his sister. "Release her and I will tell you."

Mind racing with the man's words, Haegan couldn't speak. Couldn't respond.

"He plays you the fool," Drracien said. "He had to have been there, and he wasn't."

The Iteverian smirked. "You only think I wasn't there. We can hide when we want to." He turned his focus to Haegan. "Well, prince?"

How they knew Haegan's identity wasn't as alarming as the fact that this man had information about a mark Haegan himself didn't understand. Uncertainty was overcome by a longing to know what happened. He stepped aside. Astadia was on her feet now, her hair a tangled mess. She glided toward her brother. But at Haegan's side, she paused. Touched him.

"Astadia!"

"Peace, Trale." She pushed her green eyes to Haegan with a somber expression. "The prince saved my life. The accelerant meant to harm me." Then she joined her brother and sighed. "We were told to discover why Jujak traveled so far north, away from their singular purpose—protecting the Fire King." Again, she looked at Haegan. "Now we know."

The two were backing down the path, warily watching them.

"Wait!" Haegan started forward.

In a flash Trale's arrow was nocked and aimed at him.

Hands up, Haegan stopped. "You promised to tell me what you knew."

"Sorry." The man shrugged, urging his sister behind him and continuing to recede from view. "It's information. Invaluable for bartering."

"You lied! Deceived us." The bald truth of it pressed against Haegan. "What honor is that?"

Another lift of his shoulder as he stared down the shaft of his arrow. "Not a lie, a . . . delay. I never said when I'd tell you."

"You have what you want."

"Not everything."

"We returned your sister—to what end do you linger now?"

A jeering smile. "To an end you cannot see." He glanced at Drracien. "Right now." And slipped off.

Haegan rushed down the slope after them and rounded a corner. But they were nowhere in sight. He searched the trees, the greenery. "How could they know?"

"He didn't," Drracien said. "He just heard an addled healer talking about it and thought to use it against you. And it worked."

3 6

Did the mark on his back mean something? Was that even of great import considering the impenetrable path to the Great Falls? One day. That's all he had left. He'd escaped his own father's guard in Seultrie, though not of his own devices. Then he'd nearly fallen off a hilltop because some great creature—though of this he was still not convinced—attacked him. Faced the Ematahri, babbling in a nonsense language according to Thiel, whom he trusted with his life. She might be vigilant and fierce, but she was not a liar. And then the blinding light that killed dozens of warriors. Haegan was surprised he didn't have nightmares. Maybe they'd come once he was no longer fighting for his life and Kaelyria's.

"You are disappointed the girl deceived you?"

Haegan started at the question, almost having forgotten that Drracien was walking with him back to the tent. "What?"

"The girl." Drracien flipped his shiny black hair from his face and revealed a grin. "I mean, she was pretty. She seemed to have had a mild interest in you. Then you find out she's lying her head off." He shrugged, his long cloak fluttering as he hopped off a boulder onto the path. "I'd be singed about that."

"She is the least of my worries."

With a guffaw, Drracien plucked a weed and spread it between his thumbs. "She is an Iteverian assassin! How can you believe her the least of your troubles?"

Head down, Haegan tucked all his disasters over the last weeks into a neat pile, wrapped them in a protective casing called humiliation, and stowed them beneath his pride. And his need to protect what few secrets he had left. "If she is an assassin, then she had plenty of opportunity to end my life. But she did not." He heaved a sigh. "I have one day to figure out how to get the waterfall without being seen or stopped."

"Yeh?" Tokar appeared from behind, thudding along the path with Praegur and Laertes. "Well, unless you're willing to do the Ignatieri ritual, you aren't stepping into the pool."

Haegan frowned. "Ritual?"

"As I tried to explain earlier." Praegur thumbed over his shoulder. "Just came from the center of the encampment. High marshal has a table set up. He's ordering all who want to enter the Great Falls for Kindling to register." He raised his eyebrows as he looked at Haegan.

"It ain't cheap eaver."

"Either."

"What*eever*," Laertes threw back, with wide eyes for emphasis. "What with you getting our gold stolen—"

"They were *my* paladiums."

"—don't matter who they belonged to, now does it? Because they's gone."

"They're gone." Even Haegan cringed at his correction this time. They were poor. Several dozen gold paladiums in the pocket of some thief.

"Exactly. We ain't got them. We's poor, with what little the High and Mighty"—he pointed to Drracien—"got us."

"Payment or not," Haegan said quietly as they rounded the last corner, "there's a bigger problem."

They passed a tent that smelled of fumes from a tanner, who sold leather boots, coats, saddles. Two men stood haggling with the lean but muscular owner. At the next stand, brightly dyed fabrics and knitted pieces. But farther in, the largest area offered benches and tables in neat rows. In the center of the eating area sat several large cast iron pots breathed steam, forced by crackling fires.

"Communal," Praegur muttered. "Everyone pitches in. If you don't have food, you donate time to help cook, serve, or clean dishes."

"Or do what I do, and slip away so's nobody is the wiser." Laertes laughed.

"It is a mark against your character that you do not volunteer," Haegan chided the boy.

"It's a mark against my survival if I live by their rules. They ain't looking out for no one but 'emselves."

Haegan shook his head and kept walking. Reforming the lad into an honorable citizen would take longer than a month.

"So your bigger problem," Tokar said, clearly not wanting to drop the discussion as Haegan did. "You're a wanted fugitive."

"Hey." Haegan shoved his gaze around, making sure nobody had heard. Unfortunately, several had, but they turned their backs to them. He was about to breathe a little easier when a flash of green exploded between two men.

Jujak!

Two of the royal guard. Their gazes homed in on Haegan. "Stop!"

A hand shoved him. "Go!" Drracien hissed as he simultaneously threw a punch at Tokar.

Haegan hesitated.

"You fool! Go!" He launched himself at Tokar. The two rolled on the ground, knocking into a table where a family sat eating. People scattered, the table upended.

Seeing the diversion Drracien had created, Haegan sprinted out of the gathering and back into the woods. Someone stepped into his path, but he banked left. Darted around a copse of trees and threw himself into the thick brush of the forest.

The vines latched onto him, tugging and forbidding him to pass. One caught his sleeve and yanked him backward. Eyes probing the dense vegetation for the Jujak, he fumbled with the vine, prickly and sticky with the sap of mauri trees. He finally freed himself and plunged through the sea of leaves and branches.

Through the thicket, he saw the small tent their group used and vaulted in that direction. He avoided a boulder, almost laughing at its vain effort to stop him. "Not this—"

Oof! Haegan faceplanted. He flipped over and realized his leg was caught in a vine. He tugged hard. "Stupid things."

"Here," a voice called not too far away. Not far *enough* away. "Broken limbs."

Haegan cursed his carelessness as he struggled once more against the vines. Though he tugged hard, he could not wrest his foot free. He reached for it and froze. Razor-sharp thorns had embedded themselves into his shoe and pants. Their blade-like tips sawed at his leg. He grimaced but refused to cry out. If he were caught—

"No. Don't allow the thought. Forbid it. Conquer it." His father's words from somewhere in his distant childhood seeped through the pain and panic.

He yanked hard. Harder.

Hobbling one leg to the side, he hauled himself onto his feet, hunched over. Then, not caring, he ripped away. And fell again, this time with searing pain biting through his ankle. Unless he had a knife, the vines weren't going to yield. Grimacing, he turned on his knees.

A fist collided with his jaw. Haegan went sprawling backward, an explosion of pain radiating through his head. He landed hard, needling thorns digging into his back and shoulders.

Dark and large, a shadow loomed over him. Yanked him up by his tunic and punched him. "You stupid, self-absorbed—" The fist flew again.

At the clack of his teeth and squirt of blood through his mouth, something came alive in Haegan. Heat rushed through him. *No no no.* Not against his father's elite. He couldn't unleash whatever was in him against the Jujak.

A curse singed the air.

"You okay, Captain?"

"Fine," the man growled as he pushed away from Haegan.

Hurting from head to toe, Haegan climbed up.

A long blade captured sunlight and threw it in his eyes as its sharp edge slid under his chin. Bigger and older, the other warrior almost smiled at him. "Ah-ah," came a taunting warning as cold steel pinched Haegan's neck.

Haegan hissed and drew up straight, rigid. His nostrils flared as a trickle of warm blood slid down his neck. He swallowed.

"Prince Haegan." The captain eased back as the other intention-ally raised the sword, forcing Haegan to strain upward. "Please." He nodded, a ferocity in his eyes blazing. "Give us a reason to break you."

The hatred, the fury in this Jujak's tight lips and narrowed eyes warned Haegan off. This wasn't the time to fight. Only as the captain shifted did Haegan see the Seultrian crowned flame on his tunic. Valor Guard!

The captain's hand went to the gold sheath at his belt, where he freed a dagger.

Haegan drew back.

"Make sure he doesn't move, Mallius," the captain ordered as he knelt. He swiped the blade against Haegan's pants and boot, slicing away the vine.

When he straightened, he seized Haegan by the back of the neck and hauled him to his feet. "You're the worst kind of traitor, betray-ing the Fire King. And your sister." He thrust him forward—right into the iron grip of Mallius, who'd produced shackles and secured Haegan before he could blink. "By my oath to the King and the Nine, you will pay."

37

Heat plumes warbled and danced across his fingertips. A spark leapt from one to the next, as if skipping rocks but with fingers. He'd done it since he could remember, a way to pass boredom. But this wasn't boredom. This was agitation. The other four were arguing, the boys trying to explain to the angry Thiel, who sat with her leg resting on blankets as she reclined on her cot, how they'd let the prince get caught.

"Why didn't anyone go with Haegan to protect him?" Thiel asked, her voice hitching.

Bent forward, hands dangling, Drracien met her gaze. She was pretty. Very pretty. Though she hid it with the boyish cut and drab clothes, Thiel owned beauty. But right now, she owned anger and fear more. Her eyes sparked with disapproval. He could almost read her thoughts, that he was powerful enough. That instead of fighting with Tokar, he should've spirited Haegan to safety. Or sparked the warriors. Or maybe the horses. That almost made him grin.

Drracien tore his gaze away. Perhaps she was right. He'd made a mistake.

But he could take no more rebukes. He still couldn't sort why Sir Aloing had so violently come against him, rebuked him. Tried to kill him. Forced Drracien to defend himself, which in the end, injured the high marshal.

Or why Haegan's sister transferred her gifts to him. Because that's what had happened. Had to have. Transference wasn't about physicality. It was about embers. Wasn't it?

Those who wield with great power have great responsibility. How many times had Drracien himself barked that to the sparkers in the training yard? Having the gift to wield did not mean you were better than those who could not.

"Because. What with him"—that'd be Drracien—"punching him"—Tokar—"the people went ever' which way. Plowed right into us, they did. Knocked me on my padding, what little I have." Laertes brushed his backside.

"When I looked back," Praegur said, his voice deep and quiet as always, "there was no sign of Rigar. I had no way of knowing where he went."

"Where he's gone is to the holding cages in the middle of the Jujak camp just over the next hill." Drracien folded his arms over his chest. "And if he's there, the Ignatieri will be informed."

They all stared at him now. Tokar entirely too close to the attractive brunette. The young boy, who reminded Drracien of his half brother. And the Kerguli. All watching him.

He sighed and dropped his hands to his lap again. "What happened with the prince, the transference, does not happen."

The Kerguli frowned. "What do you mean?"

"No," Thiel held out a hand, her expression fierce. "Forget that. What are you implying? What will they do to him?"

"Get the truth out of him, no matter the cost."

"His father-king won't allow that." Thiel seemed to have gone pale, even with the warm glow of their small lantern.

"Zireli is the supreme ruler." Praegur nodded.

Drracien wet his lips, hating that he must be the one to deliver the news, feeling that somehow, he was responsible for the news itself. Not just Haegan's capture. "Zireli is the supreme ruler"—a collective sigh went up—"over the land and its people."

They still didn't get it.

"The Ignatieri, the grand marshal are supreme over all matters involving accelerants and wielding."

Several blank stares met his explanation.

But Thiel sagged. "And Haegan was restored when his sister traded."

Holding up a finger, Drracien knew he must correct her. "When his sister employed the use of an *incipient*—and not just any, but a rogue high marshal—to perform a type of wielding that has been forbidden since Zaelero the Second took the throne."

Wide brown eyes glossed. "But Haegan didn't know!"

"*They* don't know that!" Drracien pushed to his feet. "The high marshals will want to question him."

"And he will beg his innocence."

"Which they will not believe." He paced, desperately wishing for the training yard to wield and work off some of the stress building in his shoulders. "So they will employ more . . . aggressive means of extracting the truth."

"Bah!" Laertes shoved both hands through his shaggy blond hair. "They'll kill him, what with him not knowin' the truf."

"He knows the truth—but not all of it," Drracien said. "Haegan doesn't know that ka'Dur has been banished from the Ignatieri for the last year."

"Did the princess know?" Thiel asked quietly.

"That is not an answer I have."

"We should find out." Thiel perched on the edge of the cot, her leg precariously propped to the side. "If . . . if she did not know, then she can save him. Speak to the king. Seek mercy and a reprieve."

"You must jest," Drracien said with a barked laugh. He held a hand out in the direction of the Jujak tents where his new friend was held captive. "How long did Zireli's son sit in a tower-like prison and rot? If he could deny the existence of his own son for ten years, he is unlikely to extend any pardon or compassion to him now."

• • •

"*Inspire them, Medric. Touch their hearts and minds. They are as much his journey as the Falls.*"

He stood in the tearing Void and saw the fledglings through it, which was no obstacle to Her or the Sent. The future had not been withheld from him. Through the raw fabric of time, he saw what would happen to the young prince should he, in his compromised state of being, enter those waters. "The transference jeopardized him."

"And the Falls are the only way to repair that."

"It will be violent, Great One." Perilous. Perhaps even deadly. He ached with concern for the one on the cusp of manhood.

"Consider the journey, Medric."

Her reprimand stung the air. He gave a nod and tucked his chin.

"Go."

Medric stood in the forest, ten paces from the tent of the fledglings. Even now he could hear their conversation, though a person at this range would hear nothing. He stalked toward them. Saw through the material that afforded shelter against the elements and corporeal beings, but not against his kind. Not against Abiassa.

"I say we clear out. Leave him. This isn't our trouble." It was the one they called Tokar. A lot of brawn. Good brains. But short on wisdom. "He's a curse. Has been since you two insisted we drag his lifeless self out of that tunnel."

"We ain't leaving no friend. No way, no how." The youngest of the fledglings had wisdom beyond his years, having fought for every moment he had lived and breathed. Clearly, his life had been sparked by Abiassa. "If we leave him, then what's to say you won't leave me some day. I ain't trusting you, Tok."

"You have to listen to us. We're older."

"And stupider." Laertes looked to Thiel. "Not you of course. Him. But I ain' leaving this mountain unless Rigar—Haegan, whateva's his name—is wif us." He moved to the cot and sat behind Thiel, as if seeking her protection and affirmation.

"He's right," she said. "We can't leave him there."

"Why not? He's with his people—those guards are his father's! He should go back."

"If he goes back now, his sister what sent him won' neve' get healed. And then that—that be what trouble we don' want."

"We won't leave him, Laertes." Thiel was so resolute.

Medric ducked into the tent. As he stood there, half expecting them to alert to his presence, they did not. They stared. Unmoved. Locked in the grip of time, which Abiassa held. To his immediate left stood the Kergulian.

No, not yet.

Stepping deeper into the gathering, he reached the lad first. He touched his shoulder. "You will see what others miss. You will guide where others are lost. You will succeed where most fail. Your loyalty is rewarded, fledgling."

Two strides carried him to the tallest of the group. Tokar. He placed his palm against the chest already cording with muscle. Medric stared into gray eyes that could not see beyond the void of time. "Restless but strong. Impetuous but skilled. You seek a path separate from him, but it will be a painful one if you choose it. Dread and death will be your only companions when you are not aligned with him. Might and honor are yours, from one sea to another, if you choose the right battle, warrior."

The weight of those words pushed Medric to the oldest fledgling, the one whose life would suffer cruelly should he seize the wrong path. Dark hair hung in his eyes. Fire roiled through his irises, visible only to accelerants, Deliverers and Abiassa herself.

"You have a strong gift. One that will take you far. As with the other, two paths lie before you. One will bring death and darkness. You are drawn, powerfully *drawn within your deepest parts, to the power wielding grants. That will be your gift, or your curse, apprentice."*

The girl. Medric knelt beside her. His large hand dwarfed her head. "Asykthian warrior you are. He will depend on your wisdom and even your sword. You will depend on him, too. Before you rides a day, mounted on the wings of a raqine and the might of a Drigovudd, that will thrust you to the other side of the planet, far away from him. Misery will be your comfort. Pain your healing. Look not for joy, for there will none in the Reckoning, warrior."

Though she could not hear him with her natural ears, she heard him with her inner being. And she would cling to the words the way a warrior does to battle. For she was a champion. A mighty one.

Medric stood. Touched the girl's hair. Smiled as he felt a trill of affection run through his fingers. She was favored by Her Lady. Her hair . . . her hair will grow. Her stature will grow. Her renown will grow. Her love will grow.

But then his gaze fell upon the Kergulian. Medric closed the half-dozen paces between them. Rich brown eyes. "Friend. Counselor. Advocate." His hand covered the entire left quadrant of the man's chest, right over his heart. Heat exploded. Light as well. "He will turn to no other for advice the way he will with you and his champion. You will serve him until the end of your days. He will rule over you but not lord over you. Abundance and blessing will be yours for the sacrifices demanded of you on his behalf. You will be Her voice to him. And to him alone will you be able to speak until the Reckoning."

Medric drew back his hand, sensing Praegur's resistance to releasing the direct channel to its Source. Those who were hungry and tasted the fruit of Her craved more. More touches of her presence. More of her righteousness. The hunger in this one bordered on starvation. And he fed as a newborn at the breast for the first time.

"Forgive me, Counselor." He patted the spot that still burned with Her Flames. "This will hurt when the Void closes."

At the door, he glanced over his shoulder, overcome with the dreadful paths facing these five. The girl and lad. The general in young man's skin. The accelerant. The advisor. An ache spread through him. What they would endure . . .

"They are but fledglings."

"Yes," She said forcefully. "But they are my fledglings."

38

Thiel blinked. All at once she heard a handful of words spoken, including her own, "Champion."

Laertes said, "Fledgling."

Drracien: "Apprentice."

Tokar: "Warrior."

Thiel drew in a breath and darted a look to the tent opening, where she would have vowed someone had entered then exited. But as she did, she only saw Praegur. He gripped his chest and crumpled to the ground with a horrible, guttural sound.

"Praegur!" She hobbled to him, catching his shoulders in her hands. "Praegur, what's wrong?"

"What happened?" Tokar dropped beside them, turned him over.

Tears streaked dark rivulets through the dirt that had powdered Praegur's face. Eyes squeezed tight, he made that wretched noise again. He arched his back. His knuckles pinked, fingers digging into his chest. He rocked back and forth.

"Stop!" Drracien was there. He pinned Praegur's shoulders. "Remove his hand."

Thiel hesitated.

Tokar grabbed the hand and pried it away, then glanced at the accelerant. "What?"

Shaking his head, Drracien stepped back with widened eyes. "Nothing."

Annoyed with futile distraction, Thiel turned to her friend. "Praegur, talk to us. Please." She pushed in closer, homing in on his face. "What happened?"

Though he blinked and his face was still red from whatever seized him, he opened his mouth. And croaked. His eyes went wild. Panic rippled through his features. He opened his mouth again.

Another croak.

"Did he hit his head? Is that why he can't talk?"

Thiel frowned. Was that possible? To lose his ability to talk because of a blow to the head? She considered her friend. He'd been the most steadfast and patient of them all. "When you fell—"

He shook his head. Rolled onto his side, once more gripping his chest. Hands propped and aided him as he came upright. He swiped a palm over his face, drying the tears and smearing his face muddy, still grunting. His mouth opened and again an empty word fell out.

"You can't talk," Laertes said, his voice a whisper.

Praegur shook his head, sagging. He lifted his hands in defeat and question. He unlaced his tunic and lifted the fabric. Cringing in pain, he tugged harder.

Was it stuck to his skin?

He craned his head back and peered into his tunic. His eyes widened. He leapt to his feet, mouth open. Ripped off his tunic. Placed a hand near—but not on—his chest.

"What in the Flames?" Tokar whispered, circling closer. "What is that?"

Feeling the heat climb into her cheeks for staring at her friend's chest, Thiel felt more alarm at the sight than anything else. About as large as a grown man's splayed hand, a marred mess covered what was once smooth flesh.

"Blazes," Laertes muttered. "It looks like what Rigar had!"

"What is that?" Tokar's voice pitched. "He wasn't near fire. He didn't fall against a torch." He pointed to where the beam supported the lone candle box. "The lantern hasn't moved. So how did that get there?"

Thwap!

Thiel pivoted. Against the black of nighttime in the camp, she saw Drracien's form hulk away.

"Double blazes—your leg, Thiel!"

She spun back to the others. Stopped short. *My leg.* She had no pain. No discomfort. She hurried to the bed. Quickly removed the wraps, her heart stuttering. The others hovered, their confusion and curiosity as strong as hers. When she unwound the last stretch, the binding fell away. With a swallow for courage, she rotated her foot.

No pain. Not even an ache. No bruising. No swelling. "I . . . I don't understand." She looked up at Tokar and Laertes, then to Praegur, who sat at the foot of his own cot, hand still over his heart, face screwed in pain. As if he wanted to conceal it. Shame blanketed him as heavily as shock covered her. "*What* happened?"

"Maybe you were faking." Tokar's words sounded small. *He* sounded small. And he shrank beneath a withering glare she shot his way. He lifted a shoulder. "How am I supposed to know? One second, we're arguing about helping that singewood, the next, he's howling, the accelerant is storming out, and you're healed."

"I know what 'vis is," Laertes said in his thick Caorian accent.

Tokar turned to Laertes, who stumbled to a cot in the corner. He'd gone pale. Seemed unsettled. His gaze roved the ground for several long seconds as he shook his head back and forth.

Thiel went to him and lowered herself to the dirt. "Laertes? What is it?"

His light brown eyes came to hers as Tokar eased onto the edge of her cot and Praegur watched, sweat beading on his upper lip. "I heard the tale." His eyes bulged. He jumped to his feet. "O blazes-singewood-seared-brain-and-all-the-Flames!" He turned a circle muttering about the sage and readers. "They was just stories what they told." He froze. Looked at them. Then turned again, wagging his head. "They was *just* stories," he repeated, shaking his hands in emphasis. "What with the reader having no hair and no friends, we thought him addled and all."

Tokar huffed. "Laer—"

"But he wasn't. No, he wasn't smushed in the brain. He was right." Laertes gave a firm bob of his head. "He was right and we couldn' see it. Cuz that's wha' peoples do—they want to feel good about themselves, so they make fun of o'vers." He spun to them, his sandy blond brows tied together in a panicked knot. "We didn' know. How's we supposed to know?"

Tokar balled his fist. "Laertes!"

"Ain' no call to go shouting at a boy just 'cause he took awhile to figure things out."

Thiel caught his shoulder and crouched to look him in the eye. "Laertes. What? What are you talking about?"

"How could I 'ave been so *stupid*?" He cradled his head in his hands as he gave them a strange expression, as if he couldn't believe something. His mouth opened, but he said nothing. Then he flung a hand to the back of the tent. "We 'ave to help 'im."

"Who?" Tokar growled.

"Rigar. Him what's the prince!"

"Why?" Thiel went to a knee, now looking up at the boy. "Help us understand, Laertes."

"How would *you* know what we need to do? You're just a boy." Tokar stood and paced to the front of the tent.

"Yeh? I might be a boy, but I got eyes and ears whats heard things you 'aven't!"

"Laertes," Thiel said as calmly as she could, turning him away from Tokar, who was as agitated as all of them combined. She stole a peek at Praegur, who had laid back on the cot, feet on the edge, knees pointing to the canopy, his arm over his eyes, and the other hand still holding his chest.

O Abiassa, we are falling apart!

"Reader." She licked her lips, drawing the boy back to her cot and sitting down with him. "You said something about a reader?"

He nodded, his blond hair rippling beneath the tease of lamplight. "And the sage. You can't forget him what got the smarts." He wrinkled his nose. "The reader has smarts—he can read the Parchments—but not what the sage has. He tells us what the Parchments mean."

"Parchments." Thiel felt herself sinking into treacherous waters with the talk of Parchments. Because that meant prophecies. Which meant religious—Ignatieri—high-handedness.

"Which ones?" Tokar stood over them, intensity radiating through his face, making him appear more annoyed than usual. When Thiel shot him a questioning glance, he shrugged. "You know how those things can be."

Yes, all too well. In part, 'those things' had been why she'd fled her home and family.

"The Parchments what tell of the world's future." Laertes lifted his arms and made a wide arc, as if mimicking the planet. He then paused, frowned and rubbed his head. "Or was it what told of . . ." He bunched his shoulders and held them tight against his neck. "I can't remember what one it was. I just knows it was told. And it done gave me terrors for weeks!" His hands motioned in his hysteria. "The Lakes of Fire spilling over like a raging sea in a storm. The ash what choked the sky. And the people. The Fierian what over'frows the king and brings the ageless war to the Nine." He swallowed and shook his head, his young face filled with timeless fear. "We ain't gonna survive this. Not if they take him. Not if he lives."

"What?" Tokar was listening now, his head craned toward Laertes at an angle. "You said 'not if they take him,' then 'not if he lives.' Which is it? Is he supposed to live or die?"

Laertes's eyes bulged and his mouth gaped. "Thems the words the sage spoke!" He dipped his head as if trying to remember and started mumbling. "'The Fierian true . . . when he lives and dies—'" He shook his head. "No. No, that ain' right. It was, 'the Fierian true went to die, but he lives.'" Letting out a long groan, Laertes fell onto the cot. "I can't remember."

"So are we supposed to help him? Or kill him?"

Thiel jerked. "We are *not* going to kill Haegan! He's our friend. We protect him."

"But if protecting him kills us . . ."

"No, we can't hurt him," Laertes said, gripping at Tokar. "If we hurt him, we will be cursed!"

"Stop it! That's—you have singewood for brains if you believe that." Tokar pushed him away.

The tent flap snapped back and Drracien stepped in, a spicy wind with him.

Thiel struggled to see his face in the waning light and glow of the torch. She stilled at his knotted brow and taut lips. The ferocity . . . "What is it?"

"You are all loud enough for the entire camp to hear!" Wind tussled his black hair into his eyes as he tossed his cloak aside.

"You rescued us just in time from Laertes's insane ramblings," Tokar said as he moved to a separate cot.

"They ain't insane. They're written. Parchments, what they are." Laertes turned to Drracien. "We have to help Rigar."

The accelerant considered him at length through narrowed eyes.

"Drracien? Is something wrong?"

He retracted his gaze and gave a long sigh. "The boy is right."

Tokar jumped to his feet. "What do you know? This isn't for you—"

"I know the Parchments." Drracien's expression and tone darkened. "You forget—besides lessons in wielding, an accelerant's primary task is to learn the Parchments. Learn them to be guided by them."

"Guided." Thiel wrapped her arms around herself, sensing a chilling turn. "Guided how?"

"To use the wisdom of the four elders who wrote them to guide our decisions and actions."

She angled away, both wanting and not wanting to hear his thoughts. Fearing that the accelerants were dividing yet another life from love and friendship. "And what do those precious Parchments say of our situation? Does it speak to the incredulity of this predicament? To a venture to the Great Falls on behalf of a friend who intended to find healing and now finds tragedy?"

"You are good at enlarging a situation."

"Our situation remains unaltered. And you have succeeded in not answering my question."

Drracien relented. "We should help him."

"But he's being held by the Jujak," Tokar objected.

"And even if we goes in there and help him, we can't just escape with him. He has to make it into them waters what have healing power." Laertes pleaded with a long look to Thiel. "Ain' that right?"

With a reluctant nod, she said, "It's a fine mess, but if we abandon him now, he'll likely die—"

"He won't die—"

"Do not negate my position."

"I only meant—"

"Hear me out. If we abandon him, Haegan will be returned to Fieri Keep."

"Which is under siege," Drracien said.

Thiel hesitated. "You know this? When we left Seultrie, the Unelithiens hadn't reached the city yet."

"Overheard the Jujak," Drracien said with a half nod.

Thiel's stomach tightened. "Then it is more important than ever that we get Haegan out of there. He cannot be returned to the keep."

"But his sister . . ."

Thiel clapped her hands over her head, frustrated. "I don't know the answers. Everything feels defeated or useless."

"It's not useless," Drracien said. "I haven't sorted all the facts, but I believe Haegan is Touched. Or protected. He is marked by a Deliverer—Abiassa does not send those without a very deliberate intent regarding the person. They do not act but at Her hand."

"For an accelerant on the run, you seem to believe their mash," Tokar growled.

"I believe," Drracien said. "In Her. Not in them. At least not all of them. And if you want to tear me apart, fine, but it needs to be later. We are out of time."

"Why?" Thiel asked. "What's wrong?"

"The Great Falls. Haegan must go to the waterfall. If he is who . . . who I think he might be, it will be revealed there."

Curiosity and a large chunk of dread spread through Thiel. "Who do you think he is?"

"The Fierian."

Thiel scoffed. But isn't that what Laertes's rambling referenced?

"That bumbling, awkward coward? No way." Tokar laughed. Then laughed some more. "If he's the destroyer of worlds, then we're singed."

"Not destroyer," Drracien said with an edge to his words. "The Reckoner."

Thiel pressed her fingers to her forehead.

"What's the Reckoner?" Laertes asked.

"Forget it." Turning away, Tokar pushed both hands over his short-cropped hair. "You don't need terrors again."

"I ain't had terrors since I was a lit'le boy!"

"Look!" Thiel snapped. "I don't care if he is"—*O Abiassa, say it's not so*—"the Reckoner. Haegan is our friend. That's what matters. And he needs our help. He's a good person. And he would give his life to help any of us. We need to find a way to free him."

"Do I get a vote?" Tokar growled.

"Not if you're going to disagree," Thiel said. "It will take all of us to free Haegan. But we have to not only get him out, we have to hide him until he can enter the pool."

"How?" Tokar stuffed his hands on his hips, his jaw muscle flexing. "The Ignatieri—"

"Will be busy with their rituals. A little fire and water are all Haegan needs now."

39

Hands tied and tethered to the horn of the captain's saddle, Haegan stumbled along behind the horse and rider.

"I say make him walk the whole way," Mallius grumbled from his mount.

"What report would there be of us if we returned the prince to the Fire King half-starved and feet worn off?"

"It's what he deserves."

Haegan started to look at the thick warrior but diverted his gaze.

"Laejan won't be happy about us taking one of his horses for the traitor prince."

"Nobody is happy about this," the captain mumbled, shooting Haegan a sidelong glance. "Traitors deserve to be flogged then hanged."

A half-dozen Jujak coalesced around their captain as they plodded up the hill. After a steep descent, Haegan side-sliding to maintain his balance, since his hands were bound, they broke into a clearing. Five hundred paces separated him from the Falls. His hope soared—could he break free and make it?

Movement in the foreground drew Haegan's eye to the row upon row of tents standing between him and his goal. The Ignatieri. The other Jujak. And just as quickly, his hope faded.

As they trod toward the center of the camp and stopped in front of the large command tent, a tall, lanky form ducked beneath the opening. When he straightened, Haegan hauled in a breath.

"General Laejan," the captain greeted as he dismounted. He passed Haegan's leash to Mallius, who jerked Haegan toward himself.

Laejan wasn't the giant General Grinda was, but he was fierce, no mistaking. Especially when one saw the scar that traced the side of his skull. "Word came that you were hunting a traitor." Large brown eyes fastened onto Haegan. "I see the king's trust was not misplaced."

The captain clapped a fist over his chest and gave a curt bow. "You honor me."

"I only state the facts." Laejan smoothed a hand over his bald head. "Why are you here, Captain? Why have you not sped on your way?"

"A horse, sir." He motioned to Haegan. "The journey is several days at a hard clip. Much longer if the prisoner is not mounted."

"Indeed." Laejan glanced to the Jujak at his right. "Secure the prisoner." He pointed to a large post in the middle of the camp, then nodded to the captain. "We should talk."

The captain turned to Mallius, and a silent message zapped between them. Mallius handed off Haegan's rope to another.

As Haegan watched, they vanished into the tent.

"Move," a Jujak barked as he hauled Haegan to the middle of the camp. There, he secured the ropes to a wench gear. Soon he was positioned so his arms wrapped the pole, forcing him to nearly hug the wood. A position that tugged on the wounds he'd incurred at the river with Thiel and compounded the splitting headache the captain's punches had inflicted.

He stood there for what seemed hours, so many that he no longer felt his arms, and his legs seemed to have a thousand ants crawling on them for the way they prickled and burned.

I am a prince! The thought rolled through Haegan's mind over and over. Both as a chastisement against his treatment by his father's best warriors and as his own judgment exerted against himself for being in this position.

He should have refused Kaelyria.

It seemed especially cruel to place him in the middle of the Jujak camp so he could see the warriors going through their drills, practicing and sparring. He'd wanted nothing more as a boy than to one day rank among their numbers. Even chained and humiliated, the lingering ache of that dream taunted him.

But there was no chance for him now, even with the use of his legs. In their eyes, he had neither mental strength nor character. They would never follow him. Strung up to a stake as the sun passed overhead, Haegan heard the hateful words spewed against him.

Cripple stole his sister's legs, left her to rot.

Only a coward abandons those who love him.

Wanted to steal the crown.

Perhaps he's colluding with Dyrth.

Then he'll pay Dyrth's price, too.

"Maybe he won't make it back to Fieri Keep after all." The new threat whispered on the wind and lured Haegan's head up.

The strong *thwap* of a tent flap drew his gaze behind and to the right.

Lieutenant Mallius had emerged, his brow twisted tighter than Haegan had seen earlier. And that worried him. A lot. Especially when the oversized warrior started toward him.

Where was the captain? Or the general?

An arc of soldiers formed behind Mallius, the storming sea headed straight for Haegan. He tried to straighten, but it was a challenge in his position.

"It would do you well to give us something, Prince Haegan," Mallius said, his voice low, "before the general comes. As one of the Three, he brings not only justice but judgment."

Though his heart hammered, Haegan stood fast. Gwogh taught that hesitation kills—and there was no room for hesitation here. Haegan knew the Codes. "There is but one who can stand in judgment over me—the king." It was true. He earnestly hoped it would be enough to fend off their malice.

Sniggers peppered the enlarging crowd as they encircled him.

"In combat," Mallius boomed, "the general has the decree of the king to do as he must to extract information from *any* prisoner. Laejan will do what it takes to find out who set you against your own father! Your sister!"

Ah. They weren't talking about legitimate judgment. "What you refer to here is not a writ of judgment, but physical discipline. Against a man without trial." *Abiassa, I beseech thee.* "Punishment." As understanding dawned, Haegan shifted, adjusting his hands once more to alleviate the pinch. "You mean to torture me."

"The punishment for treason against the crown is death!" The lieutenant's shout echoed across the open field, silencing the camaraderie of those huddled around the fire.

"And yet," Haegan whispered, "my father has demanded I be returned *alive*."

"He said nothing of how alive you had to be." His meaty fist slammed into Haegan's head, bouncing it against the stake. Spots danced across his vision as his knees wobbled beneath the spike of pain. "You have lost the right to call King Zireli your father. You betrayed them and you betrayed us all!"

"I betrayed no one!"

Mallius pressed in, taunting. "Remember your place, traitor!"

"I am no traitor. I fled—"

"You admit it!"

Haegan clamped his mouth shut as the young captain shouldered his way through the crowd. A storm had moved into the man's eyes, one that quickened Haegan's pulse. It would do no good to defend himself here. His words would be twisted and pushed back on him like a dagger through the heart.

The captain stood before him, staring down at him. "You admit that you fled the city and the condition you abandoned your sister to?"

The Jujak circled in like carrion birds.

Low songs wafted from the Ignatieri camp, drawing Haegan's gaze. The accelerants had gathered in long lines before the Great Falls, candles flickering and hissing beneath the spray.

"You've broken Seultrian laws as well as Ignatieri principles, Prince Haegan." The captain pointed to the accelerants. "They have asked us to surrender you to them, but Jujak answer only to the Fire King. And I will not fail our king in this quest to return his traitorous son. His honor demands it."

"Honor—you speak of honor? The Jujak Code demands *you* act in honor, yet you string up a man whose guilt is not proven!"

"Man?" Someone guffawed, drawing laughter from the others.

The captain's nostrils flared and his lips thinned. "Your guilt was determined by King Zireli. Dare you accuse *him* of lying? Of dishonor?"

"No!" Nearly choking, Haegan sagged against the pole. No, his father's accusation was made out of sincere belief in his guilt. "By the Flames, no." Once he had chosen a path, Zireli rarely diverged from it. But if Haegan could just talk to him . . . explain. "I will not speak to the charges until they have been formally brought and I am presented to my father-king."

"Your sister is dying!"

Haegan started, mortified to hear of Kaelyria's condition but also to hear the tremor in the captain's voice. "Dying?"

A fierce fire raged through the officer's face. He leaned into Haegan and held his gaze. Bored through him. His gray eyes pierced and amplified the fury so clearly roiling inside. "You have sentenced your own sister to her death!"

"No." A wave of grief washed over Haegan. His gaze skimmed the surrounding crowd, past the sharp lines and ceremony of the Ignatieri, to the deep blue waters crashing into the pool beneath the moon's dull glow. "If I can . . ." He must reach the Falls tomorrow. He had to. If he did not, he would never forgive himself and neither would his father. And perhaps even Kaelyria. If she lived.

But how? How could he when they held him captive?

Defeat pushed. Pressed him against the wood.

O sweet, foolish sister—your gift has become a curse. He hung his head, pained at the thought of her being ill. Of her dying because she wanted him to experience an adventure. Of her preparing herself to marry Jedric and give up the man she loved. A soldier named Graem. She'd mentioned their secret meetings and begged Haegan's silence. Never had he seen her so happy and carefree as the times she spoke of the handsome Jujak.

"You think this a joke?" Mallius's growl startled Haegan, and only then did he realize thoughts of Kaelyria had made him smile.

Another fist flew—but from a different guard. Connected with Haegan's jaw. Snapped his neck back. Blood glanced across his tongue.

Pooled at the back of his throat. He coughed, gagged on the metallic taste.

Another threw a punch.

A jav-rod poked through and stabbed his side.

Haegan cried out.

"Easy," the captain ordered. "Hey—"

But the Jujak seemed to feed off Haegan's pain and blood. Rocks. Fists. Kicks. Something connected with his eye.

"Stand down!" a booming voice ricocheted through the camp.

Around Haegan, the Jujak parted like waters at a boulder. General Laejan stormed across the field. With lips pressed into a thin line, he pivoted to his men. "Bed down before I tie every one of you to the stake. You are Jujak!"

"We serve. He wields. She rules!" the elite guards shouted in response.

"And you will conduct yourselves as such." After the mob broke up, Laejan turned his gaze to the captain. "You're Grinda's son—I expected more!"

"Sir."

Grinda's son?

He motioned to the captain and Mallius. "Take him to the cages and lock him up. And make sure he's secure!"

"Aren't you going to question him?"

Once more Laejan glared at Haegan. Then to Haegan's side, where a bloody spot stained his tunic. "He's answered enough for now." He looked to the captain. "Keep your guard in check or you'll see my anger and the king's. And it's a warm summer breeze compared to the Fire King's scorching wrath."

Captain Grinda gave a curt. "Yes, sir."

Secured between two Jujak and led by Mallius, Haegan made his way, limping and wincing toward a small line of mauri saplings cut in the same size and secured together to form cages. But stumbling aggravated the stab wound. He tried to favor it, holding a hand over the spot, and lost his balance. He dropped to a knee, jarring the injuries. Haegan cried out this time. Then gritted his teeth. Weakness would only be made sport of among these warriors.

"Weakling. You're a disgrace to the Celahar name," Mallius growled as he resumed his pace.

Thumping and murmuring floated up over the dying din of the soldiers, once more drawing Haegan's attention to the Ignatieri. To the Falls.

A jolt of fire hit his back. With a grunt, Haegan winced. Then felt the heat searing his skin.

"Fire!" the captain shouted. "He's on fire!"

Haegan glanced over his shoulder and found his tunic aflame. He yelped. Reached backward.

"Roll on the ground!" Captain Grinda ordered, shoving him down, hands peppering his shoulders.

Arms bound, Haegan rolled and rolled. Maybe he could keep rolling all the way—

"Enough." Mallius planted a boot on Haegan's chest. "The flames are out. Get up."

Haegan struggled to regain his knees with the awkwardness of being bound, but finally pushed one up to stand.

"Merciful—Blazes!" Captain Grinda exclaimed. "Look at his back!"

"We'll have the healer tend him," Mallius groused as he moved to look at Haegan's back.

Silence.

Dead silence.

"Get the high marshal."

40

Thiel sprinted away from the overlook, the others racing behind her. They made it to a narrow, curving trail when she spun around. Sorted the others and homed in on Drracien. Three sharp steps carried her to him. With both hands, she shoved Drracien backward. "What did you do?"

"I—"

"Burning him? Are you out of your mind?" Heat coursed through her, anger sped by the race of her pulse. "If we wanted him killed, we would leave him there for the Jujak!"

"I wasn't trying to kill him."

"No, just burn him alive," Laertes shouted.

"Quiet," Tokar bit out.

She couldn't shake the image of Haegan on fire. Of seeing the small ember seize the fabric and grow exponentially. "Why would you do that?" She shoved him again. "I thought you were on our side." A punch.

"Hey."

"Were your words about who he was a ploy?" She flung her hands at him again.

Drracien caught them. Heat bloomed around her wrists.

Shocked, Thiel froze.

Immediately the heat was gone.

"You—you're wielding against me now?" She set her right foot back, ready to fight.

This time, Drracien held up his hands. "Peace." He inclined his head after that soft word. "Listen. I only sparked him."

"Yes, thank you. We's what got eyes saw that pretty well. We also saw him blow up in flames!"

"No." Drracien looked to the boy, then back to Thiel. His eyes were pale beneath the moonlight. "No, Haegan wasn't burned. The kind of spark I struck him with does not burn flesh. Only material."

Thiel stilled. Blinked. "You . . . you can do that? I mean, it's possible—"

"Yes." Drracien pushed his hair from his face.

"But why? Why would you—did you do that?"

"They needed to see it." He started hiking up the hill.

"See what?"

"The mark."

"What mark?" Thiel kept pace with him, glancing back to make sure the others were still with them. "What are you talking about?" When he didn't answer, only climbed higher, she grabbed his shoulder, ready to punch him again. "Blazes!"

Drracien stopped. But wouldn't meet her gaze.

He'd always been direct. Blunt. But now he'd gone quiet. It . . . worried her. "What mark?" She shook her head, mentally scouring Haegan for marks. He didn't have any. Unless . . . She opened her mouth. "His back. The bruise?"

After an almost imperceptible nod, he was moving again and still not speaking.

"Where are we going?" Tokar asked, frustration in his question.

"That bruise came from the fall."

"It's not a bruise. He didn't fall."

"I'm sorry to say you are quite wrong," Thiel said as the incline leveled out and Drracien turned straight into a thick bramble of bushes and vines. Annoyed with his indifference and leading-the-way presumption, she lifted her booted feet over the vines. "I was there. We fell. I had the broken ankle to prove it." Well, she'd had one for a little while.

"And wha' do you mean it isn' a bruise? I saw it wif me very eyes! All blue and gross." Laertes hopped from one boulder to another. In fact, it seemed the ground had become nothing but rocks and moss and vines.

Frustration shoved her onward. Thiel lunged ahead of Drracien to get answers. To stop this madness. She hit a boulder—him.

Drracien held out a hand, stopped cold.

Hmph. Like she would listen to him when he wouldn't listen to her. She threw herself forward.

"No!" A hand snaked around her shoulders. Snapped her back. In that instant, she realized her feet dangled over nothing but air. Misting, cold air. As a scream climbed her throat, she grabbed the only thing that held her from falling to her death—Drracien's arm. Another hand clamped onto her mouth.

Shaking in the fist-hold of terror, Thiel peered down the length of her body and saw nothing but water, vanishing into a thick veil of mist.

Her palms grew sweaty. Her grip slipped.

She yelped, pure dread icing her veins.

"Quiet," Drracien hissed—louder, out of necessity.

But terror had its firm grip on her brain. She struggled for ground. To scramble backward.

"Get her back, get her back!" Tokar was there, but not close enough.

"Easy," Drracien whispered as he stepped back.

Thiel twitched her feet, searching for terra firma. Finally, they scraped rock. She slumped as he released her. She spun around and grabbed the sides of his tunic, eyes closed. Pressed her nose against his chest, unwilling to trust her trembling limbs to support her and keep her from falling into the mist.

With an arm around her shoulders, Drracien eased to the side. "It's okay."

She shuddered a breath, then sagged. Recovering, she lifted her head. Looked up at blue eyes. Without a word, she shoved backward. Drew herself straight, staring at the curtain of water. She glanced up, expecting to see a wall of water. Instead, she saw nothing. "It doesn't make sense." Where was the water coming from?

"Let me show you." Drracien crossed a ledge that would be wide enough for four people to pass shoulder to shoulder, but with the moss and the slick rocks, it'd be dangerous to do so.

On the other side, he stepped up a small path. Pointed. "See for yourself."

Thiel angled in front of him, once again sensing strange things. "What?"

But he didn't need to tell her. From that spot, she saw it. No wider than her hand, rock formed a wall that soared upward in a glistening, roaring tumble of water. That created a channel, funneling the falls behind it. A gap would allow someone to stand on the ledge, but the width was no more than a couple of feet before it fell away. That's where the waterfall roared through like a thick blanket. Water spit on her face as it blurred past. Dampness soaked her clothes and hair, but she didn't care. It was refreshing and exhilarating!

"Amazing." The wall protected the ledge they'd used to cross the narrow neck of the river, directing the flow into what basically was a spout, spewing the water down . . . down . . . down into the pool.

"Great sightseeing trip, but shouldn't we be working on getting Haegan out?" Arms folded, Tokar glowered. "Not that I really want that singewood mucking up my life again."

"Oy, great." Laertes wagged his hands at them. "Water. It's great. But what about the mark what Haegan got?"

With mist pluming before her eyes, suspended in the air above the pool, Thiel moved to the edge of the overhang.

"Thiel!"

A hand held out both reassured and silenced the others. Peeking over the side nearly sent the contents of her stomach hurtling down with the water. The queasy rush slowed as she steadied her breathing and held her balance. Her foot at the edge of the rock seemed so large compared to the pool, fifty feet below. Maybe sixty.

She understood. If they could get Haegan up here, he could jump into the water from the Falls. "What about the ritual?" Unable to take her eyes off the location, she took in the area. The way the trees seemed to reach around the waterfall with their branchy fingers. She'd always loved the satiny feel of water against her hands. Did the trees, too?

"It's a farce," Drracien said. "Maybe that's too harsh of a word. It's not necessary. They do the ritual to create a log of those who enter the Falls. Who gets healed. Who doesn't."

Thiel turned to him. "You are certain of this?"

"Nowhere in the Parchments is it written one must perform a ritual to get a miracle."

"What, you've gone and read them all, 'ave you?" Laertes's hair stuck to his brow, darkened by the mist. "The Parchments—there's a lot of them."

"I've been at Sanctuary for a decade. When we weren't wielding, we were reading. And reading. And reading."

"We get the idea," Tokar said.

Drracien shoved a hand through thick hair that hung lazily around his face. "I've read the Kindling Parchment so much, I have it memorized."

Interesting. Thiel folded her arms. "Let me hear it."

His eyebrow arched. "I could spend the next fifteen minutes numbing your ears with the Abiassian tongue, or we could get on with rescuing your friend. First—the mark." He reached for Thiel and guided her back to the side. "And why this place matters."

"The place matters," Thiel said, feeling a chill skitter across her neck now that she was not by the mist, "because Haegan can jump into the Falls."

"Uh, no," Tokar said, standing close to her and tucking his hands under his arms. "No, Haegan is still down in those cages. Beaten and"—he moved his gaze alone to Drracien—"burned."

"Would you like a demonstration of the spark?" Drracien almost seemed amused.

Challenge and anger flashed through Tokar's face, and Thiel sensed a confrontation in the works. "The mark." She brushed her hair from her face and swiped away the dampness. "You said it wasn't a bruise. What is it?"

Drracien suddenly seemed abashed about answering.

Thiel shifted closer. "Drracien?"

His jaw muscle flexed and he flared his nostrils in his reluctance. "It's the mark of Abiassa."

41

Strong winds tugged at his cloak and sleeves as he raced the mighty beast through one Ybiennese town after another then down the main road to Nivar Hold. Thurig as'Tili aimed through a tall line of trees. His brother would follow. But if he hurried, there would be time. He grinned and focused ahead. They broke through the pines into a flat stretch. Three mountain ranges sat in protection of the mighty Askythian realm. Houses littered the road. Prosperity—of soul and pocket. His father had done well by the people, and they loved him for it.

And it annoyed him. When Kiethiel had returned after her kidnapping, the people threatened and hard times descended. Ybienns so rife in their animosity and mistrust. Then his sister left, and the realm settled into a comfortable complacency. Removed from eyes, removed from thought, as the ancients had said.

He guided the beast across a pristine white meadow, sailing effortlessly from one incline to another with only a soft thump of the agile paws. The frozen breeze skimming the mountains bit at his face, a welcome after the too-hot territories of the south. Over a river steaming against the fresh-fallen snow that lined its banks. Down the snowy embankment. Tili saw a wagoner lumbering toward the main road. A bit of that rebellious side his father always berated him for took possession of him. With a tweak of his knees against Zicri's flanks, he jumped the beast over the wagoner.

"Fool boy!" the wagoner shouted, cracking a whip in the air.

Another few bounds and they broke into the open. Zicri slid, his paws digging into the snow for traction. He realigned himself, then threw himself forward. On to the tall trees that formed a protective border around the estate of King Thurig and Queen Eriathiel. The beast snorted, clearly disconcerted with the incredible pace and the wall before him.

Prince Tili pushed his gaze to the right and then to the left. Certain nobody was in sight, he leaned forward. Pressed his stomach to the beast's spine, feeling the undulating strength of the past roaring through him. Sliding a hand along the black fur, he closed his eyes. Trained his mind to the thrill surging through his mount. And though the elements tore at them and the sound would be unintelligible to any other, Tili spoke the language of the ancients. *"Eghat au'moni ighthieri, Zicri."*

With a primal scream, the beast responded. Tili gripped handfuls of fur and let his legs slide back along the spine. With an enormous *thwap*, wings unfurled from a secret fold in Zicri's shoulders.

Four meaty paws thudded against the ground and kept moving. Yards from the gates. Zicri shook his powerful neck, as if relishing the freedom to spread his wings. He tucked his head. A purr trembled through his body, warmed by the hard ride.

Noting the purr—a cue—Tili tightened his grip. With a growl, Zicri launched upward. Into the air. Over the road. Despite himself, Tili laughed. The thrill never got old. The experience new every time.

"Aha!" He laughed as the force of Zicri's rise pressed him against the black fur, borne up on the wings of one of the mightiest creatures of all time, the raqine.

Zicri gave two thunderous flaps of his wings and locked them. They sailed over the gate.

Guards shouted and pumped their fists and weapons. Tili pushed his attention to directing Zicri to their landing spot. The inner courtyard.

Father will kill me.

The thought drew a sly smile. "There." A slight crinkling carried on the wind as Zicri maneuvered his wings to catch the right current and change direction. With a graceful elegance that belied his monstrous size, Zicri descended.

Watching the cobbled courtyard, bustling with a horse-drawn carriage rolling toward the main entrance and a few servants scurrying into a side door, Tili hesitated. Searched the castle windows. A shadow moved in the far left. Father's study.

He cringed. Snapped his gaze back to the carriage. "Foul fires!" he hissed as he recognized the Earl of Langeria and his daughter entering the main courtyard.

Quickly, Tili guided Zicri over the castle wall and landed on the far side of the dens. As paws touched earth, wings tucked beneath the thick hide, and Tili dismounted. Steam radiated off the dense fur. With a hearty shake from head to tail, Zicri let out a satisfied moan and nudged his nose beneath Tili's chin—giving him a balmy blast of nostril air. Pungent but an honor.

Tili smoothed a hand along his friend's spine, which was nearly at shoulder height, and smiled. "Me, too, Zicri. Me, too."

A beefy man emerged from the den with a cluck of his tongue. "The king will have yer head if ye keep doing that." He held out a hand to Zicri, who nudged his long snout and black nose against the proffered welcome. "And if he doesn't, I will. Ye put them in danger riding like this."

"Be at peace, Klome. I would sooner give my life than put Zicri in danger."

Klome glowered, but walked alongside the raqine, who now looked like nothing more than a cat. A large cat. A *very* large cat with the strange, broad skull of a dog.

"I hope ye weren't so careless in the southlands. If the thin-bloods realize they still exist, they'll come hunting."

"I'll put an arrow between the eyes of the first man who tries." Tili gave Zicri a nod, and the raqine lumbered into the dark den. A growl-purr emanated from within.

"Chima's been mooning after him since ye called him out."

"And truth," Tili said with a laugh. "That is why I would never take a wife and why I knew Zicri needed some freedom. A man wants a ride in peace. "

"Bah!" Klome swatted the air. "The day ye think those creatures are human is the day ye die—they're so much better than us. More loyal."

"Ye chide me yet bestow human qualities to a beast." With a wink, Tili backed toward the door to the castle. "Rest ye well."

"Rest. Ha! With ye and yer brothers—" He stopped short. "Where are they with my horses?"

"Yers?"

"I muck and feed them. Yes, my horses."

"The king might have something different to say."

"Indeed," came a stern, stoic voice. "The king *does* have something different to say."

Tili widened his eyes and stilled. Slowly turned. Saw the scathing expression hidden behind the wind-weathered skin and the wisdom-streaked beard. Silver and black hair had been smoothed back and hung to his broad shoulders.

With a bow, Tili did as decorum demanded. "My father, I have returned."

"Don't think I didn't see ye flying Zicri."

He dared not look his father in the face lest he betray his amusement. "I felt it prudent to return with all haste. I have news—"

"It will wait." King Thurig turned back into the house, his broad shoulders adorned with his official cloak and the gold sash of his title. "The earl is waiting."

Freeze the Flames! Yaorid, Earl of Langeria, wanted to find a strong political connection to secure more land and raise his title—and many, many chins—all by marrying his eldest daughter, Peani, to Tili.

"Maybe when I'm sixty," Tili muttered as he slipped into the darkened passage. Took the servant's stairs past the kitchens up to the fourth level, where the private rooms offered sanctuary. His manservant, Gaeord was there, sweeping a brush over the green jacket with the gold embroidered symbol of the Asykth—the raqine. "No," Tili said, removing his dirtied cloak and tunic. "The blue one." It was less . . . just less.

"I'm sorry, Master as'Tili, but the king insisted on this one."

With a disgusted sigh, Tili stomped to the steaming tub of water behind the curtain. "He wants to shackle me to that mare."

"I think Earl Yaorid's daughter quite pretty."

"Many cows are pretty, Gaeord. And she has as much brain as one." That wasn't true, but saying it improved Tili's foul mood a little. "Where is the queen?"

"Preparing for the dinner."

"Dinner?" Tili hissed as he slid into the water and washed himself. Dinner meant dancing. Meant entertaining. Meant stiff conversations and batting eyelashes. He threw his back against the tub. "Flames, take me away from this madness! Give me wings and the sky."

"Oh, the king will take a whip to yer hide if he hears that talk."

"He's three floors down, creating a writ that will forever seal my heart to blackness and despair. He will hear nothing but the praises of Yaorid, who will be fattening his coffers and his ego."

"Ye are the eldest—"

"No." Tili whipped the tip of the bath brush at the curtain separating him from Gaeord, water spewing across the floor. "No, I am not the eldest." He scrubbed harder, trying to erase the stigma of Elan's betrayal. He soaped his hair, scrubbing furiously as he fought the tide of memories.

"And that is all the more reason to be what yer father and this realm need, master. Ye are the eldest *acknowledged* son, and as such, ye must secure a wife and heir to hold the throne."

"Secure?" Tili halted his scrubbing. "Ye *secure* a sow. Ye secure a deed." He dumped a bucket of water over his head and swiped the excess from his face. "Ye do not secure a wife."

Gaeord brought a towel and held it out. "In Ybienn ye do."

Tili flicked the brush at the curtain again, this time intentionally flinging water over it to nail the servant. Tili climbed out, dried off, and dressed. "I must speak with my mother before dinner."

"Ye haven't time, master." As if to chime in, the courtyard bell toned. The loud gong reverberated around the tiny city thriving within the walls of Nivar Hold.

While Gaeord laced boots up Tili's calf, Tili worked to dry his hair. Was there a way to thwart this ridiculous plan to marry him off? Would it be too much to wish for a world war that would draw him away for, say, forty years?

Resigned to his fate, he made it to the grand hall in fifteen minutes, having evaded Gaeord's plan to spritz him with cologne. If Peani didn't like the way he smelled, she could go back to Langeria. At the double doors, he peeked in. And frowned. How had his brothers already bathed and made it to the hall? This did not bode well.

Relig stood tall—the lanky beast—beside their father. With a drink in one hand, he held the earl's daughter captive with his gaze.

"You have hidden from dinners and balls since you were a boy."

Tili spun at the soft, endearing voice of his mother. She struck an elegant figure, her hair done up in graceful loops, each one tipped by a pearl. Her lavender gown shone beautifully against her olive complexion. "Mother." He inclined his head. "I have news!"

She raised an eyebrow and nodded to the doors. "Any attempt to stay the execution?" She smiled and tucked her hand through his arm. "Come, Peani is a vision, and you insult her with your indifference."

"In earnest, Mother. I have news." He took her hands and pulled her toward a chair. "Ye should sit."

"You will not earn me a glare from your father by distracting me." She tugged her hands free. "Come. We must hurry."

"I found her, Mother."

She froze. Her skin blanched. "You are wretched, Thurig as'Tili, to use that as a delay. I rebuke your—"

"Mother." He held her and peered solemnly at her. "I found her." He breathed a smile and nodded. "Kiethiel is well. A bit thin, but well. She is ye reborn, even with hair shorter than mine."

Covering her mouth, she squeaked, her brown eyes pooling with tears. "Please." She shook her head. "Please do not torment me with cruel jests."

"I do not." He squeezed her shoulders. "In earnest, I saw her just outside of Luxlirien. She's with"—no, he should not mention the Fire King's son—"friends."

"Why did you not bring her?" Tears slipped free. "How could you not—"

"She refused." When his mother spun away, he hurried to stop her. "But only because she felt she had something she must complete." He snorted a laugh. "From Abiassa."

Nor would he mention how Zicri had shown himself to the Seultrian prince. Raqine never did that with foreigners. Never. Not unless a bonding verse had been spoken.

"The Flames. She believes in the Flames." She turned and lowered herself into the chair, clutching a hand to her breast. "I knew . . . she could not . . ." A sob wracked her. "I will not grant you a reprieve for allowing her to remain apart." She drew a long breath and let it out, her shoulders relaxing. "But I will trust my darling girl."

• • •

The scene was all too familiar and all too humiliating. Ten years ago, Haegan had lain in bed while the finest healers, accelerants, and even a little-known yet revered pharmakeia stared at him. Poked him with needles. Took samples—all kinds of them. All trying to understand what he'd been poisoned with that would cause such a complete and debilitating paralysis. They had come to no real conclusion other than to say he would never again use his limbs.

"Be thankful he's alive."

"At least he can talk and think still."

"Thank Abiassa she didn't give him *the gift of wielding."*

Words meant as comfort proved as sharp and cruel as a blade run through his gut.

Now, stretched out with his hands tied to two posts and shirtless, Haegan knelt on ground that was perpetually damp from the waterfalls. Behind him stood a bevy of soldiers and accelerants. Inspecting him. Assessing him. They muttered. Shouted. Touched him. Pushed his back, sending shards of pain through his spine.

"It's immature," came a nasal pronouncement. "In its infancy." A huff issued forth. "*New.* It's new."

"I don't care if it's new. I want to know what it means." Many stories had been told of Laejan's intolerance for accelerants as Kaelyria sat with Haegan in the tower. How Laejan had refused to place a single accelerant on the Jujak. How he'd nearly killed a recruit when it was discovered he could wield. "If you can't tell me that—"

"Put aside your petty disdain, Laejan, and listen," the accelerant said. "It means he's marked. That's *Her* mark." Swirls of black and red swam into Haegan's view. Head to toe adornment. Glittering gems— citrine. A high marshal. But he didn't recognize this one. Head held up, the high lord cast a sidelong glance at Haegan, leaning away. As if . . . as if . . .

He's afraid of me.

Laejan muttered an oath and waved off the accelerant. "All I need to know is if this will endanger him on the route back—"

"Him?" The high marshal chortled. "Endanger *him*? My dear general, your fear should be for yourself."

"What in blazes are you talking about, Adomath?"

"If you will refrain from flinging your weak tongue and curses around, I will explain."

Armor clinked. Boots thumped. Nervousness flitted through the gathered throng. And Haegan shifted with them. He dared not speak—he didn't want to miss anything.

"You said the mark is new." That was Mallius speaking now. "Where did it come from? How did he get it—he left the tower only a month ago."

"From a Deliverer, of course. Only they walk in the Void between our world and Hers. Only they stand before Abiassa." The high marshal lowered himself in front of Haegan, but did not touch his knee to the damp ground or lean too close. His eyes pierced Haegan and narrowed. "Have you the ability to wield, prince?"

"No!" Haegan's voice pitched, but he shook his head. "No, I've been a cripple, trapped in a body that failed me long ago. I have no training. Ask Captain Grinda—his father visited me in the tower. Ask h—"

"You should be grateful for this," Adomath spoke over Haegan's words. He stood and lifted his chin. "It is a favor—"

"Don't give me lectures. I just need to get him back to the king."

"Lectures fall on deaf ears. My words are a balm. If he had the ability to wield, you could consider your lives forfeit for the beatings you gave him, but also for those who would wage war against you and Zireli for allowing this scourge to run free."

Scourge?

"I would secure him—"

"Why? He just admitted he cannot wield."

"That mark is the sign and herald of many horrible things to come. Secure this boy and hurry him at once back to his father."

"No!" Haegan shoved his gaze past the Ignatieri tents to the crashing, roaring waters. They could not remove him tonight. He must be here in the morning. And if it cost him his life, he would get to the water and immerse himself. Free Kaelyria. He cared not the price. "It's imperative I enter the Great Falls."

Laejan sneered. "Get him up. Return him to the cage."

"Please, I—"

"I would keep a close eye on him, General. Marked and empty." Adomath clucked his tongue. "There is no telling why a Deliverer marked him. History only records three such pitiful creatures. All were put to the Lakes by their families for the devastation they caused." He once more scowled down at Haegan. "It is beyond my ken to understand why he was chosen. It's never happened to one without the gift."

"Perhaps he has conspired with the Raeng or with Sirdar himself."

"What! No!" Haegan thrashed against the two Jujak who lifted him from the pole he'd been tethered between. "I have never conspired with anyone, let alone the Lord of Darkness! I would as soon end my life as—"

"Please, do us that favor." With a twirl of his robes, the high marshal spun away.

Laejan waved a dismissive hand at the religious order. "Go back to your tents. It will be good to be free of your presence come midday tomorrow."

"I would leave now. Hurry him back—"

"No. We are under orders to remain in support of the sentinels through the noon meal."

Nostrils flared, Adomath glowered. "Make sure he doesn't enter the water."

"Water? Bah, he'll be in a cage."

"Just make sure. Especially if you want to live."

• • •

Cradled in loneliness and moonlight, Haegan snapped awake.

No. It wasn't him who snapped. He had heard something, the crack of a branch. The center fire had burned down to almost embers, though two new logs sat mostly untouched. Ah. Sap must've been exposed in the log and crackled. The fire was unattended, hissing and smoking now under the mist from the relentless roar barreling down the Falls. The Jujak were asleep. As were the Ignatieri. No doubt a few sentries were on guard, but otherwise, the camp had bedded down.

Which made it the perfect time to break out. It was imperative. He could not remain caged and allow them to drag him away from the water tomorrow. Haegan rolled onto his other side, his back to the camp, his face to the bars and the foot of the great mountain that abutted the encampment. He dug his fingers into the damp earth, feeling it burrow beneath his fingernails. Hope pulled at him and he dug harder.

His finger jammed against something hard. He moved around it. Jarred again. Frustration rose quickly through his wearied body. But he dug. *Tried* to dig.

"You'll get nowhere."

Haegan whipped around, pain tightening his back. He cringed and strangled a cry.

The captain squatted before the temporary prison. "I chose this location for the cages because of the rocks"—he stabbed a dagger into the earth with an unmistakable shink of steel on rock and grinned— "impenetrable. If you can break through there, then you aren't human." He held up a tin cup and tapped it against the bars. "It's grog. Tastes like mud, but it will help."

"Nothing will help."

The captain slid the cup through the bars and set it down. Haegan accepted it and sipped gingerly, his eyes never leaving the captain's. The warmth of the brew spread through him, chasing away what felt like a permanent chill. He shivered.

"She said you were the strongest person she knew."

Haegan hesitated, wondering who he meant. Thiel? How could—? He glanced around, his mind racing through possibilities. Had they captured her? Was she in a cage, too? Or had they somehow known each other? She'd known that Ematahri warrior . . . "Who—?" But then he noticed the captain's eyes again. *Really* noticed them.

"His eyes are like the sky before a storm, gray and fierce, cut through by lightning—that's his scar. So rugged." Kaelyria's words made it through the thick fog of pain and defeat.

"You." Haegan pulled himself to a sitting position, but the short height of the cage prohibited him from straightening. "You're Graem, the one my sister—"

"I hated you." The captain balled a fist. "I've wanted to kill you since I first set eyes on her in that bed." Torment held him fast as he stared into the darkness.

• • •

"I hunted you . . .When King Zireli asked me to hunt you down, I committed my whole life to finding you."

"But he said you must return me alive."

Jaw muscle popping, Graem pulled his gaze back to Haegan. "Aye," he said with flared nostrils. "This cage is too good for you after what you've done."

Haegan lowered his chin. "I agree." He shook his head. "I never should have agreed. But she . . . she can be so persuasive."

Graem snorted. "Aye, I know."

"You love my sister," Haegan said, waiting for a slight nod, then continuing. "Please—know that I never would have—"

"I know that, too." Gray eyes stabbed him with finality. "She told me."

"Told you what?" Wariness held a tight fist on Haegan's hope.

"How she used your love for her against you."

All at once, Haegan was relieved and furious. Relieved that Kaelyria had told someone. Furious that this captain knew the truth but had not spoken up for him when the Jujak attacked him. "You can't say anything . . . "

"She broke the laws of the Ignatieri as well as Seultrian edicts by consulting with a stripped accelerant." Propped on his haunches, Graem swung toward the Falls. "She begged me to make sure you reached the Great Falls. But . . ." He scratched his stubbled jaw. "My orders from the Fire King supersede her petitions. I would lose my commission if I freed you."

Futility strangled Haegan as he stared at the waters. So close. And yet it seemed they were eternally removed from his reach. Deafening and yet silent. So strange. "If I do not enter the waters, she may die or be forever fated to suffer the torment of that tower. Is that what you want?" Haegan looked back at the captain.

But he wasn't there.

No! He was there—but on the ground. Laid out. As if he'd collapsed. Haegan scrambled to the bars on all fours. "Captain!"

A mighty explosion of fire shredded the veil of night. Fire raced across the tops of tents, sending soldiers scrambling for safety with shouts and cries.

Fingers hooked over the bars, Haegan watched as the entire plain collapsed into chaos. A shadow raced from the largest Ignatieri tent just seconds before it collapsed in on itself with a great huff that seemed to fan the flames eating through the Jujak tents. It seemed ironic. Somehow symbolic.

"Psst!"

Haegan twisted around to where the great slope of the mountain formed an impenetrable wall. There knelt a hooded figure. Haegan checked on the Jujak lying prostrate. "Pray—tell me you haven't killed him."

"Only a spark." Drracien worked a hand over the entire length of bars. Heat warbled but did not grow to flames. With knuckles almost touching, he gripped two bars and yanked them outward. The bindings snapped and the poles surrendered. "Come on! Move!"

Haegan climbed out, unfolding himself and cringing as pain tweaked and pinched his body.

A warm blanket draped over his shoulder, providing warmth Haegan had not realized he'd missed until the fabric scratched at his neck. He clamped a hand over the left side when it started to slide off.

"Just keep moving," Drracien said. "Don't stop. Don't look back." He pointed. "The woods. Go!"

After the push, Haegan started to glance back and remembered the admonishment. He quickened his pace. "Where are the others? Thiel?" Of course he had to mention her first. "Laertes? And—" He looked toward Drracien, but found no one there. Where had he gone?

Over his shoulder, Haegan searched the frenzy within the burning encampment for the rogue. Searched dancing shadows. Jujak rushed around with buckets of water, dousing the flames. Tending wounded.

There.

Drracien was dumping someone's body into the cage. Graem's. Oh, the soldier would never live that torment down. He might even lose a rank or two for Haegan's escape. He'd be blamed, no doubt. Kaelyria would never speak to Heagan again if Graem were injured. The Jujak would pursue him for all they were worth if he died.

Let him not be harmed, Haegan silently prayed.

"Go!"

Haegan blinked and found the rogue sprinting toward him. He spun and ran toward the trees, holding his side and keeping himself stiff to stave off the pain in his back.

Drracien barreled past him. "Keep moving! They saw me."

42

Haegan scrambled up the hill, no path to ease the hardship. Lying in the cage, he'd not realized how much the injuries bothered him. Now as he ran to keep up with the agile Drracien, he wondered if the Jujak had done more damage than he knew.

Or if I'm just a weakling.

Another name to add to the list attributed to him.

"C'mon," Drracien growled, throwing himself up an impossible stretch with one jump.

Huffing, Haegan considered the steep incline. Vines, bushes, and rocks waited. Wind riffled through the green, waxy leaves. Taunting him. The hill rose almost completely vertical. *Passage is impossible!*

And yet the accelerant moved like a panther in his element.

"I want the prince alive! The accelerant can die for all I care," came a voice all too near.

Hand against his side, Haegan planted his foot on a rock that rested nearly at hip height. With a great push, he launched himself upward. Another grunt and strain of his side delivered him up a half-dozen more paces. He hopped to the right. Caught a branch . . . and dangled. Blazes.

A vice caught his leg. Yanked.

Haegan lost his grip. Dropped hard against the slope.

"Come here, you worthless dung!" The Jujak grabbed him by the belt and dragged him down.

One well-planted foot in the man's chest sent the Jujak spiraling backward, down the cliff. Haegan scrambled onto all fours and continued like that up the incline, grabbing roots, branches, shoots, or embedded stones to haul himself up. It also kept him low to the ground. Hopefully a little less obvious to the warriors in pursuit.

Glancing up as he progressed, he couldn't see Drracien or the others. Had they fled? He wouldn't blame them. No sense in all of them getting caught because of him. But they had just risked everything to save him. Why would they...?

He shook off the irrational doubts. He must move. Haegan grabbed a vine.

Shards of pain ratcheted down his arm. "Augh!" He jerked his hand back, realizing too late that it was a thorny vine. Blood dribbled down his arm. He He tore off a length of fabric from his tunic and wrapped his hands before navigating in a zigzag pattern to ease the incline.

Shouts below startled him, and he swung around to see a particularly young and agile Jujak spring from the bushes not too far behind.

Haegan sucked in a breath.

A streak of fire whistled past. Down the slope.

"Auggghhh!"

Turning from the stricken Jujak, Haegan searched the foliage above and finally spotted a blur of black. Drracien.

A few more pain-numbing drags up the hillside and Haegan found the earth leveling out. And the dampness heavier. The air colder. Huffing, he pulled himself over the small ledge and took a moment to catch his breath.

A sound warbled in the air stilling him.

"Down!" Drracien shouted.

A second too late. A jav-rod whooped at Haegan. The iron head seared his shoulder. Haegan twisted and threw himself to the right. Sprinted across the almost-even ground. Through a thick bramble of shrubs and trees growing defiantly in the difficult terrain. He burst into a small clearing and stopped short, the darkness broken by a strange gap in the canopy above, which allowed the moonslight through. The others were there. They were all there. Including Thiel.

"Yeah!" Laertes pumped a fist.

Tokar grunted something.

Thiel leapt at him, wrapping her arms around his shoulders.

Surprise froze him for a second, but the overwhelming pleasure of being hugged made him smile. Tens years a cripple, he missed hugs. Feeling her warmth against him, her shaking form, he closed his arm around her. And squeezed. Pressed his nose into her neck. Breathed the relief that he was safe.

But then . . . yeah, he'd be a liar if he did not admit that the embrace gave him a hope he did not deserve. Made him too aware of her softness.

Without a word, she pushed back. Chin tucked as if she'd embarrassed herself. "Tunnel rats should know how to run faster."

"They should. And climb impossible heights." A smile barely made it out.

"We need to move." Drracien touched his shoulder. "Should we tend this now?"

Haegan had forgotten about the slice from the jav-rod. "I'm well. Let's go. I can't let them stop us."

"We won't," Drracien said.

They hiked single file behind Drracien, who navigated the mountainside as if it were a bricked path. But Haegan had not forgotten the words the accelerant had spoken. *We won't.* There was something in the way he'd said that. As if . . .

Haegan drifted back in the queue, positioning himself more evenly with Thiel. Holding her had scattered coherent thought. "Where are we going?"

She gave him a slight smile. "Up." This route wasn't easy, and her uneven breathing told him it was difficult for her as well.

"Drracien is leading."

With a nod, she smiled. "He found a way." Then she frowned. "What's wrong?"

"The mark on my back—it means something. A high marshal warned the Jujak about me." He scowled, thinking . . . worrying. "I think Drracien knows."

She caught his arm. "Wait. He's not leading us to an ambush. He's leading us to a haven." Her eyes were bright beneath the moons. "I've seen it. I think you'll be pleased."

"I already am."

She blinked, met his gaze for a long second, then glanced down.

Had the words truly escaped his lips? He should give care. Plying her affections was cruel considering he would be on his way back to Fieri Keep tomorrow. Healed.

Would he truly and forever be healed? He had never before hoped for the affection of a woman, for who would love a man who could not perform duties within the realm and produce heirs? It meant humiliation for them both.

But tomorrow, he would be set free.

The branches and brambles gave way to rocks and moss. Haegan slowed when a foot whooshed out from under him.

"We'll rest here," Drracien announced, unshouldering a pack.

Where had he gotten that? "Should we not keep going?" It was harder to talk up here, the noise of the waterfalls swallowing sound.

Pointing across a span of twenty hands, he grinned. "Soon."

Haegan frowned.

Thiel's hand slipped into his as she walked by. "Come. It's not visible from here."

At her touch a surge like the lightning that had buzzed his tower rushed through him. He followed her another half-dozen paces and stopped short. There, to his left, the raging waters of the Falls erupted from the ledge beneath his feet.

"It's a straight drop," Thiel said, shouting to be heard.

"To death?"

"It's only about forty or fifty feet."

"I've spent a lifetime with Parchments and figures—that's enough to shatter a man's legs, if not his entire body!" Though he laughed, Haegan did not find the idea of a person jumping—The healing waters.

He turned to Thiel. "You expect me to *jump*?" He glanced down . . . down . . . . "Into *that*?"

She held both of his arms. "Think, Haegan," she strained to speak loudly without shouting, then drew him back across the ledge to the others. Drracien had managed to build a fire, but with the humidity in the air, Haegan didn't know how.

Regardless. They wanted him to jump. To his death. Or to his life. To healing. "I'd die as soon as I hit the waters. If you're dead, it won't revive you. Will it?"

Drracien clenched his jaw.

"I appreciate—it is with great respect that I decline. I know you went out of your way to find a way, but . . ."

"What other way do you have, princeling?" Drracien was on his feet. "The Jujak will kill you if you return to the clearing. The accelerants will attack at first sight because of that—" Drracien clamped his mouth shut.

"That mark." Haegan tensed and squinted at the accelerant. "You knew about it, didn't you? That night with the healer. You saw it. That's why you left."

"It doesn't matter."

"It does!"

"What matters is if you don't jump, you don't get to the Falls. There's no way around to the other side. It's guarded from here. And if you try to go down, they *will* capture you, and, depending on who captures you, kill you!"

"Why can't he just step into the stream behind that wall?" Tokar asked.

"Because, the prophecy surrounding the Kindling includes the touch of the sun on the waters." With a nod to the stone wall, Drracien shrugged. "Sun won't penetrate stone."

Haegan pushed his hands through his hair and held his head. He looked to the others, who watched him. They'd been through so much because of him. They'd fought hard. They'd run harder. And now they wanted to him to jump off a cliff.

• • •

Haegan met her gaze, and she saw the way he wilted seconds before he pivoted and stalked away.

"I'll talk to him." Thiel hurried after him. She followed the snapped twigs and branches to where he sat on a rock. It reminded her of the night he'd spied on her, seen her with Tili. When Zicri had pinged him, and she'd had to invent a lie to protect him and the creature. She hiked up next to him and stilled. The view was unobstructed. She could see for leagues—even the lights of Hetaera. The paleness of the moon bathed the vast landscape in blues and grays.

"It's beautiful," she whispered as she sank beside him, legs crisscrossed.

Haegan said nothing. Just stared.

"I've heard tales of people jumping from greater heights and living."

"That's unlikely for me."

"You must belie—"

"I can't swim." His cheek twitched. His chin puckered in and out. Again, he raked his hands through his hair. "Why? Why must everything be so difficult and complicated? I just—I was happy there. In that stupid bed. With my tutor. With hours of boredom that made days feel like years. I was no threat to anyone or anything, save the dust that would have surely overtaken the attics were I not situated there."

Her lip tweaked upward but not into a full smile. He'd never spoken so openly of his life before the tunnels. It pained her to hear the truth of his existence.

"I don't know what's happening to me." He twisted and snapped a twig. "The high marshal warned the Jujak not to let me enter the waters. Called me a scourge. Insinuated I was a danger to those around me." His blue eyes came to hers. "Since I met you, that is all I have been to you, Thiel."

"No!" She shook her head. "If you knew my life before we met, you would know the falsity of those words. I have been in danger, one time after another, since I was twelve."

"Again, for your pain, I am sorry." He motioned to the Falls. "But I *can't* swim. So even if I survived the jump and got healed, I'd drown."

"Not if someone went in after you."

Haegan glanced at her, and it was only then that she realized while he looked the same, the person sitting with her now was not the same one she'd knocked down in the tunnel. He tore his gaze away. "I won't allow anyone to risk their lives anymore. I'm through. This is my decision."

"You must think you're a prince or something, telling everyone what they can and can't do," she said with a laugh.

"I beg your mercy. I only meant that I have no choice—if I don't try, Kaelyria will waste away for the rest of her life and it will be my fault. I have no choice." He met her gaze again. "You do."

"Yes, I have a choice."

A twinge of concern tugged at his strong brow, his lips flattening in a way that accented the firm line of his jaw. "Thiel, please—swear to me you will not—"

"I can swim, tunnel rat."

"If anyone it should be Drracien. He's stronger."

She shrugged. "Sorry, tunnel rat, but you don't dictate this one. Now." She stretched out her legs and pointed her toes. "When you jump, make sure your legs are like this."

"Thiel, I beg of you."

Ignoring the tug of her heart at the softness in his voice, she gave him a cheeky grin. "I like a prince who begs."

His cold fingers touched her cheek, drawing her gaze back to his. He slid his fingers around the back of her neck. "Please, swear to me."

Her heart pounded like the water hitting the pool. Not just because of the promise he was trying to extract, but his nearness. The way those blue eyes waxed nearly white beneath the stroke of the moon. The way her stomach clenched tight. Did he feel the spark between them?

He must. His expression shifted. Not much, but enough. Then his eyes lowered to her lips. She couldn't help but swallow and wet them. Craziest thing of all, she *wanted* him to kiss her. She'd never wanted anyone to kiss her. Not even Cadeif—well, at first. Theirs had been a fiery relationship, with him teaching her to spar, to defend herself. But among his people, she didn't belong, and, ultimately, that's what he'd wanted of her.

Haegan wanted nothing. Asked nothing of her, save this one thing.

"I'm stronger than you think," she said softly.

His lips parted. "I have no doubt of your strength. I see it every time I look at you."

She drew in a breath, surprised.

He tilted his head, closing the gap between them.

Thiel's heart skipped a beat, anticipating his kiss.

"Lovebirds! We need to talk."

Thiel twitched and drew back. She looked down, pulled in a shuddering breath, and let it out. She looked away. "He's right. There's . . ."

"Thiel." Haegan held her hand as they stood. "Swear you will not—"

She pried free, a sudden rush of embarrassment pushing anger through her attraction. "I give no promise to you, Haegan, son of Zaethien. My actions are my own and will not be dictated by another." No matter how blessedly handsome he was. Not even if he'd kissed her.

Thiel returned to the camp and wedged into the small space between Tokar and Praegur. Haegan lowered himself to the ground. She wrapped her arms around herself and hunched over.

"Dawn is nearly upon us," Drracien said, touching his fingers together and pointing them to Haegan. "You must enter the waters as soon as possible after the first beam strikes the water."

"Why is that important?"

"It is said the Kindling is strongest then."

"He can't swim," Thiel tossed in, her heart thudding. "I'm going down after him to help him to shore."

Silence dropped over them, leaving only the roar of the water. A thick grunt came from her left. Praegur thudded a hand against his chest. Then pointed to himself, then the Falls.

"He's right," Drracien said. "He should go. He would be healed, too."

"No—" Thiel nearly bit her tongue severing her objection, immediately regretting her outburst. Of course Praegur would want to be healed.

"Why does he need to be healed?" Haegan asked, looking at his friend in concern.

"After you were taken, he . . ." Thiel bounced her shoulders, hating the weird feeling that squirreled through her when she remembered the moment. The ice in her veins. As if she were back home in Nivar Hold. ". . . something happened. He hasn't been able to talk since."

"*What* happened?" Haegan scowled. "Did you see the healer?"

"He refused."

"A'sides," Laertes added. "He's got a mark, what like you got."

Holding out his shirt so Haegan could see his chest, Praegur grunted what sounded a lot like, "I go."

"Thank you for helping me," Haegan said. "I pray Abiassa protects us both."

Face still etched in sorrow and a measure of pain, Praegur nodded.

"You will have time to race down to the clearing if you leave now," Drracien said.

Doubt flickered through Praegur, and it seemed his thoughts were visible. As if he felt bad for not taking the plunge with Haegan.

"Please, friend," Haegan said. "Spare yourself the terror. Go!"

Without another grunt or look, Praegur trotted out of the clearing, leaped over the bushes, and vanished into the thick forest, heading down to the clearing. No doubt he'd have to navigate carefully along the edges of the camps to avoid the Ignatieri and Jujak. But Praegur was swift and silent.

Drracien looked at Haegan. "You're right. I saw the mark. It's in the Parchments. A Deliverer must have touched you."

Haegan's lips slowly parted. He gave a shake of his head, shock holding him fast. "I don't think so . . ."

"Trust me. You would have felt it. When I say 'touched,' it's not like you and Thiel. It would be strong. They do not lightly extend their hands and leave a mark like that."

"The river," Thiel said, remembering the jolt they experienced at the last second.

Haegan's eyes widened. "Yes. We were going to hit that jagged rock when we were suddenly tossed to the side."

"That fits," Drracien said.

"Incredible." Tokar grinned like a mad dog. "Then that alone should tell you that you have no option but to jump in those waters. Clearly the Deliverer wants you to get healed for your sister."

"He wouldn't have marked him if this was for his sister."

Thiel frowned. "What are you saying?"

"The high marshal," Haegan began, "said three had been known to bear Her mark and they'd all died. But horrible things happened."

Drracien nodded. "Which is why you need to make that jump."

"You think the Kindling will heal the mark?"

"Remove or heal, I don't know. But the stronger Her touch is in the waters, the better the chance, which is why I suggest being first in when the sun comes up."

"Red! Red streaks in the sky. It's coming," Laertes said.

Drracien punched to his feet. "Come, princeling! Now, before it's too late." He led Haegan by the shoulder. Thiel hurried forward, determined to be beside him when he jumped so she could follow.

• • •

Stepping to the ledge took more courage than Haegan had accumulated in his eighteen years. He inched closer and closer, the pounding of his heart lost amid the feral roar of the waters crashing below his feet. Hands braced him, and he glanced to see Drracien there.

O Abiassa, if there was ever a time to show yourself and speak, this would be it. If I am to die, please at least release my sister from this wretched curse.

"Look!" Thiel shouted. "Look at the clearing."

Haegan shifted his gaze to the thin sliver of space that allowed him to see the clearing. A gaggle of horses had rushed into the open. Nearly a dozen riders. Who were—

Haegan stiffened. He recognized the leader. It could not be. It made no sense. "It's Gwogh! My tutor."

"Sir Gwogh?"

"The sun!" Thiel shouted.

"Go!"

The roar of a mighty *"No!"* that did not belong to the raging waters raced up from below.

"Did you hear that?" Haegan shouted, his eyes locked on Gwogh, who—inconceivably—was looking up from the clearing, straight at him. Somehow, Haegan saw his disapproval. Felt. it. "Maybe I . . ." Was this a mistake?

Frantic, Gwogh waved his hands over his head. "No!"

How can I hear him? It's impossible!

"The sun," Thiel repeated.

"Wait." Haegan leaned forward, watching his old tutor. Feeling a strange terror. A strong terror. "It's a mista—"

"Go!" Drracien pushed him—hard.

Haegan pitched out over the Falls. Empty weightlessness assaulted his senses. Gravity yanked him down. Fast. And yet . . . not fast. The mists coiled around him. His legs flailed. Terror tore at every fiber of his being as the waters surged, greedy for his last breath.

But as he fell, Haegan managed to find Gwogh. Remembered Thiel's warning to keep his legs straight, toes pointed down. And in the strangeness of that experience, he saw Gwogh wield like he had never before. A field of air danced and rushed toward Haegan.

Then another spiraling plume. And another. Not just one accelerant wielding, but at least five or six! Their combined efforts created a great and glowing plume that swarmed through the air and grabbed at him. A concentrated wield by so many would singe every hair on his body.

Haegan cringed, anticipating the impact. The hissing mist. Shouts below. Screams above. Heat. Water. A blur. He looked away. Sucked in a breath. They were trying to stop him.

No. He had to do this. For Kaelyria! *"Abiassa, help me!"*

Unbelievably, their efforts hit a wall. An invisible but definitive wall. They could not reach him. It was strange. Unreal. Because he seemed suspended, the fall taking ten times as long as he'd expected. Droplets glistened beneath the bold touch of sunlight. Danced like gems before his eyes. And though he might be as lost as the Mad Queen, there was a thrum to it all.

So serene. It—*everything* was so beautiful. So incredible.

His toes hit the water. Like a brick slammed against them. The water was icy cold. Painful. But as his waist slid beneath the tumultuous surface, Haegan felt an explosion of heat. Shocked, he threw up his arms, arching his back. Fire. Burning!

A mighty clap of thunder assaulted his ears. Darkness devoured him. Water gurgled as he slid to the bottom of the pool.

He writhed. Strained against an agony that defied meaning and words. As if every piece of his body was being ripped apart. He curled inward, thrashing. Arched his back again and cried out. Water rushed down his throat. Into his lungs. Burning. Burning everywhere. Inside. Outside.

He would die.

At least Kaelyria would be free.

Death invited him into its void. *Stop fighting.*

The words tugged at him. Convinced him to surrender. Was he a coward to do this? To give up and let go? Either way—Kaelyria would be healed and Haegan would be free.

Haegan relaxed his muscles and gave in to the smothering darkness.

43

Shouts rang out from the throngs held back from the water by the Ignatieri. Family members who had come to watch their loved ones receive a miracle shouted angrily. Jujak converged on Praegur, catching him as he scurried along the outer perimeter, past the newcomers wielding against Haegan.

"No!" Thiel yelled. If they stopped Praegur, Haegan would drown! Panic ripped through her, nudging her closer to the edge. She had to jump!

"Thiel, No!" Drracien wrapped his arms around her waist, restraining her.

Wrestling against the accelerant, she searched the waters, impossibly hidden by the foamy wake of the waterfall. Where is he? "They're stopping Praegur." A sob choked her. "Haegan. I have—"

Crack!

Thiel stilled, searching the sky for the bolt of lightning she'd heard.

Pop!

A long howl flashed out.

Drracien yanked her off her feet.

"No!"

Even as he whirled her around, Thiel saw a sight that froze her blood. Mists and water converged over the pool on a flat plane. They drew in tight. Snapped like a bow string. Then flooded out, crackling and hissing. Boiling—the water was boiling!

Terror gripped her as she flew around.

"Hurry!" Drracien tossed her behind the rock wall, a curtain of water breathing against her face. She stumbled backward, the edge of the drop-off against her hand. Rigid, she hunched and squinted, expecting to be evaporated.

• • •

"You must go to him."

Seated on a chair in their private chambers, Zireli bent forward. The burdens of the raging war and the impending defeat clung to him like sodden clothes. Weighing on him. Encumbering him.

On her knees, Adrroania placed her long, delicate fingers on his knee. "Please, my love. Go. Find him. Bring back our son." Her blue eyes glossed.

He wanted nothing more than to track him down. "I cannot leave Seultrie undefended. I must remain here an—"

"He is alone! He has no strategy, no plans."

"He should have thought of that before fleeing."

She drew back, her thin eyebrows knotted. "You think him guilty?"

"Why would he flee?"

"From your anger!"

Zireli shoved to his feet, pushing away from her. He went to the beveled windows overlooking the Lakes of Fire. "Is it not justified? Have I ever wielded unjustly?"

"Do not the edicts of the Ignatieri forbid accelerants from wielding against one another?"

He spun to her. "Haegan is not an accelerant."

Surprise leapt through her face then washed away as she shoved her gaze down. "No. Of course not . . ." She wet her lips. "But he's your son. I only meant—"

The puzzle that had touched his mind at her strange expression fled before her words. "What? That our son should be exempt from the very laws I am tasked with overseeing? That the king's son can do what as he pleases?"

"*Is* he your son?" She strode forward, a fiery flush in her cheeks. "Because he has not heard your voice in years."

"Guard your tongue, Adrroania. You—"

"No." Her bosom rose and fell unevenly. "I have too long watched you bury your guilt in duties and capacity as king." She let out a sigh. "You knew how to be a father once. And a husband. I would hope you recover that."

"The Nine are falling, and you would lecture me—"

"If they fall, what are you then?" Her voice had dipped so soft and quiet it forced him to hush his own ragged breathing to hear her. "A king with no realm to rule is simply a man." Her eyes glittered with meaning. "You are no longer king, but we are still your family. Haegan, your son."

"You want the realm to fall?" He heard his voice pitch, an unseemly and girlish sound, but his ears could scarce believe what they heard.

"*I want* you to remember the man you once were—the man who loved his family!"

Anger shot over his restraint like a flaming arrow but then fizzled and clattered to his feet as if doused by the water of truth. She was right. "What would you ask of me, Adrroania? Abandon the responsibilities placed on me by Abiassa Herself to guard Her land and people?" He stalked to the window and set his back to her. "I am the king and must—"

"To Haegan, you were his father first."

"I am still his father, no matter the rhetoric. And Haegan left—fled. Like a brigand. His actions have severed my ability to protect him." He felt the decade-old wound rotting in his chest. "What little I could . . ."

Her feather-light touch came to his shoulder. "He asked for you every time I visited. Asked how you were. How your training was going. How the council meetings went. About Valor Guard selection—that, by Abiassa's Mercy, was his sorest wish, to be one of your elite." Her fingers curled around the sleeve of his tunic. "He was *starved* for word from you."

Starved . . . just as his young body had been starved of strength. As the kingdom had been starved of a strong-bodied prince to grow up and rule the Nine after Zireli. All because the mighty Fire King could not protect his own son. Seeing him in that pitiful state . . . unable to move. Needing to be carried from place to place, tended as an invalid would, it had decimated Zireli's courage.

"I know you watched him sleep."

Zireli jolted at her words, and in her eyes he met understanding.

"But he needs you now. More than ever, Zireli."

No. Haegan would want nothing to do with him. "He needs—"

Thud! Thud!

At the banging against their chamber doors, Zireli swung around, tucking Adrroania behind him. "Enter."

The doors swung open and the butler offered a bow. "I beg your mercy, my king."

Directly behind him stood Grinda, his face bloodied but steeled. The general looked . . . spooked.

"What is it?" Zireli asked as he moved forward to receive his general and the ominous reports.

With a curt bow and salute, Kiliv gave a sigh. "Reports from Hetaera."

"Graem?" Zireli's gut tightened at the thought of the young captain coming to harm.

Kiliv looked to him, then to the queen before once more focusing on Zireli. "Graem is . . . alive. A little roughed up, but following your orders."

The words were carefully chosen yet drenched in the Kiliv's lingering disapproval over having his son sent out.

"Has he learned anything of the prince?" Adrroania asked.

Hesitation held the general captive. Clearly he knew something he did not wish to share in front of the queen. "She is aware of how grave things are," Zireli said.

He sighed. "Sire, the entire land is in unrest. Asykthians have been spotted in Luxlirien, Iteverians in Hetaera, and the Ematahri are flooding out of the woods."

"They would not be foolish enough to try me," Zireli said.

"Aye, they would. And they are." Kiliv shifted on his feet. "An emissary arrived this morning. Seveirid's successor—this Cadeif fellow—is claiming a blood price."

"Blood price? For what?"

"Twenty of their warriors were slaughtered during a strange explosion."

Zireli nearly laughed. "What has that to do with me?"

"They claim Prince Haegan was there when it happened."

Zireli's breath caught. "Hae—on Ematahri land?"

"It's worse—the warriors also said a Lucent Rider helped him escape."

Adrroania gasped and stumbled back, a hand going to her mouth.

"Is that where my son is?" asked Zireli, feeling the rage of a father whose son had been captured. "With the Ematahri?"

"No, my lord. He was with brigands outside Hetaera, among them an accelerant, who held off Graem and his men while the prince escaped into the hills with the others."

"They're in the hills?"

"Yes, sire." Grinda shifted on his feet. "Laejan is there already with a contingent—sent to assist the Ignatieri, as ordered."

The Great Falls. "Blazes, has the time for the Kindling already come?" He'd lost track of such matters in his fight to protect the realm. His mind tangled with thoughts he should not be entertaining. Could Haegan be healed, completely? "So, he's there."

"Graem and his men have surely arrived by now, but . . ."

Zireli knew what was coming. "But they are not able to withstand the accelerant."

"No, my lord."

"Haegan cannot be allowed to enter the water," Adrroania said.

Both men turned to her. Zireli saw her blanched face and took a step toward her. "Are you well, Adrr—"

"General," she said, hurrying forward. "You must ride at once and order the men to stop Haegan at all costs."

Grinda frowned, darting a look to Zireli. "I . . . beg your mercy, my queen, but as commander of the armies of the Nine, my orders must come from the Fire King."

"Today is the Kindling, is it not?" Zireli said, confused about her distress. "Grinda would be too late to stop him anyway, my queen."

"Today," she muttered, her gaze sweeping toward Zireli but never quite meeting his. Was that fear in her eyes? "I . . . I'll excuse myself." She turned and left the chambers. Or was it more like fled?

Why did she look so afraid? "In light of this claim by the Ematahri, she is right in that Graem should pursue Haegan—"

"Sire, the Great Falls border the Northlands."

"I know the boundaries of the Nine, Kiliv. All the more reason for your son to complete my orders."

Another curt nod. "And the queen's words?" Speculative gray eyes held his. "Not to let him enter the waters? Why would she say that? The transference—I heard it was temporary. Why would she not want the prince healed for good?"

"I'm sure that wasn't her meaning." Zireli wasn't convinced of the words he spoke. Something about her expression and pallor haunted him. "It would be too late anyway, once your rider reached Graem and the others, to stop him."

Kiliv straightened. "Yes, sire. It is several days' hard ride on the fastest horses." He bowed low. "However, I'll send him at once to convey your command."

Zireli caught his general's thick arm. Waited for their eyes to meet. "I want him back, Kiliv." He looked to the window. "Dawn rises, and with her I want the hope of seeing my son restored—in body and to me."

Understanding pushed into the rough lines of the hardened man's face. "Aye. And—"

A searing, concussive wave of heat slammed into Zireli. Knocked him backward. Knocked him out.

• • •

Shrieking rent the morning. The sound so unusual, so terrifying that Tili launched out of bed. He cared not about the draft and his half-clothed body, only about the agony so clear in the howl of a raqine. *Zicri.* He flew from his chambers and down the hall. Barefooted, he skidded to the window in the eastern passage that overlooked the den. Leaded glass blurred his view.

But it could not block him from the fury roiling through the air.

"What is the matter?" came Gaeord's concerned question behind him.

Tili cranked open the window, clearing his view. In the yard below, Klome stumbled backward from the den, using one of the corded whips and aiming it at the opening. Tili's question froze on his tongue as the wood gate exploded. Shouts and screams ensued. A second later, a raqine soared into the open, roaring.

The sound vibrated against Tili's chest.

Zicri? As the beast angled toward the Klome, it's familiar red-tinged coat shone—Chima!

Klome shouted.

"What is the bother?" It was his father's voice this time, behind him in the hall.

Chima contracted, poised to attack, then lunged. Tili held his breath, fearing for his friend's life. The raqine soared to the top of the den. Then onto another, lower building. She ran, jumping rooftop to rooftop.

"No," Tili muttered, jogging along the windows, pacing her. Where was she going? The clearing? "No! No, no, no!" He stopped and pivoted. Checked her neck. Slammed into his father. Rolled around him. "Chima's going airborne and her collar's missing!"

With an enormous shriek-roar came a solid thwack. Her wings. She'd deployed her wings.

Warning bells from the watchtower rang through the morning.

"Why in the blazes are they sounding those—"

"Sir!" a servant shouted from the other end of the long hall. "Unauri—coming down from the Cold One's Tooth!"

Tili stared at the flush-faced manservant. "Unauri? You're sure?"

His father turned to him. "Get dressed. I'll need your help."

Tili nearly laughed. "What am I to do against giants?"

• • •

Haegan. Accelerants. Praegur. Thiel sat huddled against the wall, drenched and shivering. Trembling. She felt a bump against her elbow and pulled her gaze there. Laertes looked up at her, his brown eyes wide and dripping with water. No, not water. Tears.

She slipped an arm around his shoulder.

"Wh—what was that?" His teeth chattered from the cold and wet.

Her body convulsed, the temperature much worse here, hidden from the rising sun and warmer air. She couldn't answer his question. Her own mind wouldn't process what she'd seen. What happened after Haegan hit the water.

"What did we hide for?" Laertes asked.

"It's safe now," Drracien's voice reached into the cramped space.

"Safe of what?" Laertes crawled toward the opening and carefully peered out. "Blazes and Flames."

His muttered oath made Thiel tense as she sidled free. Tokar extended a hand.

"Thanks," she said to him, but he wasn't looking at her.

His gaze was locked onto—"Merciful . . ."

The clearing, while not flattened, wasn't far from it. Trees that had stood tall and proud, shielding the earth from the sun, were now bent to the ground, as if wishing to put distance between them and the pool. Branches reached outward, as if clawing a path to safety.

"Look!" Laertes pointed to the encampment. People were laid out, unmoving. "What's wrong wif 'em? Are they dead?"

Thiel's heart thudded. Whatever had happened . . . What would have been their fate had they not hidden? Drracien had saved them. "How did you know?"

Drracien's eyes met her, leaden with guilt. He glanced at his hand, which he flexed and contracted, frowning.

Thiel drew up her shoulders. "You—"

"There's Praegur," Tokar announced.

"—knew this would happen. How did you—" Thiel's brain caught up with Tokar's words. She pivoted. Saw where he looked and located

Praegur sprawled on the ground, surrounded by incapacitated Jujak. "Haegan." Her gaze flicked to the pool. "O Beneficent One! He's still in the water!"

"Then he's dead." Tokar sounded lifeless.

She spun. Shoved his shoulders. "Don't say that!" She whipped back to the opening. Moved to the ledge. Praegur hadn't made it to the water. That meant Haegan was drowning. She toed the ledge.

"Wait! No!" Drracien held her arm.

"Get off—"

"The banks. Look at the banks around the pool." He pointed to the water, but his eyes never left hers, a wild panic in them.

Thiel pushed her gaze to the area surrounding the water. It seemed different, but she couldn't quite tell . . .

"The explosion emptied the pool—evaporated the water. The Falls are filling it back up. If you jump now, you'll kill yourself."

"Healing waters—"

"I . . . I don't know that they will heal now." He stood straight, the implication heavy and oppressive, and flexed his hands. "Things"—he stared at his palms—"are different now."

Shouting down below caught her attention. The old man, an accelerant she'd noticed just before Haegan jumped, was moving swiftly toward the water's edge, hiking up his belted tunic as he sloshed into the pool.

"How can them be alive?" Laertes asked.

"That's Sir Gwogh."

Haegan's tutor? Thiel turned and fled down the path. Her feet slipped and slid down the terrain, but she wasn't waiting anymore.

"They'll arrest you!"

Thiel ran down the straight paths. Leapt into the air and jumped several feet where the incline was too steep. She landed, pitching into a tree. Pain struck her shoulder. She kept moving, not caring. Haegan . . . Haegan couldn't be dead. She wouldn't let him. She tripped. Scratched her arm. Scored a knee. Stumbled over rocks. Slid over mossy drops.

With a great jump, she sailed through the air, clearing the final five feet of hillside, and landed in a roll at the base of the mountain. She came up running. Sprinting. Racing for the water, ignoring bodies strewn across the grass like flowers cut down. She couldn't think about whether they were dead. The thought was too gruesome. Awful.

Thiel made it past the burned Jujak camp. Beyond the table barriers, shattered and scattered like splinters. Aimed toward the small cluster of people—Gwogh's companions?—standing at the water's edge.

"Where's Sir Gwogh?" Thiel demanded as she tugged off her leather boots.

An older woman merely aimed a shaking finger toward the middle of the water.

"The center? Or nearer the Great Falls?"

"Center," the woman answered stiffly.

Thiel waded into the water, hiking her legs as she sloshed onward, surprised at how long she could stay on her feet before diving. She swam hard, kicking and dovetailing downward. Enough light broke the surface for her to spot the tan fabric of the accelerant's garments. He was coming toward her. His gray beard floated eerily. He was, worst of all, empty-handed. Alone.

He nodded, waved her on.

Thiel dived hard past him, swimming faster and faster. Limbs aching, she pushed through water that seemed to get denser and thicker as she went. And warm! The farther down, the warmer. Wasn't it supposed to get colder where there was no light?

A glow wobbled in the pool.

Then a hand. Haegan! Thiel thrust herself at him. Grabbed his hand. Pulled. He floated toward her—then snapped back. She pulled, her lungs burning. She tried again, but he wouldn't give. Down a little further, she saw slick weeds wrapped around his foot. Always getting stuck in vines! She released him and dove to his feet. She struggled with the slippery weeds, and finally untangled him.

She nearly gasped, desperate for a breath. Pressure thumped against her temples, as if knocking her upside her head, demanding air. Gripping Haegan's belt, she aimed for the surface. His weight slowed her. Her legs burned and ached. Cramped. The return seemed twice the length. Her limbs felt like a hundred pounds each.

They started sinking.

No! Thiel shook her head and even gave her courage a mental jog. Haegan was unconscious. That meant he had water in his lungs. That meant each second was vital to his survival. She kicked harder. Harder.

She wanted to whimper but couldn't even do that. No grunt. No tears. Push. Kick. Swim. Push. Kick. Swim.

A hand swiped in front of her. Someone grabbed her collar. Thiel jolted as he pulled her backward. Up . . . up . . .

She broke the surface, gasping. Crying. "He"—gasp—"He—couldn't breathe—"

Sir Gwogh and Tokar were hauling Haegan back onto the small embankment. They dropped him, exhaustion and death forbidding them from being careful. They pounded on his chest.

Drracien helped Thiel to the side. She crumpled, her muscles twitching uncontrollably. Tears streamed down her face as she watched the others trying to revive Haegan. "I should've gone after him . . . I should've gone . . ." She shook her head, grief tightening her raw throat. "Should've jumped."

"You would've died," Drracien mumbled.

"You don't know that!" Thiel shoved to her feet. Wobbled, her feet sinking in the mud that had once been submerged in the pool. Her legs buckled, exhaustion exerting its power. She pushed forward, dropping to her knees beside Tokar, who was pumping Haegan's chest.

The prince looked horribly pale. His lips blue. Yet somehow, he was beautiful. She inched closer. "Haegan, come on."

"Keep working," Sir Gwogh ordered Tokar. "On his side, then his chest. Keep going."

"His back," Thiel said. "Thump his back—the mark."

"Are you cruel, child? The pain—" Sobered, Gwogh touched her shoulder as he turned to Tokar. "Do it—pound the mark."

Tokar scowled but complied. He flopped Haegan onto his stomach. With his fingers threaded to form a giant fist, he raised them and rammed Haegan's back.

Thud!

"There's water what's coming out his mouf," Laertes said, who knelt facing their friend.

"Do it again!" Thiel shouted.

"He'll kill me if he wakes up," Tokar said.

"And I'll kill you if he doesn't," Thiel bit out. "Now!"

Tokar was already in full swing.

Thud!

Haegan's head lifted. Eyes bulged wide. Then closed as he dropped. His shoulders convulsed. He coughed. Water spewed out of his mouth. Vomited. More coughs.

Laughing in relief, Thiel scooted closer.

Only . . . Haegan went limp. Still.

"Why's he not moving? What's wif him?"

"The Kindling—it had a devastating effect on his body," Sir Gwogh said.

"And everyone else's," came a woman's soft response.

"Why?" Freeing her gaze from the woman's, Thiel frowned. Then considered her friends. "It was supposed to heal him."

"Yes," Sir Gwogh said. "*Supposed* to." He stroked his still-wet beard, his modest clothes clinging to him.

"He's breathing," Tokar said. "Why isn't he coming to?"

Sir Gwogh used his walking stick to gain his feet and looked out over the clearing. "We must get him to safety."

At his side, Thiel glanced at the bodies. "They'll hang him for killing so many."

"Oh, they're not dead." As if to confirm his words moans popped up around the field. "They're the reason we have to get him out of here."

A shriek rent the air.

I know that sound! Thiel whipped around, searching the skies, her heart pounding. Yes—perfect! She cupped her hands around her mouth and let out a long, mournful sound, followed by a wavering high-pitched whistle.

A shadow spirited across the clearing.

Thiel shielded her eyes as the dark shape circled beneath the sun.

"Blazes," Laertes said.

Chima! Thiel laughed as the beast alighted, her hind legs touching the singed grass. She pawed the air with her front legs, then dropped down. Shook and snorted. And shook again, tucking away her enormous wingspan. She lumbered the half-dozen paces to Thiel and nudged her nose beneath Thiel's chin.

Thiel embraced the raqine. "I can't believe you remember me, Chima."

But the mighty raqine stepped free. With a chortle in her throat, Chima nudged Haegan's still form, then glanced back at Thiel.

"A raqine?" someone asked. "Is that—"

"She came for him," Sir Gwogh said, catching Thiel's arm. "Take him. Take him with you on her before they awake and see him. And her!"

Dumbstruck, Thiel froze. "Take him where?"

"Ybienn."

Thiel frantically shook her head. "I can't—"

"If you don't, Haegan dies. He needs the healer there, Pao'chk."

Healer? "My father banned healers. Banned all manner of wielding." Not to mention she had left her home, she thought, for good. She pushed the stringy wet hair from her face. "And if you haven't forgotten, my father and King Zireli aren't on speaking terms. To put it nicely. If I took Zireli's son—"

"Stop arguing! He will die if you do not do this." Gwogh hooked her arm and pushed her to Chima. He pointed his staff to Tokar and Drracien. "Lift the prince up to her. Kedulcya—your cloak."

Thiel took a handful of Chima's fur, half expecting the mighty raqine to object. Instead, Chima's muscles rolled, aiding Thiel onto her back. Legs spread wide on the massive spine, Thiel shifted as Tokar and Drracien hoisted a still-unconscious Haegan between her and the raqine's neck.

"Here," came a stern voice. The woman, Kedulcya, shuffled toward her. "You look frozen through."

"Thank you." Thiel tied the cloak around her shoulders and slid her hands through the slits before securing the belt. Warmth bathed her, the interior a thick hide. Gwogh laid a blanket across Haegan's back and legs. He then touched Chima's neck and whispered something unintelligible, something that sounded like the ancient language. The same one Haegan had spoken.

A melodic purr rippled through Chima in response to the aged man's words, then she stood and shook her head.

"What did you say to her?"

Sir Gwogh grasped her hand and squeezed it, his fiery gray eyes piercing hers with intensity. "I will come. For now, his life is in your hands. Go, child!"

44

Four years it had been since she straddled a mighty raqine, the enormous beast, so catlike in its build and movements, yet with the snout of a more canine-looking animal. And of course, wings. But to think the raqine was just an overgrown cat was to underestimate them wildly. With a killer olfactory sense, they could find their mates or riders from leagues away.

Even as Chima crashed violently through the canopy of the trees surrounding the pool, Thiel felt the years fall away. At seven, she'd barely been able to stretch her legs around Chima. At twelve, she'd almost had a solid grip. Now, though still difficult, it was manageable.

That is . . . until Chima drew her legs in, gave two brutal flaps of her wings, and propelled herself far above clouds and wind. They soared, the icy breath of morning burning off far too slowly for Thiel. Her fingers ached from the cold and wet. The cloak the woman had given her worked against her, filling with air and nearly pulling Thiel off Chima. She wanted to remove it, but she dared not let go of Haegan, who lay limp across her legs and Chima's neck. The blanket Gwogh had tucked in around him rippled beneath the strong winds.

She held a fistful of Chima's fur and a death-grip on Haegan's belt, the most middle part of him. Fear held her just as tight. If they fell, they fell to their deaths.

That's what Haegan thought before he jumped.

And he'd been right. If she hadn't sprinted down . . . Still, he'd been unconscious for so long. Underwater for too long. Would he wake from this nightmare the same person?

What was the explosion that had snapped through the air when he hit the pool? Evaporated water and downed trees?

Chima tilted her left wing down and they glided in a curve.

Thiel tightened her thighs and held on to both beast and Haegan. But he was slipping. Thiel whimpered, weaving her hand under and around his belt as Chima's angle sharpened. Fighting the tears and panic as Haegan's legs dangled almost completely straight down, as if he stood on the wind itself, Thiel bent over him, pressed her weight against him.

"Chima!" she shouted.

The raqine sensed Thiel's terror and adjusted her flight pattern. She aimed down now, slowly closing the distance between them and the ground.

Swallowing hard, Thiel rested her face against Chima's neck, which also helped shield her a little against the wind. Even as she protected Haegan and rested, she could not shake the image him falling. Of him lying there . . . dead. Of that explosion that rendered everyone unconscious.

So like the burst of light that killed the Ematahri.

But those in the clearing by the Falls hadn't died. The Ematahri had. Why? She glanced down at Haegan, at the sunlight glinting off the gold strands of his blond hair as the wind riffled its ardent fingers through it. What . . . what was he?

Many times he'd vowed he wasn't an accelerant, that the gift hadn't passed to him. But there could be no denying the events that took place with him at the center. Was he a danger? Was she bringing a danger home to Ybienn?

She lifted her head, watching the treetops. The clearings. What would Father say? He'd likely have her arrested. And . . . Mother. Her stomach churned. Her mother would want her to stay, but it could not be. Cheek against Chima, she again considered Haegan. Would Father have him killed? The son of the one man he hated most in the world. And she was bringing him to their doorstep.

But even her father would not dare harm the Fire King's son. Right?

Over Chima's shoulder, she glimpsed Nivar Hold coming into view, fear her newest and closest friend. As a low, chortling noise rippled through Chima—her call to the others in her pack, at least, that's what Osmon told her—Thiel noticed the trees rustling. Hard. Swaying.

Had there been yet another snap of air like what happened with Haegan at the Falls?

She frowned, squinting.

Then saw *them*.

Her breath backed into her throat as she realized it wasn't air rustling the trees, but Unauri. She sat a little straighter to look as Chima glided over their heads. The Unauri, at least a dozen of them, stood at the lip of the forest. Had they not been giants, she would have missed them. They stood two to three heads taller than her father. And they were watching. Watching *her*. Their firsts raised in solemn salute.

"Blazes," she whispered, a tremor of awe filling her. The Unauri had not left the safety of the Ice Mountains in . . . centuries.

Chima began her steep descent. Circling. Angling. Down . . . down.

Thiel struggled to keep her seat and secure Haegan. Why hadn't they tied him to Chima's neck? The leather of his belt cut into her arm as they circled, swooping down lower and lower with each circuit. The wind seemed as violent as that which had evaporated water and knocked people senseless. It pulled at her, angry.

Thiel struggled. Dug her fingers into Chima's fur.

Chima shook her neck and a grumble went through her, but she kept her approach.

Though she fought to maintain her grip, Thiel could not help but gauge their landing spot. The den. Inside the walls of the keep itself. Not the city. Good. They did not need talk or threats. She pressed her head down, determined no one would see her outside those walls.

Yet a half-dozen of her father's elite fighters lined up around the den, which seemed to be undergoing renovations with the wood piled— wait. Those beams were splintered. Broken. What happened here?

Chima lifted her wings then wrapped them almost in front of her. They hovered directly over the spot in the stable yard.

"Clear a hole," someone shouted.

As the men moved, Chima chortled as if thanking them, then arced her wings up to ease their landing. Thiel glanced up to make sure she could not be seen outside the walls. Assured of that relative safety, she straightened enough to search the faces around her. As she did, swords were drawn. A perimeter formed, then tightened.

Chima touched down softly, folded her wings, then slumped to the ground.

Shoulders hunched, Thiel tucked her chin, afraid the guard would strike.

"Stand down! Stand down!" Tili sprinted between the guard. Her brother grinned, his eyes alight with wonder. "How did ye summon her?"

"I need help," Thiel said, not ready for questions to which she had no answers. She lifted the blanket from Haegan's legs. "He's been seriously injured. I was told . . . Pao'chk. We need Pao'chk."

Tili moved to the other side of Chima, who sniffed then snorted at him. "Who is he?" He brushed the hair from Haegan's face. "I don't—"

"Please," she said, a shiver racing through her. "Can we go inside?"

Her brother's assessing, analyzing eyes struck her. Questions lurked there. Curiosity. A little wariness. Then a nod. "Of course." He lifted a hand. "Bring him inside to the servants'—"

"The Green Room," Thiel interjected, hating the idea of Haegan relegated to the servants' quarters. Their father would not appreciate her giving him their best guest room. But he'd also have heads if someone treated the Fire King's son so ill.

Tili's frown was bigger this time as he met her gaze in question. "The Green Room," he said as the men lifted Haegan from Chima. Holding up a hand to assist her, Tili waited.

Thiel tossed her leg over Chima's side and slid down without his help.

He grinned. "Still as rebellious and ornery as when ye left, sister?"

She arched an eyebrow at him as he put an arm around her shoulder and guided her toward the house. "More."

He laughed hard—then stopped short, staring at her. "What ails ye?"

"The Unauri." She hauled in a breath, the chill of seeing them clinging to her still. "They are amassing on the borders of the forest."

He nodded.

"I am in earnest. They—"

"Aye, they came down when Chima broke loose this morning. But there's been no attack nor ambassador to come yet. They just . . . wait."

She shook her head. "They saluted me as I flew over. There must have been a dozen."

Tili weighed her words, his brow stern and a maturity wreathing his face she had not noticed in the forest weeks past. He had grown, as she had, in the years since she'd left. "I will mention it to Father. Come, let's go to him now."

Thiel was brought up straight at the sight of their father standing just inside the entrance. Silhouetted by the sun that poured through the Sanctuary-height windows behind him, he stood as still as one of the statues of his forebears that lined the gallery.

Thiel swallowed and lowered her head. "I beg your mercy"—why was it so hard to speak his name?—". . . Father."

He shuddered as he drew in a breath. "Then it is ye, child?"

Hearing the hint of his Northlander brogue snapped something in her. A smile wanted out, but she dared not let him believe she thought light of this. "Aye," she whispered, her throat raw.

"All these years without a word, without explanation—"

"Father," Tili started forward.

But their father stilled him with a swift upheld hand. His face unreadable, almost unable to be seen for the light behind him. His beard glittered with gray.

Would he throw her out? Forbid her entrance? Her insides quivered as she bit her lip, itching to speak but terrified at the same time to open her mouth. She had dreaded this day. Feared he would do exactly as he was—

"Who is the boy ye have brought to my home?"

Thiel lowered her chin, too frightened to own up to the truth. "A friend, Father. He is in dire need of a healer. I was told to seek Pao'chk."

"Pao'chk! He's as insane as a loon bird."

"Father, I only—"

"The situation is unusual, Kiethiel. But . . . I will have him brought." He nodded to Tili. "Take her upstairs and let her bathe and dress. Both of ye in the solar immediately after." With that, he was gone.

A piece of Thiel shattered. She sagged, both relieved and rejected.

"Yer departure devastated him."

Thiel jerked at her brother's words. "Deva—I left to protect him." She jogged up several steps, feeling the strange squish of water between her frozen toes and socks, trailing her brother out of the servants hall. "To protect our family!"

"Aye," Tili said, glancing at her without stopping. "But it did all the same. I told ye in the woods ye should've sent word that ye were safe." He stepped onto the third level, the family's residence.

She brushed her hair off her forehead, swinging around to avoid barreling into him when he slowed. "Had I, he would've sent the elite after me."

Tili shrugged. "I would've led the charge. In fact, I did. Every time he sent us."

Slowing, Thiel placed a hand over her stomach. "He—he sent you?"

"Every six months." Tili strode over the worn carpet toward the chamber that had once been hers.

She stared at the richly carved door, the symbols ascribed to her when she had been born. The dove for peace. The entwined rope, the symbol of her parents' lines. The crown resting atop the head of a raqine. Peace. Power. Prowess.

Petulant had been more like it.

"May and true, he was probably more happy to have ye out of his hair than he was anxious to search for me."

Tili rounded on her. He frowned. Deep and true. "Thiel, have ye no inkling of the hurt ye've inflicted on our father? Our mother?" He placed a hand over his chest. "Me?"

She laughed. "Ye?" With a snort, she started for the door. "Mother will take a strap to ye for so many lies in the space of an hour."

He stepped into her path, nearly causing her to collide with his broad chest and leather vest. "Sister." He rested his hand on top of her head. "When ye fled, all joy went with ye."

She swallowed, her voice and courage losing potency. "Please . . . I . . . it had to be done. I had to protect our father." She raised her eyes to the thick beams, richly embroidered tapestries, expensive paintings.

"Ye forget yerself, Kiethiel. That is our charge, as men of Nivar Hold." His brown eyes reflected the light slinking through the windows above as he looked to the barracks for their soldiers. "For those who have taken an oath to defend Ybienn and the Northlands."

"No man could undo what was done to me, and that shame—"

"Ye told me yer reasons in the woods outside Luxlirien." He leaned past her and flicked open the door to her old chambers. "As ye left it." His lips quirked. "I would imagine the dresses might be a bit . . . short now." He wrinkled his nose as his gaze swept over her in a brotherly, amused fashion. "But you're still skinny enough to fit otherwise."

She would have slapped him had the sight of her old room not struck her dumb. She wandered in, as if seeing for the first time. May and true—she was. After her return here from the raiders, she'd hated this room. The frills. The floral papers on the wall. The . . . happiness of it all.

Now, having slept for years on the hard earth or on a pallet, it was hard to fathom the luxury of the feather bed. The thick fabric curtaining the bed to keep out the cold out. The hearth where a perpetual fire burned to ward off the chill of the mountains. The wall of windows draped in sheer fabric that had been hand embroidered with gold raqines, wings outstretched.

At the dressing table, she lightly touched the hairbrush. Instinctively, her other hand went to her shorn crop. It'd grown out, but it wasn't much longer than Laertes' now. A short haircut had served her well while ducking through alleys and fields, but here . . .

"It will grow." The voice, so warm and familiar, poured over her like a healing balm.

She whirled and found her mother standing in the doorway, hands clasped in front of her, doing nothing to stop the tears that spilled down her cheeks. Lavender. She knew her mother would be wearing lavender. The edges of her flared sleeves were trimmed in a gold brocade that draped almost to the floor. A choker at her neck bore the wrought symbol of the Asykthian crest and beaded down to where the Abiassa twists dangled in gold.

"Mother." Every ache, every hurt from the last four years leaked out of Thiel. She wanted to rush to her, but she thought of Tili's words. Of how she'd hurt their father. She could only imagine the wound much worse in her mother. She dropped her gaze. "Mercy . . ." There were no words that would heal what she had done.

"My darling girl." Her mother rushed toward her.

Thiel met her on the thick rug, throwing her arms around the diminutive waist. She clung for life to her mother, terrified she'd toss her away. Make her leave. "I beg your mercy, Mother. I didn't want to leave. But I—"

"Shh," she said through her tears. Cupping her face, she smiled down at Thiel. "Please tell me you are here to stay. That I will not have to bear your absence again."

"My shame—"

Her mother pressed an adorned finger to her lips. "There is no shame that our Lady cannot wipe away. You are restored to the seat of honor the daughter of Thurig possesses." She smiled at her. "My beautiful, darling girl." She kissed her, hugging her tightly, then stepped apart. "You must hurry. Your father was in rage over the boy you brought." Curiosity danced in her eyes. "Tarien will dress ye."

Dress me? Thiel only then noticed the servant moving about the room as she and her mother had spoken. She drew a green and gold dress out and hung it from the bedpost. "It's too . . ." Extravagant. Fancy. Bold. Everything.

"You're going before your father," her mother said. "You would do well to make this impression a strong one." She cupped her face and kissed her, once more staring hard into her eyes. "We will have many talks, you and I. For now, bathe. Dress." She looked over her shoulder to Tarien. "See if you can hide the bruise and cut." She hesitated, glanced at Thiel again. "On second thought, leave them."

Thiel gave her mother a questioning glance.

"He no doubt saw them already," her mother said. "Besides, they might give him pause for concern about your safety." She winked. "That will bode well in tempering his anger over this boy."

The boy. Haegan! "Mother, he—my friend needs a healer. I was told to ask for—"

"Pao'chk." She lifted her chin. "He has been sent for, although, it shocks me. Your father and he fell out years ago." She arched a fine eyebrow. "Which I'm sure adds to your father's anger." After another kiss, her mother stepped out, then turned back with a smile. "Osmon will escort you."

Osmon. Younger than her by two years, her little brother had never had an interest in her but every interest in shadowing—and annoying—Tili and Relig.

"We should hurry, mistress," Tarien said as she poured steaming pitchers into a basin behind a curtain.

She went through the motions, numb and distracted over the anger she had already aroused in her father. It would be imperative to tread softly in revealing Haegan's identity. Her greatest fear was that her father would rebuke them and remove them from the hold altogether. What would she do then?

Whatever it took. Haegan's life was in her hands. And while Sir Gwogh said those words, his gray eyes had sparked with a warning somehow.

"It's a bit loose, but I can pinch it in," Tarien said. "I'm sure once ye have a good meal and rest, ye'll fatten right up."

Thiel wanted to laugh. Fat was the last thing she wanted attributed to her. She smoothed her hand over the velvety fabric. Crystals wrapped her waist and dangled down like sparkling tassels. Her sleeves were cuffed at her elbow, then flared out with a sheer fabric. She felt beautiful. New. Restored.

Until she looked in the reflecting glass. "My hair . . ." She might have a new dress and fine adornments, but the hair would betray her.

"Not to worry, miss," Tarien said as she stretched a cream-colored fabric over her head, placed a simple circlet on it, then secured the fabric at the nape of her neck. As such, her hair—or lack thereof—was not visible. Thiel breathed a smile, turning her head as she stared back at her reflection.

Tarien slipped a choker around her neck. "Almost—"

"No." Thiel stood abruptly when she saw the Nivar crest. "I can't wear that." It would be a presumption. Audacious to presume she could return and resume her place as his daughter.

"But, miss—it's yers. From when ye were a lass. I only put it on a ribbon until the leather can be—"

"It's too soon to determine whether King Thurig will restore me."

The girl opened her mouth.

"I thank ye, Tarien." Thiel stood, a little wobbly in the heeled shoes borrowed from her mother and a size too big. She walked toward the door, and stumbled. "Oh, these won't do. I'll fall and then where's the hope he'll accept me?"

A strong rap came at the door.

Thiel considered kicking off the shoes and going barefoot, but wouldn't that be the riot if she showed up barefoot. What an insult!

"Here, miss," Tarien rushed to a wardrobe, opened the doors, and tugged out something. She turned. Gorgeous embroidered slippers. "If they're too big, as least ye won't fall."

Another strong thud.

She tried them, found them still too large, but some tissue stuffed into them worked. Straightened, she smoothed her dress. Took a slow breath and nodded.

She opened the door and froze.

The man before her stood head-and-shoulders above her. His hair was tied back in a tight queue. His cloak was rich and adorned with the Nivar crest. She flashed him a look. "I—" Then saw in his eyes. "Osmon?"

"Sister." His eyes were as wide as hers, she was sure. He offered a hand and a small smile.

"Little brother," she breathed a laugh. "You were shorter than me . . ."

His expression hardened. "People change in four years." The edge to his voice served as warning for how this interview with their father might go.

Tentatively, she placed her hand in his. "I thank ye for the escort."

Stony featured, he tucked her hand into the crook of his arm and walked her down the hall. Nerves made her anxious to offer apologies, but with each step, the realization of what would happen in the solar weighed on her. He guided her to the passage on the right. As they rounded the corner, firelight from the solar danced across the paintings of their forebears and lands.

A few steps before the door, Thiel stopped. "Wait," she whispered. Osmon frowned at her.

Hand on her stomach again, Thiel closed her eyes. This just wasn't about her future, whether she'd have a home again. This was about Haegan. His identity. His life.

45

"Afraid?"

Thiel gave a slight smile, her nerves jangled.

With a long look, Osmon moved ahead of her. "Ye should be." He slipped into the solar. "Good eve, Father."

"Yer sister—"

"Is in the hall. Afraid to enter."

Thiel squeezed her eyes, defeated. Angry, she forced herself to muster the courage Haegan said she had. She stepped over the threshold, half expecting the air to vacate her lungs. The fire danced and popped in the enormous pit to the right. Her father had donned his official coat and long cloak, as well as his plain gold circlet. Beside him stood Tili, who winked at her. And to his right . . . Relig. The dark, brooding brother who had women swooning and tavern owners barring doors. At least, that was almost five years ago. He had aged. But had he grown up?

"She's the image of ye," Relig said to their mother, who sat in her cushioned chair, perfectly poised.

Setting a glass of some dark liquid on the table before him, her father motioned to the servant. "Close the doors. No one enters."

The servant bowed and left. At the thud of the doors being secured, it was hard not to feel trapped. Suffocated. But Thiel pushed her gaze back to their father.

"Ye have much to answer for, Kiethiel."

She lowered her gaze. "Yes, Father."

"Ye don't have the right to call him that after abandoning our family—"

"Bind yer tongue, Osmon!" Father snapped.

Nostrils flared, Osmon flopped into the chair like a petulant lad. He would be but fifteen, yet he looked a man.

Chest rising and falling unevenly, their father let out a breath. "I canna' pretend there is no damage from ye running off. There is."

Thiel held her hands, afraid he'd see them trembling. "I understand."

"Do ye?"

After a long glance to him, her brothers, and their mother, Thiel nodded. "I do, much more than when I left."

"And how do ye explain yer leaving?"

"I did it to protect ye, our family, and the Nivar clan from the shame forced upon it, upon me." She swallowed, refusing to remember.

Her father lunged forward, startling her. "But that was my job, Kiethiel." A ferocity spiraled through his ruddy face. He motioned to her brothers. "Their job. To protect those beneath this roof!"

"Yes," she said firmly. "But the shame persisted, even when the blood price was extracted. When the people saw me, they saw not the daughter of Thurig the Formidable. They saw the daughter raped and held hostage for a ransom. They saw—"

"Our failings." Her father's voice cracked.

Thiel yanked her gaze to the thick rug. "Ye did not fail. It was me, Father. I brought shame. I had to leave—"

"And in leaving, ye made it impossible for me to protect ye."

She hadn't thought of it like that. Did her brothers, too, feel this way? Slighted by her attempt to protect them? "I beg your mercy—"

"The people lost confidence in House Nivar for a while," Relig said, his voice gravelly, like rocks tumbling against one another. "One house after another tried to overthrow our father in the year after ye left."

Thiel started. Looked at their father, whose face went like stone.

"Only in the last two years have they accepted that, while ye had fled, our father was still as strong and powerful as ever." Relig tossed back a glass of wine.

"Father . . . I beg your mercy!" She shook her head. "I had no idea—"

"Aye, mayhap," he said, his voice quieting, "But ye did know ye brought Haegan Celahar under my roof, did ye not?"

A queasy feeling roiled through her stomach, threatening to toss bile up her throat. She could not lie. Neither would she have. "Aye, I knew."

"And ye brought him here, knowing his father is the Fire King. The man who would as soon burn this house down as look at us!"

"No!" Thiel moved forward a step. "No, I brought him here because Haegan needed help. He was badly injured. When Chima showed up and Gwogh—"

"Gwogh." Her mother was on her feet, her face pale.

She met her mother's gaze but plowed ahead. "Haegan needs help, and if we are in a place to give, is it not only our duty but our honor to help those in need? Is that not what ye taught me as a girl?"

Her father growled. "Don't ye go lecturing me. That boy—"

"That boy has been thrown into impossible circumstances. Given no choice in what happened to him. Since I met him, he has fought for one thing—to reach the Great Falls and save his sister." She flashed her gaze around to the others. "Would not each of ye do the same for me? Did ye not just tell me, Tili, that ye searched for me? Did ye not hunt down Filcher and extract a blood price? Would ye not have gone to the ends of Primer to do such?"

Their father's eyes went wide. His mouth hung open.

Watching her, Tili smiled and leaned toward their father. "Did I not warn ye she managed to find more fire?"

She tried to laugh, but there was too much pain, too much exhaustion to endure a longer interrogation. "I beg your mercy, Father. For the shame. For my departure. For everything ye have endured because I did what I believed best. But I beg on your honor, please don't send me away—or Haegan. He was dead." Tears blurred her vision, but she blinked them away. "He was dead and we had to bring him back." Her chin trembled with the memories, the fright. "When Gwogh said to come here, I argued. Because I knew how fierce your anger could be. I knew ye would not grant me mercy. But on my life—I beg ye to grant it to Haegan. He is innocent and deserves neither your censure nor your anger because of an old wound."

He stared at her, his expression unreadable beneath the graying beard. When had he gone gray?

"Please." This time, a tear slipped free. "If ye must cast me out, then . . ." She shuddered at the thought. "I accept it, but please—will ye withhold that anger until Haegan is recovered? Please."

Three large strides carried him to her. He swept her up in his large, thick arms and crushed her against his chest. "Oh, my sweet lass!"

A sob, unexpected and its existence unknown, exploded through her. "Mercy, Father. Mercy." She cried into the stiff, scratchy fabric of his coat.

His hand was against her head. "My lass." He planted a noisy kiss against her ear. Then pulled her back. Held her shoulders as one of his large hands cupped her face. "Ye are my blood and that will no' change. Ever." He pressed a kiss to her forehead, a tear glistening in his beard. "I am glad yer home. Truly." Again, he crushed her to him. "Ye willna leave again. Promise me that."

"I have no desire to leave, Father."

46

Weightlessness. Emptiness. Haegan hovered in a blank, white vacuum. Voices warbled in and out, luring him into the deeper recesses of the nothingness. Screams. A crack-popping.

Falling . . . falling . . . falling . . .

"Augh!" He jolted.

"Easy, my lord, easy."

Haegan thrashed, fighting the water. Drowning. *I am drowning!* Sinking deeper and darker. Icy water.

"The sheets—he's caught!" Grunts. "Another blanket—he's freezing!"

Haegan blinked, the world blurring out. He lifted his head, fighting the heaviness. He groaned and forced his eyes open. Instead, the world spun, catching him once more in the barrenness.

• • •

Thiel wrapped an arm around her waist, chewing her thumbnail as the healer bent over Haegan, while Relig and Tili struggled to restrain the Fire King's son, who fought violently in his dreams.

"Hold his arms," Pao'chk ordered, lifting a concoction from a side table. "If he frees his hands—that'll be all for the lot of us." The aged man, back crooked and fingers gnarled with arthritis, took a chair and moved it closer to the bed. He sat then lifted Haegan's sweaty head in one hand and the cup in another.

A terror sprinted behind Haegan's closed eyes. He moaned, pulled his head away, then bucked. Hard. Bouncing the bed and nearly sloshing the cup the healer held.

"*Hold* him!"

Tili grunted. "He's like a newly born colt—slippery and—"

Thud!

Haegan's hand broke free and knocked Tili's head backward.

"Augh!" Stunned, her brother gave Haegan a mean glare, then attacked the job of holding his arm down. This time, the prince couldn't move.

The healer squeezed Haegan's mouth as he lifted the liquid to his lips and poured it.

"What's in it?" Thiel asked.

"A mixture of a potion to temper the fire and another to aid his recovery . . . I hope."

"You *hope*?" Thiel's own fire blazed. "Gwogh said to bring ye here. Have ye been guessing all this time, healer?"

"Easy, easy." Her brother's words were soft as Tili came and guided her back. "Ye shouldn't be here, sister. Come—"

"There's *nowhere* else I should be!" She wrested free, glaring at him. "Sir Gwogh said his life is in my hands. I am *not* leaving."

"Where is this accelerant anyway?" Relig moved into the hall.

"Father has enough to concern himself with the Drigo coming out of the mountains," Tili said, "without inviting two accelerants into Nivar Hold."

"Not Drigo," Relig countered. "Unauri. Drigo are mythical beings with the ability to transform into an ungodly size and possess incredible abilities. Unauri are simply people grown too large."

"Like ye?" Tili said.

"Ye're only jealous I'm taller, younger, and better looking—and stole yer future bride."

Thiel started. "What?"

"Don't listen to him," Tili said with a growl. "I *gave* Peani to him—keeps me from having to be shackled to the hold and tend a dithering wife." He stood behind her, staring into the room where Haegan now lay sleeping once more.

"That's what he wants us to think. Fact is, she saw me and couldn't wait to shed him like last winter's coat." Relig rested an arm on the doorpost as the three of them looked in on the healer. "The prince, huh?" He knuckled Thiel's chin. "Ye know how to pick them, little sister."

Heat climbed her neck, so she stretched, trying to hide it. "I didn't pick him. In fact, I just sort of fell upon him. Quite literally. He was lying in the tunnels like a dead rat."

"I would hear that story," Tili said.

"Ye won't."

In spite of being younger, Relig always had a way of superseding Tili. "What happened at the Falls . . ." His expression waxed serious. "The whole bailey is in an uproar over something strange that happened there and some prophecy."

Thiel nodded. "The Parchments," she muttered, remembering Laertes's excited ramblings that night Haegan was captured.

The healer stopped and glared at her from beneath his bushy eyebrows. "What know ye of the Parchments?" It sounded more like a challenge than a question.

"I don't." She glowered at Pao'chk. "Who do you think you are to—"

"Hey," Tili said, stepping in front of her and taking her arms, pushing her back.

"Get off me!"

"Hey!" His gaze was fierce, his tone worse. He stared down at her, his dark eyes piercing, his face rimmed in the shadows of the hall. Then his expression softened suddenly. "When was the last time ye slept?"

"What?" Thiel blinked. "I am not worried about me. Hae—"

"Ye should!" His shout bounced off the beams in the ceiling, but then he sighed. "If ye die from exhaustion, who will harangue the healer over how poorly he's doing his job?"

Thiel rolled her eyes. "I have to stay. Sir Gwogh put Haegan in my care. I have to—"

"What?" Tili tilted his head. "What is it ye can do at his side that I or Relig canna do for him while ye sleep?"

Thiel turned away, feeling strangled at the thought of leaving Haegan. "I can't—" Her voice cracked. She swallowed tears.

Mercy of Abiassa! Crying?

She *was* tired.

"Go, or I will drug ye myself."

• • •

Prince of the Nine. Heir of Zaethien.

Fugitive.

Tili stared at the Celahar prince as he lay unmoving. He had lain as such for the last ten years, crippled. How then was he healed? What harm had he perpetrated against his own family to find himself here with Kiethiel as his guardian?

Threading his fingers, Tili considered the damage this prince could cause. A fugitive from his own home, he would give the Jujak plenty to say if his location were made known.

That could seriously strain the thin threads that kept their families from war. But there were other concerns. Ones that made Tili consider ending this prince's life right here and now.

"How does he fare?"

Startled at his father's presence, Tili wiped the sleep from his eyes, then scruffed his hands over his face. "Quiet. Finally." He glanced at the sleeping boy. Man. "What hour is it?"

"Midnight."

Tili yawned again. "Kiethiel will be here soon."

"It is good of ye to share watch with her."

"I tried to get her to rest, to get reacquainted with our mother, but she wouldn't have it. So I insisted on splitting the watch."

"Good," his father said. "It is yer job to watch out for her. Not this . . ." He huffed and moved closer to the cot. "He has the look of his father about him, but around the mouth, I see Adrroania." Hands behind his back, his father shook his head. "I sent word to Zireli."

"Of course." Tili then noticed the grave expression his father bore. "The messenger has already returned?" It had been only two days. Had his father authorized the use of a raqine? It would be the only way to travel such a distance in so short a time.

Hauling in a long breath, his father scratched his beard. "No, though I wish he could have." He frowned. "What trouble is this Celahar bringing to my door?" His thick finger traced the leather straps. "Restrained?"

"The healer said he'd be the end of us all if we didn't secure him." Arms crossed, Tili grunted. "Father, what do ye know of the Parchments?"

"Too much and yet too little." He turned toward the door. "Why do ye ask—oh, the healer. He mentioned them?"

"Actually, Thiel did."

"Kiethiel?" He snorted. "Has she been reading Parchments as well as gallivanting across the Nine?"

"Father, ye must give her credit. She is well—mostly, nothing a little stew and rest won't heal—and she's strong." He grinned. "Much stronger than the petulant brat whining over pearls on her dress."

Something flickered through his father's expression. His beard twitched as he pinched his lips. "What I would not give to have that spoiled lass back, to wipe from her mind all the harms done against her. The failings—"

"Father . . ."

He held up a hand. "Ye will not say anything yer mother has not already said a thousand times. But I will take my leave." He looked over his shoulder. "Cover him—his hands are like ice. And notify me when he is awake. I would have words with him."

"Aye, Father." They would all want words with this young man.

· · ·

With her chair against his cot, Thiel propped her legs up on the edge, the velvet bell of her dress modestly tucked around her legs as she slumped down, head propped back. Her arm rested on the blanket covering him, and she toyed with a loose thread, all while staring at him. Her hopes rose when his eyes had darted back and forth, but instead of awakening, the terrors took him yet again. Soon Haegan would simply go limp. The same pattern. Over and over. A fortnight of this. She was losing hope he'd come around.

Would Gwogh ever arrive? What if they'd been captured? Or arrested by the Jujak, who had been waking when Thiel spirited Haegan to Nivar.

Thwap!

Thiel jolted, nearly tumbling out of the chair. She stomped to her feet and spun around, her heart galloping.

Pao'chk stood with a wretched smile. "Did I frighten ye?"

Thiel huffed and started back for the chair, but a large book now sat on the edge of the table. "Wha—?" She swallowed her question. It was a stupid one. She knew what that was. "Parchments."

This time, a genuine smile filled his face. "Some of the oldest known to mankind here."

"Here?" She laughed. "What? In the Northlands?"

"No," he said, mixing another potion to administer to Haegan. "On Primar."

"The planet! Are ye mad?" Her laugh echoed through the room. "Ye say it as if there are Parchments"—it was ridiculous even to voice it—"on other planets."

He laughed. Hard. Then straightened. "Yes." And went back to work.

The healer should use his own potions on himself. Perhaps he did, and that was the source of his crazed speech. Shaking her head, she returned to the chair and glanced at—

Blue eyes held hers.

"Oh!" She jerked forward. "Haegan! You're awake." She pivoted to the healer. "He's awake!" Then back to Haegan. She lifted his hand and held it between hers, next to her face. "How do ye feel?"

Hooded, his eyelids drooped. He breathed. Once. Twice. His eyes slid shut.

Thiel scooted closer. "Haegan, please." She squeezed his hand. "Please come back. You must."

"He will," Pao'chk said.

But I want him back now.

• • •

"Can I not have . . . simpler gowns?" Asking for pants and a tunic would send her mother over the balcony, but to Thiel, asking for less gaudy styles seemed reasonable.

"Simpler?" Her mother lifted her hand to the row of gowns that hung in the wardrobe. "I had her remove all gems, Kiethiel. If she removes anything else, ye'll stand in naught but a shift." Gliding across the room, her mother closed the distance between them quickly. "What is this, my child? Irritation only came to ye when ye were impatient. What needles ye now?"

Turning to her bed, Thiel rubbed her forehead. In earnest, she cared not about fabrics, gems, and glittering things. She wanted Haegan to be better, Gwogh to be here, and to feel like she belonged somewhere. "It's taking forever."

"Ah, Prince Haegan."

Thiel rounded. "Do not say it like that."

"Like what?"

"Like he's some whim or . . . as if ye think me a fool for being concerned about the Celahar heir."

"That you care for him is a sign of compassion and character," her mother said. "But give care where you lay your affections, Kiethiel."

"Affections?" Her face warmed. "I—"

"Kiethiel!" Her brother's shout echoed through the hall into the upper apartments.

Sprinting to the door, Thiel felt her heart vault into her throat. She grabbed the door and flung it open.

Tili skidded to a stop. Grinned. "He's awake."

After hiking up her skirts, she ran down the hall, descended the passage, using the stone wall to ensure she didn't pitch to her death in her haste. She skidded around the corner and flew down to a lower level, where the guest rooms waited.

Relig emerged as she reached the room. He considered her with a frown. Remembering herself, Thiel released her skirts and slowed to a walk. Smoothed her gown and hair. "Is he . . ."

"Asking for ye."

With a smile, she tucked her chin and eased around the corner. But the smile vanished when she saw Haegan's near-panicked expression. She rushed to him. "What's wrong?"

Relief washed over his face, his eyes brightening when he saw her. "Thiel." He closed his eyes. "My sister—"

"Shh. Be at peace. Father has sent word to Seultrie. We await a reply." When he didn't respond, she tensed. Had he slipped into unconsciousness again? "No, please stay with me." She was about to kneel when Relig slid a chair toward her. She smiled and scooted it closer. "Haegan?" Sadness gripped her that he wasn't talking now. Or looking at her. "Haegan. Are you well?"

He swallowed, his gaze on the ceiling now. "I can't feel my legs."

The sound of his voice was a relief instantly replaced with raw grief. "Are—are you sure?"

He scowled at her. "Of course, I am. Do you think—"

"Easy," she said, touching his shoulder. "I meant no harm. It's just ye've been unconscious for a fortnight. And in that time, ye attempted to kill us several times while submerged in the deep sleep. Ye had the use of your arms and legs then. Perhaps . . ."

"What? My body is still unconscious but I am not?" He snorted, his sarcasm a surprise.

She felt more than saw her brother slip into the room to show his disapproval for the way Haegan spoke to her. It had to be the potions. He was rarely rude.

A pained expression rifled his handsome features. "Mercy, Thiel. I . . . after all those years in the tower, then to have the use of my legs and arms and lose that again . . ." A lone tear slipped down his face.

Thiel thumbed it away, resting her elbow on his pillow. "Mercy, Haegan. I feared the same when I went after ye in the pool. Ye were under for so long."

His blue eyes took her in with a look of awe. "You? You pulled me out?"

With a faint smile, she felt the heat crawling up her neck and into her cheeks. "I had help. But ye needn't sound so surprised, tunnel rat.

Remember, ye are the one who said I was the strongest person ye knew."

He smiled. "I meant in heart." As his gaze shifted to the ceiling, that grief crested his amusement once more. "Why is She toying with me? What have I done to so soundly offend Her? To what end did She allow my healing then rip it from my hands—my whole body!"

Relocating her hand to his shoulder, Thiel lowered her head. Fought the emotion thickening her own throat. "I don't know."

He breathed a laugh as quiet settled between them. A full silence, brimming with regret and agony.

"Yet," Thiel said, her voice barely above a whisper as her mind journeyed through the time they'd had together, "without that gift, I would not have met ye."

A dark shape shifted in the corner, a subtle reminder to them both that Tili stood guard. "Relig went for the healer."

But once Haegan's gaze met hers. Thiel ignored her brother. Haegan was so very handsome with his wavy blond hair and eyes as clear as the Crystal Sea beyond the mount. Such a kind, earnest person, too. Though they'd only journeyed together for a month, she knew him to be one of the best people she had ever met. And a quiet, frightened part of her secretly hoped their paths never parted, though it seemed inevitable. Even thinking it alarmed her, for fear of cursing her heart's desire.

His brow dug hard and fast into a frown. Sorrow washed over his face. "I am—"

"—as thick-headed as the day I trampled yer body in the tunnel. Or the night ye tracked me into the woods where I spoke to my brother." She bobbed her head toward Tili. "Or the night ye nearly fell off the cliffs overlooking Throne Road, convinced ye saw a raqine."

"It was the same night," he said.

"Wait. He thought he saw a raqine?" Tili's voice thundered through the room, breaking their moment.

"It was dark," Haegan growled. "My eyes deceived me."

Tili's laughter was long and hard. "What madman have ye brought to the hold, sister, thinking he saw a raqine? Don't ye know, prince? They haven't existed for centuries."

"Tili," Thiel chided him, rolling her eyes.

Clearly Haegan didn't remember Chima's rescue or the flight to Nivar Hold. His face turned red. Embarrassed. Haegan looked at her brother, then closed his eyes.

"Tili, please." She motioned him out of the room.

But her brother stiffened. Scowled at the two of them. "For decency's sake, I should stay. It would not be proper—"

Thiel huffed. "I've spent the last month sleeping on the ground at his side," she said. "Think ye that sitting in a room with him will impugn me after that?"

Tili's shoulders squared, his expression dark. "I'd keep that to myself, Kiethiel." He slid a warning glare to Haegan, who did not see it. "I'll be in the passage."

With a sigh of relief, she focused on the Celahar heir, leaning closer. "Haegan."

"I was supposed to be healed." Anger tinged his words. "Have you any idea what this means for Kaelyria? For Zaethien and the Nine? With my father on the field, Seultrie is defenseless!"

"Please, no more," Thiel said, clutching his hand.

His eyebrows twitched.

"What?"

He stared at the wall by the foot of the cot. "How is it that I am paralyzed, yet I can still feel your touch? Still feel the chill in the air?"

She glanced at their hands, confused.

"That would be because you are not paralyzed, my prince." Gwogh entered the room, leaning on his walking stick.

Surprise leapt through Thiel, followed quickly by hope that her friends had finally made the journey as well.

"What? No proper greeting for your old tutor?"

"Gwogh!" Haegan looked truly surprised. "You are a cruel friend, for you see with your own eyes I cannot move."

Thiel looked to the door. "The others—"

"Are with Thurig, explaining themselves." Gwogh seemed much taller than before as he folded himself into the corner on the other side of the cot, allowing the healer to enter the room. "As for you, young prince, you cannot move because Pao'chk has been administering a precise regimen of remedies to keep your muscles sedated so your healing could be thorough."

"Then I am not paralyzed?"

"Only because of the medicine. Once it wears off, you will have your full . . . abilities."

Haegan breathed a laugh, then closed his eyes again. "I'm healed." He whispered the words, as if he feared they would suddenly become untrue.

Thiel slipped out of the chair and knelt beside his cot, her heart full of his joy. "You're healed. Thank Abiassa."

"What do you remember, my prince?" Knuckles on the mattress, Gwogh bent in. "Of your jump?"

"That it was terrifying," Haegan said with half a laugh. His hair curled around his face, blond and shiny from the baths the servants had administered as he recovered.

"Give this to him." Pao'chk nudged a cup into her hand. "Slowly. Don't spill it or choke him."

Annoyed with the implication that she would be so clumsy, Thiel rose from her knees and peered into the murky concoction. "What is it?"

"Never ye mind," Pao'chk tapped her shoulder in remonstration. "Just give it to him."

"It is the antiserum to what has kept Haegan sedated," Gwogh said with a nod.

"Oh." She gave the healer another seething look as she lifted the tin cup to Haegan's mouth, then tilted it so the contents streamed in slowly.

Haegan cringed.

"Hot?" she asked.

His face wrinkled tight. "Bitter!"

"Much like the truth, eh, Gwogh?" Pao'chk's tone was not unkind, but neither was it friendly.

Gwogh used two fingers to wave off the healer.

"What does he mean?" Thiel asked.

"Trouble is what he means." Gwogh smoothed his beard, staring at his charge with great thought and consternation. Or maybe that's how the accelerant always looked. "If he were not the best healer in the lands, I would never open my door to him."

Pao'chk snorted. "He says that because he knows I'm right." He motioned to Haegan. "Go on. Tell him. He needs to know."

"Know what?" Now Haegan seemed concerned. "Gwogh?"

The elder eased onto the edge of the cot, his size straining the wood. He touched Haegan's shoulder. "When your strength is back, we will talk. For now, rest. And remember. It is important that you remember what you saw at the Falls."

Haegan frowned. "I told you—"

"It will come." Gwogh's smile never reached his eyes. "Call for me when you remember."

"Must you always be so cryptic?"

"Yes." This time, the smile did reach his eyes, but faded quickly. "In times like this, especially. Forgive me, my prince."

47

Seven days since the concussion had hit him. Six days since he'd lain awake with the terrible awareness that he was now but a fraction of himself. But he must not let anyone know. He must harbor the secret as long as possible, even with the searing stench of Poired's breath at the gate of the keep. He felt it more than ever, the impending doom. The defeat. The fall of the Nine.

A day not so far in the past would've seen him railing, his pride filling him with anger. But this time, the woes were for his people, for his family.

Haegan.

He hadn't just failed him. He'd shamed him. Now, according to reports from the Great Falls, which had come in at breakneck pace, his son was lost. The explosion that had lessened Zireli's ability to wield had also claimed his son's life. He was completely lost to him now. And Zireli was filled—no, *consumed*—with a need to right this wrong.

"Abiassa . . ." Her name faded on his lips, his guilt stifling. Why would She listen to him this time? "Please." What could he say that might move her and the Creator? The supreme being? "For him . . . show me." Grief strangled Zireli. "Help me make this right."

Haegan was dead. What right could be made of that?

A tearing drew his attention to a dark corner of his bedchamber. He lifted his hand to send a spark into the fireplace when a shadow shifted. A dart of terror shot through him as a blur coalesced before his disbelieving eyes.

"Deliverer," he whispered. His training told him he should stretch prostrate before the Hand of Abiassa. That he should beg for Her mercy.

Instead, he plunged off the bed. Threw himself at the immortal. "I beg of you—my son! End my life if you will, but . . ." Asking for Haegan's life, which was already lost, would be foolish. But those were the only words he had. "My son."

Piercing eyes held his. Though the Deliverer said nothing, Zireli heard *"Come."* ricochet through his mind. The being turned and melted through the stone wall.

Zireli pivoted and flung himself at the bedchamber door. He ripped it open and burst into the hall, searching the darkness for the Deliverer.

"Your Majesty!" The chamber guards straightened, but not before their gazes swept him. "Would you have me fetch your robe, sire?"

"Where'd he go?"

"Sire?"

With Poired encroaching on the city, staff had been reduced and lamps were minimal in order to avoid giving away the location of the family within the keep. His eyes strained to see past the tapestries, down the hall . . .

There! Atop the stairs waited the shadowy figure.

"Wait!" Zireli sprinted after the Deliverer, who vanished as he moved. But each time the Void Walker vanished, he appeared almost instantly in another location. This time down a corridor leading to the library. Zireli rounded the corner and found himself immersed in utter darkness. He ran unyielding, the passage memorized in his youth, the steps as familiar as conducting forms. In the library, a sliver of light pushed past the closed curtains.

On the thick rug woven in the pattern of the Crown and Flame of Zaethien, he stood, waiting. Anxious for the Deliverer to show himself again. Minutes ticked by with the firm, solitary stroke of the hall clock. Each stroke a solid *thunk*, the vibration detectable against the wood floor.

But as he attuned his senses to his surroundings as any accelerant would do, Zireli knew he was alone. Why? Why would the Void Walker bring him here, then leave?

"Come on," he mumbled. "Show me your will." He twitched his fingers, aching for what had been lost. For the Flames ripped from his very veins. He ached for answers. For a way to restore all that had been lost, all taken for granted.

The door creaked open. A guard stepped in. "Sire?"

"I must wait for him."

Silence gaped. "For whom, sire?"

Zireli refused to look at the guard. "Did you not see him?"

"Him?"

Of course. Deliverers revealed themselves to only those whom Abiassa willed. *I must look the madman.* "Leave and close the door."

"Sire?"

"Do it!" Zireli snapped, then felt a tinge of remorse. "Wait outside, if you must. But leave me."

Acquiescing, the guard stepped out and secured the door.

Zireli closed his eyes. "I beg your mercy," he muttered. "Show me what I missed. I beg you—do not leave me here, in the dark. I want to defend your people, my son!"

How long he sat here, he could not say. Only that he had somehow missed the Deliverer's direction. The point. He wandered the dark, the lack of light, chilling. Frightening.

He sniggered as he stood at the empty fireplace. When was the last time he'd been afraid? Now he stood here, nearly powerless. Poired ready to tear down the walls around them. Crush the Celahars. Steal the last hope of Primar. "Do not let this happen. Show us. Show us how to stop him."

He moved to the twenty-foot painting of his father, sensing a disapproving chill that made him shudder. All those years with the ability to wield, the adherence to the Guidings, the heat.

The heat.

Zireli turned back, glanced at the fireplace. He'd not felt a chill there. Yet there was no fire. He backtracked and stood there. Extended a hand.

Warmth.

He traced the mantle, the detailed stone cool to the touch. Around the cornice . . . Chuckling, he pressed his hand against the plaster. "Warm," he whispered.

Snick!

The panel to the right of the hearth opened.

Like a tepid bath, warm air rushed over him. Drew him down . . . down . . .

• • •

"I look like a right lord, I do." Laertes stood before the reflecting glass, holding the brass-buttoned jacket together at his waist. He turned, angling his head this direction and that. His blond hair was shinier than Thiel had ever seen it. Had he let someone trim it?

She tucked a smile aside, knowing it'd irk the young lad. "And quite handsome. I had no idea yer hair was that yellow beneath the dirt and grime."

He licked a hand and smoothed it over his hair. "A little too clean, iffin you ask me."

A servant entered.

"Could we—?" Thiel straightened. Shock flashed through her. Not a servant. "Tokar."

Though his chin lifted in pride, he stood silent for a moment, his eyes traipsing over her in the burgundy dress. Clearly he was as surprised by her appearance as she was by his. But perhaps his gaze lingered a little too long.

Praegur joined him, thumping Tokar on the back.

Tokar twitched. Shifted, obviously embarrassed at the way he'd stared at her. "The shirt itches."

Rolling her eyes, Thiel approached and straightened the tie around his throat. "They're silk. Too soft to itch."

He made a choking noise. "This thing strangles."

She gave him a playful push. "Ye would do well to be grateful my brothers loaned ye clothes, or ye would be out in the bailey with the pigs."

"I'm grateful for a warm bed and meals I don't have to scrounge for, but the clothes—" He tugged at the tie.

Shoulders down, Praegur moved to a chair. Though he, too, wore a new set of clothing, what defined Praegur was his presence. Much like Haegan. Her heart hurt remembering what had happened to Praegur that night in the tent. He was still unable to speak. No explanation, though the king had a pharmakeia examine him.

She touched his shoulder. "Ye look very nice, my friend."

He nodded. His gaze roamed the room and came back to her in question.

"Haegan?" When he nodded, she smiled. "Resting." She shrugged when he groaned. "He sleeps a lot."

"Did he tell you what happened?" Tokar joined them around the table that offered a basket of fruit and warmed cordi juice. "The explosion and all?"

"And does he have special powers and all now? You know, powers what She gave him for to rule the world?"

"Grow up," Tokar said.

"I am growing up. Can't right stop that." Laertes trotted to a small sofa and sat. He tugged at the socks and stretched his legs.

"Haegan hasn't talked much, but no—he has no recollection of what happened at the Falls." She watched as her friends enjoyed the simple snack that was to them, after years traveling from once place to another, a luxury. "What of Drracien? Perhaps we should ask him. Where is he?"

Tokar chomped into an apple, then tucked the chunk of fruit to the side of his cheek like a squirrel. "Haven't seen him all morning."

Praegur rolled his hands over one another, gesturing something.

Thiel wasn't sure what he meant by that. It seemed—

"Accelerant," Laertes said around a mouthful of orange.

"Yes, Drracien." When her mute friend shook his head, she finally understood. "Oh! Pao'chk. Ye think he went down to see the healer?"

"Or the o'fer one. The tall one wif the beard what tried to save Haegan."

"Gwogh," Thiel spoke. Yes, that would make sense. Curiosity tugged at her—were Gwogh and Drracien perhaps talking about Haegan? About what happened? She rose. "If you'll excuse me—"

"What is that?" Tokar screwed up his face tight. "Why are you going all stiff on us?"

Though she felt the flush of embarrassment, Thiel held her poise. "I was just trying to be polite."

"What? Are this house and the clothes changing you?" Tokar growled.

"No."

"Because you don't need to change. We liked you just as you were. And what's with the way you're talking now? It's all . . . Northlander." Lifting his hands, Tokar stood. "If that's how this is going to be, maybe we shouldn't be here."

"This is my home—in the Northlands, in case ye didn't notice. And this is my family." Incredulous, she set her glass of juice on the table. "I know not what ails ye, Tokar, but I would strongly suggest ye exercise some humility, as ye are guests in my home."

"You don't live here!" Tokar shouted. "You lived with us. Fought with us!" His lip curled. "Are we nothing to you now? Have you changed so much in a fortnight that you do not remember your friends?"

"I *haven't* changed," she bit out, moving away from him and his condescension.

He reached for her.

"Don't ye dare." Heart pounding, she stepped back. "I might not have lived here for a while, but this is my home. And unlike ye, I've always had good manners and courtesy. Ye should try some."

"Naw," Laertes said, sinking his teeth into a cordi. "It'd just make him itch."

Tokar swiped at Laertes.

When she turned toward the door, Thiel stopped short. Tili and Relig stood there, their matching scowls locked onto Tokar. Older than Relig by ten months, Tili turned sideways, holding a hand toward the grand hallway. "Kiethiel, I would have a word."

Frustrated that Tokar, who'd been a strong friend and companion in the last two years, had made such an unfavorable impression, Thiel moved toward her brother.

Passing her, Relig gave a nod.

"Relig," she said, touching his arm—she blinked at how corded his muscles had grown since she was last home. "He meant no harm."

His slanted look expressed his disapproval quite clearly. Though he gave no reassurance, she was sure that his silence left the future of Tokar's presence in Nivar Hold up to his behavior and attitude.

"Kiethiel," Tili urged her away from their brother, offering his arm.

As they stepped into the large marbled hall, she blew a breath between puffed cheeks. Guilt hung on her at Tokar's accusations. She must admit she loved being home. Loved wearing clean, comfortable dresses. Hand laced around her brother's arm, she detected the tautness. "Ye're angry."

"He's insolent. Treated ye with disrespect and abuse."

She laughed. "If ye only saw what I have endured these last years . . ."

"I care not—nay, I do. But that is passed. Ye are here, in our father's house." Tili's jaw muscle flexed. "If I see him touch ye like that again . . ."

His protectiveness had never waned. She rested her head against his shoulder, surprised at how the years had vanished between them. "Ah, Tili. How I have missed ye, brother."

"Do not think to deter my anger with yer womanly wiles."

She cocked an eyebrow. "Wiles?"

"Aye, ye and our mother are far too practiced."

As they walked the stairs to the third level slowly in companionable silence, her levity faded. "I am so conflicted."

"About?"

"Everything. I think it will take years for me to acclimate. I just want to be here, to remember how to be an Asykthian daughter." She sagged beneath her thoughts. "He is right—I have changed."

"Do not tell him that before Relig has a chance to inflict some humility upon that impudent thin-blood."

Thiel raised her head. "What is Relig going to do to him?"

"Probably give him over to Aburas."

Thiel widened her eyes and stopped. "The captain of—"

"Colonel. He is second in command only to myself and Father now."

Thiel couldn't help but chuckle. "That will definitely teach him some humility." She stared up at the paintings of their ancestors as they walked the long hall. "Being back here, with ye and our parents, is an answer to a prayer I whispered every night though I never believed it could happen."

"Yet . . .?"

"It's so strange. The beds too soft. The dresses"—she lifted her skirt—"too . . . airy."

He laughed. "And what of the prince?"

She gave him a startled look as they stopped before the solar. "Haegan?"

He snorted a laugh, then nodded, indicating she'd just answered his question.

"What?"

Hands on his belt, he heaved a breath. "Ye address him by his given name."

"So?"

"It is too intimate! He is the prince of the Nine, Kiethiel! Were it to be heard, ye would be punished for addressing him so casually."

"He's not like that."

"He is."

"He's not!" She almost stamped her foot.

"By his very blood, he is, because he was born to that title. He is a royal!"

"As am I!"

"Who must address a future king appropriately. Even if he's not *yer* future king."

Future king. She touched her forehead at the heady proclamation. However . . . "Haegan won't be king. His sister is set to rule." He'd said that, but, of course, that was before he was healed.

Tili sighed and held her shoulders. "He is alive. No one's rule is guaranteed. Even if Princess Kaelyria should take the throne, she could be killed. Or overthrown." His dark brown eyes probed her. "As long as the prince lives, he is in the line of succession."

Thiel wrested from his grip, frightened and pained at the thought of Haegan succeeding. "He is my friend."

With a knowing smile, Tili shook his head. "Do not think me a fool, sister. There is more than friendship that lingers in yer eyes each time ye look at him."

She turned away. Searched for an escape. "Is this why ye pulled me from my friends?" Would that she had her dagger.

He huffed. "Ye are no easier to corral now than when ye were but a lass." He bobbed his head toward the double doors of the solar. "Our father would have a word."

Thiel blanched. "Why? About what?"

Shrugging, Tili opened the door.

Smoothing her hands down the front of her gown, she stepped into the solar. Their father sat in his favorite chair, a cigar in his mouth as he read documents. Mother, situated near the window with a book in hand, glanced up. "Thurig."

"Eh?" Her father shifted the papers and brightened when he saw Thiel. "Ah, Kiethiel!" He tucked his cigar in a tray and set aside the papers. "Come in, my lass!"

"As 'Tili said ye would speak to me?"

"Yes, yes." He was on his feet and ushering her toward the settee. "Please." When she took the seat, she folded her hands, feeling awkward.

He peered at her. "How are ye?"

"Well, Father. Tired, but well. It will do me good to rest and just have some peace and quiet with my family."

Her father's eagerness waned. "Yes. Well, that will happen . . . eventually."

Her stomach twisted into a knot.

"Notices were sent out this morning."

The knot tightened. "For?"

"A ball! We are inviting all the Northlands to celebrate yer return!"

• • •

"Mastering the finer art of sitting up?"

Haegan tore his gaze from the window and his thoughts from how similar the view was to what he had at Zaethien. One of Thiel's brothers propped himself against the doorpost. Haegan glanced down at the embroidered chair Pao'chk had put him in, feeling inferior in every way possible—looks, strength, position. "It was only supposed to be for a moment, but I think my absent-minded healer may have forgotten me."

"More like got lost on his way out of the tavern." Tili folded his arms over his chest. "The king thinks ye should have daily exercise on the lawn to speed your recovery."

"Oh." Haegan glanced around and nodded. "I'll notify—"

Tili stepped out, then rolled a wheeled chair into the room. "Yer carriage awaits. Have ye yer bonnet?"

Haegan wasn't sure whether to laugh or be insulted. In Fieri Keep, no one would ever talk to him as such. Yet he liked the teasing. It reminded him of Kaelyria. "Very well."

Tili lifted him from the chair.

"I can—"

And grunted. "Might lay off the stew," Tili said as he lowered him onto the wheeled chair.

Another taunt. "As I was trying to say, I can walk." Just not for long.

Wheeled down the passage, Haegan felt the draft through his clothes, though he wore both a tunic and pants. In fact, very nice clothing at that. A woman in tan skirts and a white cap stepped into the hall but jumped back with a yelp.

"Chariot races, Atai," Tili said in a warning tone as they rolled past her, then trounced down a short flight of stairs to the main floor.

A screech echoed through the entire hold.

Haegan tensed, the sound vaguely familiar and . . . haunting.

Without warning, Tili popped the chair back, thudding Haegan's head against the top, and spun around in the opposite direction. Tightening his grip, Haegan tried to pretend he wasn't startled. The king's son drove him down a long hall, passing several large rooms and a kitchen. Then through a pair of double doors onto a paved garden area at the back of the hold.

"A little slower, perhaps?" Haegan said, shifting nervously.

Tili continued, right off the stoned area where bumps were limited to the joints between pavers.

Another shriek sliced the air, then turned to a low rumble.

Haegan's nerves jounced. "Wha – what was that?" He glanced up at his driver.

Grinning, Tili quickened his pace but gave no answer as he drove Haegan right off the end of the pavers onto the pebbled path, the chair vibrating hard.

Haegan could feel the low, mournful sound as if it were in his own chest. He touched his head, feeling a faint wave of nausea. Perhaps it was a reaction to the wheeled chair and being violently pushed across the gravel and onto grassy lawn. Bumping. Jarring. Up a hill. Faster. They crested it. The other side spread out into a lush meadow with a river cutting through it.

"Tili—"

Out of nowhere, a large shadow dropped over them. Haegan froze. The chair stopped. A gust of wind blasted the back of Haegan's neck. Massive and black, a large beast swooped down and landed with a soft thud against the grass. Wings folded. Black. Muzzle. Blazing eyes. The creature launched at Haegan.

He screamed. Threw himself sideways, away from the horrible creature. The chair tilted. The world upended. Haegan scrambled, fought against weakened limbs.

Laughter—laughter pervaded the afternoon.

Haegan looked up, sun blotting out the features of man standing over him, chortling. "What—?"

But Tili only laughed harder. Wiping tears from his eyes, Tili clapped. "That was priceless."

"Ye fool, Thurig as'Tili!" Thiel's voice hissed into Haegan's awareness. He pulled himself upright and glanced to where her voice had come from. "I will end ye, brother!" Running, the skirts of her blue and silver gown gathered in her fists, Thiel barreled at her brother.

Knocked him over.

Tili laughed harder, then clamped his hands on her wrists as she fought to hit him.

"That was cruel!" she growled at him.

Haegan scrambled around, searching for the beast, surprised when he found it lying on the grass, panting softly, a look of pleasure squinting its eyes. As brother and sister fought, Haegan dragged himself off the ground. When he finally gained his feet, he started.

The creature—a raqine. It had to be a raqine—now stood. Staring at him.

Haegan braced himself, both for physical reasons but also for the terror that beset him. He took in the raqine's enormous body. The lean frame could easily have been mistaken for a cat's. But very muscular. Tautly muscular. There wasn't a spot that didn't ripple with the slightest twitch. His—her?—eyes were black, and yet they blazed with intensity and deliberate focus.

He wanted to get closer, but dare he? Haegan took a tentative step forward. He moved slowly on shaky legs, afraid to spook the creature. The raqine seemed to bob its head.

Giving me permission to approach.

"Ye have gone mad, prince," he could imagine Tili saying if he knew Haegan's thoughts. A half-dozen paces, each one oddly strengthening instead of weakening, had Haegan at the raqine's side.

"Her name is Chima," came Thiel's soft voice beside him. "She'll need to accept ye."

"Ho–how does she do that?"

Chima stretched her neck, nudging her wet snout beneath Haegan's chin. He stumbled back, the force of her nudge not violent, but in his weakened condition, nearly strong enough to knock him off his feet.

"Like that." Hand to his back for support, Thiel chuckled.

"Then I'm accepted?" He held out his hand, palm up.

Thiel turned it sideways. "Neither party—the raqine nor the human—is subservient. Give her that respect by holding your hand straight."

Chima sniffed, then rubbed her face along it. Haegan smiled. She pushed harder and stretched into his hand, forcing his fingers to run along her neck, then her spine.

His laughter grew. "They're real." He hadn't meant to say it out loud. But it was too incredible.

"She saved yer life," Tili said, arms folded once more as they watched Chima return to a spot on the grass and slump down, paws crossed. "Nearly destroyed the den and bailey escaping."

"What?" Haegan frowned.

"She woke us all out of a dead sleep with the commotion. I ran to the window in time to see her burst out of her den, which they normally give no complaint about. Then, with a shriek that would curdle yer blood, she tore into the sky and took off."

Another raqine emerged from the woods, this one a touch smaller than Chima but no less fearsome.

"That's Zicri," Tili said. "He is bonded to me."

"Bonded?"

Tili had the same dark brown hair as his sister and the same intensity in his eyes. "Each raqine chooses a human with which to bond."

"Bond? How?"

"Unknown. Chima accepted no human—"

"Except me," Thiel said.

"Barely," Tili countered. "She tolerated ye. I remember many rides she pitched ye. Thankfully within a decent range of the ground." He rubbed a hand along the back of his head. "When she spirited out of here, then returned with Kiethiel and ye . . ."

"Me?" Haegan looked between the brother and sister, unsure whether to believe this tale or not. Tili had already played him the fool about the existence of raqines. "In earnest?"

"Quite," Thiel said. "We thought ye were lost at the Falls. We weren't sure how we'd get ye out of there because of the Jujak. Then Chima just showed up."

"I don't understand." Haegan shook his head. "Why—how?"

Tili slapped his shoulder. "That's what we'd like to know." He pointed to the chair and righted it. "Now, we should get back to that room before Pao'chk takes off my head or poisons my grog."

"I'd like to walk back, if I can make it."

"Would you escort me back to my house, Prince Haegan?" Playing coy didn't suit Thiel, but right now, Haegan was grateful for her offer. When she slipped her arm into the crook of his elbow, it was not for propriety but a surreptitious effort to help him preserve his dignity. Her way of allowing him to lean on her a little.

"It would be my honor."

"Yer bloody right it's yer honor," Tili muttered. "Just keep those hands where I can see them." He pointed to Haegan as he guided the chair back to the house. "Remember, she has three well-muscled brothers and a burly father who could inflict heinous injury upon yer person."

"Beg off, Tili!" Her laughter—he really liked the sound of her laughter. Not a nasally cackle, but a light, almost melodious one. And her accent. She'd fallen back to the patterns of her homeland since she'd been here. He found it endearing.

Blazes. He must've been struck hard in the head in the waterfall. "What do you remember?"

"Sorry?" Thiel looked at him, holding her skirts with one hand as they made their way over the field. "Remember of what?"

"The Falls. When I jumped?"

"Terrific panic watching ye plummet."

"And when I hit?"

"I'll have to beg your mercy," she said softly. "Drracien somehow predicted what would happen and threw us behind that enormous stone wall. It protected us."

"From what?"

"The blast."

"What blast?"

She wrinkled her nose. "Perhaps that is the wrong word. It was like"—she shook her head, her gaze shifting from the ground to the impressive home—"Words fail me. It was as if someone had snapped a bowstring, but with light. Or heat." Brown eyes rose to his, delicately lined with concern. "Do ye not remember?"

"No."

"Gwogh said you would remember—that you must."

For her, he wanted to remember. "In truth, my main concern is getting home to Kaelyria." He did not want to weight their conversation, but the urgency had been with him since first waking. "She ordered me to the Falls. Now I must return home to find out how she fares and face my father."

Something about that terrified Thiel. He saw it in her eyes. "You're too weak still, Haegan. Even Gwogh said so this morning."

"I cannot remain here. I must—"

"The ball." She stepped in front of him and placed a hand on his chest. His pulse spiked. "Wait until after the ball. Then go."

It was hard to think past the warmth of her fingers over his heart. In that moment he realized something terrifying—he would do anything for Thiel. But Kae . . .

A cleared throat made both of them jerk.

Her brother quirked an eyebrow and looked to Thiel's hand on his chest. She drew in a quick breath and removed it.

Brains. Think. Talk. "What ball?"

"Father is holding a celebration for my return."

"Then you will stay." He'd woken with some crazy hope that she would leave with him. It didn't make sense. She was Asykthian. He was the Seultrian. Their fathers hated each other. And her brother could not stand him.

She took his arm and drew him toward the house, her chin tucked. "I think I must, Hae"—her gaze went to her brother, who shared a sidelong glance that severed Haegan's name from her tongue. "At least for now."

But in truth, what would draw her away? This was her home, her family. She'd been gone for four years. Surely they wanted her to remain as much as she needed the stability. "Of course." His voice pitched. "I understand."

They made their way across the pavers to the double doors. She continued, "And I think ye must stay as well. Perhaps we will hear from the messenger Father dispatched to your"—her gaze hit her brother once more—"the Fire King. I'm certain a good word will soon be yours."

Tili escorted them into the house. When they reached the stairs, Haegan stared up the expanse and suddenly had no energy. Defeat seemed to be his only friend.

"Prince Haegan," Tili said. "I am under orders to deliver ye to your room in one piece. Might I suggest ye take the chair and let me live a little longer?"

His tongue-in-cheek remark saved Haegan's pride. "On one condition."

Tili's amusement vanished, probably at being challenged.

"That you no longer call me prince."

"As ye wish," Tili said, his expression and tone flat.

Deflating and—once more—defeated—Haegan lowered himself to the chair.

"I beg yer pardon," Thiel said and bent to him. "But I must see to the others."

"Laertes and Praegur!" An infusion of joy leapt through him as her brother eased his chair quite gently up a couple of steps. "Could you bring them to me?"

"Of course." She started away, her gown flowing gracefully. She was every bit the princess.

The thought sent heat through his chest. Haegan's heart thudded. "Thiel!"

She spun around, her hem swirling about her legs.

"The ball."

She waited, a hand going to her stomach.

"Do you have an escort?"

Crack! Teeth clacking, Haegan grunted. Pain spirited through his head and neck when it smacked the chair after a particularly hard jolt against the steps.

"Mercy," Tili said through gritted teeth.

Thud.

"*Tili*," Thiel hissed. "Give care."

"They are stairs, dear sister." *Thud!* "Marble stairs."

She glared, but then smiled at Haegan. "I would be honored to have ye as my escort, good sir."

He was grinning like a fool and didn't care.

Crack! Thud!

48

"I would have answers!" His own voice bounced back to him, startling Haegan. He twisted away from Gwogh and Pao'chk, who stood to the side. "You promised me answers, Gwogh."

"It is imperative," Gwogh spoke softly and slowly, "that you give yourself time to heal."

"I *am* healed!" He faced them, frustration fitting tighter than a glove. "It has been nearly three weeks since the Kindling."

"Yes. Three weeks since you were completely debilitated," Gwogh reminded him. "Healing is not only in the body, my prince, but in the mind."

Shoving his hand through his hair, Haegan scoffed. "Now you suggest I am addled."

"No," Gwogh said firmly. "But your view of the Nine . . . has it not changed?"

Pacing did little to help his frustration or chase the prevalent chill from his bones, but it did alleviate the itch within him to be doing something. Anything. "Of course it has changed. There are raqine!"

Disappointment filled Gwogh's face.

"I know what you meant, old friend." Haegan went out onto the balcony and stared across the great fortress wall to the mountain that breathed its eternally cold breath on Ybienn. And to his left, the forest. "My view of the world has expanded. I've encountered Ematahri, Iteverians, Jujak, Ignatieri . . . and many people much oppressed."

"And of yourself, my lord?" As his old tutor joined Haegan, an icy breeze teased the man's graying beard.

Haegan glanced at Gwogh, who was nodding to Pao'chk inside the room. "Myself?"

"Has your view of yourself changed?"

Haegan frowned. "You confuse me."

"As I attended and tutored you, there lay a young lad not simply paralyzed in his body, but in his mind, his confidence." Gwogh lifted his wide shoulders. "Now stands before me a man who leapt to almost-certain death for the love of another."

Haegan traced the Cold One's Tooth, its tip perpetually dipped in snow. "I know not what I think of myself." He leaned his elbows on the balustrade and sighed. "These last two months have tormented me. Once paralyzed, I find myself freed but a fugitive of the father by whom I only wanted to be loved. Running through the sewers, I discover friends. Some of the truest people I have known. Then I am chased, captured, and beaten by my father's own men." He looked to Gwogh. "I don't know who I am. Or what purpose in this great jest I have. It feels . . . futile. Foolish."

Gwogh's low, deep chuckle rippled through the air. "I would give care calling the way of Abiassa foolish."

"The way of Abiassa?" Haegan yanked around and sat against the rail, folding his arms. "This . . . this journey cannot be of Her hand."

"And what convinces you of that?"

Shoulders hunched, Haegan shook his head. "First of all, it began with something forbidden to Her people."

"Mm, the transference."

"Yes! Then the struggle, the futility—it has felt hopeless since I left the keep. And now, when our goal may have been accomplished, I cannot return to Kaelyria to ascertain if her plan worked. If she is free of this spectacular insanity."

Gwogh's brow furrowed. "What plan, my—"

Pao'chk interrupted. "It's time, Gwogh." Another shape emerged behind the old healer.

"Drracien." Haegan frowned. "What is this?"

"Time for those answers." Gwogh stroked his long beard, nodding. "But they may not be the answers you hoped for."

"Cryptic as ever."

"These truths I share," Gwogh began gravely, "they will change your view of yourself, so resolutely that I fear you may lose yourself."

"Lose myself?" Haegan snorted. "Think you I have any element of myself left after these last months?"

"Let's go inside." Gwogh's stooped shoulders bent as he returned to Haegan's chambers.

Haegan entered behind him and came up sharp, his heart thudding. The room was filled with people wearing the Ignatieri tri-tipped flame on their simple black robes. They were of varying ages and heights, but their severity was unanimous.

Drracien remained quietly at Haegan's side.

"The Council of Nine," Gwogh said, sweeping a hand around the room. "For what will happen here, they must be present."

The Council of Nine. Gwogh had told him many times that nobody ever saw them. They convened in private. Guided the Nine from the heights, overseeing the Fire King and the grand marshal with equal authority. What then was this that they would converge on him? "Why? What is happening?" the question croaked out of Haegan, betraying his churning stomach. "Do they believe I hurt my sister? Is that what this is about—punishment?"

"My lord prince," the lone woman said with a smile that barely made it past her thin lips. "You needn't be afraid of us. We are here as your allies."

"Allies." Then why did he feel like their prey?

"We're frightening him," a taller, darker man with black hair said. "Kedulcya does well to encourage him, but we should just get to the meat of this."

"Well said, Kelviel." Gwogh pointed his pipe to the other graybeard. "Aoald is the eldest, next to me. He is most versed in the Parchments. I would have him lead, if you do not mind, my lord prince."

Mind? Haegan had only one mind—to run. Flee this council. Then Gwogh went down the line and introduced them with a mind-blurring list of names and provinces they represented.

"Please—sit," Gwogh said.

Haegan tucked himself onto a chair, facing the crowd as the seven men and one woman assumed seats, Gwogh to his right. Drracien stood to the side, silent, still. Shaken, Haegan pushed back against the embroidered cushion, bracing himself.

"Aoald, if you will." Gwogh crossed his legs and lifted his pipe.

With a slow exhale, the gray-haired accelerant drew a large book from a black velvet pouch. He moved his chair closer to the fire and sat, opening the book.

Haegan squirmed, feeling as if he were on trial. Was he? "Are those Parchments?"

"Indeed," Aoald said. "They've been in my safe keeping these hundred years."

Haegan blinked, wondering if he'd heard right.

"We should hurry," Kelviel said.

"Indeed." Aoald flipped to nearly the end. Clearing his throat, he lowered his gaze to the page.

> "In the days of the Flames and fires, they will have ears but not hear.
>
> In the days of the Flames and fires, they will have eyes but not see.
>
> In the days of the Flames and fires, they will have mouths but not speak.
>
> For in the days of the Flames and fires, they will have guidance but lose their way, ignorance clinging to them like the mists of morning. Their hearts, though once loyal and true, have grown calloused and cold in the soft grasses of the Lakes of Fire."

Soft grass? There was no grass and nothing soft near the lakes.

> "How broken lies the city of Abiassa. How shattered the ice on the mountains! How barren the fields of Iteveria. How thirsty the Violet Seas. Her children have abandoned the keep. The fiery lakes cry out. Her foes are her masters now. Her enemies are satisfied, their coffers

*fattened with the blood of the chosen. Devastated, she
stands watch, hearts and minds plying against her truth.
Her heart rent, she prowls the land for a warrior, one to
wield the—*

Aoald paused and looked up, squinting at the others. "We do not
have a word for this one—the *he-ahwl abiałassø.*"

"Ah, yes," the youngest of the group said. "In the original tongue
it referred to something a thousand times more powerful than the
Flames."

"The Flames?" Haegan heard the disbelief in his voice and
didn't care. "You mean, something greater than the wielding? That's
impossible!"

"Far more powerful, and quite possible with Abiassa," Gwogh
said, stuffing his long pipe, which he then pointed at the accelerant.
"Continue."

Drracien shared a look with Haegan, a look whose meaning
remained hidden.

Aoald nodded. "Right. Uh . . ." His finger traced the lines. ". . .
he-ahwl abiałassø. Arise, Fhuriætyr, arise!"

Fhuriætyr . . . why was that so familiar to Haegan? He could hear it,
like a hollow echo in his brain. A heat in his chest. Agony in his back.
He shifted in the seat, trying to wade through the thick confusion.

*"Who can stand against Abiassa's Fhuriætyr? The
armies will be at his back. The enemy before him. All
will meet his fiery judgment and succumb.*

*Answer his call, Thræiho. Let your mighty hand
wield his scythe. Strike down every adversary.*

*Defend him, Deh'læfhier. Let not his blood be spilled
or you will surrender your life.*

*The chiphliæng will be his emissaries, delivering
death to those who oppose the Fhuriætyr.*

*In the day of Riætyr, none will remain beside
him. None will prevail against her champion. Arise,
Fhuriætyr!"*

Hands moving over the pages, lifting corners, Aoald sighed heavily. "It goes on in more detail about the destruction—"

"That is enough for now." Gwogh took a long drag of his pipe, squinting at Haegan through the ensuing smoke puffs. "What are your thoughts?"

Though it was impolite, Haegan laughed. "About what? The destruction of our world?" It was hard to take in, the promise of death to all. The rise of some ferocious "champion" who would raze the world and kill every living thing.

"Arise, *Fhuriætyr!*" Gwogh's deep voice boomed across the room. "Do you know the meaning of that?"

Haegan shrugged, hating these question-and-answer sessions. Especially with a weighty matter like the world's destruction. And in front of the Council of Nine—though, there were only eight of them.

"It is the Fierian."

Haegan shook himself. "The Fie—" His mouth went dry. "That . . . he's a myth!"

"So you also thought of the raqines until a few days ago."

"That's different!"

"How?"

He couldn't explain it. Anger crept along his shoulders, tightening his throat. "Look, you said I would have the truth. What games are you playing? Give me—"

"There." Gwogh stabbed his pipe at the Parchments Aoald held. "There is your truth, Prince Haegan. *This* is what I promised."

Hands held out, Haegan scowled. "How is that the truth you promised? Truth, certainly. I would never speak against Abiassa, but what has this to do with me?"

"I think it is time you spoke, Drracien."

Startled, Haegan turned to his friend. "Why? What has he to say?"

Running his hands along his pants, Drracien wet his lips. "Do you remember when we were in Hetaera?"

"I remember when I was in Hetaera—where you were, I know not."

Drracien's gaze narrowed. "What happened to the people pursuing you was not done by someone tracking you. They were all marked—by a Deliverer."

Haegan paled.

As if reading his thoughts, Drracien explained, "Marked for death. Not like you or Praegur."

The woman lifted a finger. "The first sign!"

Pointing to the Parchments, Aoald indicated a word, but Haegan refused to get any closer. "Here. *Deh'læfhïer.*"

Haegan swallowed.

"It means 'Deliverer' in the ancient tongue." Kedulcya nodded to Haegan. "Your friend says you bear the same mark found on the bodies of the Jujak who tried to stop you in Hetaera."

Haegan jerked to his friend. "You said I was being *tracked!*"

"You were."

"Yes, but I thought you meant spies or assassins, like the two we met in the woods overlooking the Great Falls."

Drracien's lips twitched into a smile, and Haegan felt as if he'd stepped into a trap. The rogue turned to the velum pages once more. *"Chïphlïæng."*

"Sign two!" Kedulcya pronounced.

Haegan laughed—or tried to. "Does it mean assassins?" He swallowed, afraid of the answer.

"No," Gwogh said, his expression grave. "It's a word that indicates sharing the same womb—siblings."

Nausea roiled through him. Astadia and Trale were brother and sister. Siblings. "No." Haegan gripped his pounding head. "No, this . . ."

"There is more," Drracien said. "The *Thræïho* are the Drigovudd."

Haegan could not stop the laugh that burst from his mouth, barking and crazy. Like this whole scenario. "Blazes! First the raqine, now you're going to tell me the immortal giants are returning?"

"Ah, this one Drracien has wrong," spoke the quietest of the eight council members. "*Thræïho* is simply Drigo. The giants."

"Yes, yes," Kedulcya agreed. "Rightly so, Adek."

"In the time of the Parchments," Adek went on, "there was no division between the Drigo and the Drigovudd."

"Indeed." The tall, burly one nodded eagerly. "That only happened after man began enslaving the creatures, which was ludicrous! Drigo live but for one purpose—to serve. They served everyone. The mistreatment was especially cruel. It'd be like torturing a kitten because it was cute and you wanted it to be cuter!"

"They do not need a history lesson just yet, Voath." Gwogh turned his attention to Haegan. "To answer your question, yes—the Drigo are returning. They were seen coming down from the mountains the day you arrived here."

Abiassa, help him. They thought him the Fierian? "This is madness!"

"There is much more," Drracien said.

"Would you hear it?" Aoald's voice was nasal and annoying.

"No! No, I would not hear it." Haegan held his temples, pressing hard as if he could push his fingers through his brain.

"What ails you, prince?" Aoald asked.

"Oh, I don't know—the whole destroying the world prophecy." A thought lit through him, panic beating a hard cadence in his chest. "Wait." What had he . . .? He rounded on Drracien. "You said something about something worse than the Flames." He wagged a hand at his friend. "The he-all-something."

Drracien snorted at Haegan's butchering of the word. "*He-ahwl abiałasso.*"

Snapping his fingers, Haegan exclaimed, "Yes! That. You said it was far greater than wielding the Flames."

"Yes."

"So it's wielding?"

Gwogh slowly nodded. "I suppose you could call it that."

"Ha!" Haegan clapped his hands together and breathed an enormous sigh of relief. "Then it can't be me. I can't be the Fierian." Giddiness surged through him.

"Why?" Drracien scowled.

"I can't wield. Never have." Thank his Maker. Relief was sweet and victory glorious. He blew out a long breath, nodding. "And I tell you, I have no regrets that I am not this person—no, this *creature*—for what person would ever kill every living being?"

Age and sadness slowed Gwogh's climb to his feet. He lowered his pipe. "My dear, Haegan." Gray eyes shone with regret as he clamped a bony hand on Haegan's shoulder. "I am afraid that is simply not true."

49

Hand cupped over her mouth, Thiel leaned against the wall outside Haegan's chambers. Tears streamed down her cheeks as she listened to Gwogh and the others. Their words terrified her. But also explained so much.

She stymied the tears to hear what was said next and peered once more along the narrow sliver where the door stood ajar.

"You were gifted from birth," Gwogh went on.

"No!" Haegan yelled. "No, I have no gifts. The entire kingdom rejoiced in that when I was struck down with poison by Dyrth's agent."

Beneath the gray beard, Gwogh's lips twisted as if in pain.

"You have the ability to wield, Haegan." Drracien sounded so certain. So mature. "I saw you in the field after Hetaera. You were very angry with me."

"You're out of your mind."

"I'm not. The embers—that's what we call the gathering of the heat in your hands when you're first learning to spark or wield—were there. I saw them." Drracien didn't sound angry. "I said nothing for two reasons: One, it did not make sense that you could wield. Even you claimed you couldn't."

"Because I can't!"

Drracien drew in a breath. "And two—because the way you wielded, the singularity of the focus, the strength of the embers—I've never seen its like."

"I don't—No! It can't be—"

"What I saw, Haegan, was a purer light than I've ever seen before. I've trained sparkers for years, and . . ."

Thiel leaned closer, listening harder.

"What you did without even knowing it—honestly, it frightened me."

"Great," Haegan mumbled. "Now *you're* afraid of me."

"That's not what I meant."

"The most dangerous wielding," came Gwogh's firm, deep voice, "is done by someone who has the power but not the understanding or instruction."

"I *can't* wield," Haegan said again.

Thiel could feel his anguish. It echoed in her own heart.

"No, no. This can't be . . ."

"It's imperative you take instruction to protect yourself and those around you," Gwogh said. "It's why I tried to stop you at the Falls. You saw me. You saw our Council there. But did you see anything else?"

"No, what I saw was you trying to stop me—"

"And it angered you."

"Of course! I had to free Kaelyria. My one goal was to free my sister. If I didn't—"

"Kaelyria?" Gwogh asked, his tone conveying understanding. Deep understanding. "Ahhh, it makes sense now."

"What?"

"How she convinced you to leave. Why you believed a month was crucial."

"What are you talking about?"

Sympathy lurked in the crinkles around Gwogh's eyes. "My prince, I'm afraid there was no turning back. There was no recovery of her gifts or from her paralysis. Kaelyria must have known this. As an accelerant, she would have been taught—"

"No! Do not speak of my sister as such. She would not lie to me."

"To protect the Nine and her gift at this desperate hour, she probably thought it worth the risk." Sadness washed over his face. "Perhaps even more."

Bile rose in Haegan's throat. He shook his head. "I . . . that . . . no! I can't believe that."

"What we must focus on is training you."

"No." His voice went shrill this time as he punched to his feet. "No, this . . . this isn't right."

Thiel shifted, watching him approach the door.

"My prince—"

"Calm—"

"Leave off!" Haegan shouted.

"Please—"

"No!"

Thwap! The doors flung wide. Snapped against the wall. Haegan rounded the corner. Thiel straightened, locked gazes with Haegan. Agony twisted across his face, tightening his lips.

Light bubbled around his hands.

With a gasp, Thiel drew back.

Anguish washed through him as he looked at his hands. Eyes wide, he glanced back at her, regret as clear as his features. He turned and sprinted in the other direction.

"Haegan!" Thiel darted after him.

And slammed into a dark blur. Arms tightened around her. "No!" Drracien growled. "It's too dangerous."

Writhing against him, Thiel felt her own volley of anger and anguish. "Release me!"

"I can't."

"Let go," she screamed, hot tears racing down her cheeks.

"He could kill you."

She pummeled him with her fists, thrashing against his restraint. *"Haegan!"* She couldn't let him go, thinking she was afraid of him.

Pounding feet echoed though the hall. "Release her!"

"No, hold her," an older voice spoke. "She must not go to him. Not now."

"Unhand my daughter!" Her father's voice boomed like a punch in the chest.

Drracien's hands fell away.

Thiel stumbled back from Drracien and Gwogh, furious and sobbing. Tili's arms came around her, comforting—or trying to.

"Explain yourself, accelerant," her father demanded. "Who are all these people in my home?"

"It is time, Thurig." Gwogh's voice was exceptionally calm and authoritative.

Thiel pulled away from her brother. "Time for what?" She looked to her father, who seemed to have gone pale. "Father?"

"You have hidden by the mountains long enough," Gwogh said. "He needs your instruction."

"What instruction?" Thiel demanded.

Her father shifted, skating a glance in her direction but not meeting her gaze. He rubbed his fingers and thumbs together. "I can't."

Gwogh's face darkened. "You *must*."

"Whatever happened to him at the Falls . . . my gifts are lessened."

"You think me a fool? We're all lessened! You still have enough to train him."

"I can't. I promised her long ago—"

"Your vow to Abiassa is a higher oath," Gwogh growled. "And I would tread softly. Haegan has a Deliverer assigned to him." Though Gwogh stood a head taller, her father made up for his lack of height in his bearing. Broad-shouldered and bearded, he was formidable.

Her father's ruddy complexion went white. He wavered, as if about to collapse.

"It's true. He's marked." Thiel stared at the two men, two mighty men—one a king, one a powerful accelerant—arguing.

"Father," Tili sidestepped her. "What—?"

"Silence," their father snapped. Looked down. Slumped in some unseen defeat. "It's him, then?"

"I'm afraid so."

Her father gave one more shake of his head and let out a heavy breath. Silence wrapped him in an ominous shroud for several long, aching seconds. "Very well."

"Father?"

He strode down the hall after Haegan without a word of explanation, his shoulders squared, his head high.

Tili seized the silence. "What was that about? What oath to Abiassa?"

"The oath of an accelerant," Drracien said as he started in the opposite direction.

World upended by those words, Thiel dragged her gaze back down the hall her father and Haegan had taken.

"*What?*" Tili demanded. "Our father is an . . . *accelerant?*"

"One of the most powerful, next to the Fire King," Gwogh said.

"How is that possible? He detests wielding—banished it!"

With a gentle incline of his head, Gwogh gave a long, thoughtful look. He bowed. "I beg your mercy. I must see the council to safety."

With Haegan's chambers emptying, Thiel dropped against the wall. Haegan was the Fierian. The most deadly, powerful person to exist in the history of Primar. The Scourge, he had been called. She slid down, the heel of her hand against her forehead, and she cried. She cried so hard her side and head hurt.

Tili stood there, arms crossed.

When her sobs turned to stuttering breaths, she swiped her sleeves over her face.

"What happened?"

She fought another swell of tears. "He . . . I had come to talk to him, but I heard them—heard him"—she pursed her lips to the side to stop the crying—"yelling. He was so angry. They . . . then I heard them. They told him"—she cupped a hand over her mouth, a sob catapulting up with the words—"he's the Fierian."

Tili bent over. Gripped his knees, then dropped back against the opposite wall. He swept his hands over his stubble. With an oath, he moved to a crouch across from her, hands dangling between his legs, gaze on the windows at the end of the hall where their father had gone. "And Father an accelerant."

Head propped on the wall, she looked at the arched windows and shuddered. "Haegan came out—he was still so angry." She sniffled. "So angry at them—his hands, his whole body, seemed to ripple with energy." She shook her head. "It startled me, after hearing their proclamation. I jumped."

"And that made him angrier."

"I didn't mean to. I'm not afraid of Haegan—"

"Ye'd better be. I might not know the Parchments, but I know the Legends. The Fierian will destroy our world."

"No," Thiel said, her eyes blurring again. "That's not Haegan. He's a good man." She curled her fingers into fists. "He's *good*."

Her brother considered for a long while. "Ye love him."

She dropped her face into her hands.

50

Running fast enough was impossible. Escaping the horrific words hurled at him would require death. And with both arms spread wide, Haegan would as soon embrace that dark void than exist in the abhorrent reality consuming his life. He ran. Across the lawn. Down along the river until daylight faded among the trees.

He fell against a trunk, gripping the bark to stay on his feet. Bent and sucking in chunks of air, Haegan saw the ominous dance of heat around his hands and arms. "Augh!" He shook out his hands.

Sparks hissed against the forest litter.

A flame leapt to life. Then puffed quickly into a fire, breathing the rich air of the forest.

"No," Haegan choked out, stamping the spot. He tucked his hands under his arms. Defeated, unable to argue the truth, he slumped to the ground. Dropped against the tree and let out a grievous groan.

Crinkling behind him yanked Haegan's attention back in the direction from which he came. A dark blur sluiced through the shadows, glints of light poking a silky pelt.

Haegan whipped onto his feet. Watching the shadows, he held his breath. Tried to swallow against a mouth drier than a bed sheet. He held the tree to support himself, thinking to slip out of sight before whatever creature had come to end his life succeeded.

A wet mist sprayed his hand on the bark. He jerked around. And cried out, his heart thrown into his throat. Chima. A low chortle warbled from her belly, just like the heat plumes—embers, Drracien had called them—from an accelerant.

Haegan stepped back.

Chima dropped her front paws, watching him with her blazing eyes. A growl trickled through the forest, encircling his mind.

She's going to kill me. Even she knows I am an abomination.

Another step back.

"She's answering ye."

Haegan again flinched and threw the briefest of glances to the side, unwilling to take his eyes from the massive raqine staring him down. "I didn't ask her anything."

King Thurig strode purposefully between them. "But ye did, prince."

This was too much. Way too much. He could take no more. He sought escape.

"Chima answered when yer abiatasso cried out to her at the Great Falls." He watched the raqine, pride in his brown eyes. "And she answers ye now that ye have learned yer identity."

"It's not my identity! I am Haegan, heir of Zireli."

Thurig shook his head. Rubbed his beard and stood quiet for several long minutes. "Would ye like to learn a signal for Chima?"

Haegan hesitated, wondering why the king had not delivered a remonstration. "Signal?"

"She will respond to what is in ye, but there are also commands she will respond to . . . if she chooses."

"If she chooses?"

"She is not a beast of burden, young prince. She is yer ally, yer guardian." His eyes darkened as he spoke. "The raqine are the mightiest of creatures to have existed on Primar, but the moment ye think of her as a horse or donkey, she'll shake ye off like water on her coat."

Haegan eyed Chima, who watched him with a focus that never relented, even when she slumped against the ground.

"And never mistake her rest for grogginess. It takes me at least two cups of strong coffee to wake my brain. The raqine is awake at all times, even when it rests." Thurig moved next to Haegan as he spoke. "Now, here—hold yer left arm out like this."

Irritation clawed through Haegan. He did not want instruction. He wanted isolation. "I just want to be alone. I—I need time to think."

"You mean to run."

Haegan ignored the comment.

"Don't be so thickheaded. She's allowed yer companionship, now honor that gift by learning her ways." He shook his arm for emphasis. "Out like this."

Grinding his teeth, Haegan held out his arm.

Thurig used his right hand to sweep down the length of the other arm, then arced it up and touched his temple. "There. Try."

Haegan did as instructed.

Chima hopped onto all fours. With a big shake of her shoulders, she raced off.

Haegan frowned. "What—?"

The king shifted a few paces away. "Now." He rolled his neck. "Ye want to be alone?" His gaze swept the woods around them. "Ye want to abandon what Abiassa has called ye to? Ye want to be hostage to yer anger and let it control ye, then I will help ye."

Stupefied, Haegan just stared. Then looked again in the direction Chima had gone.

Rolling his hands in front of him, from top to bottom as if turning a wheel, Thurig lowered himself, then came back up, muttering words Haegan had not heard before. His eyes sparked gold, an intensity that belied his ambivalent expression.

Abiassian tongue. Haegan realized it too late.

The air popped.

And with it, gravity inverted itself. Haegan's legs flipped over his head, as if a rope had ensnared him and lassoed him from a tree. "Augh!" Suspended. Angered. Haegan lashed out. His hands . . .

Wouldn't move.

His body wouldn't respond.

"What are you doing?" He gritted his teeth, straining his shoulder muscles to free himself from the heat that haloed him. "Release me!"

Thurig watched, unmoving. Silent.

The angle made it impossible to tell if the king was angry or annoyed or . . . amused. Leaves crunched as he started walking. Walking away. Why was he leaving him?

"Where are you going? Release me!"

"Free yerself, prince." Thurig continued down a path Haegan hadn't seen before, one that led quickly into the sunlight.

"Thurig!"

Light embraced the king and carried him out of sight. Haegan tugged and strained in futility. Anger rushed in, a happy ally to feed his thirst for revenge. His hands ached. His mind burned. Haegan ground his teeth against the pain. What was Thurig doing? How had he even learned to wield?

It was a trap. *He came to punish me. He knows what I am.*

Gwogh. Haegan would kill the old tutor for betraying him. He knew—he knew all along and said nothing. Hid the truth. Lied. Deceived.

Heat spiraled through Haegan's veins, coursing with a virulent poison of fury.

The bubble around him tightened. Constricted. Haegan couldn't even move his neck or fingers now. He shook, livid. *Release me!*

He tried to open his mouth. Could not. He thrashed within his paralyzed—

No! *No!* He could not be paralyzed again. Could not be trapped within an immobile body. *Thurig, I will kill you! I will dismember every limb and feed you to the raqines. I will steal your daughter, and your wife will weep!*

Hatred dark and powerful strangled him. How long he hung there, Haegan could not tell—until he noticed the vanishing sunlight. The ache in not just his muscles, but his bones. His very soul.

Abiatasso.

He'd never had it. Wasn't born with it—that's what they'd told him. That the gift of power and wielding had been granted to his beautiful, perfect sister. Not to a weak, crippled prince. Ludicrous how life had come full circle to find him paralyzed again, as he was before this journey began.

And alone. He was alone. And an abomination. One that would destroy everyone in his wake. Everyone who knew him. Every land that he set foot on. How could this be? How was it that he, who had had no powers . . .

Defeat pressed in on him. He wrestled. Fought the imprisonment. So hard he struggled to breathe. Though he tried to shout, nothing came out. Save a tear. Then another. He moaned. He was weak. Just as his father had said. Haegan huffed, hating the truth. Hating life. Hating his very existence.

"He's cursed."

Tokar had been right.

I will leave. Tears streamed freely up Haegan's forehead and dripped from his hair. The thought of leaving Thiel forever dug a hole in his hope. And Kaelyria—he could never see her again. *I am destruction named.*

He had to get as far away from all of them as he possibly could. It was the only way to protect those he loved.

Haegan wiped the tears.

Then froze, staring at his hand in front of his face.

Free!

Giddy elation trickled through him.

Ha! Good, he would track down Thurig, make him pay—

As if of its own mind, his hand froze. His muscles once more restricted. "No!" Haegan tried to move, but the halo thickened. Glowed brighter. Stronger.

And I grow weaker. More debilitated.

Haegan backtracked, remembering what had brought about the second wave of paralysis. He'd discovered he was free. Then was happy.

Then angry, vowing to make—

Anger.

That was the key. The angrier he was, the stronger the halo.

So. How was he not to be angry?

Thiel.

The very thought of her seemed to push the sun back into the sky. Haegan closed his eyes. Thought of her touch while he lay recovering. Her hand over his. Their near-kiss at the Falls. Her smell. Smile. Curves.

Gravity exerted itself.

Air popped.

Haegan dropped. He landed with a hard thud. Pain darted through his shoulder. He held the joint and rolled with a groan to his side. He sat up and glanced back up at the spot where he'd been suspended, half expecting to see the halo there. But only leaves fluttering in the wind met his gaze.

A rustling to the side divulged a dark shape. "I thought ye'd never figure that out." Thurig emerged from a shadowed alcove of rocks and trees. He started for the path Haegan had seen him take. "Come. I'm starving."

Stunned, Haegan stared at the king. "How—how did you get there? I saw you take the path."

Booted foot on a stump, Thurig paused. Glanced back. "Ye saw what yer anger wanted ye to see."

"You left!"

Sadness pinched the lines at the corners of Thurig's eyes. "I never left, Haegan. Yer anger tore ye away from me." He pointed to the shadowed spot. "I waited there the entire time." He grunted. "Well, till my legs grew tired." He lifted a shoulder. "I may have napped. Once."

Haegan dusted off his pants as he moved toward Thurig. "I don't understand—"

Thurig sighed and started walking again. "I know, prince. I know."

"No, I mean—how did I see you leave yet you didn't move?"

"Yer anger forbade ye from seeing any other options." Thurig shifted closer. "Haegan, ye respond with anger. It's the first thing ye reach for." He held his fist out between them. "Ye clench yer fingers so tight around that injustice and let it burn."

A flame erupted with a whoosh. "It consumes every thought—it consumes ye." Thurig opened his fist and twisted, banishing the flame. "With the *he-ahwl abialassø* that canna' be the order of things. Ye *must* train yerself to reach for wisdom first."

"How?"

"Time." Thurig nodded. "And practice."

"But I still don't understand how you got me to believe you left."

"There are two different forms of wielding. Lower ranks are kept to the heat in the air, drawing the moisture from it and igniting what's left." Thurig started walking. "They are restricted to that, and for good reason. Only among high marshals who take the red sash, and the grand marshal, of course, is the latter taught. It is . . . invasive. Cruel if wielded incorrectly."

"Invasive? Cruel—how?"

"We enter the mind using a tendril of heat."

"Mind control?"

Thurig laughed—and to Haegan's surprise, it was a nice, friendly one. "Abiassa, forbid! No, we only amplify what the person allows, the thoughts they already entertain. If ye are happy, it can be enhanced. If ye are full of anger and hate—"

"You'll become furious." His heart skipped a beat. "Is that why I'm to be the Fierian? Because I'm angry?"

Thurig clapped a hand on his shoulder "No, Haegan. The Fierian, believe it or not, is not a punishment. It's a gift."

"*Gift?* The Parchments say the Fierian will destroy every living thing."

Pausing outside the door of the house, the smell of some meaty stew drifting through the cracks, Thurig stopped and faced him. "Haegan, do ye think your father or I enjoy war? That we enjoy the loss of life, cutting down soldiers?"

"No one hates war more than those who fight."

Thurig nodded. "What must be done, for whatever reason Abiassa has foreseen, must be done."

"Then . . . then you don't hate me?"

Thurig turned into the house. "Perhaps that should be saved for another day." He hesitated. "Oh, and ye might want to release Chima from her den."

"What?"

"Ye ordered her back to the den. She will na come until ye free her— ye see, yer anger affects not only yerself, prince, but those around ye."

• • •

Seven days of exhaustive, never-ending instruction. Haegan's arms ached. His mind felt numb.

Beside him, Drracien reset himself in the form they'd be practicing. Thurig watched from a few paces away. "Again."

Haegan slumped and sagged.

"Again, prince!"

Though he balled his fists, Haegan rolled his thoughts away from the anger, which was fed by exhaustion and frustration. What was the point in driving him so hard? It took years to learn to wield—they'd both had years to learn. He had but seven days. Seven endless, excruciating days.

His friends were riding horses and splashing in the river. Atop a large bay horse, Tokar taunted him, mocked him. Clearly he hadn't been informed of Haegan's new status as Destroyer of Worlds. Praegur sat on the edge of the wall, watching Haegan. His speech still gone.

Frustration blossomed—no, exploded through him. Enough! Enough journeys. Enough lectures. Enough things going wrong. Enough being cast out then cursed!

Blazes! Why was this happening? He'd asked for none of it.

"We can use your anger and turn it against you," Drracien said. "When you reach for anger, you leave your *abiatasso* unprotected. Then the enemy strikes."

"I will learn not to be easily swayed." The halo crackled and popped, sizzling against his skin.

Drracien chuckled. "If it were so easy, don't you think all would do that?"

"The enemy will know yer weaknesses. One way or another, he will weed them out and use them against ye," Thurig said.

"I have no weaknesses for them to use! I've been locked away for the last ten years!"

Thurig's bushy eyebrows rose. "Is that right?"

The tone made Haegan hesitate. But he wanted this to end. "Aye." Would they hold him here forever? If he distracted himself, that should free him, right?

Folding his arms over his chest, Thurig considered him. "I would have a word with ye, Haegan of Zaethien."

Haegan stilled, meeting weathered brown eyes. Drracien stepped away without being asked, giving them privacy.

"It has been told to me that ye asked my daughter for the right to escort her to the ball."

Haegan swallowed.

"I'm afraid I canna permit that."

Grinding his teeth, Haegan fought the anger trickling through his veins.

"Think ye that I would allow my daughter to be seen on the arm of someone who—"

"Is weak?" Haegan snapped.

"Ye have shown no valor by which to earn the right to court my daughter. Ye have no accomplishments to recommend ye."

"I've been a prisoner for the—"

"And what? That is your excuse? Look at Grand Marshal Viloren—blind and deaf, yet one of the most influential thinkers and accelerants of his time! And ye think I would excuse yer empty credentials because ye were bedridden?"

Indignation coiled around his frustration and squeezed.

"Haegan."

"What would you have had me do?"

"Use the gifts ye were given. Yer mind, yer heart. Be a man!"

"*Haegan.*"

At the crack of his name, he noticed the thrumming in his limbs. But it was too late. His vision bled red.

"*Ïmnæh wæithe!*" Thurig shouted.

The halo crackled around Haegan, subduing him. Anger spurted through his mind.

"Remember," Thurig growled as he stormed toward him, his neck nearly invisible amid his thick chest and broad shoulders. "Remember what I taught ye!"

Suspended above them, Haegan glowered at the king. Drracien stepped into view, his hands extended toward Haegan.

His anger crested the humiliation. He hated that they had beaten him. Hated that he'd lost again. That his temper could be so explosive.

"Push your mind from the anger," Drracien murmured.

Right. *Thiel.* His only haven. Tonight was the banquet. She'd wear something amazing.

"We will not be able to—"

They'd dance. Her in his arms.

The halo popped. Haegan dropped, hitting his shoulder hard again.

"Well done. Much faster." Thurig headed away, calling over his shoulder. "At least we didn't miss dinner this time."

"But it took the both of you to restrain me."

"Aye," Drracien said. "He grows stronger, while we struggle."

"The Kindling." Thurig nodded. "Be thankful, Haegan, that we are lessened. Or I might've been tempted to smite ye a few times."

"My gift is growing stronger?" Haegan felt ill. "But I can't even control what little I have now."

"Which is why yer calming *must* be more powerful and alluring." Thurig lifted a bushy eyebrow toward Haegan as he hesitated almost midstep. "What is yer calming source?"

Heat bled into Haegan's face.

"Ah." Disappointment hovered in the king's brown eyes. "I see." Apparently, he did.

And the heat rose a notch in Haegan. He looked down.

Drracien stood over him, holding out a hand.

With a defeated sigh, Haegan accepted the help. He brushed off his tunic, glancing back to the river. Thiel wasn't there now. Neither was Tokar. Haegan scratched the side of his face and turned toward the house. "Never realized I had such a controlling anger."

"I'm not convinced you do," Drracien said.

"How do you mean?"

"A couple of things—I think Thurig turned your thoughts against you—"

"He—" Haegan snapped his mouth closed, remembering what the king had taught him in the woods, about using one's own thoughts against one.

"And I think as the Fierian, your abilities are . . . concentrated, more powerful. Including your anger."

Then why should he even try? Haegan threw him a look, unable to conjure anything positive within himself at the moment, then gave a half smile to Praegur, coming their way.

"You have the *he-ahwl abiałassø*. I've been doing some research in Thurig's library. I think it means 'all-consuming,'" Drracien said, tugging off his gloves. "I believe that means whatever is in you is what will be amplified."

"Either way, anger is a deadly fire in my system."

"The wrong anger, the first-reached-for anger—yes. That will be destructive." Drracien quirked his lips. "There is such a thing as righteous anger."

"Of course." Weary of the lessons, Haegan welcomed his mute friend with a tight forearm clasp. "I would imagine you've had your laughter quota met for the day, watching the king slaughter me."

Praegur smiled, held up a finger, then lifted another. *More than one day.*

Haegan shook his head. "You can lie to me, Praegur. Nobody would know."

"Hey, princeling. Have ye learned to not burn down my house yet?" Tili shouted from the stable yard, where he was grooming his horse. With a laugh, he bent down to retrieve a bucket of water.

Haegan sent a spark flying. It struck the wooden bucket. Shattered it. Water exploded in Tili's face. Shock pulled the Asykthian straight, his eyebrows up, his mouth gaping as water dripped down nose.

A grunt beside Haegan snapped him out of his own shock. Praegur stood with his mouth agape, too. Not exactly smart. "Run," Haegan whispered. In the split second before he pivoted and took off, he saw Tili barreling at them like a mad bull.

Forget prophecies. Haegan might not survive the night.

51

Too many people. Too many voices.

Deftly avoiding a cluster of females whose dresses were too tight or too low, Haegan tucked himself into a corner, feeling crowded and unable to breathe. He leaned against the wall, working through his frustration that Thurig had overruled him in escorting Thiel. He sipped a glass of fermented cordi juice, watching the doors. Champing for Thiel to make her entrance. Then again, everyone here anticipated that moment. The ball was, after all, in her honor.

Praegur threaded through the noblemen and their wives with a plate of petite cakes and sweets. He had nearly cleared the throng when a woman reached out and took one of the sweets, no doubt mistaking him for a servant.

Praegur scowled at her.

She bristled.

Annoyed, Praegur huffed. Grunted and shoved the plate at Haegan, who smiled.

"You should've worn the other suit. You look like one of the servants in that white."

Praegur stabbed a finger at Haegan's shirt and grunted. *White.* He then tugged at his own lapel. *Not white.*

"Yes, well, they are colorblind then."

Snorting, Praegur focused on his food. A few minutes later, Tokar and Laertes joined them, the younger holding a very large plate.

Haegan laughed, "Is that a *platter*, Laertes?"

The boy shrugged. "They was out of plates."

"Liar," Tokar said with a smirk.

The idea of the boy removing an entire platter of cakes and sweets made them all laugh. And suddenly, rather than feeling like a prince, Haegan felt more like a rebel in a crowd of nobility. Somehow, he didn't mind.

Not a dozen paces from them, a group of twenty-something men stood proud and stiff, staring down their noses at Haegan, Tokar, and Praegur. One of them snorted. "As if they have a chance at her hand."

"Yeah, what's you got that we ain't?" Laertes said around some cake.

"Class, for one." The man arched an eyebrow.

"But no personality what to win a princess wif."

"A soiled one," someone in the crowd muttered.

Haegan started, searching faces to rout the vile singewood who had spoken the words. "You have no character."

The man closest stood straighter. "We have no need of character. We have titles. Wealth." Again, he stared down that long nose that Haegan itched to punch. His head wagged like a dog's tail. "What do you have?"

Haegan could feel the heat of his anger. And didn't care. "I—"

Drracien stepped between them, dampening Haegan's anger like the bucket of water that had drenched Tili earlier. "Good evening, gentlemen. I believe you're missing the grand event."

The arrogant nobles spun around.

Winging an eyebrow at Haegan's arm, Drracien stepped out of the way.

Haegan shook out his warmed hand. "They besmirched her."

"So you'd kill them? Over an insult? And this is you not being so easily moved?"

Haegan's anger had been bubbling again, awakening trouble. He slid his hands into his pockets, fixing his gaze on the grand stairs, where the doors had opened. "They don't deserve her." Breath held, he waited.

"But they can buy her, and most of the cities need the alliance and wealth of their king, so they are here, regardless of what they think of her."

"Surely Thurig will not hand her over like a prize to these buffoons."

It was then that Thurig stepped into view, resplendent in his official coat and circlet. He held out his arm and drew Thiel forward. A green dress spilled out in a rich, satiny shimmer. Her shoulders were bare, the gold ribbon trim of the dress accenting her naturally tanned skin. An elegant emerald choker rested in the hollow of her throat, pulsating beneath the lights.

"Wha—she's got hair!" Laertes exclaimed.

Tokar clamped a hand over the boy's mouth and pulled him back as people scowled at them. Clearly she had donned a wig for the ceremony, for the dark brown curls piled atop her head were more hair than she possessed. Thankfully, the applause and cheers welcoming the king's daughter drowned the boy's words.

But they could not drown the drum of Haegan's heart as he watched her so gracefully descend those stairs. Nobody would ever know the journey she'd been on. The alleys she'd slept in. The Ematahri she'd warred with.

"What say we get that prig's name and introduce him to Thiel for the first dance," Tokar suggested.

"She'd never tolerate him," Haegan said. "She'd punch him."

Tokar grinned.

Ah. "Then she'd punch *you*."

"It'd be worth it." Tokar set off to put his mission into play. Haegan remained by the pillar. As much as he wanted to go to Thiel and dance with her, keep her to himself, he could not. This was her night with her people.

And there was the whole Fierian disaster. What would these people think if they knew the Reckoner stood in their midst? It churned his stomach. He could not imagine the riots if he were revealed. The thought pushed him into the shadows.

Once the dancing began, it didn't take long for Tokar to get lured away by a pretty maiden. With each new partner Thiel danced with, Haegan grew more convinced she was lost to him. She belonged here. With her parents. With her people—Northlanders.

Laertes disappeared with one of the servants who'd carried off the empty bowls. Halfway through the night, a young woman in a light yellow gown twittered and shifted her way to the pillar Haegan propped up.

Praegur stood, frowning in consternation, but not looking at her.

"May I help you?" Annoyance wasn't anger, so Haegan was safe, right? He had no intention of dancing with her.

"I—" Her gaze flicked to Praegur. "I—" She held out her card to Praegur. "Would you dance with me? Nobody—"

Praegur's dark face went white.

"My friend—"

With a look at Haegan that said to be quiet, Praegur took her hand, tucked it under his arm, and led her onto the floor. The girl beamed, and Haegan gaped. Awareness, acute and icy, cut through him. There was no hope for him.

A sharp pang poked his ribs. Haegan arched his back. A hand clamped onto him. "Don't think I don't know what ye did."

A face slid into his periphery. "Tili."

The blade jabbed harder. "Spark and run? Is that yer tactic?"

"If it works . . ."

Tili chuckled. Patted his shoulder. "I like ye, princeling."

Haegan skated a gaze around, nervous someone would hear, but then spotted Thiel. A crowd of nobles buzzed around her as she sipped from a glass. When their eyes met, Haegan felt a strange warming in the pit of his stomach. She smiled.

And made him wish he'd stolen that kiss at the Falls.

"Don't entertain it." Tili's tone had shifted. A warning encased his words, surprising Haegan.

"I don't know—"

"Ye do." His features were stern and shadowed. "And I will take it very personally if ye pursue that path." Tili turned and put his back to the ball, angling his head toward Haegan. "Pursue her, and I will pursue ye." His dark eyes slammed into Haegan's. "The path ye are on—ye risk her life, and I will na' allow it."

Tili slapped his shoulder and melted into the crowd. As if they'd just had a friendly conversation.

Her brother was right. There was no hope for him. The cruel words sent Haegan out for fresh air. The cold wind—*was it ever* not *cold here?*—breathed down from the mountains. He moved to the stone rail that hid in the shadows, wishing he, too, could hide. From this insane prophecy. From Abiassa.

His life as good as destroyed beneath the weight of this prophecy. Once word spread, everyone would try to kill him. He had only a few more weeks—months if he was lucky—of anonymity.

The laugher and merriment were too much, pushing him from the stone balcony to the lawn. He walked the shadows, glad for the soft grass beneath his feet. The quiet. Tugging up his collar, he warded off the biting wind. He strolled until he came to a hill and climbed it. From there, he could see the mountain that hid the Great Falls. The place that radically changed his life.

Beyond that . . . home. Mother and Father. Kaelyria. His sister—another point of futility. He'd inquired about her safety almost daily, but always, they said there was no word. How long did it take to reach Seultrie? *Abiassa, show me! How is my family?*

A low purr rattled behind him. Haegan held out a hand and soon felt the warm mist of welcome from Chima. She bumped her shoulder against his side, then circled him before trotting over to the river and lapping lazily at the silken waters.

A swishing noise whispered in the night air.

Haegan turned, surprised to find a green blur rushing at him. Thiel, skirts gathered in hand, hurried up the knoll. *This must be a dream.* She would not be here with him when she had hundreds of noblemen offering their keeps, lands, wealth, normalcy for her hand. Laughing, Thiel lunged at him. "Trying to escape, tunnel rat?"

He nearly fell backward, catching her. Though he helped right her, the soft touch of her bare arm against his palm awakened something in Haegan.

"I saw Tili talking to ye," she said, twirling to face the same moon he'd been studying. But she kept no space between them and leaned back against his chest.

Haegan's arms slid around her thin waist, his chin resting against her temple. Somehow, the wind was no longer cold. It was warm. Thick. Wonderful.

"Did he threaten to kill ye if ye asked for my hand?" She almost giggled.

"I think you've had too much cordi wine."

She laughed. Then rolled her head against his shoulder so she could peer up at him. "Did he threaten ye?" Moonslight stroked her cheek and jaw, glittering on the gems at her ear and neck.

Mercy of Abiassa! She was so beautiful. So perfect.

Thiel spun and straightened, her expression tensing. "Tili threatened ye."

Suddenly cold, Haegan took her hand and drew her back to himself. "Shh." He had no idea how much time they'd have together, tonight or ever. He wanted to savor this. Make it last. And he couldn't help it as he stared down into her amber eyes, but he touched the spot at her temple that the moon kissed. Satin.

Thiel's lips parted, and she went very still. A spell seemed to have been cast—a halo, perhaps, locking them in this moment. He slid his hand behind her neck and traced her jaw with his thumb.

Thiel drew in a quick breath.

"You are so beautiful," he whispered, lowering his head.

She leaned up, their lips meeting tentatively. Her brown eyes rose to his, questioning.

Haegan waited, giving her time to push him away. When she didn't, he kissed her again, this time a bit longer. She melted against him, and Haegan threw off reserve. Kissing her deeper, he tugged her a little tighter. Liked the way she fit in his arms, hers draped around his neck.

And he was lost. Lost to the rightness of being with her. To the shared passion. To the sweetness of her taste.

The blast of a horn startled them apart.

Haegan jerked around, breathing hard, holding Thiel close. "What was that?"

"The alarm—the main gate." Thiel caught his hand and started running. "Something's wrong."

52

Halfway across the lawn and holding Thiel's hand as they ran, Haegan saw two officers in green coats exit the grand hall, joining a cluster of green-clad men gathered. His heart vaulted into his throat. He skidded to a stop. Thiel darted around him, caught off guard.

"Haegan?" She looked at him, but his gaze was locked onto the elite guardsmen.

Jujak.

Mallius spotted him first. With a cry, he raised his hand and pointed. "Haegan of Zaethien, you will surrender at once and give no struggle."

King Thurig stormed across the lawn. "Lieutenant, ye are a guest in my hold." He turned to Graem Grinda. "Captain, I gave ye entrance, but this is not what ye agreed to."

A muscle twitched in Captain Grinda's jaw, but he held out a subduing hand to Mallius. "You've killed enough people, Prince Haegan. Come peacefully. Your Father would have justice."

Thiel tightened her grip on Haegan's arm.

Haegan wanted to fight the charges, fight being arrested, but the large crowd gathering on the terrace proved too humiliating. When he saw two guards break from the troops, Haegan did not move.

"Ye canna do this," Thiel hissed at the captain. "Zireli is not sovereign in the Northlands!"

"I will cause no trouble for you." Haegan looked at Thiel even as the Jujak approached. "I . . . I beg your mercy." The two guards restrained his hands, and Haegan would have laughed were he not so grieved. If he but exerted his newfound gift, the leather straps would do little more than sizzle as they fell off.

He and Thiel most likely wouldn't see each other again, not with the state of the Nine and the icy relations between the two kingdoms. His father—

Shouts went up. "Rider! Rider!"

King Thurig waved a hand, and Tili sprinted across the lawn, hopped over the retaining wall and vanished into the dark. The king turned to the valor guard. "Grinda, ye and yer men are surely exhausted. It is well past a riding hour. Come, enjoy the feast. Ye can set out in the morning."

"Your generosity is kind, but we cannot waste even an hour."

"Why?"

"Surely you are aware of the situation in Seultrie. Dyrth is encamped about the walls. I must return immediately."

"To defend yer land, of course. But with the prince? What benefit is he there? Is he not safer here than barricaded in a beleaguered palace?"

Captain Grinda shifted, his barely suppressed rage flickering to the surface. "His safety is not my priority. He faces charges of treason." He stepped back and saluted Thurig. "I have my orders. The Fire King would have his son."

"Seultrie is besieged!" Tili's shout cut off further argument as he raced back, tearing across the grass like a raqine. He skidded to a stop before his father. "The rider—the one we sent to Seultrie to alert Zireli has returned, shot through with an arrow. He was given a warning by Dyrth that any who dared an attempt to reach the Fire King would be killed. The city is razed. Those not dead have fled to Luxlirien."

Haegan's heart thudded. "My family!" He nearly choked. "What of my sister? My father!"

"Probably on the battlefield," Relig offered.

"No," Captain Grinda said, his voice quiet, his tone dark. "My father—General Grinda—sent word the king had returned to the keep before the Kindling. With what has transpired, I would wager he remained in Seultrie to face Dyrth."

Tili shook his head. "I asked the messenger, but there is no word. The royal family hasn't been seen. Windows in the keep are boarded up."

Haegan walked a circle, hands still bound. Breathing hard. *Hard to breathe.* "Father," he whispered. Kaelyria. If she had her gift, if she had not surrendered . . . she could have protected the city while their father-king was out warring. "I must go to her."

"No!" Thiel cried, tugging at him.

He hated the panic he saw in her, but . . . "I must. She is undefended."

"Yer father is the mightiest accelerant known to exist," Thurig said. "Even I could not best him."

Though Haegan looked at the king, all he saw was death. Death if he did not go. Death if he returned to face Poired Dyrth, the hand of Sirdar. He looked at his hands. Thought of the *he-ahwl abiałassø*. Could he do it? "You are less. Gwogh is less. My father will be less, too. I *must* go. I must try."

A dark shape slipped through moonslight-filled night. Chima's pace was fast but not frantic. She was coming.

She answers you.

Haegan looked to King Thurig, the heady realization of what he was thinking sinking in deep. To go back. To face Poired.

No. To save Kaelyria and his parents. To save the Nine Kingdoms. This wasn't just about one family. Zaethien, the Celahars were the strongest obstacle to Sirdar's domination of the realm. Perhaps of the planet.

"Prince Haegan—"

He singed the leather bindings. They hit the grass with a soft *thump*. When Grinda and Mallius looked to the ground, Haegan sprinted. Sprinted for all he was worth toward Chima. She came at him, full speed.

"Stop!"

Chima's front paws rose off the ground. Her wings snapped open

Haegan threw himself at her back. Grabbed a fistful of fur. She shrieked in response, but catapulted them into the air.

53

Fly true, Chima. Fly hard.

Nearly frozen stiff, Haegan rode across the night through the countless hours toward his home. He whispered the words to his raqine many times over, praying she understood. It was only as they were airborne that he realized he had no idea how to fly her.

But that would be him dominating her. Thurig warned against that. So Haegan trusted. He blindly trusted the incredible beast beneath him. He pressed his face against Chima's coat, warmed by her relentless effort to get him back to Seultrie.

Hold on, Kaelyria. I will not fail you.

As blue streaks cracked the predawn sky, Haegan saw the glint of smoke and fire in the distance. Dread poured through him, bringing with it a jolt of adrenaline. Fieri Keep burned.

• • •

She descended the spiral steps with the elegance that had always captivated him. Even now, in this dark hour, she reigned beautiful. None in the kingdom held a spark to her, save—perhaps—their daughter.

Once Adrroania's foot hit the dirt floor, Zireli felt the presence of the Deliverer at his back, the unmistakable warmth. And though darkness held this space captive, Zireli could now see unencumbered, hours after the candle had been extinguished.

He watched in silence, concealed by the Void Walker, as she moved through the lower chamber of the library with ease and familiarity. It cemented his belief, his deduction. Broken of heart, he never took his gaze from her as she glided to the long table dividing the room.

She reached beneath the table. Then straightened. Bent again and looked harder.

"It's not there," Zireli said.

Adrroania spun, her eyes wide. "Zireli." She sucked in a hard breath. "You know . . ." Nervous blue eyes took in the room. "How—"

"*Ïmnathuæaeteçt haûĝht un mwæth.*" A trill of warmth surged through him as he quoted the phrase in the old language.

"She will make the truth known," Adrroania whispered, coiling her fist back from the table.

"You knew," he said, the words laced with the anger he'd wrestled with over the last few hours, sitting in the dark, reading the hidden Parchments with that other sight.

"You do not understand!"

"In this, you are right!"

A strange shriek rent the air, silencing them as the sound penetrated the walls and seared eardrums.

"*Go to the tower,*" the Deliverer spoke in his mind.

A terrible urgency catapulted Zireli out of the lower chamber. Though he heard Adrroania's shouts behind him, he ran with singular focus to the tower where his daughter lay, trusting Abiassa to lead him. Show him.

"She's not in the tower," he finally heard his wife cry.

Yes—he'd forgotten in that moment of panic. So why was the Deliverer sending him there? Though he could not understand, Zireli ran. Trusted. He burst through the narrow wood door.

A terrible crash exploded seconds later.

He shielded himself as glass and stone rained down on the room. When he dared look, Zireli was not sure what shocked him more—to find his son standing before him, or the raqine perched on the windowsill.

"Chima, go! High," Haegan said with a wave.

The mighty beast shrieked and tore off into the air.

His son! Abiassa had granted his last wish. Zireli hurried to him, arms out. "Haegan—"

"Stop!" His son threw out a hand.

Fiery embers rushed along the edges of Zireli's arms and face, tingling. Singeing. Zireli stumbled back, staring. Embers. "It's true, then. You . . . you can wield."

"I—I beg your mercy." Haegan swallowed. "I can't control it, but do not test me, Father." He seemed to tremble. Uncertain of himself and of Zireli's response. "I came for Kae, not your anger. I did not do this, no matter what you believe."

"I know—no. I believe you." It was true. As the Parchments foretold. His son—*his son!*—was the Fierian. How was it possible?

Stalled in his tirade, Haegan stood with a furrowed brow.

Zireli knew how. His entire body shook with the emotion, the thrill of an answered plea. "I asked Her for one chance to defend your honor, to restore what was stolen from you so long ago." His throat felt thick and raw. "I—"

Haegan's eyes narrowed. "I shamed you as a cripple, and you disowned me."

"It was my shame for hiding behind my guilt."

"Your guilt?"

"For not protecting you." He swallowed, blinking away the burning. "I was your father—the *Fire King*, and yet I could not stop them from poisoning you!"

Haegan's chin trembled, his head slowly shaking. "I—" He looked away, then back. "I just wanted one hour of your time. Was it too much to ask?"

"For me, it was *everything* to ask— I watched you sleep each night, tormenting myself with what I should've seen, what I should've done differently . . ."

"You watched me?" Haegan's voice cracked, sweat beading along his temples.

"Every. Night."

Boom!

The impact of whatever had struck the tower pitched Zireli forward. He swayed, but braced himself against the bed where Haegan had lain for so many years. "Forgive me. I beg Abiassa's mercy from you."

"You said nothing. Spoke nothing. You just . . . watched?"

The tower rumbled, the stones vibrating beneath his feet. "It was wrong—I know. But—"

Crack!

The floor beneath Zireli's feet lurched. Tiles fell away into a dark abyss of nothingness as the tower surrendered.

"Father!"

Zireli searched for firm footing, only to realize Haegan was still there. "Go!"

"Here! Take my hand." Haegan lunged toward him, but a thick shadow rushed in from behind. Dark paws wrapped around Haegan's midsection and lifted. "No!" He struggled against the ancient creature, but the raqine hoisted him from the rubble.

"It's her life's work to protect you. Let her!" Zireli felt the floor vanish beneath his feet. He tensed as he fell away.

"No!" Haegan's blue eyes flashed gold.

Instantly, a shield of heat wrapped around Zireli as the distance between him and his son once again grew. Darkness and smoke pulled him farther down. "The gate," Zireli shouted. "I'll bring Kaelyria there!"

"Hurry! He's targeting the main supports," Haegan hollered from atop his raqine.

The incredible sight inspired Zireli, sent him flying down the stairs with hope in his chest.

54

"Forgive me, Father," Kaelyria whispered into her father's neck as he carried her down the stairs. Tears saturated his fine tunic.

He said nothing but continued down.

Thud! Whoosh!

They canted to the right, her father throwing himself against the wall to avoid a falling timber. With a grunt, he pushed himself down a few more steps.

Crack! Groaan!

He looked up and started hustling, but her weight was clearly an obstacle.

"Please . . . I beg your mercy. If I am to die, I do not want it to be with guilt and your hatred—"

"I could never hate my own blood," he ground out, sweat and blood from a cut smearing across his face. "Save your strength. If you survive this, he'll need you."

"Then I have your mercy? I had to surrender my abilities—that's what Poired was after. I could not let him have my gift. He would be too powerful and Seultrie undefended."

"What is done"—he grunted and hopped over a gap in the steps— "is done. We must deal with the now. You are as much a part of the Fierian as he is the embodiment."

"Fierian?"

He coughed. "Hush. Save your breath—the smoke is too heavy."

"Mother—"

"Waiting at the door."

Kaelyria hated her helplessness. Hated that she had been deceived. Her father was right. She had bartered away her soul to protect Seultrie and still they lost everything. "At least Haegan is free." When he said nothing, she feared he still accused her brother. "On your honor, you must not blame him. It was me—I deceived him. He did not—"

"Silence!"

The world tilted. Groaning overcame the roar of the fire devouring their home.

Arms tightened around her. Her father took a breath. Then jumped. They went airborne amid a mighty, thunderous crash.

Kaelyria closed her eyes and held her breath, terror clutching her in its painful claws.

They hit the ground. Pitched forward.

Kaelyria vaulted from his arms. With a scream, she flew through the air. Hit the floor hard. Though paralyzed, she strangely felt everything. The massive impact. The agonizing pain that seemed to rend her in two as she slid across the floor and collided with a stone pillar.

"Kaelyria!" her mother screamed.

"Adrroania, the door!" Her father sprinted to her side, knelt, and scooped Kaelyria back into his arms. They headed to the great oak doors, the fire lighting the stone bridge that spanned the inner gate from the house. From this elevation, they could see the town burning. Could see Poired sitting on his horse as he had for the last two months. Watching. Seething.

His horse reared. And for the first time in the weeks since the siege began, Dyrth rode down to the keep.

• • •

Satisfaction smothers the common sense of Poired Dyrth as his Auspex and general ride down into the mouth of the dragon. So ready is he for his payment, for his right to end the life of Zireli of Zaethien, that he gives no heed to the fires. To the skirmishes happening around him.

He rides gleefully down to the gate. His soldiers, who guarded the entrance these long weeks, open the passage. Dismounting, he meets the fiery gaze of Zireli. "At last," Poired shouts. "You come from your high places and surrender."

Zireli carries a lump of flesh in his arms and carefully sets the body aside. "Your fight is with me, Poired." Beard stained with the ash of his crumbling home, he stands defiant.

"The Fire King no longer looks so shiny and pretty." Poired plucks off his gloves, one finger at a time. "In fact, you look defeated, Zireli."

The queen draws the body of her daughter aside, into the shadows. As if she can hide her. Protect her. Zireli stands in the middle of the bridge and spaces his legs shoulder-width apart, then crosses his arms at the wrist and holds them there.

Poired laughs. Laughs hard and loud as he climbs the steps to the lip of the bridge. "No, Zireli, your gift is no longer your ally. It is your foe."

Lowering his chin, Zireli draws in on his focus as all accelerants are taught. As all wielders learn in their first year. Prays Poired does not call his bluff. "I will yield," Zireli offers, "if you guarantee the lives of my wife and daughter."

Still smiling, Poired stands at the gate and raps a fist against the stone. "I knocked for two months and nobody answered. Think you that I will so easily accept that slight?"

"My life for theirs. It's a fair trade."

"No." Poired takes a step forward. "The life of a Fire King, perhaps, but the life of a sapped-out accelerant? Hardly."

The rocks at Zireli's feet explode in a shower of embers.

Poired laughs harder, his heart dark and fed by the fire of Sirdar. And with a mighty blast, he sends the Fire King sprawling backward.

Sirdar's Voice decides to be heard. "One—"

A mighty shriek severs the Voice.

Poired looks up. Cowers at the great shadowy beast circling the air. Then he stands and laughs. "There! That is what we have been waiting for." He holds up his arms. "Come down, Fierian. It is our time!"

55

Terror held Haegan in a strangling grip as Chima circled the keep. Wings splayed, she hovered above the bridge. He had no weapon. No sword. Only an uncontrollable ability.

Poired shouted at him again. "Won't you join the celebration?" With that he turned and took out his full vengeance on Haegan's mother.

Her screams pierced his heart.

"Nooo!" Haegan directed Chima down.

The mighty raqine dove, then swooped at the last minute. To his surprise, she clawed Poired's shoulder. The Dark One yowled.

Chima kept moving, descending until Haegan lifted his leg over her back and slid off, dropping several feet to the ground. "Go," he shouted to her. "Stay high!"

She screeched into the dim morning.

Haegan scrambled to his mother's side. She lay unmoving. Blood trickled from her nose and ears. She smelled . . . burnt. No life remained in her. Grieved, he lifted her—and realized she hovered over another.

His sister. "Kaelyria!"

She cried.

"Go," came his father's guttural shout. "Get her out of here."

Haegan stared at his father, his face crimson from pain. Still dumbstruck by the conversation in the tower, he panicked at seeing him so . . . defeated. "Father—"

A plume of smoke coalesced into Poired Dyrth. Lip curled, eyes glowering, he stormed toward Haegan's father.

"No!" Haegan lunged forward. His hearing popped.

Poired sneered. "Yes, Fierian. Yes, show me that anger. Show me that rage!"

Warning blazed through Haegan as he stopped on the bridge, halfway between his father and sister. Anger. Anger would weaken him. *Reach first for wisdom.*

Wisdom . . . yes . . . What was wise?

Take Kaelyria and flee?

Rescue his father?

Eyes on Haegan, Poired Dyrth swept his hands at his father.

The king arched his back with a strangled cry. And Haegan knew his fear had spoken true. Weakened by whatever had happened at the Kindling, his father writhed before him, once the mightiest accelerant in history.

No, that's me. The Fierian. They said I would destroy everything.

Let that start with Poired.

Haegan took a step forward. With everything in him, he punched.

Poired slid backward a dozen feet. And laughed the whole way.

"No," his father ground out, the veins in his temple bulging blood-red against his blond hair. He gripped Haegan's tunic. "Go! Hae . . . gan. Go!"

"Father—"

"It's not a curse! It's the great"—his father gritted his teeth, blood slipping from his nose and over his lip—"gift. Serve her! Save—" His father howled as he slammed into Haegan on an invisible wave of heat, then dropped. Lifeless.

"No!" Haegan roared.

Kill Poired.

The venom of that thought pierced his resistance. Sped through his veins. His vision bled red. His veins pulsed with the fire of the Lakes. It hurt, burned. Agony.

Laughter splintered the beckoning.

Haegan looked to Poired and realized the wicked general was wielding against him. Grinning. Laughing. Taunting.

Anger . . . Anger weakens . . .

Thiel. Thiel. Think of her. Beautiful Thiel. Her sweet kisses. Her laughter.

Poired frowned. Pushed.

He killed my father. And mother. Everyone in Seultrie.

The thoughts were acidic. Strange. Strong.

Haegan remembered Thurig's words about turning a thought against a person, using it against them. *To feed my anger.*

Poired was working Haegan's anger against him.

He's too powerful. Haegan knew he had but one chance to get free of this accelerant. He wasn't sure how to do it, but he tried to summon Chima back. If she could topple the overlook, it'd put a barrier between him and Poired. Create enough time to escape.

"You fool!" Poired stalked closer.

Kneeling, Haegan pushed forward with his hand, focusing hard to thwart the Dark One's approach.

Poired speared him. A strong bolt pierced Haegan's side. He yelped and doubled over. Holding his wound, he searched the sky for Chima. Nowhere.

This was stupid. He didn't have enough training. He should have listened.

"The great destroyer. The rioter. Reckoner. The one who breathes fire and destroys the Lakes," Poired growled as he advanced, Haegan's wielding countering one step but the mighty general taking two. "You young fool. You are no match for me."

Blood streamed down Haegan's nose.

And with a strange move to his hands, Poired split his wielding.

Kaelyria cried out behind him.

Poired hit her! Haegan shouldered into the wielding.

The laughter of the menace warned Haegan he was operating out of anger. Vengeance. Yes! He wanted this man's blood. Spilled all over the bridge. Slaughtered.

An enormous blast of heat flipped Haegan head-over-heels backward. He smacked hard against the stone. As if a thousand fiery knives needled him, Haegan clawed onto all fours. Anger tugged at him. At his will. Pushed him.

"You are *weak*! The Lakes of Fires will burn forever. Her champion is a boy who cannot even wield. His father a weakling."

No. Haegan knelt and bent forward, balling his fists. Waves of anger barreling through him. Begging him for freedom. To crush the life from the—

Poired shot a blast at his father's body, flipping it over needlessly. "Limp as a rag!"

Haegan punched to his feet. His hands blasted out. His vision became shades of blue and gray. His pulse roared in his head.

"No!" Out of nowhere a man materialized, his appearance hovering like a ghoul. He was beautiful but horrible. Powerful and terrible. His visage one of righteous rage and power. "No, you will not do this!"

Deliverer!

Confusion did little to stem the fury in Haegan as he stared past the Deliverer to Poired, who seemed frozen. "He must die!" This was his chance—while the Dark One couldn't move! He raised his hand.

"No!" The Deliverer lifted a sword. Swung it overhead. And crashed it down on Haegan's arm.

Agony buckled Haegan's knees. He wavered but stayed on his feet, the thoughts of his parents and sister fueling his fury. "He must die. Let me kill him!"

The Deliverer stood over him, both hands on the hilt of his weapon. Then there were two more, circling Haegan. "You are forbidden, Fierian," they spoke in unison. "This is not yours to do."

Haegan crashed forward, not caring.

He bounced off something—the blue haze that held the Three. Like a thin sheet. The leader, the one who had struck him, reached out and gripped Haegan's wrist. "For your rebellion, you will forever have a remembrance of this moment."

"Augh!" Fire lit through Haegan's arm, searing every muscle and nerve ending. It wasn't until he was on his knees, tears streaming down his face, that the Deliverer released him. "Ride your raqine. Save your sister."

The three were gone. But their reminder wasn't.

Poired stumbled, his eyes wide. He spun around, searching for an explanation. A foe.

Crack! Crack-crack!

Haegan looked up in time to see the overlook collapsing in exhausted defeat. It spit its supports onto the bridge. Poired scrabbled backward as the span splintered in two.

With a look to his dead father, Haegan scrambled back to Kaelyria, holding his arm to his side to avoid the daggers of pain. "Kae! Are you well?" Was she alive? Their parents were dead.

Thump. Thump.

Haegan jerked back, expecting to see Poired. Chima landed and frantically shook her head at him.

"Right. Hurry." He slid his arms under Kaelyria's shoulders and legs, alarmed at how cold she was, at how agonizing the pain in his arm. He lumbered to his feet. Stumbled over to Chima, collapsing against her. He hoisted his sister onto her back then climbed on. He scooted toward her neck and pulled Kaelyria into his tight hold. "Go!"

Chima, instead of going up, went down. She skimmed the small river that encircled the keep, then soared up out of it on the south side, avoiding the overlook were Poired's army had formed up. As she sailed into the sky, Haegan glanced back. To the bridge. Mother. Father.

Grief pulled at him. He'd failed them. Failed the kingdom. He didn't understand why the Deliverers stopped him. Why they defended the poison that had infected the planet. Why they . . . punished him.

A blaze of fire shot into the sky, snagging Haegan's attention. A warning shot. From Poired. The battle was not over. It had just begun.

ACKNOWLEDGEMENTS

Brian/kiddos – to my amazing family, who puts up with On-Your-Own meals and when I escape into my cave to write for hours at a time. God spoiled me with each of you!

Rel – My beautiful friend from Down Under – you have kept me sane, kept me laughing, and kept me writing. The gift of your friendship is one I didn't deserve, but I will gladly horde with all my might. Thank you! XOXO

Shannon – You've read everything I've ever written for the last ten years, and I just cannot thank you enough for our writing nights and "sharing." You call yourself "fangirl," but I call you "amazing friend." I praise God for the gift of you!

Reagen Reed – editor extraordinaire!! Your skillz were evident from the start, and I could never thank you enough for chiseling this molten rock of a story into something good. Thank you!

Vicky/Mom – thank you so much for your last-minute help on grammar questions, but more than that—as a writer yourself, you "get" me and have been so incredibly supportive from the very beginning (twenty-five years!!). I love you and am so honored/grateful to call you, "Mom."

Vvolt N629 – my four-legged hero. I love the way you demand attention, pulling me away from the keyboard for some true 'down' time. You keep me sane, and you keep me laughing.

Shannon Dittemore and Jill Williamson – Thank you, ladies, for not just reading but endorsing the very rough and raw chapters of Embers. Your encouragement was such a boon! Praying God continues to bless you both!

Jim Rubart – Big Brother – thank you for your mad skillz writing back-cover copy. But mostly, thank you for being my "big brother," and encouraging/challenging me in the Lord, in writing, and in life! Live Free!

Dineen, Robin, & Heather – Well, chickadees, it happened—I finally got a speculative story published. The journey started long ago, and you were there. And I promise, someday…*Marco*.

ABOUT THE AUTHOR

Ronie Kendig is an award-winning, bestselling author. She lives in beautiful Northern Virginia with her hunky hero, their children, a Maltese Menace named Helo, and a retired military working dog, Vvolt N629. The author of Rapid-Fire Fiction, Ronie and her action-packed stories transcend genres and engages readers with an exciting, clean read. She speaks to various groups, teaches at national conferences, and mentors new writers.

Ronie can be found at her website: www.roniekendig.com
Facebook: www.facebook.com/rapidfirefiction
Twitter: @roniekendig
GoodReads: www.goodreads.com/RonieK
Pinterest: www.pinterest.com/roniek